NEVER DEAD

JOE SCIPIONE

WICKED
HOUSE
PUBLISHING

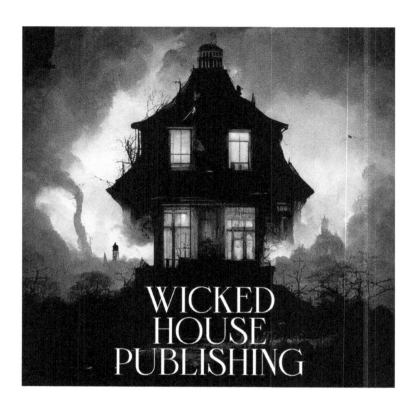

WICKED
HOUSE
PUBLISHING

Never Dead
By Joe Scipione

Wicked House Publishing

Cover design by Christian Bentulan
Interior Formatting by Joshua Marsella

For anyone I call family, the true heart of this book.

CHAPTER 1

1926

The wet ground makes it easy for Clyde to slide the spade of the shovel into the damp earth. It's been raining for most of the day, and even though it is only three in the afternoon, it feels like midnight.

"Do you think you could do this any slower?" Mr. Creighton says. Standing off to the side, the trench-coated older man supervises the excavation from under a large umbrella.

"I- I'm sorry, sir. I've never done anything like—like this before," Clyde says. He pulls up a shovel full of slop and tosses it to the side, adding it to a small pile.

"Dug a hole, Clyde? I've seen you dig plenty of holes before. Now let's get this over with. I'd rather not have anyone asking any questions about this."

Creighton is right. Clyde had dug holes before. All the time actually. As head groundskeeper at the Creighton estate, it *is* his job. It's probably the reason Mr. Creighton brought him along, but Clyde wishes he hadn't. He would rather be any other place in the world.

"Of course, sir." Clyde picks up the pace trying not to think about the fact that the hole he's digging isn't one in which a tree will be planted or a large boulder pulled out. Those holes are easy to dig. This hole is different. Under the dirt, *six feet under*, is a body. Clyde doesn't know what Creighton plans to do with the body, and he isn't planning on asking any time soon. This hole is different.

Lightening splinters the sky, and the corresponding thunderclap causes Clyde to flinch between shovelfuls of mud. Creighton remains still, motionless, watching his groundskeeper.

The pile of dirt and mud grows, and Clyde finds himself looking up at the grass above him. He tosses another shovel full of the slop up and back over his head then thrusts the shovel down into the ground again. It stops after penetrating less than an inch with the thunk of the metal against wood.

"I—I'm there, Mr. Creighton," Clyde calls up. Circumstances were unusual, but he is still a groundskeeper, so he scrapes the shovel back against the wood—the coffin—like he would any time he was digging to uncover something.

Creighton peers down over the edge of the hole. A thin smile grows on his lips. He gives a short, quick nod at his employee.

"Good work, Clyde. Now uncover the rest, so we can open it up." Creighton backs away from the hole presumably so Clyde can continue to throw dirt up over the edge.

"Open it, sir? We—we need to open it?" Clyde asks. His shovel scrapes down the sides of the hole, making it wide enough to pull the top off the coffin and get at the body inside.

"Yes, yes, Clyde. Why would we dig up a grave if not to get the body out?"

"Yes, sir. Of course, sir."

Another flash of lightning; Clyde lifts his head, peering out over the edge of the hole.

"Clyde, my friend. If you keep stopping to watch this storm, we'll never get that body out and we'll never get in from the rain. Please, just keep working so we can get back inside."

Clyde lifts his shovel without a word and resumes his work. The top of the coffin is cleaned off, and Clyde begins work on the sides of the hole, scraping the damp earth down onto the wood that now supports his own weight. He scoops the dirt off the top and adds it to the pile above. Lightning and thunder continue around him, and the wind picks up, causing Creighton to struggle with his umbrella. Clyde only notices this because Creighton never appears to struggle with anything.

Clyde has been working for Creighton for fifteen years, and although communication between the two men is limited, Clyde feels he knows the man better than most. He understands Creighton's schedule and keeps the grounds just the way his boss likes them. In fifteen years, he's never seen Creighton upset. He's never seen something go the opposite of what Creighton expects. The man always gets his way. So, when the storm doesn't cooperate, by tugging gently on Creighton's umbrella, Clyde notices. Creighton tries to maintain his composure, but Clyde sees the frustration under the facade.

Clyde gives the sides of the hole one final scrape and shovels the dirt out. Then, he runs the blade of the shovel along the edge of the coffin, making certain the sides are clear.

"I think it's all clear, Mr. Creighton," Clyde says. "But I don't think I can pull it off by myself. Even if you help, sir."

Thunder booms around them, but it is softer than the last rumble. The rain weakens.

"No need, Clyde. Stay there."

Creighton turns, retreats to his car. Cadillac introduced the LaSalle line in 1926 and Creighton, of course, was one of the first men in the country to own one.

Creighton fumbles around inside the car and emerges a moment later carrying a rope with a hook attached to one end. He tosses the rope down. Clyde looks up at him.

"Attach that hook to the top of the casket, just the top of the casket, not the whole thing. I don't want to pull the whole thing out. Just the top. Then we can get the body."

"Yes, sir. Sir what—what are we doing with the body?" Clyde asks, regretting his question as soon as the words escape his lips.

"One step at a time, Clyde. One step at a time." Creighton grins; Clyde sees a twinkle in his eye. He's never seen a look like that on Creighton's face. It is unnerving, terrifying.

But he can't think about what Creighton is going to do with the body. His employer expects work to get done, and Clyde prides himself on being a good worker. Because of that, he will get the job done.

The rain is lighter than before but still pours down around Clyde. Water drips off of his head, down his forehead, and into his eyes. It doesn't slow him down. With the sky brightening and the prospect of the precipitation ceasing, Clyde focuses on his work and is able to pry the lid of the coffin up just enough to get the hook in under the outside edge.

"It's on, sir," Clyde calls from the hole.

"Climb out of there, Clyde!"

Clyde pulls himself out, back onto the damp grass. As he gets to his feet, he looks up to see Creighton attaching a rope to the front end of the Cadillac. His boss affixes the rope to the car and climbs in. The engine roars to life, and then it backs up slowly. The top of the coffin is pulled easily up onto the grass.

"Pull it out of the way!" Creighton calls from the car, seemingly content to give orders from the dry car until he's needed outside again. Clyde does what he always does—listens to his boss. He kneels in the cold rainwater and damp grass. Clyde unhooks the rope from the thick piece of heavy oak.

With the top of the casket free, Clyde grips the wood with both hands. Though it's heavy, he drags it away from the open gravesite and looks to his boss.

"Excellent, Clyde, good work. Now, get that rope wrapped around its legs," Creighton barks from the driver's seat.

"Sir?" Clyde stands for a moment, frozen. The last thing he wants to do is get back down in the hole with that body.

"Now, Clyde, lets hurry!"

Creighton shifts his gaze skyward.

Clyde's shoulders slump. He doesn't mean to do it, would never do it intentionally in front of the boss even if he hated the task given to him. He always says 'yes sir' and gets to work. He is paid to do what is asked of him and never complain.

"Clyde, you can do this. It's almost done." Creighton surprises him by giving words of encouragement.

"Yes, sir."

He climbs into the hole, stands on the narrow edge of the casket, straddles the legs of the body so as not to touch it. The smell of death overwhelms him. He coughs and gags before setting to work. In his line of work, a dead animal here or there is nothing new; the smell of death is familiar. Dead birds killed by a cat or a wild dog left somewhere on the grounds. Or a nest of rats or mice within the walls of one of the sheds or even along the outside walls of the Creighton house itself. No, the odor itself is not new, but the intensity of the smell as it invades his nostrils and embeds itself within his head is more potent than a single dead animal or a nest of small ones. The contained and then released stench of a human body is much different.

Clyde has yet to look at the man's face, but the shoes are shiny and clean. The man's suit is dripping wet but otherwise looks new. Careful to touch only the man's shoes, Clyde wraps the rope around the ankles and then hooks the rope back onto itself. Gives it one quick tug, tightening everything. Confident the rope will stay when the inevitable happens, Clyde climbs out of the hole, steps away and gives Creighton a wave. As he does this, he gives a long hard suck of clean air and expels it, ridding himself of the deathly air below.

Creighton wastes little time and backs the car up. He rolls the car slow this time, even slower than before, Clyde assumes so as not to damage the body that he's about to pull up from what was supposed to be its final resting place.

The body lifts out of the hole and then slides back along the slick grass. Once the body is completely out, Creighton stops the car, gets out, and swings open the back door.

The sky is brighter, and the rain slows to a light mist. Creighton forgoes the umbrella and walks to where Clyde stands dumbfounded, unsure of what to make of the events transpiring. He feels more like an observer in all this, not a participant.

"Get over here, Clyde, we're almost done for today."

Clyde joins Creighton and the body. He knows what's coming but doesn't want to believe it. Can't believe it.

"Take his arms, Clyde. Let's get him in the backseat. We still have to fill that hole back in."

Clyde stares off, his face flat. He blinks, Creighton's words repeating in his head. He stands by the man's head, still refusing to look at the pale face on the former human. He reaches down and takes the body under the armpits. Creighton, doing actual work for the first time Clyde can remember, picks up the legs, and they carry him to the car.

"Go through the back. Just be careful of the tire when you climb in."

Clyde nods and backs in through the open back door, pulling the body with him. He strains and looks up, seeing Creighton not working as hard as he is, but Clyde's not surprised he's doing the bulk of the work. The body pins Clyde up against the opposite door. With nowhere else to go, the groundskeeper reaches behind him and opens the door. When the door opens, Clyde begins to fall backward but catches himself on the wet ground with his foot. The dead man begins to fall out as well, but Clyde stops the body's fall by clutching the man's cold, dead hand and pushing his arm back into the car. Once he's certain the body is in the car, he slams the door shut. Creighton shuts the door on the opposite side at the same time. The body is in the car.

"There, Clyde, not so bad right? The hard part, as they say, is over." Creighton laughs, Clyde, again, just nods.

Without a word Clyde returns to the top of the casket. Gripping the slippery wood with two hands, he drags it across the grass and lets it fall into the hole.

"It won't be hard to tell someone was here messing with this

grave, Clyde." Creighton picks up his umbrella and shakes it
off. "But they might not realize we took the body if we fill it
back up. Let's go. I'll give you a glass of the good bourbon when
we get back. After you clean yourself up of course."

Clyde picks up his shovel and slides the tool back into the
wet dirt he just finished digging. When the hole is full, they get
in the car and leave St. Patrick's Cemetery.

The Cadillac winds around the bending roads of Elk Hills.
They have to open the windows for the ride back to the house.
When Creighton got in after Clyde finished filling the hole, the
smell was almost unbearable. Creighton doesn't know how
Clyde was able to stand it down in that hole with the body. But
then, Clyde never complains. He never says no. He never asks
questions. Even with this job today, there is very little Clyde
won't do. It's the main reason Creighton brought him along.
Sure, the guy is good at digging holes, but lots of people can dig
holes. Not a lot of people can be trusted to keep their mouths
shut. Clyde will keep his mouth shut.

The ride, which is less than ten minutes, feels like it takes
forever. Finally, Creighton takes one more winding turn, and
the road straightens out and rises at a subtle incline. He slows as
he approaches the driveway. He always hated using the word
driveway because the road into his estate is so long. Private road
seems more appropriate. He rolls through the turn and comes
to a stop at the gate. It is unlocked and the guard, Terence, is
there in the gatehouse. Creighton puts his window down and
nods at Terence who hurries to open the gate for his boss.
Creighton rolls through slowly, then speeds up for the quarter

mile drive up to the house. It sits on top of a small hill in the middle of an open portion of the property. Small trees line the road to the house but there are open fields along each side of the road.

The twelve-bedroom mansion dominates the view. Though it is an immense house, it was designed to look smaller from the road. As they drive closer, the house seems to grow. Most times, Creighton admires it and has a hard time believing he lives there from time to time. This is not one of those times. He doesn't even notice the house; his eyes focus on the road in front of him. He has a task, and he needs to complete it and get a drink as soon as he can.

They approach the house, but Creighton bypasses the front entrance, which he never uses, and drives the car around to the rear of the building. He circles around the left side of the house and passes the giant courtyard that separates the two wings. From there, he pulls along the far end of the house and into the garage attached to the back. The garage and the wings cannot be seen from the road or the driveway. This was done on purpose because Creighton, his wife, and the hired architect, all agreed that the garage being visible would take away from the spectacle of seeing the house while driving up the hill, so it was hidden out of the way.

"Let's finish this, Clyde. I need a drink," Creighton says as they both sit in the car, unmoving.

"Yes, sir, of course," Clyde says. Then after a pause, "Where is it going?"

Creighton points to the bench at the other end of the three-car garage. A dark tarp covers the top of the bench. Creighton prepared it before they left, so it is open and ready for them.

"Over there," the rich man says to his lackey. "I have

someone coming later to help me with the rest of it. I just need it there for now."

Creighton looks at Clyde who nods in agreement. They exit the automobile and after a slight struggle, the man's body is lying face down on the bench on top of the tarp. Creighton is surprised that they were able to move the body that fast. He expected moving the body would take a lot more time than it actually did. Clyde is continuing to prove himself useful.

"Help me with this," Creighton says. He grabs the top portion of the tarp, pulling it down over the body. Clyde does the same on the other side.

"It won't do much about the smell, sir," Clyde says.

Creighton nods. "I know, the whole garage will stink soon, at least we won't be in here. When we're finished with the body, I'm going to have you clean up this whole garage. Get the smell out as much as you can, it will probably be tomorrow."

"Yes, sir," Clyde says.

"Clyde, I'd normally send you on your way now. After a day of work, you go home and come back the next day, but today was a different kind of work. We're both wet and sweating. Come in the house, and we can get you a shower and a drink. I know you weren't expecting this when you came to work today."

Clyde's eyebrows rise.

Creighton never socializes with 'the help.' It's a rule he's kept his entire life. He tries to keep his distance at all times. It's easier to not form any sort of relationship with the people who work for him beyond that of employer and employee. The people working at the house know that too. He greets them if he sees them, but he isn't going to talk to them about their families or ask them how their days are. It isn't his job to care about them. It is his job to make money so that they can continue working there. He pays well. They work hard. That's all there is to it. The request must have been met with confusion on Clyde's part.

"I know, I know, I'd never do this, you're right. But we smell like a dead guy, and I need a drink. If you just want to be done for the day I understand, but I'm inviting you to get cleaned up here. I can give you a room to change in and a bathroom. Margaret will bring you clothes. Once you're clean come down and have a drink in my office."

"Yes, sir, of course, sir. Thank you, sir," Clyde says.

Creighton leads the way into the main house.

"Margaret," Creighton calls one of his assistants as soon as they enter the house.

"Yes, Mr. Creighton," the gray-haired woman greets them coming from the kitchen into the back mudroom set off and down from the main house.

"Margaret, Clyde here has had a particularly rough afternoon of work, and I don't want him to go home looking and smelling like he does right now. Please set him up in one of the upstairs rooms with a shower and a bath. He will need a new change of clothes. When he's done, please bring him and a bottle of whiskey into my office. And two glasses."

Margaret nods and leads Clyde out through the kitchen.

Creighton takes his shoes off and walks through the kitchen also. His feet still wet, he leaves visible footprints on the tiles as he steps. No worries. Someone will wipe the floor.

He takes a back stairway that leads directly from the kitchen to his bedroom just above it. Mrs. Creighton is, unsurprisingly, passed out in bed. He will remove his clothes and have them destroyed. She would never ask questions about where he's been, but smelling like he does, she may become suspicious. She'd never do more than ask the question once about the smell, but that is one more time than Creighton wants to hear it.

Creighton takes his time, cleans himself and gets a fresh set of clothes. When he is fully dressed, with his tie tied just the way he likes it, he moves to his office where Clyde is already waiting, standing in the middle of the room.

"Clyde." Creighton crosses the room and heads directly to the bar in the corner. Alcohol is illegal, but no one's going to stop him. The mobsters have a monopoly on alcohol since the government decided it isn't legal anymore, but that doesn't mean Creighton can't get anything he wants. One of Creighton's men meets a contact with the mob and places an order. The next day, usually, they meet again, and Creighton's guy picks up the order. Nothing has really changed for Creighton since the days before prohibition. From underneath the small cabinet, Creighton retrieves two glasses that he knows Margaret just put there. He sets them on the counter and turns back to Clyde.

"I'm having whiskey," Creighton says. It's his way of asking Clyde what he wants, but in the back of his mind Creighton knows Clyde will have whatever he has and he doesn't care all that much about Clyde's response. Without waiting for an answer, Creighton fills both glasses with the brown liquid.

"There you are, Clyde, after a day like today it's necessary to have a drink. Sit down." Creighton sits back in an oversized brown leather chair—his drinking chair. If he's home, which has been increasingly common lately, he always has at least one drink in the chair in the evening. It's become a habit for him, one that he thinks of as a sign of his success and ever-growing influence. The chair sits in the middle of his office which is filled with the most expensive shit he could find. Some things, like the map of the United States created just prior to the War of 1812 or the musket gifted to him by President Roosevelt, he is interested in and proud to show off. Other things he purchased because they were expensive and he had the money to do so. He does it to show his money and power. At the end of the day, when he's sitting in here, alone, drink in hand, surrounded by things that remind him of his money and status, it helps him relax.

Creighton holds out his glass to the groundskeeper.

"Thank you for your help today, Clyde."

"Of course, sir, anything you need." Clyde holds out his glass. Creighton takes a sip, Clyde follows suit.

The nutty whiskey goes down smooth and slips down the back of Creighton's throat, warming him from the inside out.

"You're wondering, I'm sure, what I need the body for," Creighton says. The second sip is just as smooth as the first. He swirls the rest of the drink around the bottom of the glass. Clyde has another sip, and Creighton can see the man's face getting pink already. Maybe Clyde isn't a drinker, but he knew he'd never had whiskey this good before.

"I was wondering, sir, but if you can't tell me, I understand," Clyde says.

"You really *are* the best worker here, Clyde."

Creighton swallows the last of his drink and retrieves another, reminding himself to finish the second one a bit slower.

"Thank you, sir."

"More?" Creighton lifts the bottle to Clyde and Clyde

shakes his head. Creighton shrugs, fills his glass, and returns to his chair.

"It's not just me that needs the body you know. There's a group of us. We're not really scientists, but I guess you could say it's sort of like a science experiment we're working on." He has a sip—a small one—and continues. "Anyway, we've got a doctor we're working with, and the next step we have here requires a human body. The Doctor, he told us he could get us a body, but there's all sorts of paperwork—legal bullshit to go through. We could get it legally; it would just take longer that way."

Another mouthful for Creighton, Clyde takes a sip too, but Creighton can tell he's only pretending to drink now. His glass is full to about the same level it was after that first sip.

"I understand, Mr. Creighton," Clyde says.

"You say that, Clyde, and I want to believe you when you say it, but even *I* realize what I am saying doesn't really give much of an explanation. Please, talk to me as you would one of your friends. Just for right now, while we're here having a drink together. I'm not your employer for these few minutes, Clyde. I'm not Mr. Creighton just now. I'm Edmund. My friends call me Edmund, you know? You're Clyde, and I'm Edmund. We're just two friends sitting having a drink, for a few more minutes at the very least."

Clyde nods but says nothing.

"So, Clyde, what I'm looking for is your honest opinion of what I've just told you."

"Well, sir, I-I'm sorry, sir, I mean, Edmund. I guess my thoughts are that that man we pulled out of the ground; he is someone's father, someone's husband or brother. He is *someone*. And I wonder, I say this as your friend, what would be so important that he would need to be removed from his place of rest like that?"

Creighton is surprised and polishes off the rest of his drink to give himself time to respond. He expected Clyde to maintain his respectful manner, in a way he did; but he still got his point across. Clyde is not okay with what they did earlier. Clyde feels bad about it; if given the choice he would not have done it. But there was no choice in the matter for Clyde, then or now. He does the work because it's his job, and Clyde is a good worker. It's the reason Creighton picked the groundskeeper from the beginning.

There is one silver lining to all of this. After the test the Doctor set up for tonight, if successful, they will need a volunteer for the next test. This volunteer needs to be a live one. Creighton always assumed one of the group would step up, but his chat with Clyde gives him a better idea.

"Well, Clyde." Creighton looks him in the eye. "I'm glad you feel able to discuss this with your friend. I feel the same way actually. We *have* thought of this man's family and friends, but his body will be used to help mankind. If successful, mankind will be better off."

"I hope so, Edmund," Clyde says.

"I know so," Creighton raises his voice into and almost-shout. He nearly stands up from his chair but catches himself. He pulls air in hard through his nose and presses his lips together then lets it out, doing his best to calm himself. In just a few moments his mood is changed. He no longer wants Clyde to call him Edmund. He hates it. Clyde works for him and should be thankful he still has a job after what he just said to him.

"We are meeting tonight, Clyde, but you should go home.

In three nights, we will meet again if our test is successful. The Doctor believes it will be. I would love for you to come and see what it is we're doing. It might change your mind."

"Are we still just friends here?" Clyde says. He's a smart one, Clyde is.

"No, Clyde, no we're not. I'll see you at work the next three days, and then Thursday night you will stay late and come to our meeting. Understood?" Creighton knows Clyde will never go to the police or do anything to jeopardize his job. He gets paid more by him than he would from anyone else, and with a wife at home, he can't afford to be moral when it comes to his job.

"Yes, sir. Thursday night, sir."

Chapter 2

The newsroom is filled with people, a normal sight as the end of the day approaches and with it the deadline. It is a hard job. The hours, long. The work, stressful. But when the byline on the front page of a major market newspaper reads 'Michael Jacobs,' it's all worth it. At least it was up until a few months ago when Michael's son, Joseph, was born. Since then, Michael finds himself still caring about the job but thinking more about his time at home. The deadline, though, is almost here, and his thoughts are focused only on the story.

The noise in the room makes it hard to concentrate. Everyone finds themselves in the same situation. The quick, snapping sounds of typewriters going at least a hundred words a minute. The yelling, frustrated curses of men working to get their stories in before the deadline. A few years ago, the newsroom was one large desk in the center of the room with typewriters lined up along both sides, but a year and a half ago the bosses decided to give their top reporters, Michael included, their own desks. Now, the newsroom still has a large desk in the middle, although slightly smaller than it used to be. Around the edge sit ten or twelve small desks that allow the top contributors to spread out their notes and work away at the same furious pace as the others.

Reporters are men of habit and most of the habits are bad ones. Michael used to be a drinker, kept a flask inside his coat, and, when no one was looking, a quick trip to the bathroom involved a quick sip of rum as well. But since prohibition started, he tried to cut back. It worked, but, while he types, a cigar is tucked firmly in the right corner of his mouth, a thin stream of smoke leading up to the ceiling of the newsroom, joining the haze produced by the cigars and cigarettes of the other reporters. The smoke gives a harsh greeting to the nostrils of those unprepared for it, but it is a comforting reminder of the work to be done for the reporters who spend half their lives sitting at the desks typing away.

"What do you have for me, Mike?" Mr. Johnstone, his editor-in-chief says. He places his meaty palms on the surface of Michael's desk and leans over.

"It's almost done. That story on the murder down by the lake. The old man."

"Case closed? Cops say anything new today?" Johnstone mutters, holding a half-burnt cigarette between his lips.

"Not really. Still blaming that kid who robbed the fruit market down the street. They say the guy must have spooked him and he panicked. I don't really believe it. More likely it was one of the gangs sending a message to someone who didn't pay. I'm telling you chief, every single crime in Chicago can probably be traced back to the gangs. Since prohibition started, crime has skyrocketed because of these damn gangs. I don't have any data, just what I see with my eyes." Michael doesn't mention that this is the real reason he's tried to stop drinking. He sees so much crime and knows deep down that most of it is related, at least in some way, to the bootleggers bringing it in.

"You know my thoughts on that," Johnstone says. He straightens up and folds his arms across his chest.

"Yes, yes of course," Michael sighs. Johnstone's made it clear many times: he doesn't mind reporters working the organized crime connection into their stories, but he wants them to remember reporters who call out high-level criminals too much end up hurt or dead. It's the same reason cops arrest lower-class members of society for murders and robberies. It keeps the general public happy because they see someone arrested. The crime bosses are happy because they get to do their thing without interference from the cops. However, Michael believes that if newspapers follow suit, there's no one left to call out the real criminals.

Michael and Johnston have had disagreements over this before, and Michael doesn't want to rehash old discussions, especially this close to the deadline.

"I worked it in there in a way that will take someone reading it very closely to be able to catch it. I just don't want to let it go all the time, Chief."

Johnstone nods. He turns his back to Michael, looks out at the busy room and leans back against Michael's desk. He finally leaves without a word and makes a lap around the room, checking in with a few of the new guys. He then ends up back in his office at the far end of the room.

Keys pound up and down on the typewriter, and Michael starts in on the final paragraph. He explains again the police point of view and finishes by stating the killer is off the streets in spite of the unlikeliness that the man arrested actually committed the crime in question. It's not the most direct statement he's made in his almost fifteen years as a reporter, but an anti-organized crime statement nonetheless. It will have to do for today.

Michael gives his story a final read through. It's a little long for a front-page story, but it's pretty good. Over the years, he's developed a good sense of when the story is ready for print. He never has a typo and almost always types the word he wants to use the first time through, but he still reads the story over to make sure. Satisfied, he walks the story over to Johnston's desk.

"Chief." Michael hands the story to his boss. When he first started, Johnston would have lots of changes to the story and require a few rewrites. Now, there were hardly any. The editor takes the story from Michael and glances at the first page. Michael follows his eyes. He reads the beginning and then scans the bulk of the middle of the article. This is typical of Johnstone with him now.

"Nothing that's going to get either of us killed right, Mike?"

"No sir, I wouldn't do that to either of us."

"Alright. I'll get it downstairs then. Christine!"

Johnstone steps out of his office and back into the newsroom. He shouts to his secretary whose office is just outside the newsroom door. Johnstone's bellowing voice is easy to distinguish over the clacking and chatter of the newsroom, and Christine enters with a dark green folder in hand.

"Sir?" she says as she approaches the two men.

"This one is ready for print, add it to the pile," the boss says. He hands her the completed story, and then he turns back to Michael. "Good work today as always."

"Thank you, Mr. Johnstone." Michael nods. The two of them have their professional differences, but they've always had a good working relationship and might even call each other friends outside of the newsroom. In the end, they both want what is best for the newspaper.

"You're about cleaned up over there, too?" Johnstone says.

Michael nods again.

"You've got the new kid at home. So, pack up. Make it look nice and then get out of here." Johnstone gives Michael a quick smile. This is something new. The rule of thumb has always been everyone stays to help everyone else once their story is done. If you've got ten or fifteen different writers helping and editing your work as you finish a story, the story will inevitably be better. It also creates a team within the newsroom. One person doesn't make the paper, the team makes the paper. Working together gives everyone a feeling of ownership. That was the speech Johnstone gave when Michael first started at the *Tribune* years ago. It made sense to Michael then and still does now. The speech is why Michael has always helped out the younger, less experienced writers. He may have had his name on the front page day in and day out, but if the paper isn't any good, no one will read it. Then, it doesn't matter where his name is.

"Are you sure, sir?" Michael says, "the baby is probably asleep anyway. I'll stay until everyone is done."

"Michael, you're one of the last to leave every day. You know I see it. You'll be the last one here tomorrow in all likelihood, but always one of the first done with his story. You work as hard as anyone in this room including myself. If you want to take one day and get home a little earlier to see your new child or your wife, then I think you should go. We can hold it down here, and then tomorrow you can stay as late as you want. Go ahead and go home early, for me, Michael, if not for yourself."

"Alright, Mr. Johnstone. Thank you, sir."

Michael turns to head back to his desk to clean it up before he is on his way.

"And Michael," Johnstone says with a grin as he tucks a new cigarette in his mouth. "I don't know if you want to run this place or if you like reporting too much. But just in case you have aspirations to take my job, I want you to remember this when you're in charge."

Michael smiles. He has no interest in doing anything other than writing news stories and doesn't think he will ever want to do more. Writing is what he loves. He isn't big on managing people. Johnstone knows it, but never misses the opportunity to mention it.

"Of course, Frank." Michael gives him a quick jibe as he walks away. Whenever Johnstone brings up him running the place, Michael calls him by his first name. There are only a few people in the newsroom who can get away with it, but Michael's one of them.

"Get out of here, Jacobs!" Johnstone yells with a laugh.

Smiling, Michael returns to his desk and organizes the notes scattered across the top. Once they are in order, Michael stacks them up and places them in a new folder which he pulls from the side drawer of his desk. There are at least two hundred more empty folders beneath this one waiting for the story that will one day live inside them. He scrawls the time and date on the top of the folder, and then adds a few notes on the front so he will remember the story. He cleans up his typewriter and is returning his unused paper to the paper stack when he's interrupted.

"Did you just get fired, Mike?" It's Wilson Meade, another of the top reporters who's been working almost as long as Michael, and a close friend.

"You know Johnstone. He tells me I'm going to run this place one day, I call him Frank, he sends me home," Michael says, shaking his head.

"So, he's not serious this time?" Wilson leans a hand on Michael's desk and taps some ash from his cigar into the tray on the far side.

"He's never serious. Well, I guess he is a little bit serious. Told me to go home and see Joseph before he goes to bed for the night."

"Gosh, maybe you really are fired then," Wilson laughs.

"Yeah, I'll be the first one in tomorrow morning and Johnstone knows it."

"So, you're just never going to tell him what you really want to do?" Wilson says in a lower voice now. He brings his face in close to Michael and puts a hand on his shoulder.

Michael shakes his head. "How could I leave now? A year ago, even six months ago, maybe. Not now. I can't just go in there and tell him what I'm thinking."

"Mike, we're all thinking it. No one likes the control the mob has over the paper, but no one else can go in there and say it to him." Wilson draws on the cigar and holds the smoke in before puffing it out into the air.

"You just want me to go in there and say we don't want to report on mob crimes? Tell him we aren't fiction writers? We've talked about it before. Johnstone thinks the same way we do. I promise you that. We can't do that. We all know *why* the paper wants us to change up the facts a little here and there. It's as much for our safety as it is anything else."

"But Mike," Wilson says. "It's not really journalism if we can't even say what happened."

"I know, I know. I'm sick of making stuff up so I stopped.

Almost every story I write now, I say, 'here are the facts of the case, and here is what we hear from the police,' let the readers make up their own mind. Readers aren't dumb. At least, not most of them. They get it. I just think they expect us to give them a version of the truth. The readers will know if you write it the right way what you're trying to say. It gets the point across subtly, but it still gets the point across."

"I don't know, Mike." Wilson stands back up straight and turns around to look out at the bustling room. Then he turns his head to talk to Michael some more. "I wish there was something we could do."

"I know, me too. We could start our own paper. Write it all. Write the truth about what really goes on in the city. Not this watered-down news we write based on the corrupt police and the corrupt newspaper owners controlling everything that the people see and hear. That would never work though. We'd need start-up money at least." Michael takes a long, final drag from his cigar, closes his eyes and holds the smoke in. Then he puffs it out into the air before stubbing it out in his ashtray. "I don't know. My desk is clean, and the boss sent me home early or fired me. Either way, I'm leaving."

"See you tomorrow, Mike."

Home for the Jacobs family is only a few blocks away from the office. They live in a modest apartment. It's not small or inexpensive, but it isn't a high-end apartment for Chicago either. They never wanted to live in the best Chicago had to offer, but they couldn't afford it even if they had. When you're a somewhat public figure the way Michael is, people think they can talk about your income and your living arrangements in a way that they would never do with someone else. People assume because his name is in the paper every day it gives them the right to talk about him differently than they would someone else.

Contrary to what many in the city might think, Michael and his wife, Mary are not rich, but they are comfortable. They buy what they want and never worry about money. The rent isn't too high, which helps. It keeps them living a life they want to live.

Michael walks the few blocks home and takes in the sights and sounds of the city as he strolls through it. He always thinks of the city as a huge cave with a ceiling that stretches up out of sight above him. Some days, the sun shines bright in the morning and the warm summer air makes it feel open and freeing, but most of the time, the city moves in around him. Even in the open air, the buildings lurch above his head and press down on him like a cavern.

He works his way around and through the stalagmite buildings of the city until he reaches the door of his building. Michael climbs the three flights of stairs to his apartment, slips his key in the door, and opens the door slow and quiet in case there is a sleeping baby inside.

"Oh, hi," Mary says in a hushed tone, a finger to her lips. "You're home early."

Michael nods. "Johnstone let me off early today. He's been doing it with people every so often lately. Not a big deal, just enough to keep them happy." He kisses his wife, hangs his hat and coat on the rack by the door.

"Well, that's a nice surprise," she says and follows him into the living room where he collapses on the sofa and kicks off his shoes.

"It is. I need it. Every day it gets tougher and tougher to do the job, you know?"

She sits down next to him and rubs his neck as he leans forward. Her hands feel good on his skin. She slips her hands inside the collar of his shirt and pulls the stress out of his body with each rub.

"Just the same stuff? The—the mob stuff?" Her voice gets even quieter when she says the word 'mob,' she doesn't even want to say the word in the place where they raise their child. Michael doesn't blame her. She's not alone. For a city crawling with mobsters, no one wants to say that word too loud. Say the wrong thing and you'd have the wrong kind of people after you.

"Yeah, I mean the news isn't really the news if we're not reporting what happens. I put on my happy face because I'm trying my best. I don't think Johnstone is to blame either. He's reading all our stories and making us pull stuff out that makes the mob bosses look bad in any way, but it's not coming from him. It's the owners of the paper. They drink the top shelf booze and have mob suppliers they work with. They don't want their supplier to go away or get upset with them, or, worse yet, come after them because of something that ended up in their paper. So, they just send the word down that the paper isn't allowed to report on what might be happening with the mob. It's like they don't even exist when you read the paper. They are everywhere, but you wouldn't know it if you never left the house and only read the newspaper."

Michael sits back on the couch. Mary looks at him and stands up.

"Is there anything I can do for you? I don't know what the answer is."

"No, I know there's not much you can do. You're not there with me to hear all of the politics and stuff. But if you were, Mary, you wouldn't believe it." He knows most of the other men he works with don't share this much information with their wives. They get home from work and don't talk or think about work until they get back to the newsroom the next day. Michael has never been like that with Mary. She is the smartest person he's ever known and would write circles around him at the newsroom. If society allowed it to happen.

"It sounds like it's suffocating you," she says.

"It is, but I don't see a way out of it. I mean, I could leave, but people wouldn't get the real truth any faster that way. And we need the money."

"Do you want something to eat?" Mary says. Then, she turns back toward him. "Why don't you find different stories Michael?"

"What do you mean?" He looks up at her, elbows resting on his thighs.

"I mean you pick your own stories, right?" she asks. He nods, and she comes back into the living room and sits down on the chair opposite him. He can see her mind working but doesn't really know where she is going with this. He picks the stories that interest him, that he thinks might involve the bootleggers in the hopes that he can, over the course of days, weeks or months put small little cracks in the foundation of the thing he hates. One day, those small cracks will add up, and the whole thing will crumble. Unfortunately, the cracks never seem big enough to do anything other than increase his frustration.

"I mean step away from it all," she says, looking him in the eyes. He sits up straighter to meet her gaze. "Stop writing about murders in the city or kidnappings or robberies that are so very much related to the mob you get nothing but lies from the police. The paper covers more than just the city, right?"

Michael nods, working the idea through in his mind.

"But the major stories are those ones, the ones that involve the mob," he says.

"But if they aren't the truth, then they're not really major stories. At least in my eyes. The major stories are the ones that uncover the truth, and *you* decide which stories are the major ones don't you?"

Michael nods again.

"So, move your work out to the suburbs. Find a story that you know you can report the truth on and do *your* work *your* way. If it's not related to the mob, the bosses won't care. And they'll put it on the front page because they'll know it's the truth, just like you do. And with your name and the way you write, it will be interesting. In the end, the truth will sell."

"Because the truth..." Michael starts.

"...is stranger than fiction," Mary finishes.

"I'll make some calls in the morning," Michael says. He holds open his arms, and Mary moves to sit next to him on the couch. She wraps her arms around him and he does the same to her. He kisses her forehead, and they stay like that for a few minutes, Michael's mind already thinking about who to call to get a scoop out in the suburbs.

CHAPTER 3

Automobiles start rising up over the crest of the hill around five in the evening. They pull around and drop people off at the front door. Clyde is usually done with his work by now and on his way home, but it is Thursday night. The night he's been dreading. The night Mr. Creighton invited him to come to the meeting. But he doesn't want to go to the meeting. He doesn't want to meet the doctor Creighton told him about. He doesn't want to know what they are going to do with the body they pulled from the ground. Clyde doesn't want to know any of it. He wants to come to work, do his job and leave, and get paid along the way. If he doesn't come to this meeting, he won't get paid, at least not like he is used to. Worse than that, he could get fired.

Clyde never told his wife about the body. He could never tell her that. The only thing he said was that Mr. Creighton needed him to stay late on Thursday. It was all true, and it helped him feel less guilty. At least he wasn't really lying to her.

Creighton's words echo though Clyde's head. He said if the test was successful, they would meet again on Thursday night.

The fact that so many people are arriving—so many *rich* people —means the test was successful. The sun sets, the sky darkens, but the cars continue. Clyde wonders how long these meetings have been going on. He's never here this late.

He finishes sweeping out the garage and putting the tools back in their correct spots. It is a task that always gets pushed to the end of the list. He's the only one who sees the inside of the garage on a regular basis, so, if it's messy, he's the one that has to deal with it. He usually comes in early to clean the garage once a month, but there has been too much extra work for him to do his regular maintenance. Normally, he'd be thankful for this time, but not today.

Each time Clyde puts a tool back where it is supposed to be, he peers out the window at the people arriving. They are not all men, which is surprising. Some couples enter, others are men by themselves. Others, just women by themselves. Clyde wonders if Mrs. Creighton is attending the meeting or if she's even aware of it. He runs the broom across the floor and pushes the pile of dirt, dust and dried grass out the door. When he turns around, Margaret is standing just at the corner of the garage.

"Mr. Creighton would like to see you, Clyde," Margaret says. There is no expression on her face, but Clyde has come to expect that from her.

"Yes, of course," Clyde says. His heart hammers in his chest, and he looks down expecting to see his shirt fluttering with the hard, incessant beating. His ears flush too. He can hear his heartbeat and the blood pulsing through the veins in his head.

He wants to run. Just leave, go home, find a new job somewhere else. He wants to, but he won't. He can't.

"This way." Margaret turns on her heel, and they walk up the small hill toward the main house. They enter through a side door, and Margaret leads Clyde through the house, which is eerily empty given the amount of people he watched arrive.

Margaret takes Clyde through the two-story library, which is covered wall-to-wall with books almost to the ceiling. The room smells of old books, and Clyde would be shocked if he found out Creighton had read even a quarter of them. Like almost everything else in the house, the books were for show. At the far end of the library, away from the large double-door entrance, a small door is tucked into the back corner. The door is half the width of a regular door and shorter than Clyde is tall.

"Through here," Margaret gestures toward the small door.

Clyde had been in this room once before and noticed the small door, but he assumed it was a small storage closet.

"In there?" Clyde looks at his fellow employee, hoping she understands the situation he's in. She does not seem to care and just nods. Then, her face devoid of expression, she continues in her flat voice, "Go in and watch your head. Turn right and push, then take a step back. You will see where to go."

"Margaret," Clyde looks at her, but she just stares back through him. "What's in there? Do you know what is going on?"

Margaret says nothing at first but meets Clyde's gaze with her own. Then her eyes shift to the left and to the right quickly. She shows more life than in any other encounter Clyde has ever had with her. She looks right at him, and he understands before she says a word.

"I don't know what goes on in there, but I don't want to know," she whispers. The words flow fast with no space or pause for breath. "I'm glad I'm not you. Be careful." She turns and walks out of the room before he has a chance to reply.

He's more nervous than when he was coming into the

house. It was already something he didn't want to be a part of. He knows a dead man's body plays some sort of role in what he's about to witness and now a warning from Margaret, who might know more than she lets on.

Clyde stares at the door and sucks in a hard breath. With no other option, he pulls the door open and ducks into the closet. Inside is just about what he expected to see when he stood on the other side of the door. A small, cramped space with a low ceiling. But Margaret told him to push. Clyde turns right and puts a hand against the wall in front of him. He pushes against the wall, leans into it then takes a step back. the sound of rock sliding against rock fills his ears, and the door swings open toward him. An even smaller, narrower hallway opens up in front of him. The hall, lined with cold, dark gray stone, is only about ten feet long. Clyde crouches down and shuffles his way through.

As he slides through the short narrow passageway, Clyde hears voices and laughter emanating from whatever is at the other end. The tight space forces him to take small, quick steps. He emerges from the passageway to a steep set of stairs on his right. The same cold, gray stone that lined the passage surrounds him on all sides, even the ceiling is made from the uneven masonry. As he descends the stairs, the voices grow louder and more distinct. Although he can't make out what anyone is saying, he hears the voice of Mr. Creighton in the mass of people he assumes are somewhere ahead.

At the bottom of the stairs is a long, stone hallway. It stretches out in either direction. Along the walls of the hallway are torches. Every five feet or so, an eye-level flame burns atop a tall stick stuck into a small indentation in the floor. An even brighter light leads Clyde down the wide hall closer to the voices, but the slight bend to the left doesn't give Clyde the ability to see what lies ahead. He continues forward, part of him hoping he's not stepping into a trap or something just as evil as his actions with Creighton earlier in the week.

Clyde's heart beats faster as he rounds the bend in the hall. An opening appears, and the large, open room at the end of the hall comes into view. He sees the tops of heads of the people in the room, Mr. Creighton among them, but no one looks in Clyde's direction. He descends the steps in front of him and finds himself in a large, circular room. As with the hallway, the room is made entirely from stone. The ceiling is at least twenty feet high, perhaps taller. In the center, a fire pit filled with burning logs. The outside ring of the room is lined with more torches. These fires light most of the room, but there are some areas where the light does not fully reach. Clyde searches the ceiling for an air vent because there is no way this much fire could burn down here without some way to vent the smoke.

His search ends when Creighton calls for him.

"Clyde, there you are. I was wondering if you got lost on your way down here," Creighton says as he comes up behind Clyde and puts an arm around his shoulders. His hatred for Clyde grew every day since Monday, though he can't explain why. He also knows he needs to keep Clyde happy. Clyde needs to be involved in the process whether he wants to be or not. It would make things easier if he was a willing participant instead of having to force him. Creighton will keep Clyde close to him the rest of the night.

"Mr. Creighton, sir." Clyde smiles, but Creighton can tell it's not a real smile—

not a truthful smile. It's the smile of someone who is nervous and who doesn't trust anyone here. Creighton shrugs. Too bad for Clyde.

"Martin, James, this is Clyde, the groundskeeper I was telling you about earlier this week. He helped me obtain our friend on Monday. We owe him our thanks. If it wasn't for Clyde here, we wouldn't be celebrating tonight at all. Clyde stepped up, and we are thankful for that." Creighton looks at Clyde and puts on a grin equally as false, but Creighton is better at it than Clyde. No one knows his smile is fake. "At least *I'm* glad to have you, Clyde. Even if these people aren't."

Martin is Martin Van Nosh, owner of the largest railway line out of Chicago. When his family started the Van Nosh Railway Company almost fifty years ago, it was a small company content with moving people into and out of the suburbs of Chicago as well as providing some shipping services. When the railroads became more regulated in the 1880s, Van Nosh was out in front of the changes and laid more rail faster than the competition. They became the default or all shipping into the city. Martin Van Nosh took over for his father in the early 1900's and has been growing the business ever since. Creighton doesn't particularly like Martin Van Nosh personally, but his business capabilities are something Creighton admires, so he learns what he can from Martin and ignores the parts of him he doesn't like.

James Wallbeck, on the other hand, is a man Creighton respects both professionally and personally. Wallbeck is the person Creighton strives to be. Wallbeck's family made its money selling arms to both sides during the Civil War. Seeing the writing on the wall, Wallbeck's grandfather split his ammunition company in two prior to the war. One company—run by his oldest son along with a cousin living in the south—made as much as they could off the Confederacy and then quickly turned the cash around to purchase land. Land would always be valuable. The same couldn't be said for Confederate money. The original company, Wallbeck Ammunition, continued on in the Chicago and Indiana areas, and they saw large profits during the war as well. When the war was over, Wallbeck folded the southern company, took a small loss on the Confederate money they could not get rid of and moved the ammunition back up north. Wallbeck then had a wildly profitable ammunition company in the north and hundreds of acres of land in the south. When land prices in the south skyrocketed at the end of the century, Wallbeck sold it all off and kept the profits. Wallbeck runs the ammunition company more as a hobby and to keep spending money at the same rate, but he has enough saved to keep him and his family wealthy for a long time.

"Thank you, sir," Clyde says and smiles that fake smile again. Creighton breathes in deeply to keep his face from growing red.

"If you will excuse us, gentlemen," Creighton says.

"Yes, of course," Martin says.

"Edmund, I will be in touch about that other thing we discussed this week," Wallbeck says and looks at Creighton, lifting an eyebrow.

Creighton nods, then, keeping a hand on Clyde, steers the groundskeeper around the fire, a few steps away from where the rest of the men and women stand chatting.

"Listen, Clyde, I do appreciate you coming. That wasn't just an act. I—I wanted you to see what happened with our little project the other day. I think you deserve to at least see, given all of the work you did to help me—to help us. And the risk. We are just waiting on the Doctor who should be here any moment." Creighton looks at his watch. Still a few minutes until the Doctor arrives. He lifts his eyes to the entrance, and, as if on cue, the Doctor appears in the open mouth of the hallway.

Creighton and the Doctor have worked closely over the last eight months; it's been over a year since the two were first introduced, but the sight of the little man with the large round glasses always reminds Creighton that he is exactly what he would assume a neurosurgeon would look like. The small white shock of hair that sits toward the back of the Doctor's head sticks straight up in the air and makes the Doctor seem a little taller than his actual height, which isn't much over five feet. The Doctor shuffles into the hall like he always does, and the conversation slows as people notice him. He takes slow steps down the steep stairs; smiles at a few people as he passes. They return the greeting and then turn back to conversations that have stopped. The slow plodding movement of the Doctor suggests a deterioration of his body and motor skills. This is true of every part of his body except his hands. To shake his hand is like shaking the hand of someone forty years younger. Creighton would expect the hand of someone who looks this old to shake, or to have a delicate, weak grip. Neither of these things are true. The Doctor's hands, unlike the rest of his body, retain their youthfulness.

"Clyde, come this way," Creighton says, putting a hand on his groundskeeper's shoulder and turning him in the direction of the approaching Doctor.

The Doctor works his way through the crowd, smiling to

some people, not saying more than a word or two to anyone until Creighton intercepts him.

"Ah, Edmund," the Doctor says in his normal, rough tone.

"This is the man I was telling you about, Doctor. Clyde. The one who helped us out with everything earlier this week." Creighton smiles and pulls Clyde close into him. He already discussed Clyde with the Doctor, and they both know his role in the grand scheme of things, however, he wants the Doctor to meet the man before they continue with the events of the evening. After all, Creighton and the Doctor have already seen the results; no one else has. In their heads, they have already moved on to the next step. Once the results are unveiled, the rest of the Society will do the same.

"Ah, yes. Clyde. Thank you, sir, for your help with our, ah —our little problem. The results so far have been fascinating." The Doctor stares right into Clyde's eyes, and Clyde returns the stare. Creighton sees Clyde's mind working, trying to figure out what is going on and what it has to do with a dead body.

"Yes, sir. Of course, sir. Any way that I can help Mr. Creighton, I will do," Clyde says in his usual deferential tone.

"We may need more help here soon; and I think, after you see what we have going on here, you'll be excited to help us out again." The Doctor shakes Clyde's hand and winks at him. A small half-smile grows on the Doctor's face. Clyde smiles back.

"Yes, sir, I was wondering what it is I'm here to see," Clyde says. The little shit.

"I think we are all set to show everyone, actually." The Doctor looks at Creighton. "Right, Edmund?"

"Yes, Doc. Everything is all set. As soon as you're ready to go. Do you want any help with anything?"

"No. No, I don't think so. He's all set and we are ready to

proceed. I don't foresee any problems at all. Why don't you stay up toward the front though, Edmund. Just in case I do need help for some reason, you and Clyde will be right there."

Creighton nods. The Doctor turns and works his way back through the crowd toward the stairs into the large hall that Creighton has taken to calling the 'Hall of Life' recently. He likes the ring of it.

The Doctor lifts himself up the first three steps and turns around to face the crowd which has stopped talking. They watch him, waiting for the news. The Doctor gives a quick look behind him and then looks at Creighton. They share a short smile, and the Doctor begins.

Creighton already knows what the Doctor is going to say, but it means more coming from the Doctor than it would coming from himself. Like everyone else here, Creighton is an investor, and, although he put more money and work in than everyone else, he's still only an investor.

"Ladies and gentlemen, thank you all so much for coming today," the Doctor begins, holding his hands out to the crowd, like a priest blessing his congregation. "The day we have been waiting for has finally arrived. It actually arrived a little over twenty-four hours ago. Edmund Creighton was there with me through the whole process, but we had actual movement around one-thirty yesterday afternoon."

A low murmur rolls through the group. A few smile, and a few men nearby offer their congratulations. Creighton nods and turns his attention back to the Doctor.

"We didn't know how long the movement would last. Remember, last time we spoke we said that any movement at all would be considered a success. That *any* movement would give us the information we needed to move forward with the experiment. Movement is what we wanted, but we got a lot more. Instead of just a few small movements of the legs or arms, we were able to get total consciousness and complete regeneration of brain function." The Doctor smiles and so does Creighton. This is what they have worked for. The dead body that he and Clyde had dug out of the ground was now alive again and not just alive, thinking on its own.

They had brought him back from the dead.

"We have someone here with us tonight who doesn't fully understand what we've done." The Doctor looks at Clyde. "I would like to take a moment or two to explain to him the events that have taken place to get us to this point." Clyde looks nervous, almost scared, but the Doctor continues.

"When we started, we were looking to reanimate small things. Rats, mice, small animals. We moved onto large dogs and horses. The technique was the same because there is no real difference in the way a dog's brain and heart work compared to a human's brain and heart. The heart needs to pump blood through the body, and the brain needs electrical current to stimulate it into thinking and working with the rest of the body. No one understands how the brain does what it does, but we know we need something to stimulate brain activity. We know we need the heart muscle to work on its own to move blood throughout the body."

The Doctor looks right at Clyde. Creighton, standing just behind his employee, feels him try to back up. Creighton peers over at Clyde who returns the look. Creighton can see fear and worry on his face. The groundskeeper is not dumb. Creighton knows this, and he knows that Clyde has figured out where this is going. The terror in the groundskeeper's eyes is enjoyable to watch. Creighton does nothing more than smile at him and nod his head.

"First was the gel, inserted around the brain tissue to help stimulate and absorb some of the electrical current. We cannot, we know now, place electrical current directly onto the brain itself. The brain will fry. The gel absorbs and spreads the electrical current to stimulate brain activity in a way that is not harmful to the brain itself. The electrical nodes, combined with the gel, stimulate the brain and give us the activity we need to reanimate," the Doctor continues.

"What did you do?" Clyde looks at Creighton and whispers. "I am finished working here, sir."

Creighton shakes his head and puts a finger to his lips before pointing at the Doctor.

"Once the brain has a steady and safe form of electrical current, it can operate part of the body, though not at will. The electrical current simply allows parts of the body to move without thought. That alone was not enough for us to fully reanimate the living things we were testing. Do not be afraid my dear, Clyde, this is all safe and, as it turns out, legal. We are well within our rights to conduct the experiments. Please let me go on."

* * *

Clyde wants to be anywhere but here. At the mention of his name, the eyes of everyone in the room turn to him. He moves to step up the stairs toward the exit, but hands grip him above the elbow. He isn't leaving. Whatever this group feels they need him for, he will take part whether he chooses to or not.

"Next, my dear, Clyde," the Doctor goes on. This entire

presentation is only for Clyde's benefit it seems. "We needed to tackle the heart and lungs. Lungs provide oxygen to the blood and the heart pumps blood through the body. Together they create life in us—in every animal on the planet. The device we created for the heart is not a fake heart, but, when placed in the correct position, it will tense and release the heart, making it beat as it would naturally. The speed on the device can be slowed or sped up, but once the correct balance is discovered, keeping the heart going is relatively simple.

"The lungs need a similar device to bring oxygen into the body to allow the blood to remain oxygenated. While delicate, the device is attached to each lung and allows them to inflate and deflate as they are supposed to. We scaled these devices up in size slowly until we were able to attach them to the body— I'm sorry—the man you helped us recover earlier this week. Once the devices were attached, they were turned on and the man was able to move about independently, just as we had anticipated."

There are gasps and applause from some of the members of the large group behind him, but Clyde can't think past what he's hearing. Here, under the mansion he works at every day, they are reanimating dead bodies. He is in shock. He wants to leave.

"But there is more," the Doctor holds up a hand. "Now, Clyde, this is something everyone else is learning right along with you before we bring our new friend out. The electricity harvesting modules for the arms and legs are operational." More cheers and claps, but Clyde does not follow. "We have outfitted our friend with knee and elbow braces. The movement of his body produces electricity, Clyde. The only way we could maintain a reanimated person was to attach them to a power source to provide continuous electricity to their body. Moving his arms and legs produces electricity which is stored in the backpack and then distributed to the devices when needed. What you are about to see—the invention that I have completed with the help of Mr. Creighton and everyone else in the room—is a person who was dead, but is now able to walk into the room, speak with everyone here and function as a human being again. May I present to you all, Mr. Robert Parchesi."

The Doctor turns. At first, there is nothing. No sounds. No movement. Clyde thinks it is just an elaborate joke the group has played on him. Then, the sound of movement from the hall is followed by a shadow. Light from the torches behind him flicker and keep the face of the approaching figure shrouded in darkness. He can't be certain, but the size and shape of the man are similar to the body they pulled from the ground.

Slowly, the man reaches the top step. His face now illuminated by the fire; the group looks up at him in awe. Clyde squints and peers at the man, though the term 'man' is a loose interpretation of what stands before him. The head, once covered by a thick mat of black hair, is now shaved bald. At the crown of the man's head sits a small metallic saucer about the size of a small tea plate. The saucer is not attached to his head in any way, save for the six wires which protrude out the sides of the object and disappear down inside the skull. Three small saucers, about the same size as the one on his head, rest against his bare chest. Again, six wires protrude out of these disks and enter the man's chest where, no doubt, they operate his lungs and heart. On each leg and arm a brace made mostly of bright gleaming metal is held in place with dull, smooth leather. There are pistons on these machines, and each machine has multiple wires leading from them up to the enormous pack sitting on his back. It looks as though moving about with it would be difficult.

Clyde is shocked. Horrified. Terrified. But also, curious. He wants to know how this came about. Was the dead man happy to be back? Did he even realize he'd died? Does he remember anything about his previous life?

The Doctor whispers something to the man, and he turns around, giving the crowd a better look at the devices they paid for.

Cheers erupt throughout the room. Clyde doesn't want to join in, but his mind rolls through the reality of what Creighton and his friends and the mysterious Doctor have done. The actual achievement was close to canceling death. He doesn't know the mindset of the formerly dead man, but if he is back and can rejoin his normal life, the discovery is remarkable. Nonetheless, Clyde wants no part of it.

CHAPTER 4

It's six-thirty when Michael arrives at work the next day, but he's not the first one there. The light in Johnstone's office is on, and a plume of smoke drifts out from the top of the door. Michael was unsure of how or when to approach Johnstone about taking a break from the inner city/gang style crimes and move toward something a little different. Given the fact that he will have the man's full attention, he figures now is as good a time as any.

Michael removes his coat and hat and pulls a cigar from the bottom drawer. He closes the drawer, reopens it, and takes a second one. Then he slides them both into his pants pocket and makes his way across the empty newsroom to Johnstone's office. His shoes echo off the walls, and the sound makes Johnstone's head snap up from whatever he's been concentrating on.

"Mornin', Mike," Johnstone says, cigarette, as always, dangling from his mouth. "You look like you've got something on your mind, but you're not going to believe this."

Johnstone picks up a notebook from his desk and waves it above his head.

"What is it?" Michael asks. He wants to keep to his agenda, but curiosity gets the better of him, like it has his whole career. He momentarily forgets why he wants to talk to Johnstone in the first place.

"No, no. It's only fair. You came to me, let's do that first, then I'll fill you in."

Michael's hands rest in his pockets. His thumb rubs over the round ends of the cigars. He debates waiting until the editor spills the beans about the scoop he has in his hand. He wants the story, but at the same time, he doesn't.

"Well, it's actually about the stories I've been getting lately," Michael says.

Johnstone's eyes drop to the notebook in his hand. He sighs.

"I knew this was coming, Mike. I get it. You want to report the truth, and you're a good investigator. You know the stuff the police give you and the stuff we want you to write is not what's actually happening out there."

Michael is shocked. Maybe he isn't as good at it as he thought at hiding his hand.

"I, I didn't know you knew, Mr. Johnstone," Michael says.

"Hey, I'm here every day. I see your body language. I know how good you are. I feel the same way a lot of the time," Johnstone says.

Michael isn't sure what to say, and he just looks at his boss, his mind churning. Finally, he speaks.

"Then why don't we just print it? We go ahead and print the truth and who cares what anyone says or thinks. We just do it. Get the truth out to the people, and if the entire city knows how big and how real the criminal element is in this place, things can start to change."

"Oh, Michael." Johnstone shakes his head and laughs. "I love your positive outlook, but that would never happen, my friend. I would love to do it with you, but the aftermath would be the problem. Here's how it would go down: you and anyone else who wrote the truth would be fired within twenty-four hours. I've been told that almost word for word by the big guys. *I* would also be fired. They will find someone else to run the paper and someone else to write the stories. They don't want Michael Jacobs or Elliot Johnstone around if we're not going along with what they need. Because *their* lives are being threatened. Ours would be in jeopardy too. The gangs have the police and the newspapers under their control. If we keep our mouths shut, spew out the bullshit we get from the cops and pretend like everything is the way it looks when you read the paper, then we get to live peacefully and remain gainfully employed. If we don't play along with them, we don't really know what will happen. But we know what's likely."

"Mr. Johnstone, to be honest, I didn't—I had no idea you felt this way."

"Michael, I can't say stuff like that in front of those kids. Those young guys we have writing here now, who knows what they would do? I'm your boss, but you do what you want around here. I know it. You go along, and it's better for everyone. I'm fine with you doing what you want as long as it keeps everyone here alive. You are the hardest worker here, and I appreciate you more than you realize. But when the others are here, I'll have to be a bit of a prick. So, what do you want to do about this issue of conscience we're both having?" Johnstone takes a long drag on his cigarette and stubs the end in his ashtray. He pulls the long middle drawer out of the desk and reaches in to grab another. Michael interrupts him before he can light it.

"Sir, would you care for a cigar?" Michael produces the two from his pocket.

"Oh, always, my good man." Johnstone stands up and grabs the cigar. They cut the ends and light them. Then Johnstone looks to Michael.

"So, let's hear it Mike, because I have something to go over with you too." Johnstone taps the notebook on his desk.

"I'm wondering, maybe I leave the city for a story for a few days. Get away from the bullshit around here. Find a story where I can report the truth and get it in the paper, front page or not. Just a couple days break from—from writing fiction." Michael smiles and blows smoke up into the air.

Johnstone sighs. "I get it. Find a story not tainted by everything that goes on here in the city. Write it up and put it in the big paper. Make it a real story, do everything right."

"Yeah, yeah exactly. What do you think?" Michael's mind is already starting to work. He runs through the people he knows in the suburbs who could give him the beginnings of a story. He makes a mental list of phone calls that he wants to make as soon as he leaves Johnstone's office. He wanted to write down a real list before but decided to wait in case Johnstone said no. Now it looks like he's about to say yes, and Michael can't help but prepare for the next step.

"I want to say yes to this right now, Michael. And I *will* let you do this. I think it would be good for you." Johnstone puffs the cigar, and Michael watches as his face drops.

"But," Michael says, anticipating.

"But, the thing I need to tell you about is right here." Johnstone taps the notebook and shakes his head. "I can't let you go before this story's written. It's a big one, Mike. I need my best guy on it, and we all know who that is."

"I'm sure Wilson could handle it," Michael says and feels a pit in his stomach. Twenty-four hours ago, he was just planning on coming to work and doing the same stuff over and over again no matter how much he hated it. Now, being so close to a break from it all makes him want it that much more. The news hurts.

"Wilson is going to help. Too many angles to look at for you to handle it on your own. It's a big story, and I need my two best to get on it. I want it comprehensive though. Follow this one start to finish, and by Monday morning you'll be in the 'burbs writing fact all the way and still sitting on the front page."

"Tell me about it, sir," Michael says, his eyes downcast like a disappointed toddler. He wants to get out of the city but is also excited about this story. He's only teamed up with Wilson on a handful of occasions. The most notable time, they worked on a big story about police corruption involving cops moving patrols out of certain neighborhoods to lower land values and then buying the land cheap. It had nothing to do with organized crime, so it was allowed in the paper.

"Over on Wacker, late last night…" Johnstone starts and then looks over Michael's shoulder. He waves his hand. "Wilson! Come in here for a minute, will you?"

Michael looks behind him, and Wilson is just walking into the newsroom. He looks into the office and nods. Then he puts his bag down at his desk, takes off his hat, and proceeds right to the editor's office. Michael takes two big puffs of his cigar, and Johnstone does the same as they share the room in silence for a few moments.

"Sir, Mike, what's going on?" Wilson directs his question at Michael and looks at him first, then to Johnstone.

"Have a seat," Johnstone says.

Wilson sits down next to Michael and leans back in the chair, crossing his legs. Wilson looks over at Michael who nods and directs his friend's attention to Johnstone.

"I was just telling Mike, here, I need you two to work on a story together. It's ah- it's kind of big. Last night over on Wacker, they found the bodies of two dead cops. I just got the call in a few minutes ago. Obviously, this is going to be a big story, and we know how to handle it. They were found each with two gunshot wounds, one to the head and one to the chest."

"Jesus," Wilson says.

"And you want us both on this?" Michael asks.

"Yes." Johnstone breathes in deep, takes a long draw on the cigar then puffs that out too before continuing. "The police department has been going with the model lately of pairing new recruits with veterans whenever possible. That's what we have here. The rookie is Dennis Boyd. Started with CPD less than a month ago. Young wife, no kids, that's all I know. One of you is on his story. The other guy, we know. It's Dennis Feeley."

Both Michael and Wilson let out a groan. In a world where it seems like most police officers are corrupt and taking money from the mob to keep themselves and their families safe, Dennis Feeley is the real deal. No corruption from him, and everyone knows it. There is a lot of respect for Feeley, even from the corrupt cops and the mob. He doesn't take shit from anyone. He is as untouchable by everyone in the city as you could get.

"Wow," Wilson says.

"That won't sit well with the police. Even the dirty ones.

They won't like the fact that a guy like Feeley can get gunned down in the middle of the street," Michael says.

Johnstone nods. "I know. It's why I need two of my best guys on this. Someone works the Boyd angle, the other on Feeley. The police won't be quick to protect the people that need protecting on this. They might investigate everyone, mob or not, and we need to do our best to report the facts."

Michael and Wilson both nod.

"The way we do that is always, always, just report what the police have told us. They can't fault us for using what we're told. Even if there's more, don't follow the trail. You fellas understand? Don't follow any trails. Get this wrapped up so we can run it in the Monday morning edition. That gives you today and the weekend to get what you need and write it. Then, Mike, we can get to work on that other thing."

Both men agree and get up to the leave the office.

"Let's play this one by the book, boys. Lots of eyes on this story," Johnstone says as they walk out.

"What's the other thing?" Wilson asks as they walk back through the slowly filling newsroom.

"Oh, it's nothing. Another story I wanted to write. It's outside the city, so I asked him if he thought it was a good idea before I went and did it. Nothing really big. Who do you know over in Twelfth district?"

"Were these guys out of Twelfth, though? Just 'cause they were found there doesn't mean that's where they were supposed to be," Wilson says. He's a good thinker and thinks differently than Michael does. It's why they are good friends and why they make a good team in the few opportunities they get to work together. Michael would always call the police department where the crime happened first. Wilson would take a different approach and, if there was a victim, figure out why they were there first and then work backward.

"No, you're right," Michael says. "Feeley was First, if I remember right. I don't know about the kid. I assume he's First, also. Let's split our work here, for now. You go to First and see what you can find out over there, and I'll head over to Twelfth and see what they have. We can meet up here around lunch and compare notes."

Wilson nods and gives Michael a smirk only a good friend could give. "Sounds good to me, Mike. You know, *this* is why they want you to run this place one day."

"Why is that, Will?" Mike reads his friend's face but plays along.

"Oh, you know, we're supposed to be working together, but within thirty seconds of us working *together* you're already taking the lead."

"Come on now, Will, you know I was doing no such thing." Michael starts in. He thinks his friend is just teasing, but he can't be sure. "You know I was just getting on this as soon as we could. Could be a good story for both of us. You're the one who said we shouldn't go over to Twelfth to start with anyway—"

"Whoa, whoa, buddy. Relax. I was teasing you is all. I know we're in this together. I was just making a joke."

Michael smiles. "Yeah, I know. Two can play at that game. Now, what do you think we should do, boss? Should we head out of here and see what the cops are saying?"

Michael finds his large notepad in his desk and pulls it out along with a pen. Then, he shuts his drawer and pulls his hat back down on his head.

"Yeah, yeah. Let's go see what we can find, Mike. I'll meet you back here at noon either way. We can regroup after we see what these guys are telling people. You know someone at Twelfth, right?" Wilson pulls his own hat on and takes his small notebook out of his pocket. He flips through the empty pages and then goes back for another new notebook. He checks the pages, and they all appear empty. He shuts the drawer again and looks back up at Michael.

"I know someone everywhere," he answers with a grin. They walk out of the newsroom and down to the street. This is why he will always love his job.

Only about half of the reporters that work at the paper have clocked in when the men exit the building. It's one of the reasons they are two of the best. The two friends get down to the street level and stand in the warm spring sunshine, squinting as they look at each other. Michael shields his eyes with his hand.

"Talk to Harriet McCusty over at First," Michael says. "Tell her I told you to stop by and see what she knows, as well as whoever else you have over there. I told her I would only ever give her name to someone I trust, so she'll help you out if she can. She's the assistant chief's secretary. She doesn't get all of the information through her desk, but she hears a lot of it. Best ears I've ever seen. I'll chat up my guy over at Twelfth and see what he knows."

"Sounds like a plan, Mike. I'd give you the name of my guy over there, but he's a little squirrelly, and I'm pretty sure he wouldn't talk to anyone else again if you came poking around." Wilson lights up a cigarette and takes three puffs before storing it in the corner of his mouth.

"No problem, Will. I'll see what I can find out on my own. If we need to circle back around to these precincts we will. If we think we're good, we can move on to the families," Michael says. Will nods in agreement. Both men turn and walk off in opposite directions.

It's a nice enough day that Michael doesn't mind the walk. Most of his job involves walking around the city, and he's become accustomed to using that time to get himself ready to interview witnesses and write his story. The walk helps him collect his thoughts. Before he can really dive into a story, he needs to roll it around in his head. Prepare in advance the questions he wants to ask sources and witnesses. An entire story can get blown if he asks the wrong questions. Some people will only answer questions they're asked. Others will offer information before Michael can get a full question out of his mouth. Reporting, to him, is as much about his ability to investigate and hunt down leads as it is about his ability to write an engaging story.

Organized crime killing two cops on duty. It's been playing over and over throughout the city for the last five years. Recently there's been a decline, but that's only because most of the cops are on the payroll now. Gangs aren't going to kill a cop who's on their side. This stinks of the mob. Michael just needs to find out why, and then figure out what he's allowed to say.

Michael winds his way through the streets of Chicago until he arrives at the Twelfth. He glances one way and then the other before opening the front door and entering the station. He knows how he wants to approach the story and feels ready. Inside, he makes eye contact with the woman at one of the desks in front. Gloria is a dispatcher who has helped Michael over the years many times. She must be expecting him because she's not surprised to see him.

She holds up one finger and then points to her left at an unused office where they've talked before. Michael nods and waits there for her. It's time for him to start working.

CHAPTER 5

F ollowing the Doctor's presentation, the crowd mills around like they were doing when Clyde first arrived in the large underground room. He is wearier of the other guests now than when he first entered. They are not the harmless rich people he took them for. They are evil. They have done something no one should do. Even if it is possible—which it appears it is—it doesn't mean they should do it. Even for someone not fully committed to religion, which Clyde is and always will be, pulling a person's body from the ground and reanimating it, is wrong. Nothing could change Clyde's mind about that fact.

"What do you think, Clyde?" Creighton asks. His hand still rests upon Clyde's shoulder, for the clear purpose of stopping him from leaving his side or just leaving altogether.

"I—I don't know what to think, sir. I mean, why? Why would you do this?"

"I thought you might say that. Let's have a conversation, shall we?" Creighton steers Clyde away from the group. On the side of the room opposite the only exit, Creighton removes his hand from Clyde's shoulder. He steps away, happy for space to breathe.

His mind races. Clyde doesn't know what he thinks or even what he *should* think. What he has just witnessed is so far outside of anything he thought was actually possible.

"How could you do that? How could you do that to him, sir?" Clyde asks. He turns first toward the crowd, looking up at the Doctor and the man who has returned from the dead, and then he turns back to his boss. He doesn't know if he is ever going to leave this place. It's clear Creighton doesn't want him to, at least not yet, but he still holds a small sliver of respect for Creighton.

"Clyde, listen, I understand your outrage. Everyone here, at some point, felt the way that you feel now. We all did. Myself. The Doctor. All of us. We all could not believe we were actually going through with the experiments. But we did. And they were successful. And they are a miracle." Creighton holds his hand out in the direction of the half-man/half-robot as he slowly descends the stairs. His steps are not graceful, but they perform their purpose.

"And they *are* wrong, sir. But, why? Why did you feel the need to do this? And without his permission." Clyde runs a hand through his hair. He watches the crowd as they spread out more around the room. He has a clear path to the stairs. From the stairs, it would be a short run down the hall, up the stairs to the library, and out of the house. Curiosity keeps him in place.

"Whether it's wrong or right depends on who you ask, Clyde. And if you ask me, there is nothing wrong about it," Creighton replies. Clyde turns around and looks at him. Creighton's eyes bore into his head.

"If I asked anyone outside of this room, I think the answer

would be the same. Plus, you didn't even ask him," Clyde nods his head in the direction of the last place he saw the Doctor and the walking experiment.

Creighton laughs. There is a noise coming up behind him and Clyde turns to see the Doctor and the experiment walking in their direction. "Well, Clyde, why don't we just ask him what he thinks then, since we can. Now that he's alive again."

As they approach, Clyde gets a better look at the machinery attached to the man. There is very little mechanical equipment. Most of it has to do with the electricity production the Doctor discussed. With each step the man takes, there is an audible hydraulic hiss emanating from the devices on his legs. The rest of the equipment is silent, but the contraptions on his arms and legs make up for it.

"Clyde," says the Doctor as he arrives a few steps ahead of the experiment. "I know you two have already met in a sense, but this is Mr. Parchesi."

The Doctor gestures to the once-dead man walking up. Clyde glances at the Doctor but can't keep his eyes off the dead man for long. Clyde almost falls over when the dead man extends his hand.

"Thank...you...sir," Parchesi says in a slow, plodding cadence. He is there. His body is there, and it appears his mind is there too. But, even in the few seconds Clyde has been in this man's presence, he can tell the reanimation process is not without its complications.

Clyde shakes his hand. The grip is weak; the movement slow.

"It's nice to meet you, but why are you thanking me? It is the Doctor who, I guess, you should thank."

"These...men...told...me...what...you...did...for...me,"

Parchesi says. Again, the process of articulating the words is slow, and there is little emotion behind them. But he *is* speaking. The fact that he dragged this man out of a grave four days ago is remarkable.

"I— I only did what they asked me to do." Clyde smiles and nods at the man. "What is it like?"

Creighton smiles, watching Clyde interact with Parchesi. The horror on his groundskeeper's face turns first to astonishment, then to wonder.

"Very...hard...to...describe," Parchesi says. His thinking seems to be right where it should be. He isn't dumb. His muscle usage has slowed. At least that's what the Doctor told him. His observations of the man so far back up the claim. Speech is slow; movement slow; strength weak. But brain function is right where it needs to be. Responding to questions, carrying on a conversation with someone other than himself or the Doctor. These are good, practical results.

"Are you in pain now?" Clyde asks the same set of questions the Doctor and Creighton asked when they brought Parchesi back to life. They went through all of the questions any normal, curious human would ask. Creighton keeps his eyes on Clyde, watching, waiting for the skepticism to disappear. Once Clyde takes the bait and feels more involved in the process, it will be time to break the news of the next step to him.

Creighton also glances over Clyde's head to the rest of the group. They all know why Clyde is here. Though they are trying not to pay attention, he catches the eye of a few observing the meeting of this group of four.

Parchesi shakes his head slowly in response to Clyde's question. There is a long pause, and the Doctor, Clyde and Creighton just stare at him, knowing the response is coming, but slower than normal.

"Feel...as...good...as...ever," Parchesi finally gets out.

"So, you remember everything. Everything from...before?" Clyde looks to Creighton and then back to Parchesi. Creighton watches Clyde's mouth. The anger Clyde showed before was most evident on the corners of his lips. The man was incredulous as to how they could have done this to someone. Now, the tight, down-turned lips are gone. Replaced by an open mouth. A half-smile. Knowing the man you're talking to has died and come back to life will do that to a person. Creighton watches and waits for the right moment to intercede.

Most of Creighton's life has been about reading people—making a sale or a business move at just the right time. He grew up rich because his father was rich, but when he took over the family business, its growth didn't stop. It doubled. Tripled. He took the successful real estate business his father left him and turned it into the largest in the country by waiting until the right time to act, to make the perfect deal at the perfect time. Sales, at its core, is about reading people. It has very little to do with the thing you're selling, and more to do with the person doing the buying.

Creighton equates it to playing cards. He is a good poker player for the same reason he is a good salesman. You always have to know, or try to know, what the other person is thinking. If they have a good hand or a bad hand. His father taught him that a good poker player doesn't need to see the cards to win the hand. You're not betting your hand; you're betting the other players will fold before you do. If they fold with money in the pot, you've won the hand.

Creighton needs these skills to get Clyde over to his side. He let his temper get the best of him a few days ago and then again today. It isn't usually like that with Creighton, but Clyde is a good enough guy that he can let stuff like that go. So, he lets the conversation carry on. The Doctor backs away. This is Creighton's game now. The Doctor may run the science end of things, but working with people is Creighton's domain.

"Clyde, as you can see, Mr. Parchesi is more than happy to be back on *this* side of things." Creighton inches forward to bring himself a bit closer to Clyde. Clyde looks over at him.

"I guess you're right," Clyde says to Creighton before focusing back on Parchesi. "What about your family? How do they feel about this?"

Parchesi's face drops a little, Creighton see's the pain in his eyes, his shoulders.

"It...is...the...only...sad...thing...is...I...can...never...see... family...again." The once dead man motioned to his legs and his chest. "They...would...never...understand."

Clyde nods.

"They would want to see you, of course. I'm sure they would understand if your appearance was different. But we can't let the word get out about these inventions. You understand, we've talked about it before. But we are going to bring him by so he can see his wife and daughter again. It just wouldn't be okay for them to interact. He can see them from afar. Maybe someday in the future though." Creighton looks over at the Doctor. Parchesi and Clyde follow his gaze. The Doctor nods and smiles like Creighton told him to do at this point in the conversation.

He watches Clyde's face. His eyes squint, and the corner of his mouth turns up the smallest amount. That was it.

"What do you think now, Clyde?" Creighton asks. The Doctor steps forward, gently grips Parchesi's arm, and guides him back a few steps away from Clyde and Creighton.

"I—I don't know, sir. I guess it's not as bad as it first seemed. Obviously, anyone would rather be alive than dead."

"Yes." Creighton feigns a smile. "That's exactly it, Clyde. Who would rather be dead than alive? There are obviously some...limitations to this equipment. Some lives these inventions could never bring back. Any injury to the head would stop this from working. Any significant injuries to the heart or lungs would render these devices inoperable. But, Clyde, what we've done, is almost unfathomable isn't it?"

Clyde nods, and Creighton continues immediately. He's not positive, but he thinks his sales pitch is going to be met with an answer other than no, which is all he needs.

"Life from death. Someone was dead and now they are alive again. Walking and thinking and knowing all of the things they knew before. We've tried to find out what he remembers about the time in between, because just like you, we're curious as to what there is after death. For now, he hasn't said much, we hope more will come to him as time passes. But we're not all that eager to know death. There is another question in all of this." Creighton waves his hand in the direction of Parchesi and all of his equipment. "Although, it's still a ways off. Our next step is to duplicate Parchesi's results over and over again. Improve on them. Refine our technique. But then, once that is done, the next question needs to be answered."

"What question is that, sir?" Clyde says. He stares into Creighton's eyes. Creighton has him now, he knows he does.

Once he draws his interest, even the smallest amount, he will be able to reel him in like a small fish on a hook. There is no turning back for Clyde.

"If we can bring back the dead, Clyde, what's to stop us from making it so that people never die in the first place?" Clyde's eyes widen. Creighton goes on. He's got him. "Of course, things happen, car accidents, someone gets shot, but if we can eliminate those things, what is stopping us from putting these devices on someone already living? From preventing them from dying altogether? *That* is the next big step in all of this, Clyde. We will make these devices as perfect as we can. We will improve upon them each time, and when we have improved all we can, we will take someone still alive and make them immortal. Given your role in all of this so far, Clyde, we want you to join us. To help us as we continue down this path and see where it takes us."

Clyde tries to think of a way he can say no. It is horrifying and terrible, yet exciting and incredible. The things he's seen and heard in the past thirty minutes are more than he thought possible. And because of the small part he played in getting the body—getting Parchesi—it somehow makes him one of this group. He doesn't know any of the people here, but he saw them arrive. He sees their clothing. All wearing the finest suits and dresses even here in a dungeon beneath the Creighton house. These people are the elite. The upper class. He doesn't belong, but part of him wants to.

His heart knows what they've done is wrong. The people, Creighton, the man everyone calls the Doctor, they all did wrong, and Clyde knows it. At the same time, he is fascinated by all of it. Fascinated with Parchesi, with the man's answers. The fascination changes his thoughts. Maybe this is something good for humanity. Maybe there are people who *shouldn't* have died. George Washington, Jesus, Di Vinci, great minds, great leaders who could continue to make the world a great place if they were still alive. And with this, with the invention he sees before him, they could be brought back. If they had this invention, they might never have died in the first place. And Creighton wants Clyde to be a part of this.

How could he—how could *anyone*—say no to that offer?

Clyde looks over his shoulder at Parchesi, still standing off to the side talking with the Doctor.

"I can't really say no to that, sir. This—what you've done is amazing. I didn't think so until I talked to— talked to the body we pulled up out of the ground. It's— it's remarkable."

The smirk on Creighton's face grows to a smile, and he looks back over Clyde's shoulder and nods, then looks back at Clyde.

"I knew if you talked to him you would understand, Clyde. There is so much more to it than just bringing someone back, but that is part of it. What I asked you to do, what we all asked you to do really," Creighton gestures to the room with his hand. "It is not part of your job description. Maybe I should not have told you to do it. Maybe it would have been better to explain things to you first. But you worked hard for us, and we appreciate it. There are one hundred and three people in the room right now. One hundred monetary donors, like myself. The Doctor did not put up any money, but his value here is obvious. Parchesi also adds value, though he did not have much of a choice. And you. You have already provided value, and we hope that you will continue to add value."

Clyde looks around. All eyes are on him. The group by the stairs has moved closer to the spot Creighton originally brought him to get him away from the crowd. Clyde realizes it had been planned for him to join them. There are smiles and waves from some members. They seem happy he is a part.

"We know what skills you bring to the table, Clyde, and, like I said, we want you to continue to give us the same value you already have. You don't get to just be part of this group, Clyde. In the near future, once the devices are all perfected, once we take the necessary next steps, we will be able to sell the devices. Can you imagine, Clyde, what people would pay to stop or reverse death?"

Clyde shakes his head, he thinks he has an idea of where this is going, but he doesn't want to get himself too excited before Creighton makes it official.

"Like I said, Clyde. One hundred and three people in this room. Any money that this makes, which will be a lot according to the best business minds in the country, who happen to also be in this room, will be divided by one hundred and three. Evenly. We all add value. And we all see profit. Tremendous profit."

Creighton stops, a murmur spreads through the group, but no one says anything clear or distinct. Clyde included. The air in the large, warm room is still, and Clyde thinks about what Creighton has just said.

No one knows how much money this will bring in. But he doubts Creighton and his wealthy friends would enter into any business deal unless they were sure they'd make money on it. Plus, Creighton and the others had to pay their way in. They would have to make up however much money they'd already paid out. Clyde would make money from day one. It is a hard offer to pass up. It might even be enough for him to stop working. It would help his wife and his future children, possibly even *their* children. It could be life changing. How could he say no to that?

He can't. He knows he can't, even as he weighs the negatives. He still doesn't agree with the morality of the project. But he thinks about the money. He can't fully come to grips with the idea of bringing someone back from the dead. But he thinks about the money again. The thing that worries him the most is what else Creighton might ask him to do if he says yes. Again, he thinks about the money. He looks at Creighton and at the hopeful group behind him.

"Okay," Clyde says and shakes Creighton's hand. "Mr. Creighton, I'll join you."

A smile grows on Creighton's face. He looks at Clyde. His face is friendly, but in his eyes, Clyde sees something else. Something sinister. He fears he's made a terrible mistake. It's too late. The deal has been consummated with a handshake. He's given his word.

"I knew you would, Clyde. Smart man." Creighton looks to Clyde and then out to the rest of the group. "A celebration is in order. We have completed the first step toward our ultimate goal. There are more steps until we achieve it, but we are on the right path."

Creighton pauses, the group claps and cheers. Clyde joins them, though he doesn't know why.

"We have two new members of the Society here, another reason to celebrate," Creighton continues. "Mr. Parchesi is the guest of honor tonight for obvious reasons. Please, take a moment and talk with him as we celebrate. He is one of us, probably the most important member of our group. We need to make sure he feels at home with us. He is family now. And Clyde here, my groundskeeper, will join us for the remainder of our time together. His addition will, I am sure, prove fruitful when all is said and done."

More clapping and cheering, especially at the mention of Parchesi's name. The group can hardly contain their excitement. Clyde has already had the opportunity to speak with Parchesi, which cannot be said about most of the group.

"Ladies and gentlemen, the house is empty except for my wife who, we all know, is upstairs asleep at the moment," Creighton says. There are a few chuckles from the edges of the group. He doesn't look back but lets a small smile cross his mouth. "Please join me upstairs. Stay and drink and enjoy yourselves. We will celebrate tonight and then get back to work as we strive to reach our next milestone!"

Creighton gestures to the opening they all entered through, and the group files out. Clyde joins them, moving slowly toward the exit. He doesn't plan on staying more than a few minutes. He wants to meet a few people and then leave. He has to be back in the morning to work. As he inches closer to the exit, someone moves in next to him. Clyde doesn't have to turn his head to know who it is.

"Clyde, please stay back a moment. I've got a few more things I want to go over with you," Creighton says. He places a hand on Clyde's shoulder.

CHAPTER 6

"Here it is sir, just as promised, with only a little time to spare." Michael hands the completed story to Johnstone, Wilson at his side.

"Very good gentlemen, I'm glad you two got to work together on this. Two dead cops is not something I can give to just anyone. You need your best on it, and I know I had my best on it. The bosses will be happy with the results," Johnstone says.

Michael says nothing. He's too frustrated. He wasn't going to get sucked back into the stories in the city. He planned on a break from gangsters and organized crime. Johnstone even gave him hope that this story would be different from the others. It wasn't.

"It's not the truth, Mr. Johnstone, but it's what we were sold. Up and down from the higher-ups to the secretaries. Two precincts, one story. It matches so well there's no way it's true, I'm telling you," Wilson says.

Michael just nods. No need to go through this argument

with Johnstone again. They are all veterans in the business and know what's what.

"Alright, alright. I get it. Keep it down will you. I've got to maintain order around here," Johnstone says.

Wilson turns and walks back to his desk, but Michael remains.

"Boss, you think I could still move out to the suburbs for a little while this week? I know I can find something good out there." Michael points to the story in Johnstone's hand. "This gets a bit tiring. I need find something new to report on."

Johnstone nods and shakes the paper back and forth in his hand. He scans the room, and Michael follows his gaze. It is not the usual full-blown business that you would see on a week-night. There are still people working, but only about half the regular weekly number. With Monday stories, there is more time. Some people finish up the stories on Friday night and the stories are held until Monday. Others do the work on the week-end. His story with Wilson took the entire weekend to write. They worked straight through, finishing a few hours before deadline. Though they knew they were being fed lies, they followed every lead, talked to anyone they could to find a thread of truth. But the police department was sewn up tight. Ulti-mately, they wrote as much of the truth as they could.

"I gave you my word, Mike, and I'll make good on it. Do you need some people to talk to out there? Or do you have someone in mind?"

"Thank you, sir, I have a few people. If nothing comes of it, I'll take you up on your offer tomorrow, if that's okay with you."

Michael wants to leave in time to see little Joseph, who had been in bed when he got home each of the last four nights. He wants to see the little guy but his job is what keeps the family going, so he stays. It's easier and costs a lot less money to make calls from work than it would to make the same calls from home. There are only four telephones for the newsroom. One is in Johnstone's office, one is at Christine's desk, she's the secretary and most calls in go through her. And there are two phones at the far end of the newsroom open for business use only. Meaning you could use them if you were working on a story but you damn well better never use them to call the wife at home. Everyone follows the rules, most of the time.

Telephone use rose since they put them in when Michael began his tenure at the paper. He's been a big proponent of their use. Early in his career, most reporters were older than him. They were stuck in their ways; the telephone wasn't a part of how they did business. They'd rather go out and hustle up interviews to get the stories. Michael knew he could get more done faster by calling whenever possible. He fought for desks to be set up next to the telephones so that people could actually get work done while using them.

With the story turned in for the Monday morning edition and the go-ahead from Johnston, Michael decides to get a jump on the next day's work. He has an old friend who's now a police officer out in Elk Hills—a small town about thirty miles west of the city. Far enough away to be touched by less gangster activity than the city, and large enough to have a viable story beyond the occasional robbery or drunken fight between neighbors.

He last saw Ronald at the wedding of a mutual friend three months ago. Like it always is with old friends, they hadn't seen each other in a while, but once they were together, they fell right back into old times. They reminisced about the fun they had growing up and girls they had chased. Ronald is happy working out in the suburbs and likes that he doesn't deal with the organized crime that his city counterparts do. After the story Michael just wrote, he is happy his friend likes it out in Elk Hills also.

Michael takes his notebook and a pencil and sits at the desk by the telephones. He picks it up and gets connected to the Elk Hills Police Department. There's only one police building in the town and it's not that big of a department, so he knows he's in the right place.

"Elk Hills Police," a man's gruff voice says after only one ring.

"Ah yes, I'm trying to get in touch with Officer Weaver. Ronald Weaver." Michael hopes he's there. Even if he doesn't have anything to give him right now, at least he can set up a meeting in the morning. He won't even have to come into the newsroom. He can go straight to Elk Hills and meet up with Ronald. If this does pan out, he will have time to get home without making more calls.

"Weaver, huh? He just came in from his shift a few minutes ago. He's here somewhere. If ya wait, I can get him for ya. Who can I tell him is calling?" The man sounds older and draws out each word as long as he can without slowing his speech, so the words blend together when he talks.

"I'll hold. It's Michael Jacobs."

"Mike Jacobs, huh? Wait a minute."

There is movement on the other end of the line, then silence. The silence persists. Michael is sure the call has been disconnected, but then there's more movement and voices talking though he can't make out the words. The louder noise of the receiver being picked up.

"Mike?" Ronald says.

"Yeah, hey Ron."

"Hello. This is a surprise. How'd you catch me?"

"Luck, I guess. It's actually more a business call. The boss here wants us to diversify our stories a bit so he's sending people out of the city every once in a while, to report more on what's going on out in the suburbs. I told him I could give you a call, and, if you had anything interesting, I could write a story on it. I don't have to give your name if you don't want me to. I just need someone to point me in the right direction, then I can work on my own."

"Getting sick of the big city, huh, Mike?" Ronald says. Michael guesses this is why Ronald became a police officer. He smells the bullshit right away.

"You got me, Ron. But seriously, I'd love any direction you can give me."

A few people walk by the desk Michael is sitting at. It's not a new move, and Michael is one of the first people to notice others doing it. If it's the beginning or end of the day and someone is using the phone, they are almost always using it to get a tip for the next day. Other reporters, usually less experienced ones, will walk by and attempt to overhear enough of the conversation to poach the story. It's happened a few times and punches were thrown once. Michael was never involved. It's an unwritten rule that you don't poach stories, but reporters are competitive. It's a hard thing to stop. Michael knew when to stop the conversation or lower his voice so no one could eavesdrop.

But Ronald drops his voice too. As soon as Michael hears the lower tone and hushed voice, he knows he's going to get something good. One of the things about working the job as long as he has is that a hushed tone is a good sign.

"I actually got back from an open case. But I can't really talk about it now. Can you meet me for coffee in the morning? *Louise's Diner*, it's on Main Street here in Elk Hills. Train from the city gets in here at 9:05, and it's right across the street from the station. Let's say right then. Assuming you're taking the train of course."

"I am. That's perfect. I'll see you in the morning, Ron," Michael says.

"Take care, Mike."

Just as Ronald said, when Michael leaves the train station, right across the street is *Louise's Diner*. The perfect place for them to catch up. Michael walks across the street. There is no traffic in the small downtown of Elk Hills. On the side of the street that holds the diner is also a cobbler, a women's clothing boutique and a general store. A quick look down the side of the street he's on tells him the only public building is the town hall. There are also what appear to be small apartment buildings past the town hall, and one of the side streets leading away from the center of town has a few medium-sized buildings. That's it. Both sides of the road are lined with small maple trees. They can't be more than four or five years old, and Michael assumes that the entire downtown area was redone when those trees were put in.

He jogs across the street. It's been a long time since he took the train out to the suburbs.

When he and Mary were first married, they would take the train out this way often. They liked getting away from the bustle of the big city and find quieter areas to sit, talk and enjoy nature. But as they grew older and busier, the trips out this way didn't make sense. They only had so much time to get the things done that needed to get done. They felt like they couldn't come out this way as much. So, they stopped.

But it's good for him to be back. He breathes in deeply and smells the fresh air of the country, different air than the dirty smelling stuff that hangs over the city even on the clearest of days.

He pulls open the wooden front door of the small, loud diner. The clang of pots and pans, the sizzle of bacon and eggs, and the smell of coffee greet him when he steps in. He scans the dining area and is sure Ronald isn't there until he sees the police officer sitting by himself off in the corner of the room facing the door. Ronald is as far away from the door as he can be, and the area around him is clear of other diners in the otherwise crowded restaurant. The men make eye contact and nod to each other. Michael weaves his way through the tables and around chairs of the other patrons before getting to Ronald.

"Ronald Weaver," Michael says with a smile, shaking his friend's hand. In grammar school, the teacher always called them by their full names. They loved to joke about it when they were kids.

"Michael Jacobs, how are ya?"

"I can't complain much, Ron." Michael sits down. "Baby was born almost a month ago now. You should see the little guy." Michael rubs his hands together, they are old friends, but he's anxious to get to work. He doesn't really want to play this back and forth too long.

"Awesome, congrats! It's been a while. Good to see you."

"You too," Michael says. The waitress interrupts them.

"What'll it be today, Officer Weaver? Sir?" she says.

"Three eggs over-easy, bacon, toast and coffee for me, Lucy," Ronald says with a smile. Lucy writes on her notepad and then looks to Michael.

"Do you have corned beef hash?" Michael asks. The waitress nods. "Great, I'll have that, three eggs sunny-side, toast and a coffee."

"Perfect, I'll get those right in." Lucy leaves. Michael looks back at Ronald.

"You got the whole corner of the place just for us?"

"Not many police here in Elk Hills. If we need a favor, most people will jump at it. This is nothing."

"Not bad." Michael leans back as Lucy returns with two cups of coffee. She leaves one in front of each man and retreats. Michael sips his coffee black, while Ronald prepares his.

"I don't mean to be pushy, Ron, but I'm always on some sort of time crunch or another. You feel like filling me in on what's been happening? Sounded last night like something serious."

Ronald laughs. "You're always so direct when you're working on something, Mike. I mean, it's fine, I guess. I'm used to it by now." Ronald laughs, and Michael does the same. It's turning into an awkward breakfast for both. Michael wishes he'd just gotten his information and left. Now, he will have to wait for the food to come and to finish it.

"I guess I am," Michael says. He laughs again trying to ease the tension. "I hate the fact that I'm stuck on the damn train schedule, so I'm anxious to get as much done as I can before I have to leave for the night. Used to working in the city I guess."

"That makes sense." Ronald laughs. "Okay here's what has been happening. Like I said, it's been happening all over. I don't have all the details yet, but there's been these grave robberies."

"Grave robbers?" Michael says. He's never done a story on grave-robbers. He doesn't even have to ask; Ronald is more than willing to oblige.

"Yes. They happen from time to time out here, actually. But these are different. You see, usually, people are buried with jewelry or other prized possessions. Often time, these are valuable things. The grave robbers come, dig up a casket, loot the body. Then, most times, they put the body back in the ground. It's always been my guess that they don't want to hurt anyone alive, so they rob the dead."

"But these are different?" Michael leans forward.

"Yes, these guys aren't taking the valuables from the caskets. They want the body itself." Ronald's words hang in the air for a moment. "No one ever takes the bodies."

"Wow, so they're just stealing the bodies. Taking them with no reason you can figure out?" Michael rubs the side of his face. He pats his pocket, wanting a cigar, but holding off until after he eats. Denying himself is difficult.

"Right, we've been—" Ronald starts and then stops as Lucy comes back by. She refills their coffee cups, places their plates in front of them, and walks away without saying a word.

"We've been trying to figure out why someone would need these bodies. We've had three in the last week. St. Theresa's Cemetery. Guy named Arthur Keanally is the caretaker there. Medville had one and Brackston and a few other towns. We— our department is taking the lead in the case because as of right now we're the only ones hit multiple times."

Michael nods. "What kind of leads do you have at this point?"

"Nothing. Some tire tracks but we don't know what kind of auto they're from. We know the width of the tire, but it matches more than half the autos out on the roads right now. It doesn't really narrow it down. Nobody has seen anything. We don't even know if it's the same people or different people doing these things. Could be a whole group, not necessarily the same one or two guys doing it over and over."

"So, other than the fact we're friends, why tell me?"

"I'm taking a big risk." Ronald pauses to take a bite of his eggs. Michael does the same. "It's a risk because the Chief told me no newspapers until Wednesday. I think it's a bad idea to wait because we're already up against a brick wall here. We got nothing." Ronald snorts, smiles, then continues. "He wants to see how much we can get done before we go to the papers with it. I figure you're going to need some time to research this out before you run your story. So, you're here doing your thing and gathering up any information you can get. I don't know, maybe people will talk to you because you're not a cop. But you get a few days to write your story, and then, when we alert the press on Wednesday night, you already have a completed story. You run your story first because it's done and share any information you gather with me so the police can keep tabs on the whole thing. It's a win-win. You get to be first with the story by a mile, and I get some investigative assistance."

This sort of relationship between reporters and police officers is common in the city. Michael has the same relationship with officers or other department employees in most of the precincts in Chicago. It's rare that a story like this appears in the newspaper as soon as it happens. The police like to work without interference from the public. Once a story appears in the paper, there is *always* interference from the public.

Michael nods. "This your first time doing this kind of thing, Ron?"

Ronald laughs. "Yeah, actually. A friend of mine from the academy works in Chicago now. He says it's just the way it works."

"He's right. I've got this kind of relationship with about fifteen officers in the city. You might be a small-town cop, but you're playing like it's big time." Michael slides some hash onto his fork with a piece of egg and puts the whole thing in his mouth.

"If I'm here long-term, Mike, it's because I'm running the place. I don't just want to be Officer Weaver forever. Detective, maybe. Chief Weaver, I could see that. Is there any piece of this I'm missing? Glad I can work this out with a friend instead of someone I don't trust."

"No, trust is key," Michael says with a mouthful of food. The awkwardness of the conversation is gone. Just two friends talking like old times again. He swallows and continues. "It's harder if you don't really trust the person. I've got a few of those in the city, believe me. This will be easy because we trust each other. I won't run the story until you tell me to. I'll meet with you or phone if I get anything big. You do the same for me. The more I know the better I'll be. I never really worked these small towns, so I don't know the people to talk to. But I'm a fast learner."

"I can help you if you need it," Ronald says, but Michael stops him.

"No, no. After this we should keep our distance. Meet in private somewhere. Don't introduce me to anyone, we don't want your chief on your back; or on mine. We keep separate as much as possible so we can keep this going."

"Alright." Ronald finishes his breakfast and downs the rest of his coffee. He leans back in his chair. "There's a train that leaves for the city at six forty-five tonight. That the one you're taking back?"

"I honestly didn't even figure that part out yet, but that sounds good to me," Michael says.

"Okay. Around the back of this building is a fence separating the diner from the park. Big shrubs and trees along the edge. No one could see us if we met between those shrubs and the fence. Say, six-fifteen?"

Michael nods. "Yeah, that works. I'll see you then." Ronald looks like he wants to get up but reaches into his pocket first. "I got breakfast, Ron. Thanks for the tip. I'll see you tonight."

Ronald nods and stands up; Michael doesn't look up at him or shake his hand but continues eating and sipping his coffee.

He runs through the day in his head. He doesn't have much to go on. Just the name of the cemetery and the guy who runs the place. Michael does the math in his head. It's probably around nine forty-five, and if he's meeting Ron at six-fifteen it gives him eight and a half hours to find something the police couldn't find in the couple of days they've been working on this. The fact that he doesn't have much information to go on doesn't bother him. Neither does the fact that the police have been unable to come up with any leads. People, even if they trust the police, may not be open with them like they would be with just a guy off the street. All Michael has to do is get the people to believe that he *is* the guy off the street they want to share stuff with. He does it all the time in Chicago. He should be able to do it in Elk Hills.

With his breakfast finished and coffee cup empty, Michael stands and drops five dollars on the table. It more than covers the bill, but it is not so outrageous of a tip that the waitress will remember his face. The diner is the only part of this that he doesn't have locked up tight. Enough people saw them here today; it could cause some questions. Yes, they're old friends, but Michael is going to be around town poking about and asking questions, people might put two and two together. It's only a couple days and it's not worrisome, but he can't help but think about it.

He leaves the diner and steps back out into the bright sunshine. It's a good day to be outside and away from the city. An automobile drives past headed south. Michael watches it go until it turns, and then he follows it without any real reason in mind. As he strolls through the center of town, he sees the church stretching up into the sky. He missed it on his first scan of the downtown area because it is partially obscured by the four tall oaks standing in front of it. Now that he's closer, the steeple, protruding up between the light green leaves, is hard to miss.

Michael assumes the church is St. Theresa's, but he doesn't know for sure. When he approaches the building, the engraving on the middle step leading up to the church is inscribed with the name. His original thought was correct. He hopes the cemetery is close by.

CHAPTER 7

"Clyde, we make a good team, don't we?" Creighton says. He pulls the car around a turn in the road and brings them closer to the house.

In the back of Creighton's car is another body. The third one they've gotten so far, the second after the meeting in the basement of Creighton's house. The day Clyde realized his life may have changed forever. Clyde has worked every day since then, though not the way he used to. Creighton hired a new head groundskeeper. Clyde has other, more important, jobs now.

He hasn't told his wife the full truth. Not yet. He doesn't know if he can ever share with her exactly what he's been doing. It's easier for him to tell her he got a promotion which means more work, than to tell her what's actually been happening.

It isn't really lying. He did get a promotion. He used to work for Creighton, someone he saw on occasion and never for very long. Now he is Creighton's right-hand man. The two of them do everything together. For the last five days, Clyde has been with Creighton every second of the day while at work, and they've both been working on the same thing.

They arrive back at the house. Just like the previous two times, Creighton pulls the car around to the garage, and the two men unload the body. It's easier now that they've had practice. Once the body is placed on the table with the tarp, they wrap it and bring it down to the Doctor's lab, buried far underneath the house, tucked at the far end of the hall opposite the large room where the meeting took place.

"Ah, yes, good," the Doctor says when they heave the body in through the lab door. The odor of rotting flesh is present, but Clyde has learned that with each trip into the lab, he grows more accustomed to the stench. The bodies don't look that old though, and he's surprised at how alive they appear. The lab is more high-tech than anything Clyde has seen in a hospital, and cold. He doesn't ask questions, and he doesn't really want to know what everything in the room does. But walking in, even after ten or fifteen times, it is still an awe-inspiring sight. The tangle of electronic equipment on one side contrasts with more familiar medical equipment on the other side. There are devices that blink and beep and others that seem to have no useful purpose at all. In the center of the room, fifteen beds hold fourteen bodies.

"The next phase is ready to go, Edmund." The Doctor looks at the bodies laid out for him, ready to be brought back to life.

"Very well, Doctor. I am ready to begin whenever you are." Creighton goes to the sink in the corner of the room and washes his hands. Clyde remains still, unsure if he is supposed to do the same thing, stay, or leave. No one has told him much of anything. As usual, he's there to do his job.

"What about our friend, Clyde, Edmund? Is he joining us for this today?"

Creighton slips on rubber gloves, hooks his head through an apron, and then ties it around his waist so he's covered from his chest to the tops of his feet.

"He is one of us, Doctor. He has to work today. If we need some help, I don't see why he can't be here to witness the miracle with us."

The Doctor nods. "Clyde, we need to be able to repeat the process that we successfully completed with Mr. Parchesi. While we do that, we are going to attempt to fix some of the errors with the first subject, you see. Mr. Parchesi's slow speech and movements are not a huge problem, but if we alter the amount of electricity and blood flow a small amount, we may be able to rid these subjects of those issues."

The Doctor prepares for the procedures the same way Creighton did. "How long will it take to re-animate all of these men and women?" Clyde asks. He feels like he's stuck in a dream he can't get out of. His heart knows what's happening here is wrong. If it was right, they wouldn't be doing it in the basement of Creighton's mansion in secrecy. They'd be doing it at a real hospital. At the same time, he can't seem to get the snowball to stop rolling forward. It has started, and he continues on with Creighton and the Doctor, moving toward whatever the final result is they hope to achieve. They still have not told him that part. And what would happen to him if he said no to Creighton? It isn't beyond him to kill Clyde in order to keep all this a secret.

"Not long at all, Clyde. The blood, if you can imagine, is one of the difficult things about working on a live body. As long as the person's heart is beating within their chest, the blood will continue to pump. It gets on everything and gets in the way. Imagine, if you can, the blood of an individual pumping and covering your hands as you try to perform some delicate surgery. The blood, dear Clyde, makes it that much more difficult. These patients do not have blood pumping through their veins. When I opened up Mr. Parchesi, the heart was the last piece that I turned on, because once it starts, the new blood begins to flow. Working with organs, without flowing blood, makes everything easier."

Creighton and the Doctor begin to put instruments out on a small table on wheels, laying them out in what appears to be some sort of order. He assumes this is the order in which the Doctor will use the tools. He's never seen a surgery. But is this even surgery? There are so many working parts, not just the human element, but the electrical components.

"So, you're planning to do this all at once then? All of them?" Clyde waves his hand over the group laying across the beds.

"In a way, Clyde. I want to see how each person reacts to small changes in the way we reanimate them," the Doctor says. "We will improve ourselves with each. The procedure with Mr. Parchesi took less than an hour, and, once he was activated, he was ready to go almost immediately. It took me a few minutes to diagnose the problems with him, but I had no bodies to improve upon. Now, I do. When I go to bed tonight, everyone here will be alive again."

"And, Clyde, we know what we're doing. You will clean the instruments between each procedure. The sink is over there." Creighton points to the sink he just used to wash up. "The Doctor will monitor the new arrival, and I will begin to prep the next body. Then, we will move on to the next one until we have finished."

Clyde nods, noting the empty tin for tools as well as the cleaning solution and pile of neatly folded rags.

"Fine, then," the Doctor says. He rolls the table with the first body out, leaving about four feet of space between it and the rest of the line. The Doctor lowers his glasses from his forehead to his nose and then leans in close to the body. He pulls the white sheet down to the subject's waist. With a pen he produces from the front pocket of his shirt, he makes three small lines on the chest, two on the sides and one a few inches to the right of the sternum. The Doctor then examines the shaved head. He makes two small lines with the pen on the top part of the man's forehead and one small line toward the back of his head. "Here, here and here," he says with each stroke of the pen.

With the examination complete, the Doctor glances at the tools and equipment and gives an approving nod. For the most part, Clyde cannot tell which piece will go where. Clyde had seen all of the devices attached to Parchesi, however they look different when not on a body. He can determine the electricity gathering equipment though, because they have leather straps on them. They must not be surgically attached to the dead people.

"Gentlemen, it appears we're ready to proceed. Any questions?" The Doctor says. He looks first at Creighton who shakes his head and then at Clyde who does the same. The groundskeeper feels like he is going to be sick, or pass out, or both. Sweat drips from his neck down to the small of his back, and his hands shake, though he does his best to hide it by clenching his fists at his sides.

"Clyde, you do not need to watch this part. If you would

like to keep your back turned, you may. I only need you to do the cleaning. It takes...a certain type of person to witness this." the Doctor is trying to help, but his words only make Clyde more determined to watch; to become a full member of this little group.

"I'm fine watching. I'll— I'll be fine," Clyde says, though he's not sure he believes it.

"Fair enough." the Doctor turns and looks down at the body. "Are we ready, Edmund?"

* * *

"As ready as we'll ever be, Doc. Let's make some history, shall we?" Creighton says. Then, he looks over at Clyde. "When he's finished with the tool, Clyde, I'll place them in the tin. You know what to do from there." Clyde looks back at him and nods. "Good man."

Clyde's behavior thus far has surprised Creighton. It looked like they were going to have to take Clyde by force that first night when he saw the reanimated body of Mr. Parchesi, but he came around. Whatever problems he had with their brand of experimentation, he pushed past it and understands why they are doing things this way. He almost seems interested by it.

Since then, things have gone even better. Clyde was always his best worker, but Clyde has morals. Now, it seems, the morals have left Clyde, and he is becoming as much a full-fledged member of the Elk Hills Research Society as those people who paid their way in.

"Small scalpel, Mr. Creighton," the Doctor says, and Creighton hands the small scalpel to the Doctor. He gives a quick look over at Clyde who watches him make the incision. Creighton smiles, nods, and returns his attention to the body.

The first time they did this, the Doctor talked through each step so Creighton understood. Now, the Doctor is silent, focusing on his work. The first cuts are along the skull, the two on the front first and then the single cut along the back. These are the most difficult cuts because there is no easy access to the brain. The Doctor first makes the cuts through the skin and then, using a small hand-held saw, cuts his way through the skull bone. The air fills with bone dust as the Doctor files away bone and gains access to the brain. With the three skull cuts made and access to the brain created, the Doctor switches his attention to the chest.

Creighton looks up at Clyde. When the Doctor moves his body, they both have a clear view of the brain. Creighton looks for a reaction from his groundskeeper-turned-lab-assistant. There is none. Clyde stares down at the Doctor watching him work, but he shows no revulsion or horror over what he is witnessing.

"How are we doing so far?" the Doctor asks, his eyes still on his work; not pausing for an answer. He takes a larger scalpel and cuts along the lines he had drawn on the chest. Creighton watches Clyde again. Still no response. Even as the body is opened up.

The Doctor glides the blade through the skin and muscle of the man he hopes to reanimate. One cut for each lung; another for the heart. The organs are easy to see because, as the Doctor mentioned, there is no blood flow from the lacerations.

"All cuts have been made. We will now prepare the lungs, brain and heart for reanimation in that order," the Doctor announces.

Creighton hands the Doctor the first device. The Doctor separates the two electrodes and splays them apart. He lays the devices down against the man's chest and attaches the first electrode to the man's lung. Then, he does the same with the second electrode.

"We are attached," the Doctor says. He takes a second device from Creighton and attaches the electrodes to the other lung. "We will now close up the incisions."

The first lung incision gets sewn up, followed by the second. The devices are then sewn against the subject's chest. This is a new idea that Creighton and the Doctor brainstormed after the glue they used on Parchesi did not hold properly. They wanted the devices to stay in place better and longer, but they couldn't figure out a way to do so with just the adhesive. The devices were just too heavy to rely on glue alone. The stitches used to close up the incisions were regular medical stitches. The thread he uses now is stronger and will not break down over time. On top of that, the Doctor applies a new invention he's been working on which he calls epoxy. This will allow the devices to stay in place. More of the new invention is applied underneath the devices for even more stability.

"The lungs are complete and ready for reanimation," the Doctor says.

Creighton looks up at the clock. Fifteen minutes have gone by. He estimates the procedure will be completed in under forty-five minutes. Then, he looks down the long line of bodies and tries to estimate how long they will be here working.

"Is there anything you need, Doctor?" Clyde says.

"Patience, Clyde, patience. Thank you for your concern. Right now, I need this man to come back to life," the Doctor says as he takes a small cup of jelly from the table next to him.

This is the electro-conductive solution the Doctor had come to Creighton with almost two years ago. The Doctor wanted financial support to help test the solution. He didn't have the resources to perform the research he needed to complete his experiments. The electro-conductive jelly is applied directly to the brain. Then the Doctor takes a thin, soft sponge and slides the jelly around the exposed brain. This allows the low level of electricity to flow over the brain and help maintain continuous brain function. It is the central piece of the experiment. Without the jelly, the rest of their work is useless.

"I think the brain is sufficiently covered. Agree, Edmund?"

"Yes," Creighton replies. One electrode is attached to the brain through each of the frontal incisions, and two electrodes are attached at the rear of the skull. The Doctor is delicate, but Creighton can still see the man's soft brain give and press inward with even the slightest touch when the pads are placed against it.

"Now we close up the brain?" Clyde says. Creighton turns, glares at Clyde.

"In a sense, yes," the Doctor says, unannoyed by Clyde's questioning of the procedure. "We cannot close it up completely because I had to file some of the bone away to get at the brain. I will sew him up as best I can, then use this over the remaining brain tissue." The doctor holds up a small, white, bone-like substance.

"I will place this over the remaining opening, then attach the device over that. The brain devices are obviously smaller, as you can see, but they are also lighter than the lung devices and will stay in place easier. Once everything is on his head, his brain will be well protected."

"I see," Clyde says.

"Clyde you're handling this better than I did the first time, if I'm being honest," Creighton says. He isn't being honest, but it *is* shocking how well Clyde is doing. Clyde looks less like a scared man witnessing this type of procedure for the first time and more like an inquisitive scientist studying a new process.

"Just trying to learn, sir. If I'm a part of this now, I might as well make sure I'm useful. I can do the physical work that you need me to do. I'm sure that's why I was allowed to join in the first place. But now, I've seen the Doctor complete the actual work which, I think, puts me above a lot of the other people in the Society. Like you said the other day, I'm just adding value," Clyde says. The Doctor seals up the man's head as they talk.

"You *are* becoming more useful by the second, Clyde," Creighton says. It is amazing to Creighton that Clyde doesn't realize just how valuable he will become as the experiments stretch on. Creighton hopes he will go for their ultimate plan willingly, but if he doesn't, they will force him to go through with it. It won't matter what the young man wants in either case.

"Enough talk," the Doctor says.

Creighton stops, turns his attention back to the procedure. "Now, Clyde, I will connect the heart. Once that is complete, we will turn the machines on and reanimate. When that is done, we can go through the procedure of making the subject free of wires. But we will do that once he is conscious again."

The Doctor places electrodes onto the heart and stitches up the incision as he did with the others.

"Now, we are ready to reanimate. This is the experimental part of today's procedure. We were conservative last time, used only fifty millivolts on Mr. Parchesi. This time, we will use sixty millivolts in the hopes of speeding up the signal from brain to muscles."

Creighton attaches a cord to the end of each of the devices, then he looks to the Doctor who adjusts the dial in the center of the cord to the proper voltage.

"Let's see how it works at just a little bit higher voltage," the Doctor says. He flips the switch and Creighton watches the body. Parchesi took a few minutes to become conscious, so Creighton expects the same to happen here. He watches. The cold room sits in silence. He cannot hear the other two men moving or breathing. Like him, they watch the body for signs of life.

There is nothing. More seconds pass. Still, nothing. Creighton watches. There should have been some movement by now. Something to show the subject is alive again. But there is nothing. Nothing.

The subject's eyes flutter.

Clyde watches in horror. He's frozen in place, staring at the once-dead man on the table in front of him. The man's eyes, while still closed, move back and forth under the thin skin of his eyelids. Clyde keeps the same passive expression on his face he's kept the entire time, though he wants to run screaming from the room, out of the house and away from Creighton and the Doctor forever. But he doesn't. Something keeps him here. Something makes him watch life begin...again.

The man's chest rises up and falls back down the smallest amount. If Clyde wasn't watching intently, he would have missed it. Slow breathing, but the eyes don't open and there is no other movement. Then, the breaths stop. Nothing happens for ten seconds. Fifteen seconds. A minute. The room is still again, and they all stare at the subject. Is he dead? Is he alive? Is he somewhere in between? Clyde can't be sure.

Another breath then, another. The chest rising and falling. Rising, falling. The dead man's eyes move, and his fingers twitch back and forth.

"This— this is similar to the last time now," Creighton says. The Doctor nods: three men captivated by the historic event unfolding before them.

The man's eyes fly open, and he groans with such volume Clyde and Creighton flinch back away from the table. Only the Doctor remains stoic, watching.

"What? What is this? Where am I?" The man looks wildly around the room, his eyes gleaming but unable to focus, as if blind.

"Mr. Grimwald," the Doctor says. "You are okay. I'm a doctor, my assistants are here with us."

The man shifts on the bed, sits up. The movement is slow, labored. His bones crack and pop as they move for the first time since death. The wires tug gently at the devices attached to him. He winces, then lays back down flat on the bed. He lifts one hand and then the other. His feet rise up off of the bed and then lower themselves back down.

"What is this? Who am I? Where I am?" Questions fly out of his mouth in rapid succession.

"It appears we have successfully sped up the brain activity. Speech is faster. Body movement is faster too. More responsive than with Parchesi," the Doctor says to Creighton in quick staccato bursts. He then looks back down at Grimwald. "Your name is Mr. Grimwald and we have—"

Grimwald's movement stops him in mid-sentence. The patient sits up and glares around the room, this time focusing. He first looks at the Doctor and then at Clyde. Starting with his hands, violent tremors spread throughout his body. The bed shakes up and down, and his breathing quickens. His eyes roll back into his head, and his neck cranes backward. Clyde moves forward to help him as the bed nearly topples when the convulsions intensify.

"Stop!" the Doctor shouts. Clyde halts in his tracks, watches the suffering man. He starts to move forward then stops, thinking better of it. The blue veins on Grimwald's forehead bulge, and Clyde sees the blood pulsing through them.

The body stops. The tension that was held in every muscle in the body is gone. All movement stops. All breathing stops.

The three men wait in silence again, staring at the man that was dead, then alive, and now appears to be dead again. Like before, they wait. A minute. Five minutes. At the seven-minute mark the Doctor moves forward and takes the man's hand gently in his own. The Doctor rests his fingertips against the inner wrist of Grimwald's body.

"He has a pulse," the Doctor announces. "It appears the heart device is still operating normally. If the brain device is operating, it will tell the lungs to breathe again at some point. Then, the lung devices will begin operation. It is not lost yet."

They wait, the Doctors hand still resting on Grimwald's wrist. The dead man's eyes flutter, and he sits up like before. He breathes a long, deep breath in and lets it out.

"I am David Grimwald, who are you?" the once dead man says as he looks around the room.

Clyde looks to the Doctor and then to Creighton who both stare down at Grimwald.

"I'm Edmund Creighton, Mr. Grimwald. This is the Doctor and our assistant, Clyde."

"I— I don't know any of you, I'm afraid. How did I get here? The last thing I remember was going out fishing on the lake by my home. The— the boat I was in capsized. I was stuck, stuck underneath it and..." Grimwald trails off. His eyes look upward as if he's trying to remember how he got from the lake to this room with people he's never met. "You're a doctor. Is this—this is not a hospital."

"No, sir," the Doctor says. "This is *not* a hospital. The accident you speak of happened three weeks ago. You died in that accident, and we have brought you back."

The room is silent. Grimwald stares at the Doctor, then looks down at himself for the first time. He sees the shining metallic devices attached to his chest. The lights on each blink, indicating that the correct voltage is running through them and into his body.

"I— this can't be." Grimwald moves to get up, but the wires pull at the devices. The Doctor puts a hand on his chest, keeping him from getting to his feet.

"I'm going have to have ask you to remain still. I can get you unattached from the wall momentarily," the Doctor says and looks to Creighton.

Creighton retrieves the piston-like devices that sit on the opposite table and brings them to the Doctor.

"The devices on your body keep it functioning at the same level it did prior to your death, Mr. Grimwald. These devices will produce enough electric current to run the devices on your body. Otherwise, you would have to stay plugged in to stay alive. With these you will have the freedom of movement," the Doctor explains.

Clyde is motionless. He doesn't know what to think or what to say, so he just watches. The only thought that runs through his head is the new fact that life does not necessarily end at death.

"I don't know what to say. Is this a miracle or the work of the devil?" Grimwald says, watching the Doctor.

The Doctor ignores this comment and begins to attach the electricity harvesting devices to his legs. "Edmund, make a note that subject B has quicker speech and body muscle movement than subject A. We will try to repeat these results with subject C. If we can repeat three times, we have found our—"

Another convulsion from Grimwald cuts off the Doctor. He pulls away. Clyde moves forward as the tremors of the body rock the table back and forth. It tips all the way to one side, but Clyde grabs the table with two hands, pushing it back upright and keeping Grimwald from crashing to the floor. He holds the table steady even as Grimwald's legs buck and thrash against his arms.

Grimwald stills. The Doctor takes his wrist and looks for a pulse again. He shakes his head.

"Edmund, please flip the switch off, wait a minute then flip it back on."

They cannot do that. Clyde needs to stop this. The man was alive. He'd come back to life. They spoke to him. He had been here and alive again. His second life. They can't just turn the power off. Turning the power off is killing him. He would die again with the power off. Maybe he was already dead—again. Clyde knows he should stop this. He needs to stop Creighton from flipping that switch. But he doesn't move.

Creighton flips the switch off.

Grimwald is dead again.

They wait the minute, Clyde still holding the table, the muscles in his arms tensing as he grips its edges. While it appears as if Clyde is holding the table upright, his vice-like hold at the edge of the table is also the only thing keeping him from running out of the room.

Creighton flips the power back on. Grimwald's eyes flutter open, and he sits up, his face right in front of Clyde.

"Hello...I'm...David...Grimwald," he says, his speech slowed to a pace similar to what Parchesi demonstrated.

"Interesting," the Doctor says. "This is unexpected. It appears he doesn't remember his return to life just a few moments ago. Please make note. Edmund, prepare to repeat the process again. Mr. Grimwald, please listen to me. The man holding the end of the table there is Clyde. I need you to look at him. It is imperative that you remember his name."

"Clyde...where...am...I?" Grimwald says. He looks first at Clyde and then over at the Doctor. "I...will...remember...his... name...Clyde." The man's voice is childlike, lacking the intellect it had only a minute ago. He has changed.

A voice inside Clyde's head screams at him. He needs to stop the Doctor, to stop Creighton. He should jump over the table and grab Creighton, refuse to let him kill this man and reanimate him again, but he still doesn't move. He doesn't know why. He smiles at Grimwald.

"Now, Mr. Creighton," the Doctor says.

Creighton flips the switch off. Grimwald dies again.

CHAPTER 8

Instead of going up the steps and into the church to investigate, Michael takes a walk around the back. Church cemeteries are not always near or close to the churches they are affiliated with, but they usually are. He'd rather find the cemetery himself without having to ask around. The less people he talks to, the better. He wants to keep his relationship with Weaver and the Elk Hills Police as quiet as possible. Grave robberies where people take the bodies and leave the valuables are rare. He wouldn't consider himself a grave robbing expert, but almost every case he's heard of involves stealing the stuff in the casket, not the bodies. Whatever is going on in Elk Hills, it's interesting and front page worthy.

Michael meanders through a small copse of trees along the right side of the church and follows a path of matted grass around to the back. Still in the shadow of the large, brick building behind him, Michael follows the trail leading away from it and down a slight decline. It's not a tall hill, but it's clear the church was built on the highest point in the area, though Main Street is mostly flat. The trail of matted grass turns into an actual path when he gets behind the church. Grass that once grew here has been worn away by foot traffic and is now a trail of hard packed dirt through an otherwise empty field. Michael follows the trail down. About a hundred yards in front of him sits a stone wall. It's difficult for him to guess the height from this distance, but it's shorter than he is. A large metal gate hangs open at the far end, opposite his approach. Inside the boundaries of the wall stand rows of gravestones. Michael can't read the words on the metal gate from this distance, but he's positive it reads 'St. Theresa's Cemetery', or some approximation.

He adjusts his hat and strides down the decline toward the cemetery. He pats his pocket, feeling for a cigar. He almost pulls it out but decides to wait until he figures out what to do at the cemetery. It's a perfect day to be outside. Still cool but not cold. The sun is rising up from behind the church and warming the air and the back of his neck as he approaches his destination. Michael scans the cemetery for signs of life. It's a cemetery after all. Life is scarce, but it also sticks out. There is movement in the far corner and he focuses his eyes in that direction. Two men— they appear to have tools and a wheelbarrow with them—and are in the middle of working on something, though what they are doing, Michael can't tell. Behind them, a small, inconspicuous hut.

There is no way through the stone wall from this side. The wall is made up of large rocks and comes up just above Michael's waist. On the top row, the rocks are pointed and stick straight up. They are there for ornamental purposes and give the wall a more refined look. For practical purposes, it makes it hard for someone to climb over, especially if that person doesn't want to tear his clothes. Instead of risking it, he turns right and follows the wall, looking for a way inside. It appears he's not the first one to travel this way. The path of light dirt and matted-down grass follows the wall along with him. As he walks, he checks from time to time on the men, who act as though they haven't noticed him and continue working at the opposite side of the cemetery. When Michael approaches the corner of the wall, there is a metal door. The trail he's been on turns left into the gate, and he does the same. He pushes the gate open and lets himself inside the cemetery.

With each passing step, the view inside the cemetery changes. Although he's only ten feet away from the last time he stopped to take in the view of the surrounding area, the cemetery appears vastly different. A large tree just inside the gate reaches up to the sky and blocks the view of the church with it numerous low-hanging branches. The corner opposite him on the church end of the cemetery has the same type of large tree in the corner. On the opposite side, away from the church, a dense forest abuts the stone wall. The men are working on the forest side of the cemetery, and Michael heads toward them.

The wet grass in the cemetery clips the tops of his shoes, and they become damp as he works his way in-between and around the gravestones. A quick check of some of the dates on the stones tells him this place has been around a while. Some of the smaller, thinner stones date back over a hundred years. Michael is surprised by the condition of the stones given their age. The place is well maintained, a good sign.

As he nears the men working, they spot him and the rhythmic sound of the grubhoe being slammed into the dirt ceases. The men stop their work and wipe their foreheads as they look up at Michael. Any reason to stop, Michael thinks.

One man is taller, skinny with a long, thin face and stubble that says he only shaves one or two times a week. He has a wide brimmed hat on, but it's tipped back so the hat sits low on the back of his head. The second man is tall as well, though not as tall as his partner. His shoulders are broad, muscles visible through his shirt. He wears the same wide brimmed hat, but he takes it off when he stops working and runs a hand through his hair. Both men wear similar clothes, thin shirts and dungarees with the knees wet and dirty.

"Howya doin' there?" the taller guy says. It's only then that Michael realizes these guys are in their mid to late twenties. He's older than both of them, and it's unlikely they are in charge around here.

"Hey there," Michael says with a friendly wave and smile. "How are you? Michael Jacobs."

Michael approaches the two workers, hand extended. The taller one greets him first.

"Not too bad. Marvin Landry." Marvin shakes Michael's hand then gestures toward his partner. "William Brody. Beautiful day innit? How can we help ya?"

"Great day, great day." Michael looks up into the sky. No clouds, bright sun and a perfect temperature. But he cares very little about it at the moment. After some fake admiration for the weather, he gets down to business. "I'm actually here because I'm looking into the grave robberies that have happened around here as of late."

"You police?" William speaks for the first time. He squints his eye, and Michael can see his posture change slightly. He's defensive.

"Me? Nah, no way. Can't trust a lot of the police these days." Michael hopes he read the situation right. "I'm with the newspaper. Not out here, in the city. We heard about the robberies and wanted to see what we could find out."

William's face softens and Michael watches the tension in his arms disappear. He's read it right.

"Yeah, yeah. They came by asking about the people robbing them graves a few days ago. I told 'em the truth though: we didn't see nuthin'. We was working that day too, the first one, I mean, but it was a bad thunderstorm, and there wasn't much work to do. So, we was just in the shed waitin' for the storm to pass. The grave was up there on the other side," Marvin says and points across the cemetery.

"So, what happened then? Did you see anything at all?" Michael asks. He doesn't pull out his pen or a piece of paper, he just listens. These are the type of guys who wouldn't like the idea of someone writing stuff down while they talk. They won't have a problem sharing the story as long as it feels like a conversation. He's got a good memory. He's interested in this enough to remember the conversation word for word.

"Like he says, we were both working that day." William looks at Michael and folds his arms across his chest. It could be a sign that he doesn't want to share much, but Michael thinks it's just the way the guy usually stands. "The storm was bad. Really bad. Normally, we'd just work through the rain. It's no big deal really, but the rain was comin' down so hard it was impossible to work. We were supposed to be planting grass over in the far corner. Some skunks dug it up, and we were just gonna get the seed down. Rake out the area and re-work all the turf over there. But the rain was so hard it washed the seed away. We put down hay after we seed, but there wasn't even enough time to get the seed down, so we left it."

Michael nods, and Marvin picks up the story.

"So, I figgered we'd just get inside the shed and putter around 'til the rain stopped. The tools and stuff can always use some maintenance, so we just went through everything. Sharpened the axes'n the saws. Cleaned the caked-on dirt off the shovels and pickaxes. Reorganized the shelves up there. Normal stuff we do when we can't work outside."

"We checked the weather every few minutes or so. I was lookin' out the window quite a bit," William goes on. Michael can't help but think of the two as sharing one mind. "But I couldn't see that spot from inside the shed. I'd have to get out and walk up this way, even past here on account of that little hill right there." William points at the crest of a small mound. Not much, but it does block the view of the far corner.

"So, you fellas didn't see anything at all then?" Michael asks. He watches them, judges their reactions and tries to get a read on how much truth there is in this story. If they were worried telling the police all of this because of the hassle it would cause them, they're right. But sharing the story with Michael is a safer bet, these guys must know that. Michael gambles that he's reading them right once more. It's paid off so far. "Listen, I get it. You tell the cops what you saw and there's a whole other thing you've got going on here. It's going to lead to more questions. I understand all that. But I'm safer."

The men share a look with each other but say nothing. Michael knows he's pulled the right string and keeps going.

"I'm safer for a lot of reasons. I'm not the police. I'm a nobody." It's not entirely true, but it works for Michael at this moment. He has to get them to think there is no risk to them in all this. "You tell me everything you know and that's it. The only thing I'll ever do is write the story and tell it to people. Someone gets mad they'll be calling *me* into the station and bringing *me* to court."

He pauses, but he's got one more reason in case the groundskeepers are still on the fence.

"Finally, no names. No one but me will know who it was that told me whatever you tell me. Not the police, or my boss, or anyone reading the paper. That's a guarantee." He reaches into his pocket and palms a five dollar bill he'd put there just in case, then he reaches out and shakes William's hand, passing him the money. "I've been doing this a long time, and I've never named a source. I've been pulled into court twice over it and still nothing from me. You'll have the information off your chest. No more guilty conscience. What do you say?"

Michael gives a quick smile and looks from Marvin to William. Reading them. William glances down at his hand and the money there. They say nothing at first, just share a few glances at each other. William shrugs, and Marvin lifts his eyebrows at his partner.

"Could we have a minute?" William says.

"Of course." Michael steps away from the two and turns his back to them, retreating a few steps in the direction he came. Marvin and William retreat too, in the opposite direction. They talk in low voices. Michael can hear the sound of their voices, but with a slight wind blowing against the side of his face, he can't make out the words.

"Sir," Marvin calls out. Michael turns around, pretending that he wasn't trying to eavesdrop the entire time.

"Yes?" Michael says. He walks back toward them and looks back and forth from one to the other.

"I think we'll help ya out a little bit here," Marvin says. "But we need ta know for sure our names is gonna be out of it."

"I can't sign anything like that, but I can promise you and give you my word, I'd never do that to you. Sources are the most important thing I have. I've never given one up. And I never will."

They look at each other again and nod.

William looks to his partner. "You tell him, Marvin."

"Okay, so like I said, we didn't see nuthin' when we were in the shed workin' on stuff. But, the rain started to clear. The sky brightened first, then the rain slowed a bit. It almost stopped, but not completely. We checked outside like we'd been doin' that whole time, and when I came out that last time it was good enough to get back to work. I figgered we get the rakes and clear out the water from that spot and get the seed back down in there before the end of the day. And when I came back out, I saw it. I didn't really think much about it when I first saw it, not 'til we found that grave all dug up. Then I kinda connected it together, you know?"

A light breeze blows across the cemetery. Michael squints his eyes and gives his hat a slight tug down, though he doubts a breeze this light will knock his hat off. He nods, and Marvin continues the story.

"It was one of them expensive automobiles. I didn't know the name of it at first, but I seen an ad for it in the paper the very next day. It was a Cadillac. LaSalle or something like that. Anyway, I saw it just over there on the other side of the gate." Marvin points to the gate and the road that leads away from it. "But you can see, we couldn't see from back over there where we were. I could only see when I came out this way. And I just saw it driving away and that was it."

"And you didn't tell the police about this?" Michael asks. This is a big break. The police didn't have anything. Michael had no leads when he arrived this morning. A few questions to the right people and he was on the trail. LaSalle was the new expensive model from Cadillac; Marvin was right about that. But it wasn't just new, it was *really* new. Only the richest people would own one. The gangsters in Chicago didn't all have one yet, though there were a few floating around and Michael conducted his fair share of research on these new cars just a few weeks ago for another story.

"Naw. Like you said, it's too much of a hassle for me to tell them things. You musta heard the rumors. Chicago police is all run by the gangs, and bet it's moving out this way too. Better just to tell them I don't know anything and let them figger it out a different way. Not like anyone was hurt or nuthin'. The guy was already dead, right?"

"You're right about that," Michael says, then he looks to William. "That's really helpful actually. Is there anything else?"

William shakes his head. "I didn't see anything. I was still in the shed and Marv didn't mention it when he came in to get me because there was no reason to. Only after when we saw the dirt all dug up did he say something."

"Okay, guys. Thanks. This is a really big help." Michael turns, acting like he's going to walk away. Then, he turns back to them. This is a deliberate tactic. Sometimes people will give information if they're caught off guard. Making William and Marvin think he is done and then pulling a quick question on them might get them to give an answer without thinking. The best way to get real honesty from two guys who are admitted liars. "Oh, you guys live around here I assume. Any idea who might own a big expensive car like that?"

"Well," William starts, but Marvin coughs, interrupting.

"Not that I can think of. Lots of people with cars around here. Hard to get away from them now."

"And you'll keep our names out of it right?" Marvin asks.

"Of course." Michael smiles. He has almost all the information he needs already. He would love to have the name William was just about to give him, but it won't be hard for him to find out. He has the car they saw, and he knows that there is an obvious answer to the question about who might own it. This is why he loves his job. "Listen, fellas, if anything at all comes back to you and you want to talk again, I'll be around. You can find me at *Louise's* around nine every morning, and there again around six in the evenings. I'm not a hard person to find. If that's it, then I guess I'll be on my way. Thank you for all your help."

He tips his hat to the two men, and they return it.

As Michael walks back across the wet grass toward the corner where the gate is, he thinks about his next step. He told Ron he would share information with him when he got it. This was a pretty big step in the right direction, and it didn't take more than an hour. He could find Ron and keep him in the loop, but he feels there is more he could do before he brings him in. Also, if Ron knew he got this type of information this fast, he might be able to put two and two together about where he found it. That wouldn't be the best situation for his two new sources at the cemetery. Better, he thinks, to see what else he can find out in Elk Hills today and bring all of his information to Weaver at the same time.

It's time to find out who the rich men in Elk Hills are.

CHAPTER 9

It's been hard for Clyde to be at home with Patricia the last few days. It gets harder every second he's there. He wants to tell her everything, but he knows he can't. It would do no good to tell her what he's seen; what he's been a part of. She couldn't understand.

He sits motionless after dinner while she cleans the house. Usually, he helps her. Usually, they talk. They've always been a team. Patricia works just as hard as he does. She has a job making bread for one of the bakeries in town. She works. Most men can't say that about their wives. She takes care of the house, too. They have always been in it together, and now, now he feels like he's breaking up their team. He *knows* he is, but there is nothing he can do about it.

"Is everything okay, Clyde?" she asks.

"Yes, of course. It's just with these new longer hours and all the new work, I'm just really tired lately. I'm sorry. I'll help you out," Clyde says. As a rule, he doesn't lie to Patty, never has. But now the lies slip off his tongue faster and easier than he ever thought they would.

"No, no. You're working hard for us. Maybe too hard?" She rests her hand on the back of his neck and squeezes, relieving the tension in the muscles but not the tension inside his brain. "I can take care of this. You try to relax. You've got a lot more on your plate now than you did before."

Patty rubs his neck again and slides her hands down to his shoulders kneading the muscles and forcing a soft moan from his lips. It feels good. He doesn't know how long he can continue to lie to her.

He knows he will lose her if he tells her the truth. So, he sits, content to let her help him while the lies continue. Over and over, every time she asks him how his day was, he lies. Every time he makes up a detail about his new job to have some sort of answer to her questions, he lies. The lies eat him up. They make his head throb. He wants a drink, but he knows that will only make his head hurt more.

Clyde sucks in a long breath.

"You're too good to me, you know?"

"Why don't we just go to bed?" Patty says.

"You go ahead," Clyde says. "I— I just need to sit here and unwind before I go to bed. I have to get up and do it all over again tomorrow."

"Okay." She looks at him and narrows her eyes. It's a look he's never seen from her before. "I know there's more than just work, but I can't make you talk, Clyde. I'm here for you. I always will be."

The truth almost pours out of him then. He almost spills it all. Instead, he stops himself. There is too much at stake if he tells her. His life would be in danger and he presumes her's as well. Clyde isn't going to put Patty in danger no matter how much he hates lying to her. He has to in order to keep her safe.

He remains silent, staring ahead, not making eye contact. At last, she goes to bed, and Clyde is alone.

The way it should always be now.

"This is a big day, Mr. Creighton," the Doctor says. The two men wait in the library as the guests start to arrive. The Elk Hills Research Society has not met since the reveal of Mr. Parchesi. Though it hasn't been long, a lot has happened. They successfully reanimated all of the bodies. Since their reanimation, three have died. It is, the Doctor assures him, still a very good percentage. Two of the deaths, it was determined afterward, were the results of problems within the bodies prior to the original death. Those were inevitable. While the outcome was tragic, it helped further their research. The other death was Mr. Grimwald, resulting from applying too much electricity to his brain. He is to remain dead. No further tests will be run on him.

Creighton shakes hands with everyone who walks past, smiling and sucking on a cigarette when people arrive. With each person he greets, Creighton pulls them in close to him, keeping them off balance. He always likes to have the upper hand, even with the people he considers his equals. *They* are in *his* house; therefore, he is in control of the situation. It's what's gotten him where he is in life.

Creighton takes the last sip of bourbon in the small glass and looks to Margaret, who is at the entrance to the library greeting people. He catches her eye and shakes his empty glass at her. She nods, smiles, props the door open, and returns a few seconds later with a bottle of bourbon.

"Thank you, Margaret," he says. "You're one of the best workers I've ever had, and if I ever tell you otherwise it just means I'm tired or hungry. Or both."

"Thank you, sir," she responds with a bow of her head. Then she fills his glass and takes the bottle out of the room before returning to her post.

Creighton greets one of the members of the Society and watches him go through the closet and down the stairs. For the moment, he and the Doctor are alone in the library.

"Do you think Clyde is doing okay down there with all of the reanimates?" the Doctor asks.

"Oh, sure. They don't like us, but they like Clyde. They don't hate us. Except for that one woman. She hates us. Especially you." Creighton laughs. "She *really* hates you."

"He does seem to have an affinity for them as well. I mean, it's not like they are the same as regular people. Like you and me. Yes, they're alive again, but not really. And if they are alive, they owe everything they have to you and me. We gave it all to them. Another chance at life. They should be grateful. Even that bitch that tried to scratch my face." The Doctor rubs his fingers along the faint red line on his cheek. The scratches were worse right after it happened—very noticeable then—not so much now.

Everyone in the room that day, when they learned they were brought back to life, saved from death by the work of the Doctor and Creighton, were happy. Thankful. Everyone except Melinda McDonald. She was *not* happy. She was *not* thankful. She was angry. At first, the anger was so violent and resentful, the Doctor assumed it was a problem with the reanimation process. A small variable that he did not account for. But as they got to know the woman, they realized she was just angry about the situation. She was a devout Catholic in her first life. She had strong ties to the church and, even after death and reanimation, her strong ties persist.

"You know, I think with all of them, all of them except her, they're not so much fearful of us as they are fearful of the power it seems we possess." The Doctor puts a hand on Creighton's shoulder and leans in a little closer to him. "Clyde has been with us for such a short time, he doesn't know everything. But you and I have been through the whole thing. They know that, and being able to bring someone back from the dead is no easy feat. They are intimidated by us, Edmund, nothing more."

Creighton nods. "And McDonald?"

"Ah, McDonald is different." The Doctor laughs and rubs his cheek again. Creighton is sure the man has no idea he's doing it so often. "We were wrong to assume that there wouldn't be more of that. I think that was our mistake. Some people believe in religion if only to help their souls once they die. They live life and go to church on Sunday so that God will save their souls. We took that away from her. In reality, her belief system is wrong. Talking to all of these people, we know that now, but we should have anticipated it."

"You're probably right, Doc." Creighton takes a sip of his drink and pulls on the cigarette again, puffing the smoke up into the air. He watches it curl and float up to the ceiling, joining the haze of smoke already up there. The windows at the very top of the room near the ceiling are open, but only a crack so the smoke takes time to drift outside. "Do you think she'll play along tonight?"

The Doctor coughs and shakes his head. "No, I don't. If she doesn't that's fine. We can explain it to the rest of the group, and we can leave Clyde in the lab with her so she doesn't cause any trouble. We'll only bring Clyde out to tell him about the next step. Agreed?"

Creighton nods. Clyde has been a good sport. Better than Creighton thought he would be. He's almost starting to like the guy. Almost. There was always something about him, even before all of this, when he was working, that Creighton didn't like. Is he too nice? Creighton always thought it was that—but then watching him the past few weeks—the things he's done are not things nice guys would do. They are things a ruthless person would do. They are things someone who would stop at nothing to get ahead would do. It doesn't fit with what he knows about Clyde. Clyde works hard, not smart. But maybe Clyde is turning over a new leaf. He isn't sold on Clyde just yet. Either way, he might need some convincing to go along with the next phase of the plan.

"Clyde has been better than expected, I'll give you that. But I don't know if he will be up for this next task," Creighton says.

"I think he may surprise you, Edmund. You keep thinking of him as the worker you had for however long. He is not that anymore. He's something different. Something more. I think we can count on him. Even if he has...reservations about this. He is following through with everything we ask. His mind is in a different place now. You watch. I think you'll be surprised."

Creighton greets two more people who come in, nod and shake his hand. He stands with them for a few seconds, and then they move along. He looks back to the Doctor.

"I think that's most of the Society. I know there are a few who could not make it tonight. It's probably alright to proceed with the session now. Should we go down to the lab before we start?" Creighton says. He places a hand on the Doctor's shoulder and turns toward the closet without waiting for a response. Creighton ducks inside and goes down the stairs to the lower level. The echo of voices moves its way up and down the stone hallway. Creighton looks back over his shoulder, toward the meeting room and turns the opposite direction down the hall to the lab. It is filled with once-dead bodies. And Clyde.

Creighton opens the door to the lab, and Clyde looks up from the desk. Around him, the faces of the former dead turn to look at him also, but their turns are slow, measured, inhuman.

"Are we ready in here, Clyde?" Creighton looks at the groundskeeper, averting his eyes from the reanimates, who will only stare back at him and speak only if absolutely necessary.

"Yes, sir," Clyde says. He looks at Creighton and then the Doctor. "Except Mrs. McDonald, who says—"

"There...is...no...way...I'm—" the woman starts, and Clyde helps her finish.

"No way she's going out there, sir. I don't know what will happen with her. The others, I think—" Clyde says. The Doctor jumps in before he can finish.

"I understand that. I may not like it, Mrs. McDonald, but I understand. I don't think we should make her come out if she really doesn't want to, do you Mr. Creighton?" The Doctor steps forward and touches Melinda McDonald's arm gently. She pulls away slowly, glares at Creighton and then at the Doctor.

"Tell...them," she says to Clyde, like a child talking to her parents when she's too nervous to talk to an adult she doesn't know.

Creighton doesn't like that Clyde is getting so close with the reanimates. They are more machine than human. For every good thing that Clyde does, he does something else that irritates

Creighton. He can't wait until this meeting is over so he can tell Clyde exactly what his services will entail within the research society.

Clyde looks from the Doctor to Creighton and sighs. He can tell Clyde doesn't want to share this information. He knows it's not Clyde's request, it's Melinda McDonald's. Still, Creighton is in a shoot-the-messenger type mood. If Clyde gives him bad news; he may do just that.

"She wants me to tell you to shut her off." The McDonald woman stares at the two men. Her eyes move back and forth slowly from one to the other, her lips press tight together, her chin lifts up in the air. "She says she would do it herself if she knew how. Just tell her how, and she will do it. You won't be killing her. She just wants to be with Jesus again."

McDonald nods and waits for a response.

"I don't care what she—" Creighton starts, his voice approaching a yell, but the Doctor cuts him off.

"Just like I can understand her point of view regarding not coming out for this tonight, I also understand this. I think we can come to an understanding. But we will have to wait until after the meeting in a few minutes. Does that work, Mrs. McDonald?"

When she nods, Creighton feels his face redden. They've worked too hard and spent too much money on these reani-mates to just turn one of them off. Additionally, they've asked them all—each and every person who has come back—what they remember about being dead. Some of them have been dead more than a few months. If there is anything waiting for humans after death, these people would know. Every one of them have said the same thing. There is *nothing* after death. Nothing. Jerrold White, who died because his heart stopped while he was out working on his property, said he remembered falling to the ground, and in the next instant waking up here in the lab. There is nothing else. Nothing in between. No passage of time. No light. No Jesus. Every other person's story is just like Jerrold's. There is life, and then there is death. And death is nothing. Why then? Why would Melinda McDonald want to return to that? Why does she want them to just shut her off? It would kill her again. Creighton can't figure out why the woman wants this, and it makes him angry. But he bottles it up. The Doctor is right, this is not the time for anger or arguments. There is a meeting he must run and other reanimates who are grateful and happy to be alive, albeit weary of the Doctor and himself.

"Does that work for you, Mr. Creighton?" The Doctor looks him in the eye and nods. There is a half-smile on his face. Maybe there is a way to get through this without having to turn off the McDonald woman and the Doctor has some sort of plan. He will play along for now.

"Yes, that works for me. We certainly don't want you to be unhappy, Mrs. McDonald. We have a lot of people here tonight, and we don't have to discuss it right now. When we have more time to properly address your concerns, we will." Creighton forces a smile.

McDonald backs away from the front of the room, joining the rest of the reanimates. Creighton looks to Clyde.

"You haven't been putting ideas in her head have you, Clyde?"

"No, Mr. Creighton. She...she came up to me with it on her own. I think she truly hates this and would rather just be dead again, given the choice. The others are ready, though. If you would like to start the meeting together, I can walk them out when I hear you introduce them. It will take us some time to get down there, obviously, but they are eager to see other people. They want to return to society again and think this will be a step toward that."

Creighton lets out a loud, quick laugh then lowers his voice so the reanimated can't hear him. "If they only realized there is no way they could ever rejoin society. The only people they will ever see again are the three of us and the ones in that room." Creighton points out into the hall in the direction of the meeting room.

"Yes, sir, of course. But we— you gave them a second chance at life, and they are eager to get back to it. I know I'm just the groundskeeper, but I believe that if you let them think there is a chance they will return to their lives outside of here, they will be more willing to go along with what you need from them. I'm just trying to help, sir."

Creighton nods and then looks over at the Doctor who nods back at him, a smirk growing on his face.

The Doctor and Creighton leave the lab and begin the meeting of the Elk Hills Research Society. Clyde stays with the reanimates until it's time for them to join the group in the meeting hall. He feels more comfortable with these people than with either the Doctor or Creighton. Especially Creighton. Some days Creighton seems to enjoy Clyde's company, and on others he seems about to kill him. The Doctor, on the other hand, Clyde is certain, likes him a lot. Maybe it's because the Doctor hasn't known Clyde as long. The Doctor has not seen Clyde grow from just another worker to the most trusted worker on the property. Yes, Creighton promoted him, but Clyde can't help but think he is envious of the way Clyde has moved up through hard work. He always felt Creighton looked down on him, as though he was a second-class citizen. Now, solely because of his hard work, Clyde gives his opinion on things related to Creighton's deepest secrets. He works alongside Creighton and the Doctor, all because of his hard work. It is something he thinks Creighton could never do and it angers his employer.

He will put up with it. He can stand the sometimes displeasure of his boss if it means he gets the money they promised; it would change his life. And Patty's life. He sees no reason why they would hold out on him. Creighton seemed genuine when discussing money last week. The millionaire has always paid him on time and never tried to short him on cash. As far as he was concerned, the business side of Creighton didn't let personal problems get to him.

"You're...different...from...them," one of the reanimates says to Clyde as he waits by the door, listening for his cue to bring the group out to face the investors.

At first, Clyde cannot remember the person's name. It is someone he hasn't spoken with much.

"No, no. I'm not like them at all," Clyde says, wondering why it's easier to talk to this formerly dead man than to his wife. "I'm sorry, I don't remember your name. Lots of new faces here for me." Clyde laughs.

"John...Ferling," the man says. The reanimates have come up with a way of speaking in which they say as few words as possible. After experimentation, it turned out the electrical charge that the Doctor used on Mr. Parchesi was correct. The greater charge helped their speech, but it caused problems in the long run. They all talked and moved slow, but they were still alive, again.

"They have been doing this a long time," Clyde says to Mr. Ferling. "They tested this on animals of different sizes before they moved on to humans. They recruited me, I assume, because they needed to move the— your bodies around, and someone with a little more strength than those two was needed."

"What...do...before?" Ferling says pointing at Clyde. *What did you do before?*

Clyde looks out the crack in the door and down the hall in the direction of the meeting and listens to the Doctor. He's waiting for Creighton to begin talking. He knows what the Doctor is telling the group, and he's only about halfway through the spiel. When Creighton starts talking, that's his cue to usher the group of reanimates down the hallway.

"I've worked for Mr. Creighton for a long time, as his groundskeeper. I only found out about all this within the last few weeks." Clyde gestures around at all the equipment. Equipment that, over the course of a few days, has gone from horrific in his eyes, to ordinary. Just another part of the workday. He resents the fact that it's become normal, but the money reminds him that he has to keep playing this game if he wants to see the benefits for him and Patty.

Ferling's head goes up and down. Slow but steady. He's nodding.

"Long...you...here...we...okay," he says. *As long as you're here we will be okay.* "Good...man."

"Thank you. I will try my best, Mr. Ferling. I don't want anything to happen to anyone, but I'm not in charge either." Clyde tries to smile and almost musters one, but he's sure it looks like a shrug. He listens at the door again and hears Creighton speaking.

"Thank you, Doctor, the next step in our ultimate goal has been achieved..." Creighton starts. He will speak for a few minutes, which won't be long enough, but it will get them most of the way down the hall so that there isn't so much waiting by the rest of the Research Society.

"That is our cue." Clyde stands up and projects his voice across the room, but not so loud the crowd outside will be able to hear him. "Remember, they just want to introduce you to the group that helped make all of this possible. If we could move toward the door and work our way right and down the hallway."

Clyde backs up a few steps so that the group can get through the door. He lets them proceed ahead of him and follows the last man out. It is Mr. Ferling.

"Wait here, Mrs. McDonald. I'm sure they will talk to you after they are finished," Clyde says. He doesn't know what's going to happen to her, but he believes if Creighton gets his way, they will turn her off and back on again, try to get rid of any feelings she has that he doesn't like.

CHAPTER 10

After leaving the cemetery, it doesn't take long for Michael to determine who in the Elk Hills area would have enough money and influence to purchase one of the new Cadillacs Marvin and William saw the day of the grave robbery. It was so easy Michael can't figure out why Marvin and William didn't just tell him themselves. Under the guise of doing a piece on the ultra-rich member of the community in the suburbs, he speaks to the Priest up in the church on his way back to town and then two locals he bumps into on the street, and Edmund Creighton's name came up all three times. He might not be the only suspect or involved in the robberies at all, but right now he is the only name Michael has.

If he had a car with him, he'd be driving to the Creighton estate. Instead, he sits on a bench against the wall in front of the general store, planning his next move.

Michael checks his watch; it's just past noon. He's accomplished a lot for a half day of work. It's so much easier to get around a small town than a city like Chicago. But he needs to make a decision. If he walks to Creighton's estate, he won't get there until late afternoon, and he has to catch his train and meet Weaver around six. If he interviews Creighton and runs out of time, the man could get spooked and refuse to talk to him again. Opportunity wasted. But he's hit a one-way street. The only lead he has is Creighton. It's probably the correct one, but he has to verify. If he can't follow up on it now, what does he do with the rest of his day?

The story forms in his mind. It's something he's always done. While some guys outline ahead of time, Michael never does. Instead, he figures out which direction he wants to take with a story and dives into the research. As each new piece of information is gathered, he adds it to the story in his head. When he's finished his research, he sits down to write, knowing the whole story from beginning to end. When he finally sits down to write, the words flow out, and he knows he has all the information he needs.

The warm spring sun shines down on his face as he sits on the bench and closes his eyes. The breeze is light but cools his skin. The combination of the two, along with the fresh, clean air is something he rarely enjoys in the city. It puts his mind at ease, and he prepares the story in his head. He knows the facts of the case. He has a good idea of who is behind it, and he knows the area well enough to describe how it might have happened. The only thing he doesn't know is what Edmund Creighton will tell him and—Michael opens his eyes. The family. The families of the victims. *That* is the only piece missing from the story. That could slow his progress later when he sits down to write. Parchesi was his name. The only challenge in talking to Parchesi's family is that he might have to tell them why he's poking around.

Either way, it would be a good activity for the few hours left in the day. Tomorrow he will come back to Elk Hills and start in on Edmund Creighton.

Michael runs through the story in his mind once more, thinking of the paragraph, or possibly two, that discusses Parchesi. His family's reaction to the grave robbery. They would be distraught, upset. They might also be willing to talk if it meant finding who took him.

Reluctant to leave the comfort of the warm sun and clean air, Michael gets up and enters the general store. There is an old woman behind the counter and an equally old man stocking shelves near the front with what appears to be strawberry jam.

"Mornin'," the man says as Michael lets the door close behind him. The corner of the door hits a bell and announces his arrival, even though he's already been spotted.

"Morning." Michael smiles and tips his hat at the gentleman.

"Anything I can help you with?" the man says.

Michael looks around. He needs to buy something, and the bottles of jam look pretty good. "Loaf of bread, and actually, that jam looks pretty good, too."

The man smiles and tosses Michael the jar in his hand. He catches it, smiles.

"My daughter makes it. She owns a farm th' other side a town. Picks the strawberries fresh, makes it 'n stores it 'n then sends it over to me when we have the space ta sell it. Bread's over there 'n the corner. My wife can ring you up."

"Thanks, I'm sure it will taste great. I've actually got another question I think you might be able to help me with. It's a little bit of a different nature though, Mister..." Michael trails off, knowing the man will fill in the blank.

"Smith," he says. "Rufus Smith." He stands up and walks over to Michael and extends his hand. Michael shakes it.

"Michael Jacobs, sir. It's good to meet you. I am...I'm actually a reporter. I was trying to get some information on the grave robbery that happened here last week. Fella named Parchesi." Michael presses his lips together tight and shakes his head, knowing what Mr. Smith is going to think about the grave robbery just by the kind of man he appears to be.

"Oh, awful thing. Terrible," he says. "They're such a good family. He was a good man. Why can't they just let 'im rest in peace, you know?"

"I agree. It's awful," Michael says. "I didn't know if you knew where I might be able to talk to the family, sir."

"Oh, I don't know about that. Don't know if they want ta be disturbed right now, 'specially about this kina thing. Best to just leave them alone. You know? No need to bring it up for 'em, put it in the papers 'n stuff. They shouldn't have to deal with it." Smith leaves the half-full box of jam on the floor and the half-filled shelf by the entrance to the store. He puts a hand on Michael's back. At first, Michael isn't sure what is happening but then realizes the old man is leading him over to the bread. Michael is expecting this type of resistance and is prepared.

"I understand it, believe me. When my father died, if someone took his body up out of the ground, I don't know what I'd do. But I'd also want him to get back into the ground." Michael knew before he started the conversation that he was going to have to take a gamble to get the information he needed. At least he had a friend on the police force just in case. "Listen. Just between you and me, the police have no leads. Nothing. I think this is one of the worst things you could do to a person and their family, short of killing them. They asked me to help them out, the police that is. I just want to help get Theodore's body back where it's supposed to be. Where God wants it to be. I don't know if the family can help, but I'd feel awful if they could and I didn't at least talk to them."

The old man sighs. Michael knows he has him.

"I like to think I can figure people out pretty quick. You seem like a good person, Michael."

"Thank you, sir."

Rufus takes a loaf of bread off the wall. The one he grabs looks soft, and, when he hands it to Michael, it's still warm.

"This is the freshest loaf we have. You should take this one. It'll go perfect with that jam."

"Thank you, I appreciate it. It smells fantastic."

"Martha can ring you up. Then come back up front 'n talk to me." Rufus motions toward the counter and then walks back to the shelf by the front door.

Michael pays for his bread, and Martha puts his items in a bag for him. He clutches the bag in one arm and works his way back through the store.

"Thank you again, Mr. Smith. I'm sure it will be delicious," Michael says following one of his golden rules: if someone says to talk to them again, don't ask them the same question twice. They know what you want. If they feel like sharing, they will. With this rule in mind, Michael turns to leave, hoping the old man will stop him. It's not until he puts his hand on the door to exit the building that Rufus Smith speaks up.

"I trust you, son. Don't betray that trust, you hear me?" Rufus says. Michael says nothing but turns back to face the older gentleman. "I want the ones that took that body caught s'much as anyone. Even if you don't believe in afterlife, you feel for that family, you know? Two things: you keep my name out of it. Don't tell them where you got their address 'n don't put nothing I'm about to tell you in the paper neither."

"Of course," Michael says. He wonders what else ol' Rufus has in mind. He just wants a location of the Parchesi family. Anything more is gravy.

"They're about ten, fifteen minute walk from here. Jefferson Ave, I think it's one-twelve Jefferson, but I can't be sure of that. You'll be able to tell it's their house. Dark brown wood, red shutters. It's the only one like it on the road. They walk to the Catholic Church up there every Sunday. Jefferson's just off Main Street past the church, there on the left. Ya can't miss it."

"Thank you, sir. Like I said, I just want to get his body back where it belongs, same as you. Any information I can get could be helpful, even if the family doesn't think it is." Michael shakes Rufus's hand and turns to leave again, following the same rule as before. If he wants to share more, he will. Michael is still not going to press him.

"There's one other thing, son. I don't know if it's pertinent, but if it can help catch whoever's doin' this, then I can be a good Samaritan s'much as anyone."

Michael looks back at him, waiting for the next line to come.

"I'm sure you know about the other grave robberies that have been happening around here lately," Rufus says. Michael nods, and the shopkeeper continues. "I assume you think they're all connected 'n that the police think that, too. It's the rumor anyways. I hear a lot with this job. Anyway, another rumor going around is that the bodies are all ending up at the same place. Maybe you're only looking into the first robbing or maybe you're looking into all of them. Either way, they're supposedly all going up to the Creighton place."

Michael tries to keep a straight face, but he realizes he's let Rufus read him when he stops talking and looks at the reporter. Whatever Rufus sees, it's enough to throw him off for a second.

"I'm guessing this ain't the first time you've heard the name in your research, then. Well, I don't know the man very well. He keeps to himself up there 'n doesn't like to mix too much with us locals. He's here for the land, not the community. He pretends to be one of us, but he's not. Anyway, rumor is he's got all the bodies up there at his place, but no one can even guess why. He certainly doesn't need the money from stealing the jewelry from them or anything. The Parchesi's know this too, but they might not pass it along, so that's why I'm telling you. If you already knew the name, then at least you know you're headed in the right direction. It also might serve as a warning for you to be a little cautious when you talk to 'im. He'll be a hard person to nail down."

"I— um, I *have* heard the name come up, actually. But it was just like you said, a hunch more than anything substantiated," Michael says, lowering his voice, though the store is empty other than Rufus, his wife and Michael.

"It's all I'm givin' you, too. Rumors. People don't like to mess with Mr. Creighton. He's a powerful man, no one would want to cross him, so I'm not surprised it's just rumors you've heard."

"I understand what you're saying, sir. The only person who

will have their name on this thing is me. I'm the only one that has to worry."

"Okay, son. I appreciate what you're trying to do. Please be good to that family," Rufus says and returns to his jars of strawberry jam.

"Thank you, Mr. Smith," Michael says. The man nods but doesn't look back and Michael leaves the store.

It is a quick walk through the center of town back in the direction of the Church. When Rufus mentioned Jefferson Avenue, Michael was sure he saw it on his first foray around the church. He was right. He finds the street and walks down it, looking for the dark house with red shutters.

It's unlikely that Creighton, who by all accounts has plenty of money, would actually walk into cemeteries and take the bodies out of their caskets himself. He would pay someone to do it for him. However, Marvin and William said they saw the expensive Cadillac leaving the area the day Parchesi's body was taken. That, in Michael's mind, means Creighton *was* there. He wouldn't let someone else drive an automobile like that and throw a dead body in it without being present. Most rich folk have drivers, but they also love their expensive possessions. He wouldn't leave something like this up to chance. Creighton might not have been alone, but he was most certainly there. The question in Michael's mind then becomes: why would Creighton go forward with this on his own? He'll know for sure tomorrow if Creighton is involved.

Tonight, on the train and when he gets home, he will have to come up with enough questions about the fake story he is writing on Creighton and suburban wealth to be believable. Those questions tomorrow will be critical.

The questions he will ask in a few minutes, while not critical to learning the events leading to the grave robberies, must be good enough to help round out the story and give it the human element that sells papers. In the end, people want to feel good about things. He knows people will respond to the crime. The difference between a good story and a great one is connecting it to people. This interview with Parchesi's family, and humanizing or demonizing Creighton, will be the connection.

Jefferson Avenue bends slightly to the right and rolls downhill. As it turns, Michael scans and studies each house. Straight in front of him is a modest house, dark brown, bright red shutters. It's not the biggest house on the street, not even close. It's not the smallest, either. It is well maintained and the plants and shrubbery in front make it warm and welcoming.

Michael strides up the front walk, attempting to keep a caring, somber look on his face. He needs to maintain a balance between friendly and understanding the tragic situation. He knocks on the door three times like Goldilocks, not too loud, not too soft. There is a moment of silence, and Michael remains motionless, listening for movement on the other side of the door. At first, nothing. No sounds. Then, a piece of furniture sliding on hardwood, footsteps, and the metallic sound of locks being disengaged. The door opens six inches and stops. A chain connects the door to the jamb and obscures the woman's face behind it.

"Ah, hello. Mrs. Parchesi?" Michael says, doing his best not to sound rehearsed.

"Yes, that's me. What can I do for you?" There is no smile on her face. She wants to know who he is and why he's here

before she sends him on his way. This is going to be more difficult than he thought.

"I am, I'm actually here about the tragic events that have
happened to your family lately, ma'am. I'm very sorry to hear
about what happened at the cemetery," Michael says. His
mouth downturns, his eyes look down as well.

"Thank you, I don't think I know you. Did you know
Teddy?"

"No, ma'am. You don't know me; I didn't know your
husband either. I—please ask that you just to hear me out,
though." Michael looks at her, and she just looks back at him
for a second as if mulling over his request. Then she gives a short
sharp nod and looks back at him through the cracked door. "Do
you think we could open the door, ma'am?"

"No. I can hear your words fine. I'll hear you out and then
decide if I want to open the door. This is still my house. Please
go ahead."

"Of course, ma'am," Michael says. He's sure this isn't going
to proceed the way he wants it to. "I am a reporter."

This one statement causes Mrs. Parchesi to inhale sharply.
She almost closes the door in his face, but appears to be a
woman of her word, so remains still and lets him finish. Michael
knows she will slam the door in his face the moment he is done,
which means he only has one chance to change her opinion.

"I know you don't want to hear from me, or talk to me, and
I can understand that. After what happened to your husband,
and then what happened to his body, there isn't much I could
say or do to make you feel better. And I wouldn't want to. And
I also wouldn't want to exploit you for your story. That's not
why I'm here. I didn't ask for the story, which is something I
always do." A small lie, but she would never know. The rest of

what he's about to tell her will be true, so he feels okay about it. "The police are having trouble with the investigation into your husband's disappearance. They don't have any leads, as I'm sure you know. The unfortunate part of this is they don't have the resources to continue investigating the crime the way it should be investigated. Elk Hills is small, and they are trying to investigate all of the other robberies as well as anything else that comes up in a normal day. They're running thin."

She looks back at him and nods. He can't tell if she's angry or about to cry, but he presses forward.

"I've investigated every kind of crime. I might even go as far to say I'm better than the police when it comes to investigating crimes. And a friend of mine on the force asked me to investigate—to help out. Yes, I'm writing a story, but I'll only include what *you* tell me to include about your family. My main purpose for being here is to get Theodore back where he belongs. And *that* is the truth, ma'am." Michael finishes and silence fills the air between them. He waits for the door to close. Her bottom lip quivers. Here it comes: the door slam is imminent. But it never comes. The door closes softly instead. Another metallic rattle, and the door reopens. Mrs. Parchesi, eyes wet, looks back at him and turns her mouth to the side, making her lips tight before speaking.

"Come in," she says.

Without another word, Mrs. Parchesi leads Michael into a sitting room. He looks around, making mental notes, figuring out how he might describe the inside of the house. Small and cozy. Warm and inviting in spite of the sadness that he feels being in here. She lost her husband, not once, but twice in the matter of a few weeks. It is enough to bring anyone to tears.

She sits down on a dark leather chair in the corner of the

room next to the brick fireplace. The once red bricks now tran-
sitioning from red to gray to black from years of use. Michael
sits on a couch opposite her. The curtains are drawn making the
room dark, but Michael can imagine—with the curtains open
—it being one of the brighter rooms in the house, especially in
the afternoon when the sun would shine on the front of the
house and in through the windows behind him.

"I appreciate this," Michael says as he sits.

"I told the police I would do anything to help get Teddy
back and I meant it. If they think you can help them out, then
I'll help you out. I'd like, though, to leave our daughters out of
anything that appears in the paper. They've been through
enough."

"Agreed on all accounts, ma'am."

"Please, call me Abigail. And what shall I call you?"

"Michael Jacobs. And thank you again. I hope we can figure
this out for you." Michael stands up and extends his hand. She
leans forward and grasps it gently.

"Nice to meet you, Mr. Jacobs. What can I tell you that I
haven't already told the police?"

"I'm guessing they asked you all the questions I am going to
ask you, ma'am. I'm sorry, Abigail. But when I've done this in
the past, I've found that re-asking the questions lets me get the
information firsthand. Sometimes that can lead to different
thoughts and results. It's more about getting my head in the
right spot, and it's more effective to be here talking with you.
One answer might lead me down a different path than the
police."

"I understand. But I have a hard time talking about this for
very long. I'm sure you can understand."

"Yes, I will try to be as brief as possible. I don't need to know about your family back story, for example. I can skip over any questions like that."

"Yes, that would be best." Abigail shifts in the chair, lifting one foot off the ground and crossing it over her leg. She looks comfortable, but there is also a sign of worry on her face.

"Then let me ask you about people that may have been angry or upset at you or your husband when he was alive."

Abigail shook her head. "No, no. Everyone loved Teddy here in town. He was the sort of person everyone wanted to be friends with and be around, you know. We would walk down the street, and everyone would say hello and ask him how he was doing. He knew everyone and what was going on with their families and asked about other people. We went to church and did everything that good people are supposed to do. Because we were good people. We are good people. He was...he was just really great."

"Thank you, it must be hard for you to talk about him," Michael says. "I know the police probably asked you about that as well. What about you, Abigail? This may not be a crime against Teddy after all. In actuality, the perpetrators may be targeting people *they* think it will affect the most. Which, in this case, means you. Do you think you have any enemies? Any people that feel you may have wronged them recently?"

Abigail's eyes widen. He's already hit on a question the police didn't ask the first time around because she's not expecting it. She was ready to just rehash the same answers she told the police, but now she had to think.

"I— I don't think so. No. I mean, I'm sorry, I just wasn't expecting that question."

"It's okay. Take your time."

"I can't think of anyone who might be angry or upset with

me. I guess you're right. If someone doesn't believe in God or getting into heaven, they might think this is a way to hurt me instead of this as a way to hurt Teddy. I guess it makes sense." Her eyes shift back and forth. Michael can tell she's thinking, and he gives her some time. "I honestly can't think of anyone. Just like Teddy, as far as I know, people like me, like us, like our family."

"Okay, I understand. You certainly seem like a nice family. Although I didn't know your husband, what I've read is basically the same as what you've told me. I'm not saying this is *why* it was done, but I have to look at all the possibilities," Michael says. Abigail nods and he moves on. "What about leading up to — to the robbery. Was there anything out of the ordinary at the grave site? I'm sure it's hard to go and visit, but if something was out of the ordinary any of the times you visited, it might give us some information."

She shakes her head. "No, nothing was moved or touched except by us any of the times we were there. They have good workers over at the cemetery, so I'm sure if they saw something out of the ordinary, they would have told the police during the regular investigation."

Michael nods in agreement, knowing the truth. "They are on my list of people to talk to next."

There is noise out in front of the house. Abigail leans to the side and looks out the window. Michael turns and looks with her as a car rattles by. When the noise subsides, they both return to their original positions.

"Was there anything of value buried with your husband that went missing in the robbery?"

"Well, yes and no. He had a pocket watch he kept with him as long as I've known him. His grandfather gave it to him before he passed away. He loved that thing. His grandfather worked on watches and did all the repairs to the watch himself. When the watch stopped working, Teddy refused to get it repaired because 'only his grandfather should work on the watch'. So, he just kept it with him even though it didn't work. When he was buried, I placed the watch in the front pocket of his suit. No one but me knows it was in there, and it isn't really worth much. But it had value to Teddy, if that makes sense."

"It does. It's valuable, but not the kind of thing someone would try to sell."

"Yes, that's right."

"Abigail, I actually can't think of anything else." He has one more question, but that one is all about timing. He has enough information to fill a paragraph about Abigail, the family life of Theodore 'Teddy" Parchesi, and the home he lived in prior to his death. That information is covered. But as far as his real investigation, there is one more question left. He stands up, she does the same. "It was nice to meet you. I'm glad I made the trip out to talk to you. I'm sorry we had to talk about these kinds of topics."

"It's alright. Like I said, I just want him back where he belongs. I hope there is something I've given you that can help. But the police have all of this information already."

They walk toward the door, and he extends his hand to shake hers again. She grips it gently, like before.

"I hope we can find him also. I will do my best, Abigail," Michael says.

"Thank you, I appreciate any help you can give us," she says. "If there is anything else I can help you with, you know where to find me."

Michael takes a step out the door and then stops and turns back toward her.

"Actually, Abigail, I just thought of this. It is probably nothing, but I'd hate to bother you again."

"Yes, of course."

"I was wondering if your husband ever had any dealings or contact with Edmund Creighton."

Her eyes narrow and then shift from side to side like before, as if thinking before she answers. Michael tries to read her, but he doesn't know her well enough to get a good idea of what she's thinking.

"I, well— I mean he really keeps to himself up there. So, we don't have a lot of dealings with him personally. But at the same time, he lives in town and has a lot of money, so people end up dealing with him indirectly."

" What do you mean?"

"For example, he owns land—lots of land. If people are looking to expand their farms, they are usually buying their land from him. He owns several businesses here in town, but he doesn't run them and never visits. Just owns them. So, while he wouldn't have had contact with me or my husband, we would have had dealings with him, I'm sure."

"I understand," Michael says.

"May I ask why?" Abigail says. He can tell by the look on her face that she is curious. He thinks he has a better read on her now, at least about this. He can tell she's being honest. If her husband ever had any face-to-face dealings with Creighton, she doesn't know about them.

"No real reason," he says. "His name has come up when I started looking into these events, and I want to make sure I cover all my bases."

She nods, and Michael backs out the house, turns, and does not look back. He wonders if there's more she's not telling, but he doubts it. He doesn't want to come back and push her more unless absolutely necessary.

It's early, but he's going to head back into town and wait for his meeting with Ronald before heading home for the night.

CHAPTER 11

The house is different.

Mrs. Creighton is usually a rare sight around the house, but now she never comes out of her room. Clyde isn't sure if she stays in there willingly or if she's been told not to come out. The first-floor curtains, usually opened by Margaret during the day, are now always closed. All the other employees are gone as well. Workers who usually filled the house during the day have gone. Save for Clyde, who remains working despite the disappearance of his colleagues. He hopes the workers have just been sent home, but, at times, he fears something more sinister has happened.

But the house is not empty. If anything, it has more people in it now than it did a few weeks ago. The reanimates now run the house with the Doctor, Creighton, and Clyde overseeing their work.

Creighton sold it to Clyde as a way to be sure there are no cognitive delays with the reanimates. The Doctor said they needed to look at long-term repercussions of the procedure. So, they put the reanimates to work doing regular household chores. The kind of things Creighton would normally pay for.

Clyde is the middleman between the reanimates and Creighton. A slavedriver for these new, reanimated slaves. He isn't an equal with either the Doctor or Creighton, but he *is* in a position of power, delivering assignments to the new workers of the house.

The Doctor stays in the lab most of the time. Creighton lives in the house as if nothing has changed. Clyde is the go-between for the two of them, also. They only come together when they both feel it is necessary.

The former groundskeeper emerges from the basement stairway and enters the library. There are two reanimates there when he enters through the false closet. Clyde acknowledges them. They turn their heads toward him, slow and steady as if to return the nod or perhaps greet him, but he has no desire to speak to them or anyone else at the moment. Instead, he continues out of the library before either of the slow-moving men can say something to stop him. It is one of the advantages of not being a reanimate. The people Clyde sees most on a daily basis have slow reaction times. They rarely get in his way, and, if they do, he can simply walk away.

Clyde feels bad, but he finds himself doing it more and more. He wants to spend less time with the reanimates and more time with anyone who moves and speaks at the same speed he does. He doesn't know why it happened, but he notices the Doctor and Creighton doing the same thing, rushing out of rooms to avoid any interaction with people who have returned from the dead.

Clyde finds Creighton in his office, looking over paperwork. When he enters, Creighton covers the papers before Clyde can catch a glimpse of what he's working on. Creighton is also, per usual, drinking.

"Clyde, yes, come in," Creighton says. He touches the half full glass on his desk but does not pick it up. "What can I do for you? Something from the Doctor?"

"Yes, in a way, sir," Clyde says. He senses Creighton's dishonesty, but he can't figure out what his employer is hiding. And why he feels the need to hide it from Clyde after everything he's done to help the Research Society the past few weeks. Clyde is all the way in. At this point he has to be. He is going to go ahead with anything the Research Society asks him to do. He's done too much for them already. Changed, or just completely ignored his morals is just the start. Because of that, he can't fold his hand now. Letting this play out as far as it will go is his only opportunity to cash in on his portion of the money. It's only fair considering how much he's given to the cause. If he quits or leaves or gets in an argument with Creighton, he won't see a penny. He has no choice but to remain a model employee.

"Well, let's go, Clyde, out with it," Creighton says. Before working with Mr. Creighton so closely, Clyde would have assumed this kind of response was impatience. But he knows now that it's just the way Creighton works. He is always on edge. Always waiting for the next thing. His mind is always working, thinking, striving for that next cent. His ambition and work ethic are like nothing Clyde has ever seen. The seeming impatience comes from the fact that Creighton cannot stand to be idle. If he sees no useful reason for doing something, he doesn't do it.

"He told me to let you know that he's done all of the preliminary analysis of the findings from the reanimates and that he believes he has enough information to proceed to the next step in the project. He knows this is earlier than expected, but he's confident the next step will be a success."

"We should all hope so. Is he ready for us to come down?" Creighton smiles and picks up the glass now. He swirls the brown liquor around in it, then raises the glass to his mouth and tips it back. Creighton puts the empty glass down and holds the liquid in his mouth for a few seconds. He swallows loud enough for Clyde to hear, then opens his mouth and lets a puff of air out.

"Us, sir?" Clyde says. He wasn't planning on going back down there with Creighton. Since the other workers at the house were gone and the inside work was taken care of by the reanimates, Clyde has taken any free time he has to return outside and continue his favorite job of grounds maintenance.

"Yes, of course. You're a member of the Research Society now, aren't you, Clyde? When any of us are here and there is another step in the process, we meet together. We cannot have the entire Elk Hills Research Society live here, at least not yet. So, we will have a small meeting, just the three of us, to discuss the next step. I believe the Doctor may have mentioned the next step to a few of the other members at the last meeting. They were excited at the prospects, but we should go down and discuss this with the Doctor before we get too excited."

"What *is* the next step?" Clyde says.

"Ah, Clyde. There are some things that are better shown instead of told. This is one of those things. But, if this is successful, we will have accomplished the goal we set out to achieve so long ago." Creighton rises from behind his desk, takes the stack of papers he was working on, and piles them on a shelf behind him. "Come, and we will show you, Clyde."

Creighton breezes past Clyde and walks down the hall and into the library. Clyde follows.

"I don't mean to be short with you, Clyde. I hope you know that," Creighton says as they descend the stairs. Creighton is in front, Clyde a few steps behind. He doesn't want to spoil the surprise, and he hopes Clyde will go along with it. He's tried to be as nice to him as he can, but it's been hard. He doesn't like the guy and he can't put his finger on why. The Doctor, it seems, has taken a liking to him.

Creighton looks back toward the former groundskeeper. From now until the time the Doctor breaks the news to Clyde about their future plans, he has to be as nice as possible.

They reach the bottom of the stairs and his natural instinct tells Creighton to keep going; Clyde can catch up. Instead, he stops and waits for Clyde so they can walk together. He reminds himself again to be nice to the man.

"This is exciting, Clyde. I know you're new to the process, but this is terribly exciting. A bigger breakthrough, much bigger than that last one, if you can imagine that," Creighton says. He smiles, and it is genuine. He isn't lying to Clyde, at least not about this. It is a huge step. What they have done so far is amazing, but both Creighton and the Doctor believe this next step is an even greater accomplishment.

"Sir, we've already brought someone back from the dead. Lots of people. What could be bigger than that?" Clyde asks. He understands Clyde's question. It was the same one he had when he first met with the Doctor years ago. Back then Creighton, too, thought the final step would be to bring someone back. There was money in bringing people back to life. Sell the technology or mass produce it; either way, they would make more money than they knew what to do with. Creighton would add to his already tremendous fortune. But while the Doctor was still creating his prototype devices for use on rats, he broke the idea to Creighton. The final step would not be the simple reanimation of the dead.

"After you, Clyde," Creighton says. He holds his arm out, and Clyde enters the lab. Creighton follows him in and sees the Doctor where he would expect him to be, bent over his large wooden desk in the far corner. He doesn't look up when the pair enters but instead continues writing with a small pencil on a tiny flip notebook that he carries with him at all times. He appears to be nearing the end of whatever he's writing because his pace picks up as the men enter. The Doctor hurries though a few more words in the notebook, flips it closed, and shoves it in the front pocket of his lab coat.

"Edmund, Clyde. I trust Clyde has given you the good news, Edmund," the Doctor says as he rises from his seated position at the desk. He walks around the desk then leans back against it.

"Yes, he has. We are um...ready for the next step in all of this?" Creighton eyes the Doctor who gives a quick nod and a half smile in return before Clyde can see the gestures.

"Would you care to go through the next step with Clyde, since he doesn't know what we've been going on about for so long? I think it will make more sense coming from you." They planned this out in advance. Given the delicate nature of what they were going to tell Clyde, what they were going to ask of him, and what they ultimately might have to demand from him, they felt it was news that should come from a friend. That meant the Doctor had to give the sales pitch this time.

"Yes, of course. Shall we sit?" The Doctor motions to the chairs stationed around his desk. He sits back in the chair he was in when they first entered the lab; Creighton and Clyde sit on the other side, opposite him.

"Clyde, I know you're curious. I can understand it, too. I didn't know what to expect when the Doctor first told me what we might be capable of doing. It's remarkable," Creighton says, gesturing toward the Doctor.

"Yes," Clyde says. "Like I was saying. I think what we've already done, what *you've* already done, Doctor, is brilliant. Tremendous. Apart from the religious problems people might have, there is not really any reason to be against it. I didn't understand that at first, but I do now."

Creighton smiles on the outside, but he clenches his fists and hides his anger. How could Clyde—even if it was a slip of the tongue—try to take credit for this? *He* hasn't done anything but dig up and move dead bodies. The Doctor and himself have done the real work, from the beginning. Clyde has done none of it. Nothing! And he's already trying to take credit like he's been here the whole time.

"I'm glad you've come around on that, Clyde. Don't you agree, Edmund?"

"Yes, yes, of course," Creighton replies. He smiles but his lips stay together. Behind them, his teeth clench.

"So, what *is* next then?" Clyde asks.

"Ah, that brings us to today. We successfully reanimated all but one of our subjects. That one failure, while tragic, actually helps us to move forward with more confidence. We were able to see what the brain looks like with the minute increase in electricity we used with Mr. Grimwald. We were able to observe his brain operating at full capacity for the few seconds he was with us. What it tells me is that we cannot artificially introduce enough electricity into the brain to allow a human to function as they did before their death."

The Doctor looks at Clyde who nods. Creighton studies his face, watching for any sign of understanding. He's ready in case Clyde decides the next step is too much and makes a run for it. He doesn't think he will but can't take any chances. Clyde knows too much to leave now.

"So, I turned the electricity down just slightly, and it was enough to reanimate the rest of them without any difficulty, except for the single side effect we've all seen—the slowness in muscle movement. While I can't be one hundred percent sure, I do believe the slowness is most likely a delay in the message being sent from the brain to the muscles. I do not believe their thoughts are slowed in any way. Their minds are as sharp as they were when they were originally alive." The Doctor pauses and studies Clyde. Is Clyde going to figure this out? Is he going to run when he does?

"Are you following so far, Clyde?" Creighton asks.

"Yes. So, what you're saying, Doctor, is that it's impossible to put the correct amount of electricity into their brain for them to function at a normal speed?"

"Correct," the Doctor says, waits.

"Then we are stuck with reanimates who cannot function normally in society. We can bring them back, but we cannot create a new race of reanimates, for lack of a better word."

"I guess that's right, Clyde. They could never join society because of the speed with which they move. But we can still bring them back. They were all once dead, and now they are alive. They have feelings and memories of when they were alive. Loved ones could reanimate a dead relative to have a chance to say goodbye or have them continue to live with them. Grandma will always be there when you need her, even though she's well over a hundred years old." The Doctor is starting to talk with his hands, a sign that he's getting excited and is about to move on to the meat of this discussion.

"Money can be made from this, Clyde, but there is a next step. Something we can do, greater than letting ol' grandma slowly shuffle around the house and spend ten minutes trying to spit out a sentence. We can move well beyond that!"

"What is it?" Clyde says. He's leaning forward in his chair, intently listening to the Doctor, his excitement matching the Doctor's.

"Think about what I said before, Clyde." The Doctor points to his temple with his middle finger, eyes glued to Clyde's. "I said we could not *artificially* introduce electricity into the brain and get the results we truly desire."

Creighton watches the color drain from Clyde's face, but he doesn't move. He looks like he has something to say, but the Doctor presses on without waiting.

"But that does not mean we cannot get the electricity into the brain naturally. The way we do that, Clyde, is by performing this on someone who is not dead." The words hang in the air, but no one says a word. A smile grows on the Doctor's face, and he continues. "We do not need the dead body if we have a live one, Clyde. The live body already has the proper amount of electrical current inside it to run the brain. We do not need to add it, we simply need to maintain the level that is already there. It's something I've been working on and have already begun constructing. In fact, it is almost finished. But then, you might ask, and I can tell by the look on your face you have already figured it out, but I will tell you anyway. You might ask, why would we need to perform this procedure on someone who is already alive? The answer, Clyde, is simple. With the heart and lungs always operating due to the devices and the brain constantly receiving the proper amount of electrical current to operate, we can allow a person to live for a long—possibly endless—amount of time."

"So," Clyde pauses, thinking through the reality he's just been told. Usually in a case like this the Doctor—or more likely, Creighton—will speak up and try to force their opinions down his throat. Neither man does so in this situation. Creighton and the Doctor let him have his moment. Once he feels he's ready, and prepared for the answer he knows is coming, Clyde continues. "So in theory this would allow someone to live forever?"

"In a manner of speaking, yes," the Doctor says, and stands up. "Just like with our current reanimates. It all depends. If they were to have some sort of significant brain injury, they would still die. We cannot account for accidents. A person's heart will never stop working. They will never stop breathing. The heartbeat will be regulated, and there is no worry of a heart attack. If we can get the subject to avoid unnecessary risks, they could live for a long time, perhaps forever if they continue to do their best to avoid those risks that can lead to accidents or death."

"That is incredible," Clyde says. "The next step would be to try this on live animals like you did with the other experiment?"

"No, Clyde," Creighton jumps in before the Doctor can answer. "We have already completed those experiments as we went through the process."

"But you never mentioned—" Clyde starts, but Creighton cuts him off.

"We didn't want to scare you away, Clyde. You can understand that can't you?"

"Sir, sorry. But if raising the dead didn't scare me off, why do you think this would?"

"Because, Clyde." The Doctor is behind Clyde now. Clyde turns to look at him as Creighton prepares himself to leap up from the chair if needed, but the Doctor has Clyde's escape blocked off well. "We need a volunteer to try out this experiment. Someone strong and very much alive."

The Doctor smiles and looks down at Clyde. Creighton sees the full realization on his face.

"Me?" Clyde asks. He looks at Creighton and then back to the Doctor.

The Doctor nods.

* * *

Clyde realizes he's played his part too well. Throughout the process, he's wanted the men to think he was fully invested in this. He went along with everything they'd done. He convinced them he understood why they did what they did. The whole time he wanted them to believe that he thought the reanimation of a dead person was not a moral problem for him. He played his part so well he even started to believe it himself. But now he realizes, did his job too well.

Now they are here, asking him to be their guinea pig. Their test subject. The Doctor stands behind him and Creighton sits next to him. Both men ready to pounce, worried he's going to make a run for it.

Clyde ponders his situation. He doesn't mind the silence that hangs in the air. They are asking him to do something he'd never in a million years thought anyone would ever ask of him. If he wants to think about this for ten minutes, he will.

"Clyde, listen—" the Doctor starts and puts a gentle hand on Clyde's shoulder.

"No." Clyde shrugs off the Doctor. "Give me a minute."

He needs to think. Are they even asking him? Or are they telling him? Was this destined to be his role in the Research Society from the beginning?

When Clyde jerks from the Doctor's touch, Creighton begins to jump up like he is preparing to intervene. He looks over Clyde's head, relaxes and sits back in his chair.

"I understand, Clyde. Take some time," the Doctor says.

His mind races. There are so many questions that he cannot even begin to think in a way that makes any sense. His first thought—the one that keeps popping back up in his head—is Patty. If he decides to go through with this, what will become of his relationship with her? Will she still want to be with him?

"Why me?" Clyde asks. He stands up, and Creighton joins him, getting a little too close for Clyde. He's had enough being an employee. If they want to do this to him, if they even want to ask him to do this, he needs to be treated as an equal, and he will act like it. "Back off, *Edmond*."

Creighton recoils and then grabs Clyde by the upper arm.

"Son of a bitch," the rich man says.

Clyde is stronger than the usually stagnant millionaire and twists his body out of his grip then glares back at Creighton. "I said, back off."

"Edmund, it's okay," the Doctor says. He puts a hand out toward Creighton, calming him. Creighton snorts out his nose, lips curling back, baring his teeth. He turns his back as Clyde walks away. The Doctor moves with Clyde.

"Those people, we didn't ask. We took them. We brought them here, and we brought them back to life," Clyde says. His voice echoes through the lab, probably down the hall and into the large round meeting room. He doesn't care how loud he is. Doesn't care who hears him. If he is going to be this much a part of all of this, he will do what he wants.

"Correct," the Doctor says. The Doctor is always sure about what to say and when to say it, but now, his words are tentative, slow and shaky.

"So, fine. We could not get the permission of a dead person to experiment on them. I can *almost* understand that. For the most part, they are grateful for a second chance at life. Let it be. We deal with the issues as they come up. Mrs. McDonald, we let her rest again, and morally I think that was the right decision. But there is no going back from this decision. If...if the devices are placed on the subject while they are alive, is there any going back?"

The Doctor shakes his head. "Once the devices are placed, taking them off would end the life of the subject. The subject could always be brought back, of course, but we know what that is like."

Clyde nods. It's a one-way decision. He can never come back from this.

"What about my— what about the subject's family? A wife or a husband. Could they go on living their normal life?" Clyde says. This question even causes Creighton to turn around and pay attention again. Maybe Clyde's slip tells him he is actually considering it.

"I'm not sure, Clyde. I think it is something we would have to discuss as a group." The Doctor looks at Creighton, who rejoins the other two, closer to the door. Clyde's back is still to both men.

"Well, we should discuss that now, then," Clyde says. "There is one other thing. You told me every one of the members of the Society will get paid, equally, if and when the technology is sold. First, I don't believe that. You don't have to tell me, but I assume you two will get paid more than everyone else when all is said and done. I also believe that the reanimates won't see any money, and, if they do, they won't be allowed to give it to their families. You'll keep them here and never really have to pay them at all. I want to get paid. If I get paid more than the two of you, so be it, but I want ten percent of whatever amount of money this thing makes. I know there are over a hundred people down here total. Subtract out the reanimates, because I doubt you're planning to pay them. Take your percentage and the rest of the Society can have their percentage too. But I want ten percent. I have more risk than anyone else. *No one,* not even the reanimates, is putting their life on the line."

Clyde turns back toward the two men. He doesn't know if he can trust them, but he's never shown this side of himself before. This is the real him. The side he hides from Creighton when he's at work. The side he has hidden from everyone since he first helped Creighton dig up a dead body. It is good to be himself again. Their eyes are wide, both men speechless. Clyde has to keep a satisfied smile hidden as he watches Creighton's face turn various shades of red.

"Maybe you just think of me as the gardener or groundskeeper. Or you did before all of this. Just because I work for you, *Edmund,* doesn't mean you own my life." Clyde spits his former boss's name out at him. It feels good. "As a

member of the Elk Hills Research Society, this is what I want. If
you don't feel like doing business, I will leave. I know you want
to try to stop me. But I won't let you. My wife knows what to
do if I don't come home from work at the Creighton place."

Clyde isn't sure if the threat is a good idea, but it's already
left his mouth before he can reconsider it. It's an idle threat at
any rate. He's been working strange hours the past few weeks
and been distant with Patty when he's at home. If he stopped
coming home, she would probably think he ran off on her. He'd
never do that, but what else would she think given the past few
weeks?

Creighton reacts to the threat as Clyde would expect: he
moves toward him, arms outstretched like he's going to grab
him and throw him through the wall. He's mad enough that he
might actually be able to do it, but the Doctor intervenes. He
puts both hands on the rich man's chest and pushes him to the
other side of the lab. Clyde stares at Creighton, who continues
to try to push past the Doctor.

"You son of a bitch. I'll kill you. I'll fucking kill you if you
think you're in control here! You hear me?"

Clyde doesn't shout back, instead he just watches, observes
and is unable to stop the corners of his mouth curling upward.

The Doctor whispers to Creighton. Clyde can't hear what
he's saying, but he's not sure it matters. He knows the gist of it.
He's trying to calm Creighton down. Trying to tell him that
they will make so much money it doesn't matter how they split
it up. And he's reminding him that they have a possible willing
participant in this portion of the experiment. Someone willing
will be easier to work with.

Creighton nods and holds his hands up in the air.

"Alright," he says to the Doctor. The Doctor moves and lets Creighton walk in front of him. Clyde stands his ground.

"Clyde, I think Mr. Creighton might have a proposition for you," the Doctor says.

"I'm listening."

CHAPTER 12

Michael arrives home from the train at seven o'clock and finds baby Joseph still awake. He's surprised because when he usually gets home around this time, the baby is asleep. The train ride back into the city was useful to run through his thoughts and begin to formulate a strategy for tomorrow's discussion with Edmund Creighton. By the time he gets to his door, he's done thinking about work.

"Who is this?" Michael asks the baby, who naturally responds by staring back at him without answering.

Mary smiles and watches him take off his hat and suit coat. He walks over to his wife and takes his son out of her arms.

"Is this little Joseph? What have you been doing all day? You must have been sleeping all day if you're awake now," Michael says. He kisses the baby on the forehead then does the same to his wife.

"Actually, just the opposite. He woke up right after you left this morning and skipped both naps. Now, he won't go to bed. I'm glad he gets to see his daddy, though." She folds her arms and watches Joseph's fingers curl around Michael's index finger. "How was the country?"

"Ah, interesting, actually. A genuine mystery. But I think I might have got to the bottom of it already, if you can believe that. I'll know for sure when I go back tomorrow. I'm going to interview this guy, Edmund Creighton. He is, ah, he's kind of like the John Rockafeller of Elk Hills. Lots of money. Lots of land and holdings. A king, almost. The people in town, they're scared of him." Michael rubs Joseph's back and sits down on the couch. The baby rests his head against his father's shoulder, drooling on his shirt, and his eyes start to droop. Michael whispers, "Hey, look at this."

Mary smiles at the two men. "I don't care how you do it, as long as he stays that way."

"Must be my voice. Anyway, there's been these grave robberies out in Elk Hills, and other surrounding towns. I talked to Ron Weaver, and he said no witnesses, no leads, no nothing. I believed he was telling me the truth, but I was pretty sure the locals were hiding something. Small town like that, you know, people keep lots of secrets from the police."

Mary nods, and he keeps going. He always talks to her about work, the stories he writes, but doesn't get into too many details because she lives here. He reports on crimes in Chicago and lives in Chicago and doesn't want Mary knowing all the details about what is happening right outside her door. This story isn't happening in Chicago. Elk Hills is not that far away, but far enough that he can tell her these things without thinking she might worry too much.

"I was right. These two guys that work at the cemetery there saw something the day the first body was taken. A car. Turns out the only person who would own a car like that in the area is this guy, Edmund Creighton. Rich, like I said. Estate on the far side of town. So, I didn't have enough time to get over there and interview him the way I'd like. First thing tomorrow, I'm going, though."

"Be careful," Mary says.

"I always am. I don't think this guy is that dangerous anyway. Not like these Chicago guys. If I can survive the streets of Chicago, I can survive just about anything. You don't have to worry about me, Mary."

"I know. But I will anyway. Do you want to eat?"

Michael had smelled the food when he entered. But he wanted to see his son before he ate, even though the growls in his stomach grow louder by the second.

"Yeah, I'll put him in bed first." Michael eases himself up off of the couch, careful not to jostle the sleeping baby too much. There is a wet spot on his sleeve from the drool. He looks down at the child in his arms and sees a mixture of himself and Mary in his face. When his small lips pucker, they look like Mary's when she sleeps. He smiles. He's never successfully put Joseph to bed. He wakes up every time. It's a process that Mary has perfected, but Michael is still working out the kinks. The good news is that he's already asleep. If Joseph wakes up, it will hopefully be only for a moment.

Michael moves quietly through the apartment and into Joseph's room. It's already dark, but his eyes adjust quickly. He arrives at the crib and lowers the sleeping baby in then carefully slips his arm out from under his son. Joseph transfers from Michael's arms to the mattress without so much as a whimper.

For a moment, Michael watches Joseph sleep. He smiles and listens to the breathing. People told him watching his child sleep would be life changing. He never understood why they would say that to him until this moment. Joseph doesn't stir, so he stands a few more seconds. Then Michael creeps out of the room trying to avoid the spots in the floor he knows will creak.

"Shepherd's pie," Mary whispers when Michael returns to the kitchen.

"I know, I could smell it." Michael sits down at the table while Mary scoops the meal onto two plates.

"It sounds like you're into this story then." She puts a plate and a fork in front of him and then sits opposite him. Michael takes a bite and then responds.

"I am. I mean, I always get into my stories. Sometimes more than others, but this one is good. It's— it's just what I needed. Enough of a crime to be interesting. People don't want to tell stuff to the police, but they open right up to the reporter who will keep their names out of the paper."

"Yes, and the guy, Clayton?"

"Creighton," Michael corrects her.

"Yes, yes. It's been a long day. Anyway, tell me about Creighton."

"Not much to tell, except that it seems like the townspeople either don't like him or are scared of him, or both. Those guys at the cemetery didn't want to tell me his name. I had to do some asking around to find out who might have owned that car. Talked to the widow of one of the men whose grave was robbed. She was surprised by the question when I asked her if her husband knew him or dealt with him at all. She said everyone deals with him indirectly because he owns or used to own so much of Elk Hills."

"Oh, you had to talk to the widow. That must have been sad. And worse than a regular death because his body was taken."

"Yes. I can't begin to imagine what it must be like."

"I bet it's like having him die all over again. The funeral can be hard, but then, once it's over, it's over. Now, if his body is ever found, she'll have to bury her husband for a second time."

Michael nods. He needs to stop talking so he can eat. His stomach rumbles even as he fills it.

"So, are you glad then you took my advice and moved out of the city for a while?"

"Absolutely," Michael says, food still in his mouth. He swallows then continues. "It's one of the best things I've done professionally in a long time. Gets me back to my roots a little bit more than I've been in a long time."

"And you met with Ronald?"

Michael nods, chewing. He waves his spoon around in a circle, and then, when he's finished, he answers her. "Yeah, yeah. Twice actually. I told him I'd share what I learned. I told him that this morning at breakfast. He was good with it. He just wants a chance to act on anything before I run a story, which makes sense to me. So, I'm gonna keep him filled-in."

Michael doesn't know if it's a look in his eye or something about the way he talked, but Mary sees through him better than anyone he knows. It's a good thing she's his wife and not someone he is investigating, because he would get nowhere.

"But you didn't tell him everything did you?" she asks.

Michael pauses, trying to think how to word it.

"You know," he says and then pauses again. "I don't really know how you know that, but yeah. You're right. I met with him again before I left. I told him some of what I learned. But I didn't tell him about the car the cemetery guys saw. And I didn't tell him about the Creighton guy because there really isn't anything to tell yet."

"So, you told him nothing he didn't already know," she says. It is a statement, not a question.

"Right. But for a good reason. Tomorrow, I'm going to meet with this Creighton guy, first thing. If something comes from it, then I'll tell him all I know. It's not like I'm going to run the story before they arrest him. I'm going to tell him everything I learned. I'm just doing it on my own schedule."

Mary nods, looks at him. He knows the look: she's teasing him a little, but there's also some wonderment in her eyes. She knows how freely he lies when he's working, to get the information he needs. She must wonder how much he lies to her.

"It's not right, I know that. But if I tell him about Creighton and he goes up there and questions him before I do, it will blow the whole story."

"I understand."

"This job is less about writing and more about reading people and playing them off each other. Knowing what people want to hear and telling it to them," he says.

"I know, I know, I've heard this before." Mary laughs, but Michael keeps going.

"People want to talk, but they don't want to inconvenience themselves. It's why no one talks to the police. It's too much work. So, they..." Michael says, but Mary finishes his thought for him.

"...talk to you because they don't have to do anything else, and they still get to share their story. Michael, I know all of this."

"Okay, okay. I'm done. Back at it tomorrow." He laughs, and she joins him. They finish eating in silence. There is no need to talk. The silence is enough for them to realize how much they appreciate each other. They clean the dishes and go to bed. Michael wraps his arms around Mary and holds her tightly against himself. They both sleep naked, and he smiles at the feel of her warm smooth skin against him. Before long, they are asleep.

* * *

A few hours later Michael wakes and slips out of the house before Mary or Joseph are awake. He is on his way back to Elk Hills. It is a big day.

Michael doesn't have to meet with Ronald when he arrives in Elk Hills. The night before they decided to meet at the end of the day, unless something groundbreaking happened. In that case, Michael would get in touch with Ronald immediately.

Michael doesn't think he's going to find out much at the Creighton house today, but if he does, he plans to let Ronald know right away. Creighton is rich. Even here in the suburbs of Chicago, rich *could* mean connected. The last thing Michael wants is to go after an ultra-rich, suburban kingpin. He's never heard his name in the mafia or gang circles, but that doesn't mean he's not involved. Everyone with money runs into the gangs at some point. If Creighton ran things like they do in Chicago, he would have already bought off half of the Elk Hills police force and at least attempted to kill the ones he couldn't buy. He would have created his own alcohol pipeline from Canada, through Wisconsin, and into Elk Hills. And the people of the town would be terrified of going against him. The people *were* scared of him, but they weren't terrified. If they were terrified, Michael wouldn't even know his name.

It all works to Michael's advantage. He's investigating the richest, most powerful man in town. Despite his wealth, the guy lives on the outskirts of town. No one knows him well. He's not really part of the community. It means Creighton thinks he's untouchable. He thinks no one can hurt him. He isn't worried about getting caught if he *is* doing something illegal, because most people are afraid of him. Michael is not scared. Michael hopes to catch him. Or have the Elk Hills Police catch him. That would make the best story. It's what Michael wants more than anything.

He strolls down Main Street. Michael passes up the big breakfast at Louise's Diner in favor of an apple and a banana at the local fruit stand. He eats the banana first as he walks. Going to the Creighton house under the guise of a reporter working on a fluff piece about the wealthy individuals living in the suburbs of Chicago, Michael thinks that will allow him access to Creighton without making him too suspicious. It's been a long time since he's written a piece like that, but it's an easy way to get Creighton talking. If rule number one is everyone wants to talk as long as they aren't inconvenienced, then rule number two is rich people love to talk about how rich they are. Especially, if it will be in the paper.

The day is gray. It might rain, but nothing is wet, and Michael hopes it holds off. If it does rain, he hopes it's not until he's on his way back. Ronald would give him a ride most of the way there if he asked. The walk is good for Michael though, it gives him more time to think. A few cars buzz past him as he strolls along the edge of the road through town. He turns right and follows the directions he received to the Creighton house.

A cool wind picks up as he gets closer. What had started as an easy walk through town has become a long walk up steep, narrow roads and through thickening woods. Then, he sees the row of trees that is lined a little too straight along the edge of the road. A fence comes into view behind the tree line and past that, a gate. He's made it.

In the center of each door of the gate is a large metal 'C,' in case you didn't know who the property belonged to. Just inside the gate at the gatehouse, a man sits holding a newspaper. Michael is glad there are no stories by Michael Jacobs on the front page.

"Hiya, there," the man says as Michael gets closer.

"Hi, good morning." Michael gives a wave and a big smile. "That the *Tribune?*"

"Matter of fact it is. How'd you know that?"

Michael laughs. "I work for them, actually. Reporter." He pulls out his wallet and flips it open to his press credentials card.

"Mr. Creighton didn't mention a reporter or nuthin' today."

"No, no. He wouldn't have. I just got into town, actually. I'm supposed to be writing a piece about the wealth in the suburbs of Chicago, and his name was actually at the top of my list. I'm sorry, I should have phoned first."

The man runs a hand through his hair, exhales and looks back toward the house that Michael can barely see over the slight rise in the driveway.

"I'm just supposed to check and make sure people are who they say they are, not really supposed to stop anyone. I'm not even allowed up at the house anymore. I show up here in the morning and then leave by six o'clock. Haven't been up to the house in a few weeks. Lemme just get a better look at that reporter card, then."

Michael takes his wallet back out, pulls the card out this time and hands it over to the gatekeeper.

"It's me, I promise." Michael smiles but watches the man's

face as he studies the card. The man is only doing his job. He doesn't care too much about Creighton, at least he doesn't act like he cares. But Creighton probably pays well. He doesn't want to mess up, Michael understands that.

"Alright, looks good to me. I'll let you through. Don't make any trouble up there." He opens the gate, lets Michael through, and returns the ID card.

"I won't cause any trouble, just a few questions. The more he answers, the better, right?" Michael smiles again, then because he can't resist the opportunity to get a little bit more information, "Creighton get a lot of visitors usually? Or does he keep to himself?"

"Ah, well, actually, the answer would be both. Most times, no one comes through. But, a couple days a month, he has, I guess, these big parties up there. He asks me to stay late those nights. They start coming around three o'clock, and they don't really stop until six or seven. I leave after that, but they're all gone when I get back in the morning."

"I see," Michael says. He puts his wallet back in his pocket. "Must get pretty crazy here on those party nights."

"I never heard nuthin' out of them. If they get crazy it's gotta be after I leave. Even when I was allowed up by the house, I never saw or heard those people. Not after they come through the gate."

"Any names you recognize?" Michael asks. He realizes he's pushing but he can't help himself. The gatekeeper realizes what's happening too and clams up.

"Ah, I don't know if I should be talking to you about this. You know, newspaper and all."

"I understand. We're off the record though, just a curious

guy who wants to know how the rich live." Michael tries to save at least this one last question.

"I recognize some the names. You'd recognize them too. Big business type people. That's all I'm gonna say."

"Alright, fair. Thanks. I guess I'll see you on the way out then." Michael takes the brim of his hat between his thumb and index finger and tips it toward the ground.

"Good to meet you. Just head on up there and knock. Someone will be there to answer the door and show you to Mr. Creighton."

"Thanks again." Michael turns and walks toward the house. The driveway is steeper than it looked standing back by the road. He takes it all in. There is no way to know if the visit will yield anything of value, but he contemplates a description of his surroundings in the event it does. The wind whips past him as he reaches the top of the incline and the ground levels off. From the road, and without the ability to see the whole thing, the house appears modest, small for a man as rich and powerful as the locals make Creighton out to be. Now, seeing the entire house, his view unobstructed by the gentle hill, he realizes the house is as large and gaudy as expected. The main part of the house is large; two stories of windows are visible, but the roof is angled in such a way that there may be a third story hidden up there. The dark red brick is immaculate and shows no wear and tear along the corners of the house, indicating it was recently laid, recently replaced, or well-maintained. From the center part of the house, two wings are barely visible from the driveway. This is possibly a deliberate action to hide them from those who venture too close.

At first, Michael doesn't understand why someone would build a house this way, then smiles to himself, knowing the disorienting nature of a house that appears larger on the inside would have on any guest or businessman coming into it. The house would give Creighton an advantage.

He steps up to the front door and lifts the knocker. It's heavier than it appears, and Michael lets it drop three times against the door. He runs through his story and his questions once more in his head. Any piece of information will do, but he wants to know the truth. If Creighton has a body—or bodies—here, he needs to know. If he's allowed to move around the house, it will help his investigation.

Footsteps behind the door, then two metallic clicks and the door opens. Michael makes a mental note: two locks on the door. In front of him stands a large man. He is not tall, but wide. Though his shoulders are broad, the middle of his body is wider. His gray hair is thinning, and he has the faint impression of a beard and mustache. He is dressed in a suit, but the jacket appears to have been thrown on. He's not wearing a tie. Michael finds it hard to believe a doorman or butler would be allowed to dress in this manner.

"Hi," Michael says, putting on his brightest smile. "I am Michael Jacobs. I am with the *Chicago Tribune,* and I'm looking for Edmund Creighton."

"A reporter? Why?" the man says.

"I am, ah, I'm sorry, I'm doing a story on wealth in the Chicago suburbs. If I could just have a few minutes with Mr. Creighton—maybe more—to ask him a few questions, then maybe—"

"I am Creighton," he says. He pushes his shoulders back and lifts his chin up a bit higher in the air, making him seem taller, more intimidating. Michael doesn't get intimidated.

"Oh, I apologize, sir, I didn't realize. Do— do you think

you would have some time to answer a few questions?" As he speaks the breeze picks up, and Michael grabs his hat before it flies off and into Creighton's face. "Maybe if I could come in, we could talk for a while, and you could show me around."

Michael puts his hand on the door to keep Creighton from letting it swing closed on its own. He's here. He's already gotten the face to face with Creighton. It might not last long, so he wants to make the most of it.

"What's the story about, again?" Creighton says. His eyes squint with the wind in them. It's helpful. "Here, come inside. I didn't know it was going to get this windy today."

Michael tries to keep his excitement in check as he steps into the house.

"Wait here," Creighton says, and he leaves Michael in the entryway of the house. Off to his left, stairs lead up to the second floor. There is a large coat rack and a bench on the opposite side of the room as well as two doors on either side and one directly in front of him. The entrance itself is large enough to fit twenty-five or thirty people. Even though he caught the piece of architectural trickery outside, Michael is still surprised by the size of the house on the inside.

Though he can't see anyone, Creighton is speaking to someone. The words are muffled, unintelligible. Michael roams closer to the door Creighton left through, pretending to inspect the intricate wood designs on the wall. He listens intently, but cannot make out any words, only the low mumbles from somewhere beyond the door.

"Thank you, go now," Creighton says louder so Michael can hear. There is a slow shuffling of feet on hardwood floors. At least two or three different pairs of footsteps. The conversation is over, Michael spins and looks toward the narrow window next to the front door, trying to appear distracted.

"Mr. Jacobs, was it?" Creighton says as the door bangs open behind him. Michael turns back to face him. The rich man is composed now. He has a smile on his face. It looks as though he's run a comb through his hair as well. He looks kinder, gentler than he did when he first answered the door. This is the fake Creighton, the one he wants the world to know.

"Yes, sir." Michael looks back at him.

"I've had my assistant get my office ready, we can speak in there if you like. I wish you had let me know you were coming. I don't have a lot of time at the moment. We could have set something up, and I could have given you the full tour."

"I wish I could have set something up, too. You know how deadlines are. The editor gave me this assignment this morning and told me I needed to have the story done first thing tomorrow. I don't know why. Anyway, he said get at least one interview done and squeeze the others in if you can. I just rode the train out to Elk Hills without really knowing who I was going to interview. Your name kept popping up so here I am." Michael is louder than normal. He needs to come off as some half-wit reporter, not an investigative one.

"Oh sure, sure. I understand. Here, follow me this way, and we can sit down a spell in my office and talk. I'll answer as much as I can, at least for the next thirty minutes or so." Creighton leads Michael through the door next to the stairs.

Michael keeps his head forward but scans the house as they walk through. The rest of the house has the same ornate wood designs adorning the walls that he saw in the foyer. His eyes shift back and forth. He catches movement out of the corner of his eye but by the time he's able to focus on the spot, there is nothing there. It feels to Michael like there are other people in the house, lots of other people, but there's no sign or trace of them as far as he can tell. More movement down a separate hall to his right. Again, he turns to focus on it, but there is no one there. Knowing Creighton may be digging up bodies doesn't alleviate the unease. Creighton is silent as they make their way through the house. They pass a kitchen on the left. Michael gets a good look inside, but no one is there. Creighton pushes open a door, and they enter what is obviously his office.

"Here, have a seat." Creighton gestures to the chair in front of the large, dark, wooden desk. Michael sits and the subject of his story works his way around to the other side. "I know it's early in the day, but if you care for a drink, I can make you one."

"No, thank you. If it was later in the day, I'd say yes, but I've got to get some work done first, you know what I mean?"

Creighton smiles and sits. "What can I help you with, then?"

"Well, I mean, nothing too in depth to be honest. I'm just looking to get to know the wealth out here in the suburbs. Everyone knows the powerful business owners in Chicago. It's all the same group; they run things, have all the money. People talk about them and know who they are. But out here, once you get away from all of that, there are a group of people, not unlike yourself, who have just as much money, power, and influence as those city guys, but no one really knows much about them. About *you*." Michael pauses but only for a moment. He wants to say his piece before Creighton starts going again. He can tell Creighton is eager to guide the conversation. "We want the people to know a little bit about you. Tell the people more about you and give them some insight into the incredible house you have here. I'm writing the story, Mr. Creighton, but it's *your* story. So, we could take it any way you want to take it."

"Alright, I like your style. I can understand all that. Tell me what you'd like to know about me. Really, I'll be as honest as I can, maybe we can look around the house a little bit too, but not too much."

"I appreciate it, sir. First off, can you tell me a little bit about yourself? Your family and your everyday life."

CHAPTER 13

Creighton leans back in his chair. At first, he wasn't sure what to think of this reporter. He shows up at the front door—unannounced—and wants to do a story on him. He's happy to do it. He's always felt like he's taken a back seat to the big Chicago business owners, even the ones he knows well. They have less money than he does, own less property. Yet they're always in the papers because of some deal they made or a big land purchase. He makes bigger land purchases, makes more money, and it never gets any press. Because he lives in the suburbs instead of Chicago. One look out his bedroom window, and it isn't hard to figure out who got the better end of the deal. The lush green grass and thick trees are all his, as far as he can see. In Chicago, if you look out a window, you'd be lucky to see trees and grass at the same time. He's the winner in all of this, and no one realizes it.

Except maybe this kid. He seems interested. Maybe a little too old to be writing this kind of story, but that isn't Creighton's concern. Clyde and the Doctor shuffled all the reanimates down into the basement so that the first floor would be clear. The reporter wants a tour. He will have to check with Clyde to make sure the floor is empty before he takes this man around. But maybe the story will be worth it.

"Well," he says, getting back to the original question. "It's not much of a family when you pin it down like that. I live here with my wife. We have no kids. She's been sick for some time, rarely leaves the bedroom anymore. She can't, too weak." Creighton shakes his head, looks down, turns his mouth down too, just like he's supposed to when he talks about his wife. He's practiced this move in the mirror, and it always gets a concerned head tilt from whoever he's talking to.

"I'm sorry to hear that," Michael says, his head tips to one side.

"It's okay." Creighton nods.

"What does she have?"

"I'd rather not discuss it. Please keep that out of your article if you don't mind. I'd just like to mention that we both live here. We've been through a lot together. She wouldn't want people thinking of her the way she is now."

"I understand, Mr. Creighton. I'll leave it out, of course. Tell me about yourself then. How did you end up in Elk Hills?"

"Sure. I inherited most of my money from my father; he was in real estate, I just continued it after he died. Buy low and sell high, and you can't really go wrong. It's all about getting the best deal, you know? If you can make a good deal on the purchase and another good deal for yourself on the sale of the same property, you've doubled-up your good deals. You end up with a lot of extra money." Creighton has gone over this in his head so many times he doesn't even have to think about it. It's the philosophy he uses for every deal he makes. He doesn't want to talk about his personal life too much, so he deflects the questions to the business side of things. "I got such a good deal on this piece of land I almost sold it, but I decided to build on it instead."

"Interesting." He writes in a small notebook he's taken out of his pocket, nodding as he puts the words down. "Did you design the house yourself? Use an architect? The style is...unique."

"I worked closely with an architect, but I had very specific plans. I wanted to go with a lot of different looks in the house. Some rooms, like this one, feature a lot of gold and have this sort of look to it. Others are cleaner, less shiny. Others use wood as decoration versus gold. It gives every room a very different look and feel, but it still has a good flow."

"Ah, so you were very involved in the building aspect of the house. Well, then, I can tell you have incredible taste, sir. The house is truly breathtaking. I'm sorry, I have a bit of interest in building design. Though I've never taken a class on it, it's more of a hobby really. I find it interesting."

"Thank you. I'm glad you like it; would you care for a tour? To help your hobby, of course." Creighton is excited to show off the house. He will need a minute to make sure the first floor is empty. The Doctor or Clyde could be around, but he'd rather not have the reporter bump into anyone at all.

"I'd love a tour; we can walk and talk, right?"

"Of course, just give me one moment." Creighton stands up and leaves the office. He lets the door go behind him; it almost closes but remains slightly ajar. Creighton hurries to the library and into the false closet leading below the house. A glance over his shoulder says the reporter didn't follow him. Creighton calls down the stairwell in a combination whisper and yell. "Clyde!"

Silence. He waits. Fucking Clyde, not doing what he is supposed to be doing. He whisper-yells again, knowing he has to get back to the reporter before he gives himself his own tour. The experiment is going forward tonight as planned, and he can't complain about Clyde at this point. He's done everything they've asked of him, including putting his life on the line for the research, but the man still drives him insane. He calls again, this time a bit louder. "Clyde!"

An echo of footsteps from the bottom of the stairs, then Clyde's voice, "Yes, sir."

"I'm going to take the guy around. Just the first floor. *Everyone* needs to stay down there. When he's gone, I'll come down. Stay quiet. I don't think he'll hear, but let's not take any chances."

"Yes, sir."

Creighton shuts the door inside the closet quietly and then shuts the door in the library with just as much care. Then he turns on his heel and makes his way back to his office. The reporter is still in the chair he left him in, looking down at his notepad, maybe writing the beginning part of the article.

"Getting a head start?" Creighton asks. The man jumps, unaware he was back in the room.

"Ah, well, yes. I guess I am, yeah. Just writing some impressions of the house walking up. I think I'll start with that and get into your personal stuff later on."

"Whatever works for you is good with me. I trust you, Mr. Jacobs," Creighton says. "Come on, I'll show you around. Just this floor if that's okay with you. My wife is upstairs, and I don't want to disturb her if she's sleeping."

He nods, and that's enough for Creighton. He doesn't really care what the reporter says. If Creighton doesn't like a question from the reporter, it won't be hard to remove him from the house. He wants the positive story. Loves the idea of the guys in Chicago and the rest of the guys in the suburbs seeing him in the paper, but it's not worth risking their research over. Kicking out the reporter will lead to a negative story, but that is nothing compared to what they are trying to accomplish.

Creighton takes the reporter through the house. He talks as he goes in and out of each room, telling him about the reason they put the room where they did. Sometimes he makes up a story to fill the air. Small stories about his mother and father or about being an only child. No one would be able to corroborate the stories, and they will look good in print. It doesn't matter if they are true or not.

The two enter the library, and Creighton wants to move this part of the tour along quickly. He's done. It's been almost an hour; it's time to move on.

"This is amazing," Michael says. He cranes his neck to look up at the two stories of books towering around him. "I've always been an avid reader. To have a library like this. Oh, it would be a dream come true. You must be proud of this room."

"Yes, yes, I am. I always make it a point to bring visitors here when they come. Most have the reaction that you just did," Creighton says. He puts an arm on the reporter's shoulder, wanting to escort him out of the library toward the front door. However, a loud thump emanates from the direction of the false closet on the far side of the room.

Clyde!

For a moment, Creighton forgets the reporter is there and whips his head around, looking toward the far end of the library. His face tightens and a fist balls up. If Clyde comes through that door, he will become just another reanimate corpse in a few hours. But the reporter speaks up and brings Creighton back out of his rage.

"What was that? Is everything okay, sir?" he asks.

"Oh yes, yes. I'm sure. A dumbwaiter in that wall goes upstairs from the kitchen. Something must have come down or fallen over on its trip. I think I need to be getting back to work, Mr. Jacobs."

"Yes, of course, sir." The reporter turns, and Creighton hazards another glance toward the closet door. He turns his head back, and the reporter is looking in the same direction. "This way out, Mr. Creighton?"

"Yes, yes, through this door and to the right." Creighton is losing focus. He needs to be nice and get the reporter out of the house. Then he can deal with his second, more pressing problem.

They arrive at the door, and Creighton plasters on his large, fake smile again. "It was good to meet you, Mr. Jacobs. I will be looking forward to reading the story."

"It was a pleasure to meet you too, Mr. Creighton. I will get working on this right away You should see it in tomorrow's paper. I crank these things out pretty fast."

"I'm sure you will. I get most of the local newspapers daily here so I'm sure yours will be at the top of the reading pile tomorrow. I usually read them all," Creighton says, still trying to make nice. The incessant talking makes it harder by the second. The reporter finally opens the door and starts to step out but turns, his body still inside the threshold, stopping the door from closing all the way.

"Oh, Mr. Creighton, I didn't realize you were an avid newspaper reader. Just out of curiosity, what do you make of these grave robberies that have been happening in the area? I learned about them this morning, and it's just, you know, an unusual story, so it caught my eye."

Creighton feels his nose flare, his cheeks get hot, and he can tell his temperature is rising.

"I, ah, I only know what I read in the papers. It *is* a strange story, that's for sure. Thank you again, Mr. Jacobs." Creighton holds the door tight with both hands, and as the reporter backs up, Creighton is already pushing it closed behind him. He has to deal with Clyde and whatever the hell happened down there.

"Clyde!"

He can tell Creighton is yelling from the very top of the stairs down into the basement. His voice is still loud even given the distance, and it echoes throughout the large stone chambers. One of the reanimates, a woman named Martha Closton, has been losing the ability to think clearly over the course of the last few days. Cognitive degeneration is the term the Doctor uses regarding her situation. The way Clyde sees it, Martha is getting dumber. She could think clearer and had thoughts like the rest of the reanimates did at first. Now, her movement has become slower, less purposeful and her speech, while still there, makes less and less sense each day.

It was Martha that Creighton heard. Clyde waits by the door of the lab for Creighton to arrive. When he sees him turn the corner and bound down the hall toward him, Clyde backs up a step. He's never seen the man this irate.

"What the fuck happened, Clyde?" Creighton grabs Clyde by the collar of his shirt. He doesn't think the man will actually hurt him. He also knows if he fights his former boss, he will win, so there isn't much he is worried about.

"Sir, I apologize. Martha, she got past me and the Doctor. We missed her in the head count. A few of the others want to leave the house. They are done here. They don't want to be here anymore, and now they're worried they're going to lose their minds like Martha. They don't want to end up like her, sir. Anyway, I was dealing with them—we both were—and she slipped out and down the hall. I caught up with her trying to get back upstairs. So at least I caught her before then, sir. It is still my fault though. I am sorry."

"They all want a mutiny, do they?" Creighton says. His face is redder than Clyde has ever seen it. He doesn't want any of the reanimates hurt, but better them than himself. The Doctor leaves the lab and joins them. He nods at Creighton; Creighton returns the greeting.

"I believe so, sir. I don't have an answer. But if, I mean, when we are done with tonight, we might not—we might not need them anymore. I think the Doctor would think so too."

"Yes, I do agree." The Doctor straightens his body and puffs his chest out, standing taller. "After tonight, which we know will be a success, we render these reanimates obsolete. The technology is still useful to others, but by giving the people Clyde, we will be able to show them that they will never die. So, why, then, would we need technology that reanimates the already dead? After the events of this evening, we will be offering life, not simply the reversal of death. From now on, we, or at least I, will always think in the positive, Edmund. I suggest you do as well."

Clyde nods. He agrees with the Doctor. His palms sweat at thoughts of tonight. He's nervous, but the upcoming procedure will not only help him and Patty for the rest of their lives, but their children and their children's children. His family will have money. He will be able to buy what he needs and save the rest so he can leave his family well-off long after he is gone. He's always had to work hard to get places. It's easy to stay rich, but hard to climb the ladder. Hard to go from a low-class hourly wage worker to the rich upper-class. Clyde was born into that lower class. But, through hard work, he's made slow progress up that unclimbable ladder. This one sacrifice will let him jump to the top of it. He is nearly there—that thought drives the nervousness away.

"Tonight then, we need to lock them up," Creighton says.

Both Clyde and the Doctor agree.

The day passes faster than Clyde wants it to. Creighton settles down as the three of them begin preparing for his procedure. He still hasn't told Patty. He doesn't know how he could explain it before having it done. It will be easier to explain once the devices are already implanted. The Doctor assures him that he will look mostly normal, and, if he wears a hat, he will look even more so. Clyde can only believe what the Doctor says. Unlike Creighton, whom he knows he cannot.

The lab is cleared of all of the reanimates, and they are locked in a room in the upper part of the house. The windows have been barred in the room for years. Creighton guarantees the reanimates cannot escape. If they do, there will be many questions to answer.

Clyde is prepped much like the reanimates. His head is shaved as well as his chest.

"Do not worry, Clyde. This is easier than the other procedures. At least there is less of a chance for error. It is more difficult because of your blood flow. The dead, remember, do not have blood flow, making it easier for me to see what I'm doing. But," the Doctor sighs, "I've been working with flowing blood my entire career. It is nothing new. You will be fine, and we will see you in a few minutes."

"Clyde, for all of the tension between us, I am grateful for you." Creighton smiles, and it seems almost genuine. "In a few minutes you'll be the first man with the ability to be immortal. Let it sink in. Good luck."

"Thank you." Clyde looks from one man to the other as they stand over him.

"Here comes the mix of drugs," the Doctor says. He puts a mask over Clyde's face. His heart pumps faster, and he takes a long breath. He begins to doubt his decision-making up to this point, then takes another breath.

As he's about to take a third breath, his eyes close.

* * *

"Clyde." He wakes up to the Doctor's voice.

"Clyde," the Doctor repeats. Clyde is aware of where he is, of what has happened, but can't get his eyes open, not right away. The echoing sounds of the lab tell him he's come through the procedure alive. He doesn't know if it's worked, but if it has, he is immortal. If he takes care of his body, keeps from destroying his body, he will live forever. His brain, his heart, and his lungs will never stop working. They will forever run with the power of the devices the Doctor has implanted in him.

"Oh, look. See, he's waking up, he's smiling," Creighton says. Then silence, as they watch him, waiting for him to open his eyes and acknowledge them.

He wants to open his eyes, but they feel glued; he cannot

open them. Clyde feels his fingers move, but when they do, they do not fully follow the actions his brain is telling them. There is —*oh shit*—there is a delay. *No, no, it can't be.* Clyde's eyes flutter open five or six seconds after he tried to open them.

"Clyde." the Doctor looks down at him. "How do you feel?"

I feel okay, Clyde wants to say. *But I'm sore. My head and my chest.* No words leave his mouth. He waits a second or two and then hears his voice.

"I...feel...okay...But...I'm...sore...my...head...and...my... chest." Clyde's stomach drops when he realizes what this means.

"Shit." Creighton slams his hand against the metal table, the metallic bang echoes throughout the lab.

"No, no, it may be okay, Edmund. We need to wait. I was expecting this might happen," the Doctor says. "Clyde, you're regulating your own body, but the devices are assisting you. The extra electrical charge from the devices inside you is creating the delay that we see in the reanimates. But your brain is also producing its own electrical current. Once your brain becomes accustomed to what is happening, it should adjust the electric charge it needs, and your body will adjust and return you to normal. It should only take a few seconds."

Clyde thinks about nodding. A few seconds later, he nods.

"I'm sorry I didn't tell either of you about this possible side effect, I didn't think it necessary to needlessly worry either of you. Especially you, Clyde. You had enough to worry about leading up to the procedure."

Clyde nods again. He doesn't want to speak, not until his body and his brain get back in sync. The Doctor thinks it should be for a short time. It's only been a minute or so, and

Clyde already hates the feeling. It's the same feeling the reanimates go through, but there is no hope for them. He understands why they are restless. Their bodies are slower, much slower, but their minds are working as fast as they always did. The restlessness he feels inside him is almost unbearable. He hopes the feeling and the effect won't last much longer. He is trapped, trapped in his own body. He may be able to live forever, but at what cost? When will this end?

"Clyde, it may help if you get up and move around. The more activity, the faster everything will move throughout your body," the Doctor says.

Creighton watches, unable to take his eyes off of Clyde. Clyde thinks through the act of getting up, but then slows down his mind to match his body. He gingerly gets up. The pain in his chest is dull but constant. His head throbs. He wants to know what he looks like but is afraid to look in a mirror.

Finally, he is up on his feet.

"Good, good, Clyde. If you can, walk around the table a few times, the effect should begin to wear off any minute now."

Clyde walks around the table then around the entire lab. He stretches his slow, plodding steps in an effort to get the blood flowing through him faster. But the effect remains constant. Clyde counts between four and seven seconds between thought and action. After ten minutes of walking around the room, he realizes the inevitable, maybe even before the Doctor does. The effect—slowed thought, slowed brain-to-muscle function—the Doctor was so worried about in the reanimates, has happened to him. It is not going away.

Clyde is stuck in this slow-moving body. Forever.

CHAPTER 14

It's him, Michael thinks. He can't walk down the driveway and away from the Creighton house fast enough. He needs a plan. If Creighton didn't personally rob that grave the day the two caretakers at the cemetery saw his car, then he knows who did. Michael is certain it was Creighton, though. Why would he be so secretive, then give the job to someone else to do? He wouldn't. It only makes sense if Creighton did it himself. Maybe with some help, but he was there. Michael runs through the conversation. He recalls the look in Creighton's eyes, the reddening of his face. The rich man tried to play it off like there were no problems, but Michael saw a combination of anger and fear.

The interview went according to plan. It could not have gone better. He got a tour, and there was that noise coming from the wall of the library. Michael made sure to glance back on the way out; the kitchen does not back up to that part of the library.

The wind gusts and almost knocks Michael's hat off. He

catches it and continues down the driveway toward the main road.

"How did the interview go?" the man at the gate says as Michael passes through on the way out.

"It went great. Keep reading the paper, okay, friend? Might be you even make the story," Michael says and winks.

He's going to spend the rest of the day in Elk Hills. At the library perhaps, because he needs to meet with Ronald. He feels bad because he's going to lie to his friend again. But, tomorrow night he will get the rock-solid information he needs, and *then* he can share everything with Ronald. By then he'll have the story mostly written and the evidence to corroborate it. Creighton will be arrested the same morning the story runs. It will be perfect. It will sell papers. And it will feel good.

After a day at the library organizing his thoughts and getting pen to paper writing pieces of the story, Michael leaves to meet up with Ronald Weaver. He has most of the story written, the part about the grave robbery itself, pieces on the Parchesi family and Theodore Parchesi, and the background on Edmund Creighton. He leaves space for paragraphs explaining why Creighton stole the body, if there is a reason, and what the next steps are in the court case he hopes will follow. But he won't share any of this with Ronald. All he can do is tell him he's working on a few more things and hope he doesn't ask too many questions.

Michael goes to the meeting place and checks his watch. He's early but is surprised to find Ronald waiting for him.

"I heard you made some progress today, Mike. That's

good," Ronald says. It takes Michael by surprise. It's the first time he's been surprised working on this story, and it catches him off guard.

"Oh, yeah?" Michael says, switching strategies on the fly. Not his best skill, but it's all he's got right now. "Who'd you hear that from, if you don't mind me asking?"

"Mike, it's a small town. New guy comes in asking questions, people are gonna start talking, you know how it is? I heard it from a few different people, actually, that you were asking questions about Edmund Creighton. Then I heard you went up there to talk to him first thing this morning. Well, they guessed you were headed up that way, no one to confirm that for sure, I guess. But knowing you, I don't think you would just go up there unless you had a reason to talk to him. What'd you find out?"

"Ah, listen Ron. I didn't say anything because I didn't know anything yet. I need to go back to be sure. Once I made sure, I was planning on telling you everything. You understand that don't you?" His friend isn't happy because he broke their bargain, sort of. He wants them to remain on the same side in all this.

"We said you would keep me updated, Mike."

"I know, Ron. I was going to update you. That's why I'm here. I couldn't tell you yesterday because it was just talk. Nothing definite. I know you understand that." His friend doesn't have to know that he never had any intention of telling him about Creighton today either.

"Yeah, I guess I do. So, lay it out for me. Do you have a plan moving forward?" Ronald looks anxious now and back to his normal self. He's not mad about being kept in the dark, he's mad because he thought his friend was lying to him. A quick fix and easily explained away. Now, Michael has to figure out how to get the information he needs, possibly with Ronald's assistance.

"Well, like I said, I think this Creighton is involved. But I can't know for sure. He didn't say anything that would make me think that when I met with him today." Michael recounts his interview with Creighton and the noises he heard in the library. "Still, I'm telling you, Ron, if he didn't do it himself, he knows who did it and why. So, I was going to go back, tomorrow night I think, to get more information."

"Okay, I'll let the Chief know, and we can get a couple guys to go with us, you, me, maybe two more. We can call a couple guys from surrounding departments to be on call just in case—"

"No. No, we can't do it like that, Ron," Michael interjects in the middle of his friend's verbal brainstorm. "We can't go in hard like that. He'll clam up. Shut his mouth and shut the door. We won't get any information that way."

"So, what do you want to do? Keep up the reporter act?" Ronald takes off his department issued cap, pushes the hair back off his forehead, then pulls the cap back down on his head. His eyes move back and forth, not dwelling on Michael for too long before he looks somewhere else. This is going out of his element. Ronald is already working outside the rules by having Michael do some investigating for him. Now, Michael is asking him to bend the rules a bit more, and Ronald is uncomfortable with it.

"No." Michael hesitates. He's going through with it if Ronald is there or not. He'd rather just do it on his own, but if Ronald wants to join him, help couldn't be a bad thing. There is always the possibility that Ronald just arrests him instead. "Ron, I want to break in there."

"What?" Ronald's eyes get wide, and he looks at his long-time friend in disbelief. "Mike, you can't be serious."

"I know how it sounds, but listen. I go in late at night. No one will see me. I— um, I've done this kind of thing before. Hopefully, Creighton is asleep. His wife is sick, she doesn't even go down to the first floor. I find what I'm looking for; evidence that he was in on the grave robberies, or I find nothing. If I find nothing, I leave. Simple as that. If I do find something, you can call your boys in with a warrant. Get the proof you already know is there, arrest this guy, solve the case. I run the story. There really isn't much to say no to. I don't see how it could go wrong."

"Well, the whole thing is wrong because it's breaking and entering, Mike," Ronald says. "I don't know how you can just tell me this and expect me to do nothing."

Michael checks his watch, only a few minutes until the train arrives. He needs to smooth this out with Ronald because he's coming back tomorrow to break into Creighton's house. The last thing he needs is to avoid police at the same time. Or get arrested trying to solve this crime for the people who couldn't solve it on their own.

"I understand that, Ron. You let me go with this because you kept hitting dead ends. There are things I can get done that you guys, frankly, just can't. I got Creighton's name because the people who knew stuff didn't want to talk to the police. People would just rather keep to themselves. They saw this, mostly, as a crime with a victim who was already dead. No one got hurt, so why hassle themselves over it? I wish they didn't do things that way, but it makes sense." Michael sees Ronald about to speak, but he keeps going, needing to make his point before leaving. "The point is, sometimes the rules police have to follow slow you down or make it impossible for you to do your job. I don't have the same rules. My only rule is to tell the truth, which is what I intend to do. You'd have to get a warrant, then search the house. As soon as you knocked on the door, he'd hide whatever it is he doesn't want you to see, the same way he did with me. He'd get your warrant, and he'd be ready for tough questions about the grave robberies. He wouldn't be caught off guard. If I go in without anyone knowing, he can't hide stuff. I get to see what's really going on, then tell you where to look. And I don't need a warrant."

"I get it," Ronald says. "I don't like it, but I get it. I guess if bending the rules got us this far, a little bit more bending can get us what we need."

"Right. Think about it. You could close this case tomorrow night," Michael says, knowing *that* is his ultimate goal.

"Alright, we do it your way, then. Just don't mess it up, Mike. What time are we meeting then?"

"What?" Michael is caught off guard again.

"What time are we meeting tomorrow night to go in there? I'm not gonna let you do this on your own. We'll go together. Just you and me. No uniform. We never broke into a house before, but it'll kinda be like old times, I guess."

In the distance, the train whistles. Michael needs to leave or wait for the next train. They don't have time to talk it out.

"I can do it on my own, Ron, really."

"I know you can. But if I'm gonna let you do this, I'll be there with you. Sorry, only way it's going to happen."

Part of Michael doesn't want to get Ron involved. Part of him thinks the less people that know about this the better. But it's Ron. He knows he can trust him. He takes a long breath and then exhales.

"Alright. This train coming in now starts in the city." Michael leans in closer to Ronald and lowers his voice. "I'll take this one out from the city tomorrow and meet you down in the trees on the other side of the cemetery behind the church. You know those trees? We can't let anyone see us together, so if anyone sees you going in that direction, keep walking until you're by yourself. I'll do the same. We'll have a few hours to plan stuff out in those woods, and we should be all set. I think I know how to get in anyway."

Ronald says nothing but nods.

"And wear dark clothes."

"Okay, Mike. I'll see you then."

Michael nods and turns to leave. He jogs across Main Street to the station. After a few minutes of waiting, the train pulls in. It hisses and comes to a stop. Michael gets on, headed back home. He has some of his own planning to do. He's seen the inside of the house and has a mental map of the layout. What he really wants to do is get to the library and figure out what made that sound behind the wall. The answers he's looking for are there.

That night when he gets home, he tells Mary everything. She's the only one, other than Ronald, who knows the whole story beginning to end. She isn't happy about his plan to break into the Creighton house, but she understands why he's doing it. They both agree, it makes it worth the risk.

* * *

The next day slides by as slow as any day he can remember. Michael debates going into the newsroom and pounding out as much of the story as possible, but he doesn't. He stays home and writes what he can. It could be a late night. If the police move on Creighton after they find whatever they find at the house, he needs to be ready to run with the story, so he gets extra rest. It's going to be an all-nighter of breaking, entering, and writing.

The time comes. Michael kisses Joseph and Mary goodbye, leaves the apartment, and boards the train for Elk Hills.

The town looks different later in the day. He gets off the train at the time he usually leaves. When he steps off the platform, it's the small things he sees; the lights in the general store are dimmed. Only the light by the back of the store near the register is on. Rufus must be closed for the night and counting up the day's earnings before leaving. The same goes for *Louise's Diner*. Though Michael has only been in there once at breakfast time, he'd noticed people there for lunch, too. Now it is dark, empty. Fewer cars are on the road. A few people walking, but their heads are down, focusing on the ground in front of them. It's cool and Michael tugs his coat down at the lapels and then heads toward the church.

The sun sets fast, and, in the short walk from the train station to the church, the town is more dark than light. A slight breeze picks up, and Michael feels it through his coat. He shivers and works his way around the church through the copse of trees and down toward the cemetery. Instead of cutting though the cemetery, Michael follows the perimeter wall and enters the woods on the far side. His feet crunch over dried leaves and broken sticks. He could try, but he would never be able to make his movements quiet.

There are separate crunches sounding in opposite rhythm to his own footsteps, and he slows his pace.

"Ron?" Michael whispers. He doesn't know why he's

talking quietly; chances are the only other person in earshot is Ronald.

"Yeah," a voice calls. Then a light shines off to his right.

"Alright, we made it," Michael says.

"I gotta tell you, Mike, I'm still nervous about all this." Ronald holds the light at waist level, illuminating the bottom half of his face and sending strange-shaped shadows up toward his forehead. It's hard to read him, but the only thing Michael sees is excitement. A good sign.

Each minute they stand in the woods, the waning light of the sun dims. The darker the better. The sun will continue to drop, and darkness will engulf the night as they walk to the Creighton house. They won't do anything until the night is dark and the lights in the house are off.

"I know you're nervous. It will work out, though. And this is your first time, so we can be gentle." Both men laugh and Michael can feel the tension easing in his friend. "The front door has two separate locks on it. I heard them unlock when he opened the door and lock them again as soon as I left."

Ronald nods.

"But he let me walk around the outside of the house after my tour, so I got a good idea of everything around the house. Inside, there's a door in the kitchen that leads out to that garage. The door only has one lock on it, and it's keyed. I didn't see a lock on the garage door itself. We might be able to get in that way. Just pull it up a few feet and roll in underneath. If that kitchen entry door is locked, I can pick it. If not, we can just walk right in."

"Pick it?" Yesterday, Ronald's face would have shown anger or fear, tonight the only thing Michael sees is a bit of a smile.

"You'd be surprised what you learn as a reporter in the city." Michael smiles.

Ronald shakes his head. "I don't even want to know."

"Alright then," Michael says. "Once we get inside, we have to get into the library. Something he didn't want me to see or, I guess, hear, is in there. Pretty sure if we can figure out what's in the library, we'll be able to figure everything out."

Ronald just nods again.

"Ready to go? Should take us a little while, right? Then we just wait until it looks like the house is quiet and dark. Everyone will be asleep, hopefully. Then, we are in and out."

"We can stay off the road, too. There's a path through the woods up this way. It's how I came in here. It'll keep us off the road almost the whole way, and it's an easy walk. Less people that see us, the better."

"Now you're thinking like a reporter." Michael pats Ronald on the back.

"Or a criminal." The detective laughs.

They weave their way through the woods and settle in on the trail. It doesn't make their walk that much easier, but at least the trail is clear. Still, it is narrow. Ronald leads the way with his flashlight. Even the moonlight doesn't penetrate down through the thick canopy. There is no other light for the entirety of their walk. They walk in silence; Michael visualizes the interior of the house as the path becomes steeper. If it's dark, he wants to be able to move around and figure out where he is without bumping into anything, so he reminds himself of the interior as best he can.

"Hold up here," Ronald says, pulling Michael out of his thoughts.

"What is it?"

"The road's right up there. We'd have to walk along the road up to the Creighton house. Same road you took yesterday. Or, we go the rest of the way through the woods. It gets even steeper and rocky, though."

"I think we stay in the woods. Can we get around to the back of the house this way?"

"Yeah, yeah, I think so. I don't know these woods that well, but I chased a kid through here once. I think I can put us behind the house."

"Let's do it." Michael nods, and Ronald leads the way. It doesn't feel like they are on separate sides anymore. He wanted to do this on his own, but he's glad Ronald is here with him instead, especially now that his heart is in it.

They pick their way through the woods again, and Ronald is right; the terrain is more difficult to traverse. They climb over sharp rocks and duck under fallen trees held up by larger ones. Twigs and branches snap and pop under their feet, and Michael hopes no one hears their approach. Light appears off to their right. They've curled up around the back of the house, and it's lit from all sides. Outdoor lights shine on the house, keeping it illuminated even at night.

"Shit," Michael says as they draw up right to the edge of the woods. The open grass between them and the house is dark, but the house itself is bathed in light. "Looks like we'll have to work in the light for a while."

"It's hard to tell if the lights inside are on," Ronald says.

He's right. The shades are drawn, and the outside lights are bright, casting shadows and throwing pools of light up onto the house.

"We'll just have to guess. What time is it?" Michael looks at his watch and waits for Ronald to shine the flashlight on it.

"Eleven-thirty. Wait until midnight and then go in? It's just a guessing game right now."

"One?" Ronald suggests.

"Sure. One works. Gives him some extra time."

The pair back deeper into the woods and wait until one o'clock, passing the time whispering about their younger days and reminiscing about their friends when they were younger and wilder. They laugh more than they should, given the situation, but the memories relax them. Before they know it, it's after one in the morning. They give the house a final once over, again trying to determine if the lights inside are off. Not knowing what the house is like behind the drawn shades, they run over the plan once more and decide to keep their talking to a minimum once they start toward the house. Michael gives a nod, and they move across the lawn.

The pair stay low and get to a small shrub close to the house. Michael ducks behind it and Ronald follows. The light doesn't reach through the thick shrub, which provides a perfect cover as they peer through the leaves at the house. The garage is about thirty feet to their left; Michael still thinks it's the fastest, easiest way in. He points to it and Ronald nods.

"Me first, then you," Michael says.

Quickly, they move in front of the light, up the lawn, and over the gravel to the garage door. Michael gets there first and crouches low, Ronald grabs the handle of the door.

"One, two, three," Ronald counts. Then he pulls up hard, and the door rolls up. He stops it at about two feet off the ground and holds it there. Michael rolls through the open door, stands up on the inside, and holds it open for Ronald, who rolls in after him. Once they are both inside, Michael lets the door down slowly, noiselessly.

At first, he didn't notice the smell because he was focused on getting Ronald in with him, but now that the door is closed, the stench of death hits Michael hard. The garage is dark, but the light from outside shoots in through the small windows giving them just enough light to get a vague idea of what is in the garage.

The car, the one the cemetery caretakers saw the day of the first grave robbery, is there on one side, parked against the wall. The rest of the garage appears empty. A table with a piece of tarp stands on one side, but no tools. Ronald investigates the table, lifting up the tarp.

"Nothing here. I don't know where that smell is coming from, but it's not over here."

"Whatever it was, must be gone now. I think we both know what it was," Michael says. "Let's see if we can get inside."

Still crouching, though he's not sure why, Michael shuffles over to the door and looks back at Ronald, who nods at him. He grabs the knob and turns. He expects the door to be locked, so he doesn't realize when he turns the knob that the door is already beginning to open for him. The kitchen is dark, but his eyes have adjusted to the low light. He can see the room clearly enough. Just as he remembered it. Two doors out of the room on the other side, the one on the right leads them to the main hall; the double doors that lead to the library are just down the hall on the right.

They cross the kitchen without a need for the flashlight and slip through the door into the hall. It is just as dark as the kitchen. They glide down the hall in silence. Michael leads and stops once when a creak echoes around them. At first, Michael thinks it is someone moving on the second floor. Then he's sure one of them made the creak on a loose floorboard. But they hold still as a gust of wind whips by outside, causing the house to groan again. Michael realizes he's been holding his breath and exhales. Then, he continues down the hall.

The house is silent again, their movement quiet. The doors to the library, propped open the last time, are closed tight. Michael grasps the smooth, glass doorknob and twists. The knob emits a soft squeak, but Michael doesn't think the noise travels more than a few feet around them. He pulls the door open and slides inside. Ronald closes the door behind them, and Michael begins his search. Ronald does the same on the opposite side. They remain as silent as possible, listening as much as looking. Michael gets across to the far side of the room. A small door sits there, tucked in between the tall bookshelves. It reminds him of a small building in the city nestled between two of the larger skyscrapers standing watch on either side. Creighton looked this way when he heard the noise yesterday. Michael pulls open the door and looks inside. Just a small empty closet. That in and of itself is not unusual, but Michael ducks his head in and looks around anyway. The noise he heard came from in here. He's positive. A thin line of light emanates from the edge of one of the walls. He leans in closer, examining the light. The wall is not really a wall.

"Ron," he half-whispers to his police officer partner. "Come check this out."

As he calls, he puts a hand on the wall and pushes. It doesn't move, but his finger catches a thin, invisible edge. He tightens his grip, and the door swings toward him.

"I knew it!" Michael says. He doesn't wait for Ron but hears him coming up behind him. He turns his body, slides down the narrow hall, then starts down the stairs, until he hears shuffling at the bottom. There is no one in sight, but the slow steady shuffles continue. Michael slows his pace, trying to peer around the corner.

A tall, gaunt, pale man with dark, death-like eyes stares back at him. At first, the man says nothing. Michael recoils out of fear and repulsion. A device sits on top of the man's head, more devices attached to his arms and legs. On his chest is a similar square shaped device. *What is this thing?* The man opens his mouth as if to speak. Nothing comes out at first, and Michael backs up to the second step, wanting some distance between him and the pale creature. This is it. This is what Creighton was nervous about. But what is it? And what does it have to do with robbing graves?

The thing finally speaks.

"You...should...leave," it says. Its speech is slow, effortful.

"What?" Michael says. He doesn't know what to say or do. He wants to ask Ronald if this is enough for a search warrant, but before he can turn, there is a noise behind him. He starts to whip his head around, but something heavy hits him in the back. He crashes down to the stone floor beneath him. The side of his head slaps against the hard slabs of rock. He tries to push himself up but can't keep his eyes open.

Everything goes black.

CHAPTER 15

"He's waking up," Creighton says to the Doctor. He looks to Ronald. "Stay over there for now, out of sight. Then you can talk to him."

They are in the middle of the lab. The reanimates and Clyde have been moved to the other parts of the house. The doors are locked to keep them from leaving, which is becoming more and more of an issue. They are mad at him and the Doctor because, while they were once grateful for a second chance at life, they are not simply happy to be alive again. They want to be alive like they once were. They do not even realize that what they have done is next to impossible. They've brought them back from the dead, but they want more. Don't they realize they have the gift of *actual* life after death? Even Clyde is ungrateful. Clyde is angry because he wants to move and think with the speed and dexterity he once had. The Doctor wants that too, as does Creighton, but a small flaw in the procedure gave Clyde the same delayed thoughts as the reanimates. But, Clyde does not seem to care that he can live forever now. He wants more. All of them, they all want more.

The Doctor believes he has fixed the issue, but he needs another test subject to run the experiment on. Thanks to Detective Weaver and the wonderful Elk Hills Police force, another subject dropped right into their lap. This subject, however, will not be dead or willing.

"Completing the rest of the research on your story, Mr. Jacobs?" Creighton asks. He likes this. The reporter is tied up and still waking up from a few minutes of unconsciousness, leaving Creighton in control with all of the power. The son of a bitch fooled him last time. He doesn't like to be fooled.

"What? What happened?"

"You fell down the stairs, Mr. Jacobs. *After* you broke into my house, you slipped and fell down my stairs."

"No, no I didn't, I was— I was pushed!" The groggy reporter shakes his head a few times and then pulls at the rope holding him against the chair he's in. "Let me up! What is this?"

"Well, you broke in, Mr. Jacobs. I was just holding you until the police arrive. I wouldn't want you to get away." Creighton smiles as Jacobs looks back and forth, trying to see around him. He can see most of the lab, but Ronald Weaver, his former friend, is hidden from view.

"Only because you stole those bodies. And, I've got the police with me already. Where is Ronald? What did you do with him?" Jacobs pulls harder at the ropes, rocks the chair back and forth.

"Oh, yes, Mr. Weaver. He's right here." Creighton nods, and Ronald Weaver steps around in front of Jacobs, joining the Doctor and Creighton.

"Sorry, Mike." Ronald doesn't smile, his face turned down. He's already told Creighton how much he hates doing this, but in the end the money and his job were more important than his friendship. Creighton has found that is almost always the case.

"Ron? What's going on? What did they do to you?" The reporter looks at Creighton and his police officer friend. Jacobs has tears in his eyes.

"I know, Mike, I— I..."

"You helped them? Ron, they took those bodies. What about moving up? Running the place? Doing what's right?"

"I know, Mike. This is how I get that job. I didn't have a choice. It's the only way I will make Captain."

"What are you going to do then, Ron? Let them kill me?"

"I don't know what they're going to do, Mike. I don't. I promised not to ask questions. Don't worry about Mary, Mike."

"Jesus Christ, Ron!" Michael presses his body hard against the restraints.

"They're going to think you died in a fire on the train home. I'll make sure Mary and Joseph get taken care of, okay? You don't have to worry about them."

The police officer's eyes fill with tears. The salty fluid drips down his cheeks. Jacobs fights hard against the ropes holding him in place, the legs and arms of the chair rattling as he throws himself from one side to the other. The ropes don't budge.

"Ron! Ron! You don't have to do this. Don't do it, Ron!" the reporter shouts at him. Creighton has seen and heard enough.

"Mr. Weaver, thank you for your help. It's time to go." Creighton puts his arm around the dejected police officer and looks to the Doctor, who takes his place and guides Weaver out of the room. Weaver gives one look back at his tied up, screaming friend and then puts his head down. Creighton shuts the door to the lab behind them when they leave.

"You son of a bitch!" Jacobs says.

Creighton ignores the comment and moves on.

"Since we're going to need you, Mr. Jacobs, I guess we should fill you in on exactly what's going to happen to you tonight."

"You're not going to do anything to me." The prisoner tries to force himself out of the ropes binding him, but again he fails. Creighton sees the muscles in his legs tighten and relax at various intervals as he continues to try to break free. He makes no progress.

"You will do whatever we need you to do. You do not have a choice in the matter. And after you broke into my house, you should count yourself lucky you're still alive. Now, keep your mouth shut so you can understand what will happen to you, because you're going to want to know."

He stops talking and waits for a smart retort from Michael Jacobs, but the man is silent, maybe he's finally learned his place.

"We need your body to test a few devices that we have invented here recently. You will not be the first person we have tested the devices on. The first person went through the procedure willingly. We did not coerce him in any way. It was his choice, and he is now part of our group. He is one of us. But we need a new test subject."

At this, Jacobs strains against the ropes again but with the same amount of success as the previous attempts. The Doctor reenters and joins Creighton. They exchange a nod, and the Doctor opens his mouth to speak. Jacobs yells over him.

"Who the hell are you?"

"I understand your frustration in this situation, Mr. Jacobs. I do. But you must understand our position. Mr. Creighton's position as well. He has done nothing to you except give you a tour of his home. He did not invite you back to his home, and you entered it illegally. Your friend informed us that you were looking for dead bodies here. As a Doctor, I can assure you that there are no dead bodies in Mr. Creighton's home."

"Who are you?" Jacobs asks again. Sweat drips from his forehead as he clenches and relaxes his muscles, trying to get out of the ropes. He will tire out at some point.

"Everyone here just calls me the Doctor, and I'm okay with that. You can call me that too, if you'd like."

Creighton folds his arms in front of him. He's done with this guy. As far as he's concerned, they should just knock him out and see what the Doctor can do with him. If the procedure works, then great. They can move on to the final step. If it doesn't work, they need to get another subject or just trust the Doctor that the next time will be a success. Either way, Creighton knows he's not going to spend an eternal life trapped in a body that doesn't respond the way he wants.

"You always perform procedures against the will of your patients, doctor? Because if you do and you're taking lives instead of saving lives, you're not even a doctor in my eyes. In which case, I'll call you a criminal like him and Weaver and anyone else you work with. Just a bunch of low-life criminals."

Creighton stifles a laugh, but he can't contain it. His deep laugh echoes throughout the room.

"If there is one thing the Doctor does better than anyone else on the planet, it's keep people alive," Creighton says.

Creighton shares a look with the Doctor. They both smile.

"I like that you're not afraid of me, or of us. You should be.

I mean, look at you, tied up. We could kill you and no one would know. Your friend, Officer Weaver, said as much. You're going to die in a fire on the train. Your wife will be sad, I'm sure. But she doesn't know where you are. She will think you're dead. But you're not going to be dead, Mr. Jacobs. You're going to be here. And you're going to be very much alive," the Doctor says. His eyes widen and almost glow in the low light of the laboratory.

Creighton had not seen the man look this way before. It wasn't the fact that he was about to perfect his procedure, because even though there were some flaws, he'd completed the procedure on a live subject before with Clyde. This was a different look. With Clyde, he had wanted the procedure to succeed. But here, with this, Creighton realizes, the Doctor has as much anger toward this reporter as he's ever had toward anyone. Deep down Creighton wonders if the Doctor doesn't want to see the procedure fail this time, just so they won't have to deal with the reporter anymore.

Creighton has considered that option as well. The reporter can cause nothing but problems if he is alive and they are about to make him immortal. He hopes, if the experiment is successful, he can convince the Doctor to remove the implants and let the reporter die once they have their success. There is no need for him to continue living.

"So, you're just going to keep me here, then? Like this?" Michael struggles against his ropes yet again.

This time it's the Doctor's turn to laugh. "No, no. Not at all, Mr. Jacobs. We're going to perform an experiment on you. We've performed it before, but it was only partially successful. We need to perfect it, and need a new living subject. I didn't know what we were going to do until we found out that you were coming tonight. Now you're here and my experiment is ready to go. If it fails, you will never know. If it succeeds, you will end up thanking me."

"What? What experiment? What are you going to do to me?" The reporter's eyes widen. He stares at the two of them, fear slathered across his sweaty face. He isn't the confident man that came to interview him the other day; he isn't even the man that was yelling at them demanding that they let him go just a few minutes ago. The word 'experiment' does something to him. It changes him from fearless to terrified. He has no idea what the experiment is or what it entails. He only knows he has very little say in the matter. Creighton smiles at Jacobs' terror and he realizes how much he likes it; how much he enjoys seeing that kind of fear. He's had people afraid of him before because of his power and money, but that is different. The fear on Jacobs' face is unlike anything he's seen before. Fear for his life. Fear for his body. Complete fear of the unknown.

Creighton doesn't just like seeing the fear on Jacobs' face, it brings him joy. This is new to him, and he wants to produce more of it. The feeling is different, something close to arousal. He leans in close to Jacobs and puts both hands on the arms of the chair he's tied to. He gets his face close to the bound man. So close, their cheeks are nearly touching. Creighton breathes in deep, smelling the sweat and dirt and fear on the man. Then he gets his mouth close to Jacobs' ear.

"You shouldn't have broken into my house, Mr. Jacobs. But now that you have, we're going to experiment on you until you beg us to let you die." Creighton breathes in the smell of fear once more, lingering there, letting it flow into him through his nostrils. Then he backs away slowly. The rapid breathing and low whimper that Jacobs produces nearly sends him over the edge, he *is* aroused and needs to back away to calm himself down. He never expected to enjoy this so much. If he knew what this was like, he would have been doing it his whole life.

After a long, deep breath, one that calms his own breathing and slows down his heart rate, Creighton looks at the Doctor.

"Are we ready to go?"

The Doctor is across the room at the table, and even though he has his back to the lab, Creighton can tell he is preparing the devices for their attachment to Mr. Jacobs.

"Yes, we are ready." The Doctor turns and stares at Michael, whose breathing increases to the point that he makes himself pass out in the chair. The Doctor and Creighton share a smile and move toward him, the Doctor with a drug-soaked rag in his hand. Creighton holds the rag over Jacobs' face, his eyes bulge and close once, then snap open then close again. Jacobs strains against the ropes for a few more minutes with diminishing intensity while he continues to breathe in the vapors. Eventually, he passes out once more.

With the devices in place and Jacobs strapped to the bed, Creighton, the Doctor and Clyde sit and wait for him to wake up. Clyde can tell Creighton does not want him here. As far as Creighton is concerned, Clyde is no different than the reanimates—a faltered step toward the ultimate goal. A failed experiment. All but useless. Clyde's feelings about himself are not much different: he is useless. Most of his life was spent using his body to work hard and complete tasks. He cannot do that anymore. He is trapped. The thoughts are there. His mind works. But his body won't cooperate.

The three of them sit. Creighton and the Doctor talk, and Clyde stares, listening. He doesn't know who the newcomer is, but the straps and the bump on his head tell that he is not a willing participant. He was alive when he got here, so Clyde assumes he was alive when they put the devices on him. As he sits, he wonders if it worked. If this time, the Doctor was able to get the results he wants without the unfortunate side effect that Clyde and the other reanimates have suffered.

Eventually, the man on the table groans, his leg moves and tries to lift up before it is stopped by the strap holding it down.

Clyde remembers the feeling well. He thinks about pointing and telling them the subject is moving, but before the words can leave his mouth, the Doctor notices and speaks over him.

"Here we are, Edmund," he says.

The Doctor and Creighton rise and stand over their newest subject. Clyde follows after a few seconds, standing at the man's feet while Creighton and the Doctor flank him on either side. The Doctor loosens the straps. The subject sits up, looks around. Clyde watches his eyes. He looks for the delay. If there is going to be a delay, he will be able to see it in his eyes.

Clyde isn't sure how to feel about his situation. He knew the possible risks, even though the Doctor said they were minimal. He knew going in what might happen. He became a large part of the operation and the experiments of the Elk Hills Research Society, and now he wants to see it through until the end. He knows the Doctor and Creighton and the rest of them want to make themselves immortal. That has to be the ultimate goal. Then they might sell their technology. But he wants to see it succeed. He wants to make his money. Even if he can't go back to his wife, he can send her the money. She will be set for the rest of her life. He needs this to work.

When the man's eyes dart back and forth, when they seem to move at a normal speed, Clyde's heart skips a beat.

"Michael," the Doctor says. His voice just above a whisper.

The man, Michael, doesn't say anything, his eyes still flick back and forth as if figuring out what he's seeing. Clyde remembers the confusion at first, and he had been prepared.

"Michael, can you speak?" Creighton says, placing a hand on the man's shoulder.

"Yes, yes I can speak," Michael says, answering Creighton immediately. Clyde thinks about smiling. Six second later, he feels his mouth move, and a smile forms on his lips.

CHAPTER 16

The three men are happy with the results. They are as happy as he thought any three men could be about the well-being of a fourth man they barely know. He doesn't understand at first. The Doctor, Creighton and the slow-man, no one ever told Michael his name, they celebrate when he comes to.

He has devices on him now. On his head, on his chest, his arms and legs. He only knows that whatever they were trying to fix must have been successful, because all three men are pleased with the outcome.

But now he is chained up. The chain is attached around his waist. Creighton and the slow-man did it while he was still only half conscious. Then they left the room.

The door does not shut all the way, and Michael can listen in.

"We need to get everyone here right away," one voice says, he thinks it is Creighton.

"I agree, call them now. Let them know."

Michael wonders what they are planning. They've only been out of the room a few minutes, and Michael's body is still exhausted from the hike in the woods to get to the house and the events that followed. He moves to sit and rest his legs and ease the pain growing at the small of his back, when the metal door of the room he's in slams open. The Doctor breezes back into the room by himself, the other two have gone.

"I wouldn't sit for very long, Mr. Jacobs," the Doctor says, approaching but staying just outside the reach of the chain.

"Why not? What did you do to me?" He sits if only to protest the fact that the Doctor doesn't want him to.

"Suit yourself." The Doctor shrugs and tucks his hands into the low pockets on his white lab coat. "You might have a different take on things once you have all of the information."

"Well, give it to me. You know I'll be getting out of here someday. You won't keep me here forever. I don't care what Ron tells my wife or anyone else. I *will* get out of here."

"No, you won't," the Doctor says. His casual tone makes Michael want to strangle him. When he can get to him, he will. "Here is what you need to know. Do with the information as you will, I am just giving you the facts."

He was more approachable than Creighton. The Doctor seems almost like he was a real Doctor at some point in his life. Even if he isn't any more, he has the bedside manner of someone who understands the value of messaging. Creighton and the Doctor are saying the same thing, but their delivery is different and it has an effect on Michael.

"Okay. What is it then? I'll hear you out."

"You are now immortal. Barring some horrific accident, you will not die. You can live—"

"What?" Michael cuts him off, but before he can go on, the Doctor continues.

"The devices attached to you are keeping your heart and

your lungs operating, as well as keeping the slight electrical function in your brain at a normal level. Should you become sick, your heart might try to stop, but the device would keep it beating. Should you develop a cancer that your body cannot fight on its own, you heart and lungs and brain will continue to function. Only an injury to these three organs can kill you. Otherwise, the devices will not allow your body to stop functioning."

"The slow-man that was here with the devices on him. Is he...? I mean, does he..." Michael trails off. The Doctor smiles and nods understanding at what Michael is trying to say.

"Yes. That is Clyde. He is also immortal. But something went slightly wrong, and he has a delay between his thoughts and his physical actions that I cannot undo. He will be like that forever. I don't mean until the end of his life, I mean forever." The Doctor pauses. Michael is still trying to process everything, so the Doctor continues. "The devices on your arms and legs are attached to your other devices. The friction that you produce when you move your arms or legs in any direction is enough to keep the devices operating without the need for an outside power source. If you do not move your arms or legs, we could hook you up to a power source to keep you alive. When you move your arms and legs, the power will be stored up, and you will be able to live without being connected to a power source. If you do not have power coming from your arms or legs or from an outside power source, the devices will stop working and you will die."

With that, Michael jumps up, picks up his legs and begins to move his arms back and forth, anger bubbling up inside of him, more than before the procedure. "You mean I have to do this forever?"

The Doctor laughs but Michael glares back at him.

"I'm sorry, Michael. It's not funny. The power generators can store three days of power to run your devices. You don't have that much stored yet. Obviously, you have to build up the energy. Once they are full, you could not move for three full days and still be alive."

"But what about my heart and lungs? And my brain? They were working fine before this. If I run out of power, won't they just continue to work on their own?"

The Doctor shakes his head, his mouth turns downward.

"The unfortunate answer is no. Your organs will no longer work on their own. The only thing that keeps them operating now are my devices. I— I tried to create something like what you describe." The Doctor, for the first time, seems to lose some of his confidence. "It was the ultimate goal, but the procedure puts too much strain on the organs. If the devices cease working, the organs cease working, and the body does as well. Imagine something like that. You just slip it on the organ and if it fails, the device takes over. Maybe someday, but not yet."

"Why am I like this then? I mean, you just did the procedure on me, but I'm not really in any pain anywhere, just a little sore in my arms and legs."

"I cannot explain that, Mr. Jacobs. You're the first successful one we've had, and I was not expecting you to be active this fast. I assume it has to do with the electric current in your brain. Perhaps the charge is off just enough to reduce the amount of pain you feel. It is actually one of the first things I plan to research tomorrow once things settle down. I don't even really need you for that part. I can use Clyde."

"Then why can't I leave? Why can't I go back to my wife and child with...with this gift?" Michael may have a device attached to his head, but it hasn't affected his thinking at all. He senses the Doctors vulnerability and goes for it.

"You're not an idiot, Mr. Jacobs." The Doctor shakes his head. His expression changes, and he looks at Michael the way a father would look at a misbehaving son. "We can't let information about this technology leave this house. At least not yet. We didn't tell your friend, Officer Weaver, anything. We couldn't. If he knew, we'd have to keep him here indefinitely. I'm a doctor. I'm here for the science behind what we're trying to do. I really am. That's how Mr. Creighton got me to join up. But there is another side to all of this. A business side. I'm not the best when it comes to business, but Mr. Creighton is. I trust him with that more than I trust anyone else on earth. That includes my own mother, Mr. Jacobs. There is a lot of money riding on this for me and for everyone in the Elk Hills Research Society. But only if we follow the prescribed business plan. Which means all of this stays in the house until the time is right."

"And Creighton decides when that is, I assume," Michael says. The Doctor nods but says nothing. "What happens next then?"

"Ah, Mr. Jacobs, next is actually a very special event. We've been planning it for a while, but we obviously needed to wait until we had a successful test before we went ahead with it." The Doctor's eyes widen, and Michael remembers why he was fearful of him to begin with. He may have a nice side, almost a caring side, but he has another, darker, side. Michael sees it in his eyes every time he thinks about his experiments and his technologies. Creighton might be crazy, fear might have excited him, but the Doctor is too controlled to be anything but evil.

"And that would be?"

"Immortal Night." The Doctor's eyes return to normal. He

turns to leave, then turns back to Michael once more. "I must go help Clyde and Mr. Creighton get ready for it. One of us will be back to collect you for the event once we are ready."

"I am needed for this?" Michael says, not wanting to be a part of anything else.

"Oh yes," the Doctor says. The wide, mad eyes return behind the glasses. "You're the guest of honor."

Michael's breath quickens at the newest piece of information. They are going to show him off to the rest of their crazy group. They couldn't have this Immortal Night without his procedure being a success. Now, they will invite the rest of the group to see him. But Immortal Night? It makes it sound like the entire group is becoming immortal. That's exactly what is going to happen, he realizes. The Doctor is going to perform the same procedure on everyone in the group. They will all live forever.

Michael waits. He has nothing to do but move back and forth to charge the devices on his arms and legs. His thoughts wander. First, he's defiant. He wants nothing more than to break out, report Creighton, the Doctor and everyone else in this Elk Hills Research Society to the *real* police. The police that will actually do something about what has happened to him, as well as the graves that were robbed. The cops here in the suburbs are just as dirty as the ones in the city. Maybe there are no *real* police. If Ron would turn his back on him, anyone could be bought, and they all probably were. Going to the police would do nothing.

He could just run the story. Escape, write his experience and expose the whole thing. It would probably get justice the fastest. Creighton couldn't hide behind the police when everyone in the Chicagoland area knew what went on inside his home. But there was a problem with that—and every other plan: he needed to escape, and he couldn't see that happening.

Then sadness comes. Ronald is going to tell Mary he died. He's even going to produce a fake, burned up body for her. She will believe it. No reason for her not to. She won't look for him because she trusts Ronald. She won't try to find him. She will have a funeral, and he will be gone. She will move on, and he will never know his son.

That part makes him angry again.

He tries a few more times to pull himself from the wall. The chain around his waist is large and heavy. He isn't going to break it, but the bracket attached to the wall looks less heavy duty. He might be able to get it loose enough to shimmy it out. He channels his anger and yanks hard against the chain. It clinks. There is a loud metallic crack as the chain slams against the side of the bracket, but it doesn't budge. Michael is out of breath after just one pull, the chain heavier around his waist. He doesn't think he can pull it hard like that more than one or two more times. He gathers up the chain and pulls it all as close to the wall as he can. With his free hand, he grabs the bracket and wiggles it back and forth. He hasn't loosened it at all.

Michael stands with his back to the wall and gathers up as much of the chain as he can. Some links still lay on the floor, but he's holding ten or fifteen of the thick heavy links in his arms. He pushes off the wall and explodes forward as hard and as fast as he can. He makes it only six steps before the chain yanks him back hard. He falls flat on his back. There is a metallic clang when his elbow hits the cement floor, but the device on his arm doesn't fall off and seems operational. Sweat drips down his forehead, and he has a hard time catching his breath. He pauses a moment to collect himself.

He wants to just give in, to stay there on the floor, but the thought of his wife and little baby forces him to his feet. He's still sucking air, but it feels like his lungs won't expand far enough. Something to do with the procedure maybe. He drags his exhausted body back to the wall and tugs again on the bracket. It still doesn't move, and Michael is out of ideas. He will have to wait until they move him somewhere. He won't be able to get loose of this chain without a little help.

It could have been hours or minutes. In the back corner of the lab with nothing to look at and no windows, time passes differently. Michael might have fallen asleep, but he's not sure— if he did, he doesn't know how long he was out. The slow-man, Clyde, shuffles into the room. The slam of a door gets Michael's attention. If he was dozing, he's not anymore. Clyde doesn't scan the room, but he does make sure the door is shut behind him. Then he goes right to Michael. Clyde's movement is slow, but direct. Even in this state, it's clear the man is in a hurry.

"They...will...be...here...in...minute," Clyde says while he crosses the room. It takes forever for the words to get out, but Michael is patient, knowing there is nothing Clyde can do to change it.

Michael isn't going to interrupt or respond. This man is here for a reason and Michael needs to know what it is.

"Want...show...you...off...then...kill...you...liability," Clyde says using as few words as he can to get his point across.

"Can't...change...minds...stay...close...I'll...try...help...
you...sorry."

Clyde walks past him and to the bracket Michael couldn't
get out from the wall. He begins working, slowly pulling at the
chain.

"No, don't be sorry," Michael says, when the metal door
slams open again and Creighton and the Doctor walk in.
"Thanks," Michael says so softly he can barely hear the words in
his own ears.

"We will keep you here, Mr. Jacobs, until I have explained
the occurrences to the rest of the group. Then, Clyde and the
Doctor will escort you out to the main chamber where you will
meet everyone. Once that is done, Doctor, we will continue
with Immortal Night. Mr. Jacobs will be introduced and
brought back here to the wall. I'm afraid, until I am able to
figure out a better living situation, you're stuck here. On the
one hand, you broke into my house, and you should be
punished for that accordingly. On the other hand, you are the
first person to become immortal in a fully successful procedure.
Clyde here had a bit of a small problem. He's still a good man,
but you, Mr. Jacobs, you turned out to be perfect."

Michael knows there is no better living situation in the
works. He is fighting for his life. He wants to cause as many
problems as he can. He isn't sure what to expect, but if what
Clyde told him is true, the worst that can happen is they will kill
him, which they plan to do anyway.

Creighton spins on his heel and leaves. Michael keeps his
eyes on Clyde in case an opportunity presents itself. The
Doctor joins Clyde against the wall and finishes removing the
chain. The Doctor holds the chain and wraps it up in his hands.
For the time being, he is still their prized possession. It won't be

until after he's introduced that he becomes expendable. This might be the best time to try to make his escape. The Doctor won't be expecting anything, and he's smaller and weaker than Creighton. He'd try to be gentle with him because of what he means and because of the equipment attached to him. He doesn't remember which way to run if he gets outside the lab door, but getting out is the only thing on his mind. Creighton is a big guy, and he thinks he can outrun both him and the Doctor if he has to. Once he gets out of the Creighton house, he will need to get himself lost in the woods until he can call for help.

Michael turns to face the Doctor. He reassesses the older man. The Doctor may be evil and a little bit mad, but he's also old and frail. Not a threat. He steps toward the Doctor, about to shove him backward into the wall, when the door slams open and Creighton's voice booms in the room.

"Change of plans," Creighton says. Michael jumps, spins around. "I'll introduce you first, Mr. Jacobs. It's Immortal Night, you should be a part of the whole thing. Let's go."

Creighton crosses the room and gathers up the ends of the chains. He unwraps Michael, then tosses the chain to the side. The ease with which he throws the heavy chains makes Michael raise an eyebrow. Creighton may be older and out of shape, but he's strong.

"You won't need that chain right now, Mr. Jacobs. I hope we can trust you."

Michael nods. Creighton leads them out the door. They make their way down the hall toward a large open chamber filled with people. The group is well dressed and happy—the rest of the Elk Hills Research Society.

"Ladies and Gentleman," Creighton starts. "Welcome to

the night we have been waiting for. Welcome to Immortal Night. We have a special guest with us. Mr. Michael Jacobs came to us rather unexpectedly. But his arrival turned out to be perfect for us."

Creighton goes through the entire story, starting with Michael's arrival the other day for an interview and ending with their arrival in front of the group tonight. Some members of the Society nod when Creighton mentions his name. They have obviously heard of him. Creighton explains how he has used to police to cover their tracks when it comes to their new reporter friend. At the end, he puts an arm around Michael and looks out at the group standing before him. They begin an applause, but Creighton interrupts it and continues.

"In the end, I'm okay with it all because we got here," Creighton booms. "We got to the place we've been striving for. The procedure is done. There is no delay in Mr. Jacobs. The delay that we saw in the reanimates. The delay we saw even in Clyde, is not present. The Doctor has assured me one will not develop. He is aware of why the delay developed in Clyde and adjusted for it. Clyde will not become any less delayed than he already is, and Mr. Jacobs will remain as he is. The delay occurs just before the activation of the devices. There are no more problems."

Creighton looks to the Doctor on the other side of Michael, and the Doctor nods, takes a deep breath, and then continues the commentary.

"Yes, all of this is correct. With the procedure perfected, we can now begin with the rest of us. I have called in an assistant to help me. I can perform the procedure on most, if not all of you, starting this evening. We will continue through to the morning. My assistant will perform the procedure on me, and then I will perform the procedure on him, if he so desires. Soon, all of us will be immortal. There is very little healing time, at least there was for both Clyde and Michael. I expect this to be the same across the board. This new solution I have developed to keep the wounds clean will make the chance of infection next to nothing. Mr. Jacobs is only twenty-four hours out of his procedure right now, and he looks, speaks and acts as if nothing happened."

The Doctor continues, but a wave of dizziness passes over Michael. It has nothing to do with the procedure. He's lost an entire day somewhere. He entered the Creighton house late at night and assumed it was still that same night, or possibly the next night. But it's been twenty-four hours since the procedure. It could be as much as two days since he first entered the house, maybe longer. He doesn't know what day it is, and the feeling makes him uneasy. Mary has already been told he's dead. She may have already seen the burned-up body Ronald told her was her husband. Anger courses through him, but he steadies himself, blinks his eyes. Focus on the current problem; how is he going to get out of this place?

Keeping his mind on what he needs to do, Michael shifts his gaze to Clyde just on the other side of the Doctor. The Doctor surveys the group in front of him and takes a step forward to address the rest of the research society. Clyde is looking out at the crowd, but Michael knows he has to wait before Clyde is able to return the look. So, he flicks his eyes back forward, waits a few seconds and then looks back at Clyde. This time, Clyde returns the look, but there is no more. Nothing else Clyde offers beyond the glance; they both return their eyes to the crowd before them.

"We will complete the procedures in the lab one at a time.

The utmost care will be taken to ensure that each procedure is a success. We will be immortal—the one thing we have a plethora of is time. I do not want to rush through—" The Doctor is interrupted by Creighton.

"I disagree, Doctor," Creighton's voice booms. "We are prepared. We have completed the test. The most important thing now is getting all of the procedures done as fast as possible. We mustn't wait to become immortal. This is Immortal Night and we will all become immortal on *this* night."

"Yes, I can understand your anxiousness, Mr. Creighton. I'm sure we are all feeling the same way. We can discuss more about timing in private." The Doctor squints at Creighton then turns to continue as though he hadn't been interrupted. Michael notices this small change in Creighton and wonders if there is more to it. He files the information away in case he can use it later.

"As I was saying," the Doctor continues, "Clyde will keep track of who is up next and will go back and forth to help us stay organized. He will bring you all back out here as you recover."

"Also." Creighton puts an arm around Michael again. He tries to pull away from the taller man and cringes at the touch. "We need someone, or maybe a few of you, to keep an eye on our friend, Mr. Jacobs here. We can't have word of this getting out, especially not when we are this close to having this completed. I had him chained up in the back to make sure he didn't leave. That will be hard to do out here, but it is imperative that we keep an eye on him. He is ambitious, and I don't think he takes too kindly to being held here. So, he will try to escape. We need to be ready for that as well."

A murmur of approval ripples through the crowd, a few of

the taller men toward the back of the group nod and stare at Michael. He could try to escape now but knows it would be pointless. He needs to wait until the right time. It's not the best plan, but the only one he has. Soon all of the people here, Creighton and the Doctor included, will be recovering from the procedure, and he will have his chance.

CHAPTER 17

The night went almost perfectly, Creighton thinks as he tugs on the chain wrapped around the reporter's waist, pulling him back toward the lab. As he suspected, the reporter made an escape attempt when he thought the group was at its most vulnerable. Most of the Society members were recovering. Creighton was in the lab helping the Doctor. Yelling echoed down the hall, and Creighton rushed to see Jacobs running toward the stairs with Clancy Black—one of the first men to sit down for the procedure—holding onto the reporter's waist. Clancy would not have been able to stop him, but he slowed him down. It was all Creighton needed. He got to the sprinting reporter and lowered his shoulder into his gut. Creighton was careful not to hit him in the chest and damage the equipment. He could give a shit about Jacobs, but the equipment is not easy to come by.

For now, the crisis is averted. Creighton strings Jacobs back up in the lab. There are only two procedures left in Immortal Night. Creighton will go second to last, and the Doctor will be the last one.

The Doctor wanted to take his time with it. He wanted to turn Immortal Night into the Immortal Week, going slow and methodically through the members of the Elk Hills Research Society until the job was finished. Creighton helped him to see the error in his thinking.

The technology is ready and they must all be immortal as soon as possible. It is the only thing that makes sense. If the Doctor can be safe doing the procedure in less than an hour, why wait longer?

Luckily, after using the sales techniques he's so adept at, Creighton convinces the Doctor to move at a much faster pace. And now, Immortal Night—the way Creighton always envisioned it—is nearly complete.

Clyde makes eye contact with Jacobs as they watch the Doctor's new assistant perform the procedure on the Doctor. He will be the last person to become immortal. Creighton made it clear that the assistant will not be alive at the end of Immortal Night. Creighton is already back and conscious after his procedure. He may not kill the assistant right away, instead waiting until the Doctor is back to normal. But the man is not going to leave the lab alive. Clyde is becoming increasingly worried about Creighton's decision-making ability. It is as though the anticipation of what is to come is clouding his judgement. Now that he is so close to the end, Creighton is no longer able to hold it together.

Clyde knows Jacobs wants to escape, but he should have waited. There isn't much he can do to help Jacobs now. He will end up in the house with the rest of them for the rest of his life, or he will end up in a hole in the ground next to the assistant.

* * *

With the Doctor's assistant buried deep in the woods behind the house and the Doctor's plea to keep the reporter alive with them, the work is done. Everyone is immortal and with the only witness to the entire thing buried where no one will find him for a long time, Creighton is happy, but still unsatisfied. There is one more thing gnawing at him, an idea he can't shake. He knows it will be unpopular with the group but he sees it as a necessity. It must be done. The Elk Hills Research Society gathers once more in the cavernous room underneath the Creighton house. Creighton has one more speech to give them, and it will be a difficult message to deliver. In the end, they will do what he wants them to do. He always gets his way, and he can be very persuasive.

He stands before them feeling more powerful than he has his entire life. He is no longer just an ultra-rich man living in the suburbs of Chicago, he is immortal. He and the Doctor have pulled this off. It is quite possible that he is the most powerful man in the world at this moment. But the real power will come later, and that's the message he has to deliver to the rest of the group.

"We've done it," Creighton says. His eyes scan the group that has made their life expectancy infinite, then he looks to the back of the room where Jacobs stands, chained to the wall, in what may turn out to be his permanent location. Creighton smiles. A cheer goes up through the small crowd. Not a single one is delayed. The Doctor did a perfect job. There were no complications. "We have the Doctor to thank for this, and, soon, we will begin to see the monetary benefits as well." Another cheer, but it's time to let them all down.

"But I need to be serious. The Doctor says we barely need food to survive, we may grow thin, emaciated, but our organs will still operate, we will not die without food." His tone is grim, and he sees it reflected on the faces of the rest of the group. "My friends, I have set up a water retrieval system so fresh water is pumped into the lab on an ongoing basis. We will never run out of water."

Whispering through the crowd.

"What are you saying, Edmund?" It's James Wallbeck talking. One of the leaders.

"James—everyone—what I'm saying is that the time is not right for us to come forward with this idea." Shouts in the crowd, but he needs them to think about it before they just react against it. This is a last-minute decision by Creighton, not a well thought out one. He'd had the discussion with the Doctor about food and set up the water merely as a precaution. Since his transformation into an Immortal, however, he's come to realize that this is the only correct course of action, and he doesn't care what James Wallbeck or any other member of the Society has to say about it. "The time is not right to sell this idea. The world is not ready for it. We will be looked on not as visionaries, but as madmen. We cannot come forward with this now. We must keep an eye out and wait. We must wait for the perfect moment to put our idea out there and make the most of our investment. James, would you make a land purchase or buy a stock the moment the price goes up, and sell it for a small profit? Or would you look to the future and wait five or ten years for a huge profit?"

Wallbeck nods. Creighton can see him figuring this out in his head, but he will not leave the rest to figure it out on their own.

"The downside of waiting to cash in on an investment is that you have to cash in at some point, because you can't wait forever for your return. But if you are immortal, you *can* wait forever. You are all smart enough people to understand this fact. We cannot be shortsighted. The rules do not apply to us anymore. We need to rewrite the rules for ourselves. The best return on our investment is not now, or in ten years, or even twenty years, the return is in eighty years, ninety years, when technology moves forward even further than it already has. Don't dismiss it. Think about what I'm saying first. We stay down here, away from the rest of the world. We wait, and we watch. I can have newspapers delivered, and we can read them every day for decades until we are certain the time is right for us to return to the world and sell our invention for more money than we could imagine. We will be richer than we ever thought possible."

The group gets together and talks. They talk longer than Creighton thought they would. But they have as much at stake as he does. He wants them to come to the decision on their own, but will force them to follow his lead if they decide against him. The knowledge of the process and the technology lies with himself and the Doctor. In the end, if they don't follow along with his lead, they will find themselves without the riches they desired when they agreed to join up. He knows he's right even if they don't.

In the end, they agree with Creighton. They are smart and know without the Doctor they are at a loss. As long as the Doctor and Creighton are together, there isn't much the rest of them can do. He's already hired someone to check on the house, he's told them he's going away indefinitely and that the Doctor will be using the library for some research. The only job the person has is to walk the house perimeter once a day at four o'clock. When he does that, he will move the newspaper from the front gate to the library so that it is available for the Doctor if he needs it. Each day Clyde will retrieve the newspaper so that they may keep an eye on the news of the world.

Everyone has an opportunity to make telephone calls to family explaining their extended absence and to set up succession plans, because they will not be returning for many years. The money is still theirs, however, and, when they do return, they will get their money back. Think of the money.

Once that is finished, the Elk Hills Research Society will remain inside the basement of the Creighton house indefinitely.

CHAPTER 18

Present Day

K at Jacobs wakes up and rubs her eyes. The shallow, soft breathing of Laura still asleep next to her gives her comfort. A smile grows on her face. Laura is the third woman she's slept with since her break-up with Crystal, but the first one who is still there the next morning. They've been on four dates; it's a real possibility something is there. The problem is that she was *sure* Crystal was 'the one.' She believes Crystal thought the same thing about her. It wasn't the relationship. They were in love they always had fun together. They never fought about anything—except Kat's job. It was the job that broke them up. Crystal didn't want to share Kat with her job, which was understandable. She spent a lot of time working, maybe too much time. But she loved her job. Did she love it more than she loved Crystal? She didn't think so, but Crystal did. That's why she left. Now, she doesn't know if she will ever have a relationship like the one she had with Crystal. But she wants it. She badly wants someone to be with her for the rest of her life. Someone she can call a wife. She had been certain that person was Crystal, but she is gone.

It's hard not to compare the two. Laura is great, Kat likes her a lot. They have fun and get along well, but she isn't Crystal. Maybe it's just a phase of getting over a long-time girlfriend. Kat hopes so, because she wants to move on. And she likes Laura.

The first thing she does every morning is check her phone. It doesn't matter if it's the weekend, or a vacation day, or Christmas. Kat will check her phone first thing in the morning. When she first started working at TheBeltway.com, it was a small D.C. news outlet that would get scoops from time to time, but the stories were small and often uninteresting. As the Internet grew, so did TheBeltway. It is now one of the biggest political blog sites in the country, and Kat is one of the leading reporters on the site.

She scrolls through the six text messages received overnight; nothing needs her immediate attention. Her email has only two unread messages. Those, she is certain, can wait. Another thing that has changed since she started at TheBeltway out of college, is the way people get in touch with her. It used to always be email. Everything was in an email, and her old Blackberry constantly had her writing, responding, and checking her email. Now, all real information comes through text messages. Any email she gets is usually about new company policies and other Beltway announcements. Never anything urgent.

It's a Saturday morning, and though she will work most of the afternoon, Kat is technically off. She gets out of bed, dresses, then slips out of the room and into the kitchen to make breakfast. Because it's their first night together, Kat is excited to see the relationship progress forward, even if it's just this little step. Their first date was a breakfast date, so she knows what Laura might like for breakfast and pads across the apartment to the kitchen to start a pot of coffee and scramble up some eggs with spinach.

She keeps her phone in her hand—always with her in case something comes up that needs attention. Luckily, the first half-hour of her Saturday turns out to be a quiet one. Kat fills the coffee maker first and then makes the eggs.

"Oh, I thought I smelled coffee." Laura comes out wrapped in the bedsheet. Her hair hangs mostly down at her shoulders, but a few pieces stick out in random directions. Kat smiles. It's cute.

"Yep, and eggs with spinach," Kat says. "On the far-right of my closet on the shelves are t-shirts and sweatpants if you want to wear those instead of a sheet."

Laura laughs. "Thanks. I was hoping I wouldn't have to put that dress back on. It's too early for a dress, let's be honest." She goes back to the bedroom.

"You look good in it," Kat calls after her.

She slides the eggs out of the pan and distributes them evenly onto two plates, then stops and gives Laura a little bit more than she gives herself. She brings the plates over to the table and fills two over-sized coffee mugs. Kat sets down the mugs as Laura comes back out with one of her old t-shirts and a pair of sweatpants on.

"Were you a cheerleader or something?" Laura says, holding out her Parkview High football shirt.

"Ha! No, my brother played. He was the team captain, and so we got lots of shirts and stuff all the time. He stole the smaller ones for me because I liked to wear the shirts to his games."

"I get it." Laura sits down on one side of the table, Kat on the other, kitty corner to her, so they are close and still able to look at each other. They eat, and there is a long silence, at first uncomfortable, but then it becomes a relaxing silence. Kat smiles. Even the silences are becoming enjoyable.

"What are you up to today then?" Kat says after swallowing a mouthful of egg.

"No plans. I have to be up early tomorrow; I'm having dinner with my parents tomorrow night, but today is pretty much wide open. What about you? Some big story you're working on?"

The mention of a big story causes Kat to check her phone. She knows it's a bad habit, but she can't help it. A big story is just one text message away. The person that gets to work on it first could be the one to break it. When the President cheated on his wife in the White House about three years ago, Kat broke the story because she acted the moment the text message came in telling her to look into it. It was the story that moved her from one of the many voices at TheBeltway to *the* voice. The pressure has grown every day since.

"At the moment, no breaking news to report," Kay does her best impression of a TV newscaster. It's a corny joke, and she knows it. Crystal would have laughed at it. She waits a beat, and Laura laughs. "I thought, I mean...I had fun last night. If you want to stay, don't feel like you have to rush out."

Kat knows her face is red, her cheeks are burning. It's been a long time since she's done something like this. It's different and awkward, but it's fun, too. She's glad to be bouncing back.

"Yeah, I'd love to stay for a bit today, actually." Laura smiles.

They finish their breakfast; the conversation flows naturally. Kat's thoughts don't turn to Crystal, and it feels good.

"Do you mind if I use your shower?" Laura stands up, stretches her arms over her head, and then twists from side to side. Her spine creaks and cracks.

"Of course not. There's other clothes in that part of the closet if you wanna grab something else for after your shower, too. Towels are in the closet in the bathroom. Make yourself at home," Kat says.

"Thanks." Another grin crosses Laura's face. She spins on her heel back toward the bedroom and the connecting bathroom. Kat listens and hears the bathroom door shut. The shower turns on, and only then does she realize she's still smiling. She hopes Laura is too, smiling and hoping for many more mornings like this one.

She clears the table, loads the dishwasher, pours herself more coffee, collapses on the couch, and flips on the TV. It is already on CNN, the first thing she watches when she wakes up, and the last thing she has on before bed. Kat can't stop working. Even when she's relaxing, she thinks about it. Though she hopes her website is ahead of CNN in terms of breaking news, it's easier to sit, watch and listen to someone telling her the news than it is reading about it. It gives her brain a bit of a break. On CNN there are three talking heads bashing the president for the latest in a long line of what they perceive to be poor choices. Maybe they are poor choices. One thing Kat has learned working in Washington, however, is that everyone makes bad choices in politics. It's just a matter of what gets reported on and what makes headlines.

Kat tries her best to stay above that. She writes about what *she* believes is the most important thing for the people to know about. It doesn't have to be the president or a high-profile name. Whatever story affects the most people is the story that should get written. And she writes them better than most.

A quick flip of the channel, and she's watching five talking heads discuss the same topic on MSNBC. She flips the channel again to FoxNews and listens to them talk about the same decision. Kat doesn't even need to listen to them talk to know where everyone stands on the issue at hand, in this case appropriating money and who should get how much. The good news for Kat is that none of the stations have the 'breaking news' ticker scrolling at the bottom of the screen. She didn't miss something overnight. She flips the station again to ESPN. Sports always clear her mind for a few minutes. She wants to be fully present today while Laura is here, so clearing her mind is a good idea. She watches SportsCenter for a few minutes, and her phone vibrates in her lap.

Kat mutes the TV and picks up her phone. She flips it over —it's her mother. Her parents call a few times a week, but never this early in the morning. Kat's heart skips a beat; something might be wrong. Is Dad okay? She answers the call.

"Mom? Everything okay?"

"Hi, Katherine," her mom says. She's the only person in the entire world that still calls her Katherine. It's been almost fifteen years since she started telling people to call her Kat, and everyone does. Everyone except her mom. It doesn't bother her anymore, it's just the way she is.

"Is everything okay, Mom?" she asks again.

"Um, no, actually it's not, Katherine. It's Gramps. He's taken a bad turn here the last few days. They...the doctors, told us it could be any day. Just a matter of time."

"Oh no," Kat says. Her response is soft, probably inaudible to her mother on the other end of the line, but Kat doesn't know what else to say. Growing up, Gramma and Gramps lived only a few houses down the street. With her dad being an only child, Kat and her brothers were the only grandchildren, so they spoiled them every chance they got. She was closer to Gramma and Gramps than her brothers. Though she lived the furthest away from them now, growing up, and through high school and college, Kat was always there. She always came home from school for holidays, and those were always spent at Gram and Gramps' house. As she got older and found her career, she started to talk with Gramps about more serious topics. Gramps' father had been a reporter in Chicago during World War I and into the 1920's. When she told him she was going into journalism in college, he shared the story, throwing in the fact that no one else in the family knew much about his father, Michael Jacobs. He expected it to stay that way.

Kat learned that Gramps himself didn't know much about his father either, just that he was a reporter and that he died in a train fire researching a story. But Gramps seemed to look at Kat's success as a reporter as a connection to the father he never really knew. Before he got sick, they talked on the phone once a week, discussing her latest story or the political climate in Washington. He kept up on all of the latest news, so when they talked, he was able to have an intelligent conversation with her.

They grew closer over those years. Kat's father even got his parents a tablet and taught Gramps how to use it so he could keep up to date on whatever Kat was working on. Then Gramps got sick, and things changed. Not at first, but over the course of eighteen months, the cancer took its toll on him. The calls were not weekly, and, when they did talk, Kat could tell he was out of breath just from talking for a few minutes. The calls became shorter. He didn't watch as much news and slept a lot more. It was hard for Kat, especially because she couldn't see him, but she was still very aware of his deterioration.

The silence between her and her mom lasts ten seconds, twenty, maybe a minute, as Kat thinks through her options.

"Mom, how much time does he have?"

"They didn't tell us much. Your father is at the hospital. I'm just home now getting him some clothes, and then I'm going back. I am calling your brothers next, but I wanted to call you first," she says.

"Thanks, Mom. I think...I'm going to try to get on a flight today. Please, when you get back there, will you tell Gramps I'm on my way to see him?" Kat says. She sees movement out of the corner of her eye and only then remembers Laura is still here. She must have heard the last part of the conversation because Laura turns around the goes back into the bedroom, giving Kat some privacy.

"Katherine, you don't have to do that. You can work, and we will keep you updated. There is no reason to—"

Kat cuts her off. She knows she is trying to help, but her mind is already made up. "No, Mom. I have to come. I have to be with him."

They make small talk for a minute or two, but Kat isn't paying attention. She has her laptop out and is looking at flights from Washington to Chicago, to see how soon she can get there. Kat doesn't stop working, even there, but she does less work there than anywhere else. They say goodbye, and Kat keeps searching for flights. The earliest flight with seats open is tonight. That works, but she hopes she can get to the airport sooner so she's there in case seats open up on an earlier flight. She books a flight leaving at eight and decides to head to the airport and get on stand-by for anything earlier. If she gets there sooner, great. If not, she has her ticket.

"Hey," Laura's soft voice calls from behind her. "Everything okay?"

Kat finishes entering her information to buy her tickets and clicks 'purchase.' She waits for the confirmation screen to pop up on the computer. When it does, she turns her attention back to Laura.

"No, my— my grandfather is sick. Like really sick." She feels the tears coming. She doesn't know Laura well enough to cry like this in front of her, but she can't help it. "He won't make it more than a week at most, so I've got to fly out to Chicago to be with him. Sorry about today." Laura doesn't say anything, but pulls Kat in to her, rubbing her back. Kat returns the hug, her head on Laura's shoulder.

"It's fine. I understand. Be with your family."

The hug is comforting, almost loving. Even in her mental state, Kat feels the embrace as something comfortable and welcome for both of them. It makes her feel better.

"Thanks," Kat says into Laura's shoulder.

"Do you need help packing?"

"No, no, I can do it." Kat leans back and blinks the tears from her eyes to look at Laura. "Thank you, though."

"Well, I'm not gonna just leave you right now, so why don't you do what you need to do. I can do your dishes and get the trash picked up out here so you can be all set to go. I'll leave when you leave."

"You don't have to do that, really," Kat says.

"I know I don't have to, but I want to."

Kat gives Laura another hug and they kiss. They stand there for a minute before she retreats into the bathroom. She showers, gets dressed, and grabs her already prepared go-bag she keeps in case something pops up for work. The rest of the apartment is ready for her to leave. The last thing Kat packs is her laptop and anything she might need for work—just in case. Laura is going to walk back to her place, and Kat called a car to get to the airport. When they get outside, Kat turns to Laura and takes her hand.

"Thank you for your help, and for being with me," she says.

"It's nothing. I like being there for you," Laura says. "Keep me updated please, and I'll be here whenever you get back."

Kat smiles and nods. "I will."

Then she leans in and kisses Laura. Not a long one, but more than a peck on the lips. Her ride pulls up, and Kat gets in.

"Bye," Kat says. "Thanks again."

CHAPTER 19

They've become accustomed to the darkness over the last ninety years, but that doesn't mean they like it any more than they used to. The fires kept them going for a while, but there was only so much wood they could burn. When they ran low, they began saving wood for special occasions. When the wood ran out completely, they just stopped the fires altogether. They were plunged into darkness. Their eyes adjusted over time. Creighton didn't think they ever would, but living in darkness for that long changed them. They could all see in the dark now. If someone from the other side—someone from the lighted world—joined them in the darkness, they would be blind. But the Immortal could see almost perfectly. They were now creatures of the dark.

For a while they would open the door to the closet in the library once a day, at night when it was assumed the house as empty. Clyde—it was always Clyde—would retrieve the newspaper and it would get passed around until everyone had read everything they wanted to read. Over time, that practice went away, and it became a weekly task. Then a monthly one. Just enough to gather some information about the outside world.

As per his instructions before disappearing below the house, Creighton's house is now the Creighton Estate Museum, Clyde discovered on one of his trips topside. The house appears very much as it did when Creighton lived there, though visitors to the house are limited. It makes Creighton happy to know that people are still enjoying his home and the things in it.

The Doctor had been correct. They needed no food to survive. The hunger was almost unbearable at first, however, over time, they got used to the feeling and, after a few decades, all of the Immortals barely noticed it. The water system worked as it was designed to work and kept them hydrated. They couldn't have these bodies drying out on them, especially after all this time.

As anticipated, no one died. They have all survived here under the house, unknown to whoever is running the museum and taking care of his house.

They have a lot of time to think, and Creighton remembers back over the last ninety years, as he sits on the bottom step of the stairwell that leads up to the rest of the house. He thinks about the struggles between the society and the hatred of him and the Doctor, along with Clyde. As long as Creighton controlled the Doctor, everyone had to do what he wanted. They lived together, they were always on the same team, but there were decades of struggle to get to this point. He thinks, also, of house he hasn't seen in almost one hundred years. And most importantly, he thinks about the next move, because the Elk Hills Research Society has taken a vote and unanimously decided the time to return and reveal their invention, is coming soon. But they must go about it the right way.

The Doctor shuffles over. His emaciated body looks like a skeleton wrapped in a thin layer of white skin. Creighton supposes they all look that way, but the Doctor was thin and bony to begin with. The time spent down here only makes it more prominent.

"Thinking, Edmund?" the Doctor says as he leans on the wall next to where Creighton sits.

"Always thinking. Always planning," Creighton says. "How can we do this?"

"Edmund, look at me." The Doctor holds out his arm and shows Creighton his elbow, the entire joint is visible through paper thin skin. When he bends his arm, the entire joint flexes. "Look at my face."

Creighton doesn't want to. He's been avoiding looking at anyone's faces for the last ninety years. They are all skeletons wrapped in skin. This brought even more tension over the years, many in the Society wanted to leave, if only to return their bodies to the beautiful sights they once were. The Doctor's sunken eyes make dark circles usually reserved for skulls. His jaw and cheek bones clearly defined, his hollow cheeks and face, expressionless. The man before him is nothing more than a living, breathing skeleton.

"I realize what we look like," Creighton says. He knows where this is going, he's thought about the same thing for the past ten days, but he doesn't say anything. He wants to know the Doctor's point. Does the Doctor have a solution?

"What kind of business deal can we make looking like this, Edmund?"

Creighton shakes his head. "Not the kind we want, or the one we deserve."

"Right," the Doctor says. It's then that Creighton realizes the old man has an idea. Creighton would love to hear it, because right now he doesn't have much. "It's not the best idea because it would require us to open our circle a little bit wider. We make contact with someone from the outside world. Someone who could be the intermediary for us and everyone else. We can make our deal with that person, then we can go back and live in the house for a while. Eat food, slowly build up our bodies until we look normal enough to return to society and enjoy the life we have worked so hard for all this time."

The Doctor touches on something Creighton has been thinking also. They'd been in here, in the dark through almost an entire century. To the people in here—the Immortals—it is still 1926. They may have known about some of the things that have happened over the years, even some of the technologies that have arisen in the last hundred years, but they still do not know the world. Not like someone who is alive now would know it.

"I agree, Doctor, but I worry if we get help from the outside, we could risk everything. Could you imagine waiting all this time and not being able to reap the benefits of our hard work?"

"I have thought of that too," the Doctor says and rests more of his body weight against the cold wall of stone. "But do you really think if we procure someone to help us that they will just turn around and betray us?"

Creighton shakes his head. "I don't think they will. We wouldn't even have to tell the person what we've done down here. We could just have them bring food and provide us with electricity down here so we can become acclimated to this new world before we try to go make a business deal with the large technology or medical companies. However, and this is the tricky part, Doctor, are we willing to put a century's worth of waiting on the line? Are we willing, as a group, to say 'we've done all of the hard work. We've suffered down here for a hundred years, fought each other, and now we are going to put all of our trust in this person we don't know, who says they will help us?' I don't know if I'm ready to do that. I don't know if they're ready either." Creighton points a thumb in the direction of the large room that has become the hideout and sleeping quarters for the Elk Hills Research Society.

The Doctor looks back in the same direction and nods. They are in agreement on this. There are few people in that group, some of whom have lost their minds over the years, but all of whom have stuck it out because of the promise of money. At first it was the disagreement over staying down below the house instead of clearing the house and living in it away from the rest of the world. But Creighton refused. They needed to be hidden. The risk was too great. At some point after that, the screams in the darkness started. For days on end some in the Society would scream and yell and attempt to ram their heads into the stone surrounding them. Fortunately, there were enough sane to keep the insane from destroying the priceless devices attached to them. Even Michael Jacobs, former reporter, has become one of the good ones. He protected the devices and agreed with Creighton—understood why the need to wait was so important. It's amazing what time, confinement, and extended periods of time, will do for a relationship between two humans.

When he first told them of his plan, there were people who

wanted nothing to do with it, but in just a few hours, they understood the necessity. Once they were sealed in, there was a lot of excitement and apprehension. Jacobs and a few of the reanimates were furious. The reanimates, on several occasions, tried a mass suicide, but their bodies moved so slow that the Immortals were able to prevent them from destroying the equipment. It didn't work and they were all still here, though moving at a slower pace than the rest of the Society.

Then the group began to fight. Every fight was for the same reason: when to leave their seclusion. The fights happened every five to seven years. Whenever someone thought the time was right to resurface and claim their fortunes, an argument would break out. Creighton would always come out on top, because he still had the Doctor. There was nothing the others could do. Once the fighting stopped, the silence replaced it. Hardly anyone spoke. For years at a time the basement of the house was filled with mostly silence. Eventually, tempers cooled and they began talking again, until the next fight broke out and it started all over again.

Through it all, the Doctor, Creighton and Clyde stuck together. They were civil to each other, but Creighton knew no one liked him. Everyone claimed their own space. Michael Jacobs was the worst of the group. Everyone else was given a choice. He never was, and he resented everyone for it.

Eventually, with only a few exceptions, the fighting stopped. People started getting along. Maybe it was acceptance of their situation or the prolonged period of time living together. Whatever it was, for the last thirty or forty years, there had been very little fighting. Michael became friends with Clyde and the Doctor, and even grew to understand Creighton. Creighton will say now that Michael Jacobs is a friend. And he is sure

Michael would say the same about him. The demeanor of everyone changed, and for that period of time, things have been peaceful. Discussion started about when they would begin the process of leaving this place once again. Usually when that became a topic of conversation, the fighting would follow. This time it was different, though. This time Creighton agreed.

The time is right. Technology is evolving rapidly in the world. It might not be too much longer before someone is able to repeat the experiment they perfected a hundred years ago. They can't take a chance on that, so Creighton agreed, it is time to act. There has been no fighting. No arguments. Creighton is ready for them in case they happen, but so far, things have been peaceful.

Creighton kept his inner circle close, though. In the end, if he and the Doctor and Clyde and Michael are the only ones to leave this place, he would be fine with that. More money for him, the rest of them could kill each other for all he cared.

* * *

Clyde doesn't expect to see the day when the Doctor's technology gets sold. He resigned himself to that fact a long time ago. He's played his part all these years, waiting for the correct moment to right all of the wrongs. A century of darkness, trapped inside his own mind in a body that doesn't quite work. Being in his mind so much gave him the chance for a lot of deep thought. He'd done this originally to help him and Patty. She's long gone now, but he still thinks about her every day. He wonders what happened to her. He tried to help her back then, but he knows he ended up hurting her. He just disappeared. Left and never came back. For years, he was depressed, unsure what to do about the guilt. He thought many times about ripping the devices from his body, smashing them and dying like normal people—like Patty. But he could never bring himself to follow through with it. Then, Michael came to him with a plan to get back at Creighton for everything. Everything the man did that ended them up here in this place, suffering for a hundred years.

Clyde couldn't say much, but he wanted to be a part of it. They discussed opening up their idea to some of the other reanimates, and even some immortals down here with them, but they decided they couldn't trust anyone other than themselves. The plan was risky, and it involved getting closer to Creighton and the Doctor. It would take time, but time was something they had a lot of, so they put it into place.

It was hard for Michael to become friends with Creighton, for obvious reasons. It wasn't going to be easy, but they managed it. They wanted it to feel as though Creighton, the Doctor, Clyde and Michael were a team. They wanted to discuss everything together as a group. They wanted to laugh with them and scheme with them, and Clyde and Michael wanted the four of them to always agree on the next step toward their ultimate goal of selling these devices. Clyde didn't have too much acting to do. He spoke slowly, and Creighton often didn't have much patience for the slow members of their group. However, Michael helped Creighton take Clyde under his wing. On more than one occasion, Creighton told Clyde that he thought of him like a son. And Clyde believes every word of it. The plan was working.

Now, Creighton is getting ready to go back out into the world. A place none of them really know.

Except for Clyde and Michael.

* * *

"Clyde," Michael whispers from the far end of the great room, away from most of the rest of the group. This end of the room has become *their* side. Michael, Creighton, Clyde and the Doctor have taken this area and maintained it as their home base for the last thirty years. He's amazed at how much it feels like home, even though he's been planning his escape, and Creighton's downfall, that whole time.

Clyde moves slowly over toward where Michael sits. Clyde is as gaunt and skeletal as the rest of the Research Society. The lack of food has affected them all in pretty much the same way. Pulled in skin, taut against the bones of the face, a skull wrapped in fine, flaky parchment. They all look the same—all suffered the same, except Michael.

He's been planning and preparing for a long time, and his patience has made his difference almost invisible. For most of their time down here, he fought with Creighton every chance he got, like everyone else. Once he and Clyde figured out the best course of action, Michael began taking weekly trips to the surface. By then, the place had been turned into a museum and it looked almost exactly the same as it had when Michael first stepped foot inside the massive home. The land around the mansion was turned into a nature preserve as well, with trails leading from town up to the house, through the woods he and Ronald had walked through many years earlier.

When the transformation of the house happened, Creighton's old office was turned into an office for the museum, while the rest of the house remained untouched. Michael only went up at night to avoid any of the tours or the staff working at the house. With the entire population of the

Elk Hills Research Society asleep under his feet, Michael would explore. He learned about the world and made the most of every second he was above. When they moved a refrigerator into the office, he would eat. Not a lot, because it would be noticed by Creighton and the others, but enough to keep him a little bit stronger than everyone else. He would grab one thing and eat it each time he went to the surface. His cheeks might have been a little pudgier; but no one noticed. His muscles may have been a bit more defined, but he never heard anything from any of the others. Creighton tricked him once before, but Michael would get the last laugh when it came to Edmund Creighton.

His trips to the surface became more frequent as the group discussed revealing themselves to the world. The group was getting ready, but so was he.

As Clyde shuffles over, Michael knows he will be doing most of the talking. If Clyde has something to say he will put a hand on Michael's thigh. If he agrees and understands everything Michael says, he will say and do nothing. It's become their way of communicating quickly. They are in this together, but with Michael's increased strength from the food he's been eating over the years, and his speed compared to Clyde's, it only makes sense that he carries out the physical part of the plan.

"There's been no response yet, but I still think we need to give him some time. I don't know if he will even try to write back to me or just start looking into it. It's just kind of all up in the air at this point," Michael whispers. There is noise throughout the room. They've managed to keep time in the dark, and the Society sleeps at night and is awake during the day. They found it best to keep themselves sane in the unending darkness. It is daytime now, and the group is talking in low murmurs, making it easy for Michael and Clyde to mask their conversation with the other noises.

"If there is a response, I don't know what it could be, but we need to be ready for anything. I want to try to get out three times this week. Today is Monday. If I can get out Monday, Wednesday and Friday, I can keep building my strength up and keep an eye out too. Maybe I can even use the telephone this time to try to make contact."

A tap on his leg, Michael stops.

"You think that's a bad idea?" Michael says, then pauses to give Clyde the chance to speak.

"No...call...Risky...Patience." Clyde whispers over the course of almost thirty seconds.

"I know, I know. A call from the house during a time when no one is supposed to be there might cause questions. We've waited a long time. I guess there is no reason to push things now."

Clyde gives a slow nod.

"But you still think I should get up there three times this week?"

Clyde nods again.

"Because of the food, right? To be stronger than anyone else down here."

Another nod.

"Okay. The Doctor and Creighton are over by the stairs talking. He has to have some sort of plan in mind. I can't see a bunch of skeletons with skin crawling up out of this cave and then running to a huge company trying to sell technology for billions of dollars."

Clyde's eyes widen, Michael looks at him confused at first, and then realizes the problem.

"Oh yes. A big deal like ours is going to be billions of dollars in today's money. It's incredible to think of. Creighton wouldn't be that rich by the new standards."

Clyde nods again.

"Alright, I'll get you once everyone looks to be asleep."

Again, Clyde gives a nod and then slides back over to the spot against the wall where he usually sits.

A loud cackle explodes from the far end of the room in the direction of the stairs. It is Creighton laughing, presumably with the Doctor. Michael pushes himself up off the ground, and his knees crack at the sudden movement. He may be stronger than everyone else here, and immortal, but he still feels old as hell. He shuffles and slides through other thin bodies of people he considers friends now, as he makes his way across the room. A few of them greet him, others just nod as he walks past. The mood in the basement has changed. The Society is cordial with each other, but everyone knows Creighton and the Doctor are still in charge—Clyde and Michael are lumped in with them because of their association. There is always going to be some distrust between the four of them and the larger group.

Michael navigates, feeling his increased energy as he makes the walk. When he was eating less, this walk across the room would have made him winded, but now it feels like he could make the walk even faster. His muscles are not as weak as everyone else's. The strength is good.

"Ah, here he comes now," Creighton says when Michael turns the corner and draws within sight of the two men who have kept him captive for almost a hundred years.

"Talking about me again, Edmund?" Michael says, and laughs.

"Actually, yes, we are. We've been trying to figure out who

would make the best candidate to either represent us when we first reveal ourselves to those up there," he says as he points up the stairs. "Or who the best person would be when it comes to persuading someone to help us. Get us food. Make us look a little more...presentable."

"And my name came up for that job? You're the salesman, Edmund."

"Yes, it did my friend." The Doctor claps Michael on the back, but not very hard. Touching someone else has become a risk. Everyone looks like they could break at the lightest possible touch. There are numerous broken bones throughout the reanimates and the Immortals. The Doctor, who knows the medical reality of the situation, is just as concerned as everyone else.

"I don't know if I'm all that presentable, Edmund." Michael pulls himself up straight and thrusts his shoulders back as far as his frail body will allow. He tries his best to suck his cheeks in when he knows they are examining him. He wants to match the others as much as possible.

"He's right, Doctor, as much a skeleton as the rest of us. He can't pull it off," Creighton says.

"Maybe so, Edmund, but look at his color. His eyes. I've noticed this for a while now. For some reason, he doesn't show all of the wear and tear that the rest of us have. I don't think he should go meet the public or anything like that. But, if we cover him up as much as possible and send him up to find someone to help us, he would just look like a frail old man, no?"

Creighton studies Michael, and then slowly nods his head, approving.

"Maybe you're right, Doctor. He talked his way into my house way back then. I'm sure you still have your slick tongue, don't you, Michael?" Creighton's laugh echoes around them again. Even underground, even when they were trying to be quiet and unassuming, Creighton had outbursts. He couldn't help himself. He is still, and probably always would be, someone who needs all of the attention on him.

That is good for Michael and Clyde because if all the attention is on Creighton, they can do what they need to do. Especially if Creighton, the Doctor, and the other members of the Society send Michael up to be a liaison with the people on the surface.

CHAPTER 20

The plane lands at Midway Airport seven minutes earlier than scheduled, but it isn't fast enough for Kat. She wants to be at the hospital already. She needs to see him and to talk to him before—before it's too late.

Her mom offered to pick her up from the airport, but Kat knows how her mother drives and told her she'd just take a car to the hospital. It would be quicker and less of a headache.

Kat sits in a ride-share car on the Stevenson, headed out of the city and toward the western suburbs. At first, it looks like there will be traffic the whole way, but, after a few exits, the traffic breaks up. Then it's smooth sailing to the hospital.

Kat talks to the woman at the reception desk and gives her grandfather's name—

Joseph Jacobs— in return, the woman gives Kat vague directions, but she makes it to the room nonetheless.

She pauses at the door, her hand holding the cold, silver handle. Out of nowhere, it hits her as to why she's there and what is going to happen over the next two or three days. Her bottom lip quivers, but she presses it up against her upper teeth.

She might cry, she's sure she will, but it's not going to be now. A passing nurse gives Kat a look, and she knows she has to go into the room or the nurse will ask if she needs help finding the right room. The last thing she wants to do is talk to someone she doesn't know. Not wanting a conversation, Kat pushes the handle down and enters.

It's dark, though the glow of the machines and monitoring devices are muted by the brighter glow of the TV hanging from the ceiling. Dad and Gramps are both asleep, with sports replays running quietly over their heads. She watches her grandfather sleep, his chest rising and falling slowly, the oxygen attached to his nose, along with all of the other instruments. But, under all of those wires and electrodes, he's still the man she always knew. She smiles and stares for a minute, happy she made it but wishing she didn't have to make this trip at all. It's been a long day and Kat just now realizes how late it is. She doesn't want to wake her grandfather, who needs all of the rest he can get, but her dad has always been a night owl. She can wake him up. There is an empty chair directly underneath the TV. Kat places her backpack on it and crouches down next to her father. She lays a gentle hand on his shoulder.

"Dad," Kat whispers. It is enough to rouse him.

He breathes in deep, squeezes his eyes tight, and then opens them slowly. He blinks a few times, looking straight ahead and then turns to her.

"Hey, Kat," he whispers, then looks over at his sleeping father. "Let's step out for a minute and talk."

She glides across the floor and goes back out into the bright hall. She'd only been in the dark room a few minutes but still needs to squint at the brightness of the lights. Her dad shuts the door softly behind him, smiles and turns to face her.

"It's so good to see you," he says. He stretches his arms wide and hugs her.

Kat notices right away this isn't his normal hug. She holds on to him, and he squeezes tight. He rocks back and forth. Finally, he lets go, sniffles, and rubs his thumb against the bridge of his nose.

"Wish I could come home for something a little happier," Kat says.

"I know, me too. It's still good to see you. You got here fast." He puts his arm around her—like old times.

"It would have been faster if they had better flight times."

"Yeah, airlines are like that. Plus, they like to fill up the planes, so it's hard to get a flight last minute."

There is a long pause. Neither of them want to talk about the real reason she's here. Kat would rather continue with the small talk, but she takes the plunge instead.

"So, how is he?" she asks, her eyes drift toward the door and then back to her dad.

"He's alright, actually. Weak, and he knows what's happening, but he's actually okay with it all. It makes it a little easier right now, I guess. He's still cracking jokes, you know him. He's asleep most of the time because of the meds, but when he's not asleep he's coherent, just a little...slower. The meds make him feel better than he really is. If it wasn't for them, he'd...well, he'd be in a lot of pain."

"But it could..." Kat trails off, her dad reads her mind.

"They can't say. It won't be the next few days, but beyond that, they don't really know."

"Okay." Kat puffs out a deep breath. Part of her was afraid her dad was going to tell her it would be any minute. Knowing that she at least had some time makes her feel a little better, for now.

The same nurse that walked by earlier comes back from wherever she went, gives Kat's dad a look and smiles. He nods back at her.

"I know, I know, we can't just stand here in the hall," he says.

"Yes, but he just had his meds. He won't be talking or seeing anyone until the morning, at least. You gave me your cell number, right? We will text you if anything happens. If you want to take a walk, talk, get some food at the twenty-four-hour cafe," the nurse says. She smiles at Kat and seems nicer now than she did a few minutes ago.

Dad nods.

"You won't believe me," Dad says, "but the cafe here has some of the best french fries you've ever had. I'm not even kidding you, Kat. They even have that good ranch dressing we can dip them in."

"Ugh, I freaking hate ranch, but you know me and fries. Let's go check them out. I bet they're not as good as you think they are." Kat smiles. It's not the most ideal situation, but she's back and she gets to spend some time with her dad. They haven't talked very much on the phone lately because she's been so busy at work, so this is good. Needed.

They talk as they make their way down to the first floor. The cafe is nicer than expected, considering it's just a smaller version of the hospital cafeteria, but there are people working and the food is hot. Kat hasn't really had a meal since breakfast with Laura, which seems so long ago now. They get two orders of french fries; her dad dips his in ranch dressing and she gets some ketchup, but they are so good she eats them without needing to dip. While they eat, they catch up. Her dad asks about her dating prospects.

This is the only part of the breakup she hasn't been able to deal with: her whole family loved Crystal. When Crystal left, she didn't just leave Kat, she left the whole family. They'd spent many holidays together. Everyone was heart-broken when she left, and only very recently has anyone in her family asked if she was seeing anyone new. They were all healing, and the conversation shows that Dad is finally getting over the break-up.

When the cardboard containers are empty, they clean their table and return to the elevators. They've exhausted the topics they can talk about without talking about the reason Kat's really here. Other than the quick version up in front of Gramps' room, she doesn't know much about what's been happening.

"He'll sleep most of the night because of the meds he's on?" Kat asks as the elevator doors slide closed.

"Yeah, I forget the name of it, actually, but it's a pain killer that makes him very drowsy too. He's taking it around seven at night and then again at one or two in the afternoon. It's only when he needs it. He's pushing the time to stay awake, fighting right up until the end, you know? When he asks for it, they give it to him, but within a few minutes, he just can't keep his eyes open."

The elevator doors slide open, but it's not their floor. A woman in a white doctor's coat boards. Kat and her dad stop talking and wait in silence as the elevator goes up to floor twelve. They get off and continue talking quietly as they walk down the hall.

"He'd rather be in pain than be on the pain meds. Figures," Kat says, nodding her head and smiling. Gramps wasn't the kind of guy who took a lot of shit from people. He fought in

World War II, but never wanted to share. He didn't like to talk about himself. But if you asked him, like Kat did one night, you would hear the kind of stories you found in history books and on 60 Minutes—stories of being on a ship in the Pacific, about landing on one of the Japanese controlled islands, stories about his survival there, stories of a hero. When he told those stories, he always referred to his friends, the ones he fought beside, as tough sons of bitches. Kat knows her grandfather is a tough son of a bitch too.

"Yeah, pretty much," Dad says.

"Listen, Dad. I came all this way. I want to be here when he wakes up. They said he should be okay today. Why don't you go home, get some real sleep and come back in the morning? I'm sure mom would like it. I can stay with him." Kat holds her dad's hand and looks up at him. For half a second, she is ten years old again asking her dad to buy her something at the toy store, knowing he'll say yes if she looks at him in just the right way. She is still his only daughter. That has to count for something.

"I don't know, Kat, what if something happens? There's two chairs in there. We can both sleep here."

"If anything happens that you need to be here for, I can call. She said it's going to be fine tonight and probably tomorrow, and the next couple days too. You might as well get some sleep while you can." Kat gives her dad the toy-store-look again.

"Alright. You're probably right, anyways. I'll go home and sleep and come back in the morning with your mom. I'm sure she's anxious to see you. Maybe your brothers will show up too. They had to find babysitters and get the time off and stuff, but I'm sure they'll come by after work, at the latest."

"Good, you've still got to take care of yourself, even with this stuff going on," Kat says. "Do you need anything in there?"

"I just have to grab some stuff from my bag," he says.

Kat slides back into the room noiselessly. The glow of the TV glints of the metal pole holding his IV bag. She steps in as her dad finds his bag and gets his things. She watches Gramps' slow steady breathing, happy, at least, that the tough son of a bitch isn't in pain at the moment.

Her dad gathers his things, and they step back out into the hall. He gives her a hug, and she kisses him on the cheek. He leaves, thanking her and telling her how good it is to see her. She returns the sentiment. It's a visit home, but with lots of mixed emotions for Kat this time. It's the first time she's come back for a reason that isn't a happy one, and she doesn't know quite how to deal with it.

Kat gets herself settled in the chair her father slept in not that long ago. The rhythm of Gramps' breathing and the hiss of medical machines could make it easy for her to fall asleep, but her mind is spinning. So, she does the only thing that feels natural. She works. Kat takes out her phone and scrolls through text messages she got during the flight. A few texts from co-workers asking if everything was okay—she'd told them she had to take a few days off for family reasons, but that was it. They were good friends, so she filled them in on the situation. Then, the meat of her texts—the tips.

She has a few DC sources. Most of the information they give her turns into nothing, but she still has to cross reference what they tell her with what is expected that day, or that week. If they give her something she expects to hear, it's not really a story. Every so often they give her information that isn't expected; *those* are the tips that lead to stories, sometimes big stories. Those little bits are what keep Kat curious. She can't help it. If she sees a small string, she has to pull it.

Kat scrolls through messages about meetings between senators and representatives, nothing major. She doesn't have the time to put a puzzle together right now. She's looking for the anomaly. There's just nothing in her messages that fits the profile she needs. Nothing out of the ordinary. Normal, for the most part, is normal in Washington. Kat doesn't want normal right now. She needs something abnormal to distract her, to take her mind off of the other stuff.

She dozes off without realizing it, and her eyes flutter open when the nurse comes into the room to check Gramps' vitals. Kat is confused at first, but then she notices her phone laying on the floor. It must have slipped out of her hand. She picks it up and smiles at the nurse.

"He's my favorite you know," she says.

Kat just nods, assuming she says that to all of the family members of all of the patients she sees.

As if reading her mind, the nurse continues. "I'm not just saying that. When he's awake, he's the sharpest person on this floor, and so funny." The nurse smiles in the nice way that nurses do. Kat isn't sure she's nice enough to be a nurse.

"He is funny. Ask him about growing up during the Depression sometime. He's the only person who could make the Depression sound funny," Kat says, smiling and remembering listening to his stories about being an only child and the son of a widow. Again, not something that would seem funny, but the way he told the stories, they just were. You couldn't help but smile when you heard them.

The nurse finishes getting her readings and turns to leave.

"He sometimes wakes up around now for a little while. It's

best to talk to him right after he wakes up, if you can. See you later," the nurse says and then leaves.

Kat watches Gramps. His chest still rising and falling. Noise from outside the room filters in when the nurse opens the door to leave, and he stirs for a moment. Then his body relaxes, and his mouth moves as if drinking water from an invisible water fountain. His eyes twitch as if something is caught under the thin skin of the lids, then he opens his eyes.

She doesn't want to scare him and remains silent until his eyes focus on the TV screen still playing silent sports highlights over his head. Then Kat whispers to him.

"Gramps?" she says into the dim room. It's loud enough for him to hear it but quiet enough not to startle him if he thinks he's alone in the room.

"Must be these drugs," Gramps says, a small smirk growing across his face.

"Why is that?" Kat says, hearing his voice and falling back into the old conversations they'd always had. It doesn't matter if they're in person, over the phone or in a hospital. They get to know each other, and her smile grows faster than his.

"Because, it looks like the famous Kat Jacobs is here to write a story about me. That can't be true, so it must be the drugs. Must have slipped me some of that LSD when I wasn't looking, I'll have to talk to them about that." His smile is bigger, and his eyes glisten in a way they hadn't when he first opened them.

"Yep, I'm not really here, but I think it was mescaline, Gramps." She stands up and goes to the side of his bed.

"Well, in that case, I think we can let it slide," he says. He reaches his arms out as far as he can toward her. Kat leans over and hugs him. They kiss each other on the cheek. "Good to see you, kid."

"You too," she says. She feels the smile disappear a little from her face.

"Don't let this get you down. It's all good in the end, right? I survived all these years. It's not really a bad thing. I'll be better off this way, Kat. It's hard to think of it that way, but it's true. This is for the better, so I don't want any crying."

"Well, I can't promise that," Kat says.

"Alright then, I don't want to see it then. Do that at least."

"It's a deal, Gramps. So how are you feeling?"

"Ah, I don't want to talk about that," he says. Kat notices a scratch in his voice that she's never noticed before. It reminds her again of how different this is from other visits. Every moment could be the last one. She tries not the think about it, but Gramps has other plans.

"I was hoping you'd come. I was going to have to call you today if you didn't," he says. Kat looks at him, trying to figure out what he is getting at. "I have to tell you something. it's important I tell you now, in case..." he trails off. He doesn't have to finish the sentence. They both know how it will end.

"Anyway," Kat says, switching back to the topic.

"Anyway," Gramps goes on. His jaw moves back and forth as he talks. She's never seen it do that before. She doesn't like it. "I've never told anyone this before, Kat, and it has to be you I tell. My mother told it to me on her deathbed, and I never really did anything about it. Maybe I should have, I don't know, but it's always eaten away at me since."

"Jeez, Gramps, what is it?" She slides her chair closer to his bed and sits down, holding his hand, feeling a possible Gramps story incoming.

"My mother, your great-grandmother, was an amazing woman, you already know that. You've never met her, obviously, but you've heard enough of the stories to know what she was like. My father died in a train fire. I wasn't more than a few months old when he died. I don't remember him. Never really knew him, so my mom raised me by herself. She did a damn good job. We had enough money from the newspaper to survive through the Depression without too much loss of comfort. Anyway, she said she never completely believed it was just an accident when my father died. He had a friend on the police force in the town where he was killed. The friend assured my mom it was just an accident and she moved on. But she told me she never really believed him. Dad's friend went on to become Chief of Police in that town not long after.

"She knew what my father was working on when he died, a story about a law-breaking, suburban millionaire named Creighton. Anyway, he was investigating this guy, and the next thing my mom knows, her husband is dead."

Gramps stops and catches his breath. Words had been coming out of his mouth fast, and his lungs can't keep up. Kat remains quiet and lets him catch his breath. Then he continues.

"Shortly after my father died, the Creighton guy just disappeared. It wasn't reported until later, but he was just gone. Not there anymore. No one knows what happened to him. He and some other rich people from the area at the same time. My mom didn't know if the Creighton guy was involved in my dad's death or if the same thing happened to both of them, but she was sure it wasn't just a train fire."

Kat nods and starts to speak, but Gramps keeps going.

"She told me all this and wanted me to look into it. I didn't right away. At first, it was sadness over her death. Then I met your grandmother, and before I knew it, I was married with a child on the way. Looking into the train crash seemed like a monumental task that I didn't have time for. I checked the local papers at the time and found information about the Creighton guy, but everything said it was just a train crash, nothing more. As far as I could tell, Mom was suspicious because of the other disappearances at the time. But there wasn't much information about those either. Just police investigations that led nowhere. Researching beyond that, when I had so much else going on, didn't make much sense to me." He stops again to catch his breath. Kat squeezes his hand tight and looks him in the eye.

"You've never told this to anyone?" Kat asks. She wonders if he's all there. He could be making this whole thing up. She doesn't think so, but it's possible.

"No, I knew it had to be you a few years ago. Right when I got sick, I started thinking about it more and more. I knew I would tell you before I went. I had to. I couldn't...you know, without telling someone first. It's all that's been on my mind since they put me in here and told me...told me about the time left."

"So," Kat starts, but he interrupts her.

"It was all just a story, you know? Just something my mother told me, and I chose to believe maybe there was something there, but not something that would make a difference in my life one way or the other. And then I got this." He points over to a bag in the bottom of a small closet along the wall next to where Kat sits.

"In here?"

CHAPTER 21

"Are you ready for this?" Creighton asks Michael.

They've done their best to make Michael look presentable. Most of their clothes have worn out over the years, but some were resilient. Creighton and Clyde looked through the clothes of every member of the Society and determined which were the best to give to Michael for his first trip above. The first trip will be at night, when they are sure the house is empty, so he can get his bearings. Though Creighton knew this was a good idea from the start, he had to convince Michael and the rest of the group at large. People even suggested Michael before Creighton himself had to, making it seem like their idea instead of his. It was perfect.

"I'm ready," Michael says. There is a smile on his face. Creighton can tell Michael's excited. Anyone would be. The first time in almost a hundred years he's been up out of this cavernous, dark basement. It's only natural.

"You know what you're looking for? Just gather any information we might need to help us with negotiations," Creighton says, going over the plan they've already discussed at least five times. He's repeating himself, but he's just as excited as everyone else. It's almost time to reclaim his glory.

"Maybe you can find some food too. If you find some, eat it —up there, though. The healthier you look, the better," the Doctor says. Creighton isn't as big on this part of the plan. They are all so hungry, they don't even realize it anymore. Knowing Michael is eating might start a riot and make the next few weeks unbearable. He just wants everything to go smoothly, but also understands the reasoning behind it, so says nothing.

Michael nods. "I got it. I'm just going up to gather information and learn what I can."

"Yes, yes, but this is the first step forward. We've been waiting a long time for this. It is momentous. Years from now, they will write about this in history books," Creighton says, still thinking he's downplaying the importance of what they plan to do. Clyde shuffles over next to them. The rest of the group looks on from behind Creighton as Michael waits at the stairs ready to make the first trip up, with the exception of Clyde, since the whole thing began. Creighton turns toward the majority of the Elk Hills Research Society and joins Michael on the bottom step to look out at them. He prepared a speech but decides to talk off of the top of his head.

"Ladies and Gentlemen, we began our life down here almost one hundred years ago," Creighton says. He looks out and scans the faces in the crowd. Though it's dark, he can see everyone's face, but he recognizes none of them. A mob of rail thin faces stare back. The ability to show facial expressions is absent from the muscle-less faces. Their eyes, though alive, missing the spark that they once held. The excitement they had at the beginning of the journey is gone. When he thinks of the people in the room with him, he thinks not about what they have become, but about what they were when the door was sealed. "We were hopeful back then. *I* was hopeful that we could turn our invention—the idea the Doctor had, the research we financed—into riches. More money than we already had. I believed we were right back then. I still believe we were right. Mike is going up there tonight to allow us to reclaim what is ours. Our money. Our fortunes and the profits from our struggle down here are not far away. We've lived this long down here. We've waited so long for the right time. Now, the right time is almost here. Now is not the time to give up on our ideas. Now is the time to embrace them. To realize what needs to be done to make our patience worth it."

He scans the crowd again. A few people draw their thin lips back, showing more of the prominent teeth in a bastardized version of a smile. A few nod; most do nothing. Say nothing.

Did they wait too long? Creighton doesn't think so. The technology is not so far-fetched now. They will be taken seriously. And just by looking at them, everyone will know the technology works. They just need to get some food in here and get these people looking and feeling healthy again. Then the immortal will regain their lives.

Michael leans down and whispers in Creighton's ear, "Ready, Edmund?"

"Yes," Creighton says under his breath. Then to the crowd: "Good luck, Michael, the next step as begun."

Clyde leads Michael up the steps, making a show of the fact that Michael has not been up on the outside since they first sealed themselves in. Michael puts on a similar show, taking deep breaths, putting his head down in contemplation. But once they get up top, it's more of the same; the only difference is now the people below know they are both up here.

As usual, the first thing Michael does is get some food. Clyde stays with him as best he can, shuffling behind him as he moves from room to room. Making his usual lap of the downstairs. The pair have settled into a good routine when they come up above, the only difference is that now they don't have to do it in secret, and they can spend a little more time up here. They are prepared, but time above is always a good thing. Clyde cannot wait until he can live out under the sun once again.

Michael makes a lap of the downstairs and returns to the entrance to the library with a newspaper in his hand. He's scanning it and Clyde slowly joins him. They look over the paper, Clyde scanning most of the headlines over Michael's shoulder, while Michael probably reads a bit of an article, as well as the headlines.

Clyde moves away from Michael and they both head toward the back office, formerly Mr. Creighton's office. There is a computer in there. Over the years, Michael has taught himself to use it. Clyde has watched and, given enough time could operate the computer if needed. At the same time, it's frustrating knowing he will never be as important to the group as anyone who moves at normal speed. Clyde doesn't have the speed ability to use the computer quickly the way Michael does. Their time is limited, Michael uses it, clicking and typing things while Clyde observes.

Clyde sees everything. He sees more than even Michael realizes. Just because he moves slow and doesn't say much, doesn't mean he doesn't notice. Everything Clyde sees, he remembers. As if all of his brain power is focused only on memory.

A few years ago, Michael looked up his son, to see if he was still alive. Clyde had wanted him to look up his wife too—he just wanted to know what happened to her once he left. Clyde didn't even have to ask. The next time they came up, Michael used the computer, and the first thing he did was look up Patty. It was impossible to find anything on her, though. From then on, the first thing they did when they used the computer was look for information about Michael's son, Joseph, and for Patty. They were always the first two searches they conducted.

Joseph Jacobs, it turns out, is a very common name, and at the beginning, the results were massive. As the internet grew, so did the number of results. The task has been daunting and they never have enough time. The search for Patty, under both her married name and her maiden name, produced nothing of value either. If she remarried, there is no way of knowing what name to look for. She is lost to the abyss of time.

They always came up empty, until a few weeks ago. Michael punched his son's name into what was called the search engine. A picture came up, and when Michael clicked on it, the resemblance was unmistakable. The old man was either a healthy Michael Jacobs, or it was his son, Joseph. Michael's hand trembled when the picture popped up on the screen. They searched around, tried to learn more about the man in the picture, but again, the mountain of information was too much to sift through in the time they had.

The next time they came up they searched for him again, the same picture came up, but with a different approach, Michael was able to find an address that he thought might be Joseph's. He couldn't help himself. He had to mail him something, but he didn't know what to send. In the end, he sent him a note on a piece of paper torn from a notepad in the office. The note was simple: he addressed it to Joseph Jacobs and asked him to look into the history of the Creighton house if he wanted more information about his father. Maybe he would be resourceful and find them. Maybe his son grew up to be a reporter, Michael had said to Clyde with a look of pride on his face. He stole an envelope and a stamp and slipped the note into a pile of mailings stacked up ready to go out.

So far, there has been no response. They don't even know if Joseph had gotten the note.

Michael types in his son's name again. It's become a ritual. It took a long time to figure out how the computer worked the first time he sat down at one, but over the years, he learned and got better at it. They didn't have passwords before, but the technology improved and so did the security. Luckily, the password to the computer is taped right next to the power button. When the password on the computer changes, so does the word written next to it. Michael performs the search for Clyde's relatives as well, but there isn't anything new. Even the search for Joseph Jacobs is starting to be more of the same now. After he saw the picture of the man who was, and still is, his son, and found an address, there hasn't been anything new. He doesn't know if the man got the note and, if he did, if he would actually follow through. Also, Joe Jacobs is over ninety years old. It's likely that if he keeps searching for the man, he will end up on the obituary page. It's one of the reasons Michael wants to keep the process of them getting out of the basement moving forward. If he could see his son, talk to him, even for a moment, it would make all of the waiting worth it. Michael still doesn't think about the money.

After the quick search is over, Michael goes to the Internet sites he is most familiar with: the news websites. When they started coming up here and realized the importance of the computer in the modern world, they decided to let the computer, and to a lesser extent the newspapers, become their window into the present day. By becoming the most knowledgeable person about the present day, Michael would become the de-facto leader of the group. He'd know more. They'd *have* to listen to him, regardless of what Creighton or the Doctor said or did. With the knowledge he held, he was more important than either of them. As the leader and spokesperson for the Society, Michael could then turn in the Doctor, Creighton and the rest of them. That was the plan.

Michael stands up after reading through the main stories on multiple news websites, reading the major headlines to Clyde as the slower man sits and watches. Michael is never sure how to read Clyde. He knows the constantly blank expression is not Clyde's fault. The experiment made the reanimates slower, and Clyde got dumped in with that group, even though he was not a reanimate. For the most part, the reanimates are treated like second class citizens. In a way, they are. They already lived and died. They weren't the same as the rest of them. They had their chance at life, then their turn at life was over. Michael, Clyde and the rest of them never died. Though it often feels to Michael like he has lived two different lives, it's just a single long life with an unbelievable path.

Michael goes to the refrigerator in the office and opens it. There is a candy bar in there. 'Snickers,' the package says.

Michael has had this before. It's good, salty and sweet and filling. He looks to Clyde.

"Clyde, you should have this. I mean it, just eat." He holds out the candy bar to his friend and waits.

Clyde stares back at him then shakes his head.

"You…need…strength," Clyde says.

"There is other food in here, hummus again," Michael says. "I'll eat that, you eat the bar. I mean it, we don't have that much longer down there, eat the food while you can. At least you'll have something in your body, in case…you know, in case something happens."

Clyde stares at him then slowly shakes his head again. As far as Michael knows, Clyde has not eaten since they first went down below. Even early on when they still had food, Clyde refused.

"Why not, Clyde? You will feel so much better. Stronger." Michael holds the bar out to him.

Clyde shakes his head yet again. "When…out…for…good… I…eat…something…to…work…for."

"Are you sure?" Michael looks at him.

Clyde nods. "There's…not…much…I…can…do…if…something…happens."

Michael knows Clyde is right. He's on his own. It's not the first time they've had this discussion. If Michael tries to take the control and power away from Creighton, if he tries to turn him in or have him arrested, he and Clyde can only hope some of the others follow his lead. If the others in the group don't join them, he will be outnumbered. Yes, he will be stronger than the rest, but there are too many of them for him to expect to overpower them all. He needs people on his side. The problem is everyone talks. He can't spread the word about his plans to have the Doctor and Creighton arrested without them finding out. He just hopes the others are as fed up with Creighton and the Doctor as he is.

The night draws to an end, and, after eating as much as his small stomach will allow and reading as much information off of the computer as he can, Michael shuts everything down, leaving it all the way he found it. It's become routine for Michael and Clyde. The last ten or fifteen minutes are spent just scanning the rooms and returning everything back as it was. The only sign that they were there is the food Michael ate. But their visits are so infrequent that he doesn't think anyone has noticed. If the visits become more common, he is going to have to figure out another way to get food.

Satisfied everything is back to normal, Clyde gives Michael a short nod, and they file back into the library. Clyde goes first, pacing them with his measured footsteps, Michael following.

"Until tomorrow, hopefully," Michael says.

Clyde gives an approving nod, and a smile grows on his face. Michael returns the gesture.

Michael enters through the closet first; he pulls the fake stone wall closed behind them as they descend the stairs and return to the bowels of the house. When he gets to the bottom of the stairs, the crowd that was there when they left is gone. only Creighton and the Doctor greet them upon their return.

Darkness surrounds him as he reaches the bottom of the stairs, and he can't see as well as usual in this lightless world. His eyes need to readjust.

"How was it up there?" Creighton's rough voice asks him through the darkness. Michael can only just make out the thin shape of Creighton's slight body.

"Amazing, Edmund. To...to be up there again," Michael

feigns wonderment. "It was incredible. I cannot wait until we all get to share it. The Elk Hills Research Society has had some of the greatest days in the history of humanity. But, when we rejoin that world, tell them what we have to offer, show them ourselves...it will be one of the greatest days in human history."

"Did you eat, Michael?" the Doctor asks.

"Yes," Michael says. "Something called Snickers. It was good."

"We have to keep you eating. You should go back up tomorrow night, just to eat, and come back down. We need you stronger. Healthier looking."

Michael looks to Creighton.

"Yes, yes. Keep eating. You'll look nearly human." Creighton agrees with the Doctor's assessment. But Michael is starting to get a funny feeling. The Doctor and Creighton seem different somehow. Since they've become more friendly, it's always been the four of them. The Doctor, Michael, Creighton and Clyde. It's rare for the Doctor and Creighton to have a planning conversation without Michael and Clyde there, but it's clear to Michael now that they've been talking.

He knows, the thought crosses his mind, but he pushes it away. There is no way Creighton could have any idea about what Michael has been doing. About what he and Clyde have been planning. He knows no one overheard, which means the only way Creighton could be aware is if Clyde told him. Michael shakes his head in agreement and tries to get a read on either Creighton or the Doctor. He doesn't get the idea that any of them are hiding something from him, but the realization sets in that he might have picked the wrong guy to be on his side.

CHAPTER 22

When her dad and mom arrive early the next morning, Kat is still asleep. She doesn't remember falling asleep, but her phone is in her hand when her father puts a hand on her shoulder and jolts her awake. She greets them both and, with Gramps still sleeping, they go down to the cafe to get some breakfast so Kat and her mom can catch up. After they eat, Kat stands up and groans at the table as she turns her torso from one side to the other.

"Oh Kat, are you okay?" her mom says, always ready to take care of her little girl. Kat is fine, but she knows if she pretends to be either tired or sore or both, her parents will kick her out of the hospital, which is exactly what she wants to have happen. She has work to do. It's not the work she usually does, but it still involves an investigation. The method will be the same.

"Oh, I'm fine mom, just sore from the plane last night and then sleeping on that chair. I was up most of the night. I can't remember when I fell asleep, but it wasn't too long before you guys got here, to be honest. I just sort of sat there 'til I finally passed out, I guess."

"Oh honey," mom says. Here it goes. Kat has her now. "Listen, you gave your father a break last night, but now it's our turn. Let's go say good morning to Gramps, then you can go up to the house, take a nap and a hot shower and then come back later this afternoon. Your brothers will be here then, too."

"Um, I don't know. I mean, I came all this way," Kat starts and looks to her dad, but her mom cuts her off. It all happens the way it played out in Kat's head.

"No, no. I insist," Mom says, again putting her arm around Kat's shoulders. "We'll be fine here today, right, John?"

"Right," Dad says, knowing there's no reason to argue with her at this point.

"Alright, I guess," Kat says. She feels bad manipulating them, but she needs to get to the Creighton house, and she needs to do it today. She doesn't know what she'll find, but Gramps asked her to do it. There is no way she's not going. If there is a mystery there, she needs to uncover it. Not for a story. For herself, for family. "Just a quick stop home though, and then I'll be back."

"Okay," Mom says. "But listen, if you fall asleep, just stay there and sleep. You'll feel better later."

Kat nods. "It's a deal."

They go back to Gramps' room, and the nurse tells them she just gave him his meds because he was asking for them. He won't be up for a while now. Kat makes both her parents promise her they'll call if anything changes. Somehow though, Kat doesn't think they will call. Gramps promised nothing would happen and, though he doesn't have much control over it, she believes him. She has to work fast, but she isn't worried about Gramps.

The day is still young and the sun low in the sky when Kat

steps out of the hospital. She's already called a ride-share, and when she steps down off the curb, it's there waiting for her. The address typed into the app on her phone is not the address of her parents' house. She's already looked up the Creighton house, now called the Creighton Museum, out in Elk Hills. She's exhausted and sore but, just like with her work, when she sees a story, she jumps on it. She can rest once she knows the truth. Right now, she's only concerned about the secrets of the Creighton Museum.

The ride is about an hour and, though she wishes she could close her eyes and fall asleep for the ride out that way, she can't stop her mind from working. She goes over the story Gramps told her in her head. She unfolds the piece of paper he got in the mail with no return address on it, examines it closely for anything that might make it stand out. Except for a small green spot near the torn edge of the paper, it's blank. She tries to figure out the connection between this guy, Creighton, and her great-grandfather. She googled Edmund Creighton and learned as much as she could about his life. There wasn't a whole lot of information, just that he was among the Chicagoland ultra-rich during the 1920's. He loved to show off his wealth, but he wasn't involved with the mobsters of Chicago as much as most of his other ultra-rich friends were at the time. Kat is sure the guy must have drank, and probably had connections to the mob to be able to get alcohol illegally during prohibition, but he had no business ties with any of the organized crime in the Chicago area. That, in itself, was rare. Supposedly, her great-grandfather, Michael, was doing a story on this guy because he was dirty or breaking the law or something. But when she looked up Michael Jacobs and Edmund Creighton together, nothing came up. Not even a mention of the fact that Michael Jacobs was doing a story on Creighton when he died. She finds very little at all about Michael Jacobs other than that he was a reporter for the *Chicago Tribune* and he died along with six other people in a train fire in Elk Hills.

What Kat finds the most interesting of all the research she does on the ride between the hospital in the city and the Elk Hills suburb, is the fact that right around the time Michael Jacobs died, Edmund Creighton disappeared. A few other of Chicagoland's well-known wealthy men and women also disappeared around the same time. The police had very little information as they all set up trusts to take money out of their names prior to this disappearance. This tells Kat they were either worried someone was coming for them, or they planned to disappear. The rumors at the time were that one of the mob families wanted the business of the rich and powerful in the suburbs as well as in the city. When they found out these people, Creighton included, weren't using them to smuggle alcohol, they had them taken out. Creighton may have gotten wind of a threat on his life and moved his money before they could get to him. Apparently, it was well known that the police were pressured to abandon the investigation after only a few weeks, with questionable effort. It's likely they did this to protect themselves and their families. The claim is based on rumor and innuendo, but it fits with everything Kat knows about the mob. The mob story was the easiest to explain, so the police went with it. It cleared the case for them and allowed them to move on, while keeping the public happy because they didn't have to worry about more disappearances.

It seems plausible to Kat, but she can't accept it as fact without doing her own research.

The driver pulls off the exit, and Kat refocuses as they pass through the center of Elk Hills. The center of town doesn't look all that different from the pictures she's seen online. Multi-level stores line Main Street with what appear to be apartments or condos above them. At the end of the street, the road splits in two directions out through the rest of town. She notices the train station on her left as they drive past, and she tries to imagine what it looked like almost a hundred years ago when her great-grandfather used it to get out here from the city. Cars line the street, and the sidewalks are full of people moving from shop to shop, or just out walking their dog on a nice warm morning.

They bear right at the end of Main Street. The car follows the road past the church and a cemetery, then eventually turns up a hill. Finally, the car slows down at the gate of a green, well-maintained lot surrounded on all sides by woods. The gate is closed, but there is a parking lot near the house. The driver stops. Kat says nothing as she pulls up the hours of the Creighton Museum on her phone. It doesn't open for another twenty minutes. That gives her time to check out the grounds before going into the house itself. She climbs out, makes sure she hasn't left anything in the car, and thanks the driver.

She waits on the side of the road for him to turn his car around, and then she crosses, hops over the low brick wall on either side of the gate, and makes her way toward the house. As Kat approaches the house, she wonders if Michael Jacobs ever even made it up here to the house. She wonders if he walked the same path she's walking now. Maybe he was on his way to the house and the fire got him first. Too many questions with no answers. She doesn't like it.

Kat walks up the driveway to the house. The building grows as she nears it. The small hill hides part of the house until she gets closer. There are two cars in the parking lot at the front. A sign sits, nestled into the shrubs on the right side of the front door.

'If you're here prior to opening,' the sign reads, 'please do not knock. The doors will be unlocked promptly at ten-thirty.'

Kat checks her phone again, eight more minutes. Enough time to walk the perimeter of the house. The landscaping around the house is impressive. According to the museum website, the interior of the house, except for a few rooms, have been preserved exactly as they were when Creighton disappeared in 1926, as per his wishes in his will. It doesn't mention anything about the landscaping. But they are trimmed short, which she assumes was the style in the 1920's.

She evaluates the house as she circles it. Most striking to her is the condition of the bricks that make up the exterior walls. Though they don't appear to be original, they are all in good shape, with little wear and tear. The more she examines the house, the more she realizes the level of maintenance that has gone into keeping the place in excellent condition. Along the edge of the grass, out by where the woods start, there are signs and maps of trails through the woods. She makes a mental note to check the trails out after she sees the inside of the house. The note her grandfather showed her specifically mentioned the Creighton *house*, so everything else on the property, Kat deems less important than the house itself.

After her lap around the house, marveling most at the way the house changed with each step she took, Kat ends up back at the front door. She checks her phone again, ten-thirty on the nose. She grasps the doorknob and turns; it opens, and she enters. Her footsteps echo on the hardwood of the entryway, but she sees no one.

"Hello?" Kat calls out. The doors that lead out of the foyer are open, and a sign rests against the left-hand wall, telling her to wait until someone comes to help her. She does as the sign says, examining the intricate woodwork along the walls. Footsteps echo down the hall, getting louder. Kat turns and is greeted by a small, older women coming down the hallway toward her, a smile on her face.

"Hello. You're here early," the woman says.

"Oh, I'm sorry, I thought you opened at ten-thirty."

"We do. It's fine. We just don't usually have people that get here this early. By the time the sun comes up and the hike up here from town, it's usually around noontime when guests begin to arrive." The woman stands with her hand behind her back in an obviously practiced pose.

"I'm sorry, hike?" Kat asks, remembering the markers and the trails she saw leading into the woods behind the house.

"Oh, did you come right up to the house? Yes, there are trails in the woods. They lead all the way down into town and usually the only visitors we get are the ones who hike up here. They come in the house, take a look around and rest for a bit before heading back down the hill. We have a parking lot up here, but no one other than me and Rebecca actually use it. Everyone else that comes here hikes up one of the trails."

"That's awesome. I didn't realize there were trails coming up here. I'm from D.C., just here visiting family. I wanted to check this place out. So, I searched the house and got the address. I didn't know about the trails."

"That makes sense. Not many people from out of town use the trails. Mostly locals, I guess you could say. What brings you here to the Creighton house then?"

At first, Kat can't figure out if the woman is always prying into the guests lives or if its specific to her. But just like every-thing else, her questions are practiced. She's done this before.

"My grandfather, actually. He, um, he's sick, and he's always wanted to visit the house and never got the chance to. I told him I'd come and check it out for him. He didn't mention anything about a hiking trail, though, so I just drove right up. Well, I got a ride up here," Kat says, keeping she story as close to the truth as she can.

"Oh, is he from around here?" the woman asks.

"A few towns over," Kat says. She stops there. The woman doesn't really need much more information about them than that.

"Well, I can show you around if you'd like. Usually, we wait until we have a larger group, but you'd end up waiting a while, so it can just be you and me. I'm Joanne." She extends her hand and Kat takes it. Used to the firm handshakes in and around D.C., Kat finds the dead-fish handshake unsettling and breaks it off quickly.

"Yes, that would be fantastic," Kat says. "Even just from here I can tell the house is fascinating. Easy to tell why Gramps always wanted to come here."

"It is an amazing place. I'm here every day, and I see all of the stuff in this house a lot. I like to give tours because people who don't see this every day give me a different perspective on it. I love seeing peoples' reactions." Joanne leads them out of the foyer and down the long hall she entered through. "Everything in the house is exactly the way it was when Mr. Creighton lived here during the late nineteen-teens and early part of the nine-teen-twenties. With the exception of my office, which we will walk past at some point. The office had to be modernized, but we still left as much of it the same as we could."

"I don't know much about Mr. Creighton," Kat says.

"He was a different sort of man," Joanne says. They reach the end of the hall, and she looks back at Kat, hand on the door in front of her. "He designed much of the house himself, and you'll see different influences in different rooms. He was married, but his wife was sick for much of their marriage and almost never left the second floor. If you believe the stories, which I personally don't, she didn't even realize Creighton was missing for almost two months after his disappearance. By that time the police had already ruled his disappearance a murder by one of the Chicago gangs.

"This hall is wide enough to fit three people down shoulder to shoulder, as you can see, and the doors leading off of it connect to the rooms downstairs. But the rooms also connect to each other. It's possible to move about the house without ever using this hallway, because each room is interconnected."

"That's incredible," Kat says. "And the woodwork. It's impressive."

"Yes," Joanne says. "I've visited other restored or maintained homes from the same time period, and our house has the most remaining detail of any of the other houses. I know Mr. Creighton was a stickler for detail, which is why he hired one of the best carpenters in the area back when the house was built, to make sure each piece of wood was absolutely perfect. This way into the kitchen."

Joanne leads Kat into the kitchen. The older appliances still sit where they did when the house was lived in. A table occupies the middle of the room with wooden chairs surrounding it. The chairs are smaller than kitchen chairs today, but back then, they were probably average sized. Kat remembers reading something about how people, on average, are taller and wider today than they were a hundred years ago. Which might explain the small chairs. She finds the old house interesting, more so than she thought she would. Kat has to keep reminding herself that she is here to do a job, not just take the guided tour.

"Shall we move on?" Joanne says, still smiling.

Kat examines the kitchen once more, worrying the entire time that there is going to be something simple that she should catch.

Kat nods. "Yeah, let's see some more."

Joanne leads Kat down along one side of the great hallway. They see the dining room, a downstairs bathroom, a sitting room, and then finish in the library.

"I usually slow the tour down here. People love to look through the books in here. There is a lot to see, so, please, take your time and look around. Then we can continue down the other side of the hall. You'll be able to see Mr. Creighton's office and a few of the other downstairs rooms.

Kat welcomes this break in the tour and wants to spend some time just looking around. Joanne sits on one of the chairs close to the door leading back to the main foyer area, while Kat turns to look at some of the books lining the wall of the library.

"Because we always stop here, we've swapped out the chairs in here for newer versions of the same furniture. The old chairs are in storage, and it's hard to tell the difference," Joanne says as Kat wanders through the room. "People always wanted to sit in here and we always had to tell them no, so we just got chairs that matched the ones Mr. Creighton had in here. That way people could sit if they wanted. I'll tell you something though, as I get older, I'm glad I have a place to sit." The older woman laughs. Kat smiles and lets some air out through her nose.

"These books are amazing. I know I can't touch them, but

some of them look to be in great shape for their age." Kat leans forward, getting her face as close to the books as she can, but puts her hands behind her back to remind herself not to touch.

She still doesn't really know what she's looking for. There is something here, there has to be. And someone knows enough about what might have happened to send Gramps that note telling him to look here.

"His disappearance was kinda strange, wasn't it?" Kat says, hoping Joanne can shed more light on the whole situation. She lives and breathes Edmund Creighton. It's possible she knows things about the man no one else does.

"Yes, yes. It was. I think in the end the police got it right, though. Maybe they never found out exactly who it was, but they knew what kind of person it was. Someone from those gangs. It's the only thing that made sense at the time. It's still really the only thing that makes sense."

"But he was able to move all his money before they got him?"

"Yes, yes. He must have known they were coming after him and moved it so they couldn't get their hands on it and it could stay in the family. Not that Mr. Creighton had any children or siblings. The money just stayed here, which is why we are able to take care of it the way we do and keep it maintained. I like to think Mr. Creighton would be proud of how it looks here."

"Was he well-liked in the community?" Kat asks. She wonders if she's prying too much, she doesn't want to seem too curious.

"Actually, no. He did a lot of things for the community, but also owned a lot of land. People were always dealing with him, even though they didn't realize it. He stayed secluded up here so much people started to resent it. I don't think he was a bad guy though. Just misunderstood by the people of the time."

Kat nods and moves toward the back of the room, a small closet door with intricate woodwork on it, like the walls, but it's the only door with that kind of woodwork she's seen so far.

"What's this room?" Kat asks. She runs her hands along the detailed carvings of the door itself.

"Just a small closet. Mr. Creighton didn't want to waste any space when he designed this place, so he fit small rooms and closets into every nook and cranny he could find. There's a few others I can show you on the other side of the house. Should we head that way?"

Kat takes one final look around the immense library and walks back toward Joanne, who has since stood up. Her hand slips into her pants pocket and her finger slides along the edge of the folded paper Gramps gave her. What did it mean?

"Yeah, let's see what else is here," Kat says with a smile.

Joanne takes Kat across the foyer and back down the main hall. They look first at another sitting room. Included on the walls is a painting of Edmund Creighton. It's the same one that Kat saw on the museum website when she looked up the address, but it's much larger in person. On the website, all she could see was the face of the man who once lived in this house. The painting shows him from head to toe. He looks tall, though it's hard to tell from the painting because there are no reference points. His broad shoulders match his wide body, and Kat finds herself surprised that he's exactly the type of person she would expect to live in a house like this. If the sheer size of the painting wasn't enough, it sits in a gold frame as detailed and ornate as any of the carvings on the walls, and at least three inches thick.

"That's the man, huh?" Kat asks, lifting her chin up to the

painting.

Joanne nods. "That's him. Supposedly this is the most accurate likeness we have of him. A few photographs exist, but not many, and they are only from the shoulders up. As far as we know, this is the only full body likeness there is of Mr. Creighton."

"Seems like a big guy. How tall was he?"

"Supposedly six feet which, back then, made him taller than average."

Kat looks again at the painting and follows Joanne to the next room.

"This next room was Mr. Creighton's private office. Once he moved into the house, he conducted all of his business out of here. Part of it, you'll see, has been converted to the museum office, so there is a fridge in there and a microwave, a copier and printer along with my computer and stuff to run this place, but the other half is basically untouched. We moved some of his furniture over to that side, so it's a little cramped, but you'll get a sense of how he worked."

Joanne leads her into the office and Kat's eyes are drawn to the difference between this room and the others. Most of the house is made with dark wood. It makes the house itself very dark, even in the rooms with lots of windows and light from the outside. This room is light wood, Creighton's desk is even light, as is his furniture. There are fewer windows here than in some of the other rooms, but it has a brighter, lighter feel to it. Kat scans Creighton's half of the room, examining his desk, looking for something on it that might give her a clue as to what she is doing here. There is, of course, nothing and she moves on. She turns to leave the room and glances down at Joanne's desk as she does so. A piece of paper catches her eye. It is blank, except

for the museum letterhead at the top and bottom. The words
'Creighton House Museum' appear at the top, and the phone
number and address in much smaller type at the bottom. Kat
sticks her hand in her pocket again, feeling the note sent to
Gramps, and remembers the small green square she saw at the
top of it. It's the same shade as the words that appear on the
letterhead.

Kat gives the paper a long stare, then follows Joanne out.
She has to approach this carefully because she doesn't know if
Joanne sent the note or not. She seems to know a lot about
Creighton, but also doesn't really question his death. Someone
who sent that note would probably question his death a little
more than she does.

"I don't think I told you the reason my grandfather was so
interested in this place," Kat says, doing her best to sound like
she's still just making conversation and not probing for more
information.

"No, no, you didn't. This way." Joanne takes them to the
stairs leading up.

They ascend to the second floor. Kat has a focus now; she
needs to know everything that Joanne knows.

"Well, my Grandfather's father was Michael Jacobs. I don't
know if you've heard of him," Kat says. A woman with this
kind of knowledge regarding Edmund Creighton and the house
probably knows a lot about the town of Elk Hills at the time. If
she isn't the one that sent the message, she might still be able to
provide some information.

"No, I don't think I've heard of him before." Joanne
reaches the landing at the top of the stairs. Kat arrives just
behind her and studies her face as they talk, trying to get a read
on her.

"Oh, he um...well, he was my great-grandfather obviously, but he died here in town, in a train fire in 1926. He was also a reporter for the *Chicago Tribune*." Kat studies Joanne's eyes as she speaks, looking for any sign of recognition. Her eyes widen for a moment, but then a nod.

"Oh yes. I do remember something about that in one of the old newspapers we have in storage. He took the train in from the city and then a fire or something. He and a few others perished if I remember correctly." Joanne nods and smiles as she talks. Kat doesn't read anything more than that in her face.

"Well, my grandfather says—according to his mother—Michael was on his way here to do a story on Mr. Creighton. But obviously, that didn't happen."

"Oh, my goodness," Joanne says. It's the most typical thing she could have said. She doesn't know anything, Kat concludes. "I had no idea. What an interesting little piece of history. I love that about history. There is so much to learn about, and little pieces that only a few people know that could get filled in at any time. I'm sorry your grandfather couldn't be here himself."

"Me too, he's very sick. He just—I guess he always felt a connection with this place because he never knew his father. And he knows this was where he was headed. He always wanted to come but never made it. I guess this is his way of helping his father complete the trip...through me." Kat makes herself sick. She hates this kind of gushy stuff, but she can tell Joanne is eating it up. She hopes to have an ally in here, so the gushy stuff is worth it.

"Oh, what an amazing story," Joanne says. "You're an incredible granddaughter to come here and do this for him. Let's continue on, shall we?"

Kat nods and wonders: who else works at the museum?

CHAPTER 23

The once-large, rich man sits on the bottom step in the cavernous room that feels like the only home he's ever known. There are times when Creighton looks down at his body and wonders how he got in this position. He used to have it all. Money, power and size; he could intimidate almost anyone. He could back people into a corner, tower over them until he got what he wanted. In lots of ways, his size was his best business advantage.

That advantage is gone. He is still the same height, though the Doctor told him it is possible his body shrunk over the years. Something about the space between his bones. He still has his wide frame; but a frame is all he is. There is not much else to him. His once broad shoulders now point out to the side, and his shirt drapes off his body as if it was hung in his closet. Down here, they all look the same. If he hadn't lived with these people for so many years, he wouldn't be able to tell them apart.

Next to him sits Michael. Clyde stands in front of them, and he doesn't know where the Doctor is. His team. The four of them were a team through all of this, but now he finds jealously rearing its head. He's always been a jealous, angry man, but for decades, that was gone. Now that the outside world is starting to creep back down below with them, the person he was before—the one that made money and wanted to keep it, the one that started the Elk Hills Research Society— is starting to come to the fore. Part of him likes it. He likes to be the one in control, and *that* Edmund Creighton was always in control. He hopes that if *that* Creighton comes back, it will be like old times again. But he also likes the friendships he's built down here, away from that world. He's closer to the people down here than he's been to anyone in his life. His wife included. He's torn, but there are important matters they need to prepare for. His feeling must wait.

"Michael, you're looking healthier than ever. Well, healthier since we've been down here."

"Thanks. Physically, I feel great. Mentally," Michael starts and then pauses. "Mentally, it's just hard eating and knowing everyone down here hasn't had a thing to eat in years. I wish I could get food for everyone."

Creighton nods. Clyde, after a moment, does also. Why does he have to be so nice about it? It would be easier to get mad at him if he pretended to be better than everyone else because he got to eat the last few days.

"We will get our chance. The more you eat now, the more approachable you become. And the more approachable you become, the easier it will be to find someone who can help us. Once we get that person, we all can come up, and we all can eat. We need to do it this way to have the best outcome. I'm sure of it." Even when he whispers, Creighton's gravelly voice carries throughout the room. People look up. They never voted him the leader. They all are supposed to have an equal stake in this, but he can't help but take charge in situations like this.

"I am trying, Edmund. Thanks for your trust in me." Michael nods again.

Creighton smiles. Even the people he thinks of as equals, the Doctor, Michael and Clyde, look to him as the leader. He *is* the leader. He will continue to lead them.

"Honestly though, Edmund, how do I look?" Michael says. He stands up and turns to face Creighton.

"You look like an old man. I guess we all do." Creighton laughs and repeats himself. "I guess we all do. The difference here is, you look like a somewhat healthy old man. The rest of us look like already dead old men."

"What's...next?" Clyde asks, looking from Michael to Creighton and back.

"Next?" Michael asks. They wait.

"How...much...longer?" Clyde says in his typical herky-jerky cadence.

Clyde looks at Creighton, and Michael does the same.

"I don't know. Another night, maybe two, then we try to make contact. Listen, I may have come up with the idea for all of this, but it doesn't mean I have all the answers. You're up there, Michael, you know what is happening in the world, you've seen more than me. When you think the time is ready, just do it. Make contact."

* * *

Michael nods at Creighton. The nervousness he felt about Creighton may just have been guilt. Creighton isn't treating him any different than he has these last years. It must just be in his head.

From the darkness, the Doctor appears, approaching slowly, stepping over and around the thin bodies of immortals laying on the floor around them.

"Edmund, Michael, Clyde, please join me in the lab. I have a thought I'd like to run by you," the Doctor says in his usual hushed tone. When he first met the Doctor, Michael was much younger than him. Now they look the same age. They all stand and let Clyde go up the five stairs to the main hall of their self-imposed dungeon first, as it will take him the longest the get to the lab. Clyde leads them into the lab. Edmund, Michael and the Doctor sit while Clyde positions himself against a wall. The room is hardly used anymore. Many of the Doctor's tools and equipment sit in the same place they were when the Doctor performed the last procedure.

"I know we've been planning for Michael to make the first contact with the outside world. I do think this is the right step, but I have an idea that may bring us even greater success." The Doctor is talking to all of them, but he is looking at Creighton. This is somewhat normal. He's telling them all, but only has to sell Creighton.

"Let's hear it," Creighton says.

Michael, and then Clyde, nod.

"We continue as planned. Michael makes contact with someone from up there," the Doctor says, flicking his eyes upward. "But instead of just finding someone sympathetic to our cause and willing to help us as much as necessary, he recruits someone. Someone who will come down here, meet us all, and then join us."

The Doctor gestures in the direction of the rest of the lab. His tools, his devices are still here, probably still in working condition.

"You mean, make them—" Michael starts, and Creighton finishes his thought.

"Immortal."

"Yes!" The Doctor's, old, sunken eyes widen and gleam. It's a look Michael has not seen on his face in a long time. The look of someone who is a little too excited about something. The look of someone whose mind is teetering on the edge. This is not just an idea the Doctor came up with recently. It is an idea the Doctor has had for a long time. He's just been waiting until the right moment to spring it on them.

"Are you sure you can still...you know, perform the task, Doctor? It's been a long time," Michael says.

Creighton sides with Michael on this. "I agree. We are not as steady as we used to be, Doctor. It is an idea that deserves some thought, but I'm not sure that it is the proper next step. What if something happens, like with Clyde? We have proof the concept works right now. If we push it too far, we could end up hurting our value."

"I am steady as ever," the Doctor says, falling short of holding his hand out to prove it to them. "And look around you. All three of you. How many people are down here? How many of us have died? *I* have done this. I can *still* do this. It will be the greatest display of our technology. When someone comes forward with the procedure already completed upon them and these business types look, not at a frail old man, but at a young, strong person who is immortal, they will pay even more money than if they are looking at Michael. No offense, of course, Michael."

Michael nods. The Doctor does have a point, but the amount he's thought this through only solidifies the fact in Michael's mind that this is not just some new idea that popped into his head. Just like Michael and Clyde biding their time to bring Creighton and the Doctor to justice, the Doctor had been waiting until the time is right to bring this forward. Creighton's head tilts to the side, Michael can tell he's considering the possibilities. He looks at Michael. The Doctor is right, and they all know it. Someone in their thirties trying to sell the technology and make a deal with medical or technology companies is going to have an easier time of it than Michael would. They will speak the business language, or an approximation of it. There are a lot of positives to what the Doctor proposes.

All Michael really wants to do is alert the police the next time he goes topside, about the fact that he was taken captive by the Doctor and Edmund Creighton in 1926, but he knows that isn't the correct way to go about it. There are people to protect down here. As soon as Creighton or the Doctor get an inkling that something is wrong, they won't hesitate to terminate the lives of everyone below. The reanimates and Immortals alike. They have lived together a long time and, if Michael knows one thing, it is that Creighton can be ruthless when he needs to be. He wouldn't think twice about pulling the devices off the frail bodies down here. He'd start without warning, and their deaths might be silent. He could murder a lot of them before anyone even knew.

"I...think...he's...right...but...also...wrong," Clyde says.

"How do you mean, Clyde?" Michael says, wishing he had more of an idea what Clyde was thinking.

"Someone...younger...for...deal...but...no...need...immortal."

"We need someone younger for the deal, but we do not need to make them immortal to do that." Creighton summarizes Clyde's thoughts.

Michael nods in agreement, but is still trying to figure out how this all fits into their plan to make Creighton pay for what he has done to them.

"It's marketing, Edmund. Think about it." The Doctor isn't giving up. His eyes are still wide. He can't wait to perform his procedure on another person. "Would you give more money to someone who looks like Michael does now, or someone that looks like Michael did when you first met him?"

"Yes, but like Clyde said, we can achieve that without performing the procedure on them. One thing fails and it—"

"I will not fail!" the Doctor yells. It's the first time in a hundred years Michael has heard the Doctor raise his voice. His shout echoes down the hall, and Michael knows it reverberates around the large central room.

Creighton glares at the Doctor, Michael knows the look. It is anger.

"No one is saying you will fail, *Doctor.*" If Creighton still had the size he once did, Michael knows he would have stood up and marched toward the Doctor, using his size to intimidate him. And he does stand, but probably realizing his lack of size, just draws his body up as straight as he can and looks toward the Doctor. "These devices are old. Very old. Why would we jeopardize something happening when we can sell the technology with the help of someone younger, like you're suggesting, and take our money and move on? Let someone else make the mistakes after we have the money in our hands."

"We will get a better deal if the person helping us is invested in what we are doing. If they are physically involved in what we are doing, they will be forced to get us the best deal possible."

"I understand your thoughts, Doctor" Creighton sits back down, his words coming out in slow shallow breaths. He's either trying to calm himself down, or resigned to the fact that he and the Doctor will not see eye to eye on this matter. "But I feel there is too much at stake here if something goes wrong with the equipment. It will jeopardize everything we have waited for. All of the hard work each and every one of those people out there have done to get to this point. If we push our luck, we may end up with empty pockets after all of this. I can't accept that for myself. There is too much money on the line, and I won't allow it."

Michael tries to hide a smile. A friendship that has lasted over a hundred years between Creighton and the Doctor can survive almost anything, except Edmund Creighton's love for money.

The Doctor looks to Clyde, who returns the stare, and then at Michael before he turns and leaves the lab. They hear his footsteps echo as he makes his way back down the long hall.

"He will be okay. This is the first disagreement we've had in a long time," Creighton says. "But not the first disagreement we've ever had. We usually think along the same lines. A few years ago, I was actually thinking about a plan similar to his, but never brought it up with anyone for the reasons I just mentioned. I think finding someone to help us is enough and, though he says he's fine and would still be able to perform the procedure, I have my doubts about that as well. None of us are as nimble and dexterous as we used to be. Michael, I'm sure you couldn't type with the same speed and accuracy you used to. Clyde, you think you could pick up a shovel and dig a hole right now? I doubt it. We've all changed over the years. But we are still alive and will continue to be so. We need to keep with the plan. I will talk to him again, and we should be fine. Thank you for your input and for backing me up."

"I was backing you up, but only because I believe the same thing you do, Edmund. Now is not the time to take chances. We took chances a long time ago. Now is the time to play it safe and cash in on our risks," Michael says.

"Same," Clyde says.

Edmund nods. "Let's plan on you going up again tonight, Michael. If you happen to go up a little earlier than usual and there is someone in the house, let's make contact. If not, let's think of some way to make contact. Even if it's not face-to-face."

"The office up there," Michael looks up at the ceiling. They all look up. "Your old office, someone is there on a regular basis from what it looks like. That would be the easiest person to make contact with, but I don't know if it's the best person. It's a woman, at least from the pictures on the desk and the name tag we found. Her name is Joanne. She appears to be older, and it was my thought that we wanted someone younger."

Edmund and Clyde nod.

"Do you think she could help us find someone younger?" Creighton asks, the only natural question.

"I do, but I worry she would want to understand it all if I do make contact with her at first." Michael stands up, walks over to the table and examines the equipment on it.

"I trust your judgment on this, Mike, Clyde. I think I speak for everyone down here with us. Even the Doctor. Whatever decision the two of you make up there, we will support. We only want what is best for the group, and I know you do too. The Doctor will come around."

Michael and Clyde nod and move to leave the room. Creighton holds open the door as they exit the lab. He is the last person to leave and lets the door click shut behind him.

CHAPTER 24

Kat continues her tour of the upstairs and checks out each of the bedrooms. Under different circumstances, she would have been fascinated by the history, but right now she is trying to find out more about who may have sent the note to Gramps.

Joanne doesn't seem to catch on, which makes Kat believe she knows nothing about the note.

"That just about finishes the tour," Joanne says as they leave the last bedroom upstairs.

"It really is amazing," Kat says for at least the tenth time. She does think it's amazing, but she lays it on pretty thick to keep Joanne talking. The more Joanne thinks she likes the house, the more she will tell her, at least that's the hope.

They go back down the stairs and end up at the front door. It's obvious Joanne wants her to leave now, but Kat isn't finished in the house yet, not until she knows how the piece of paper with the Creighton House letterhead got into her grandfather's mailbox.

"Does the house have a basement?" Kat asks.

"Boy, you really do love this place, don'tcha?" Joanne smiles.

"Just love the history. I'll keep myself busy outside too, but I think the basement would be interesting in a house like this, too. I know it's untouched up here, but imagine what you could find in an old basement. It's probably—"

Joanne cuts her off. "There actually isn't a basement in the normal sense of the word. Because of the hill the house sits on, there was never any worry about water getting in or underneath the house. So, they didn't build a standard basement. Instead, there is a foundation and a very small crawlspace, but not a full basement. There are stairs down, but there isn't even space for two people to stand down there. A crawlspace goes under the rest of the house, on the off-chance water does get under it, it would collect there and not in the house itself. Supposedly, even in the worst storms the area has ever seen, there has never been water in the house. Which, well you must know growing up in the area, it's rare for a house to never get any water."

Kat nods.

"But it's totally empty down there, I'll let you go take a look if you want, but, like I said, nothing really to see down there. Just lots of old rocks."

"No, it's fine. Thanks."

"No, thank-you for coming. It's nice to have someone who is really interested in this stuff come through and look at the house. For the most part, it's just hikers that are looking for a place to stop before turning around and heading back toward town. They aren't doing this for the house, they're doing it for the hike, which is beautiful, but it's a different crowd usually than the one that comes to see the house."

"I understand that. I love history and stuff like this. There's so much to be learned. Even the people who know a lot about history know such a small percentage of the things that happened on a day-to-day basis. They know the presidents and the famous events. But this kind of stuff," Kat waves her hand out toward the rest of the house, "this is the stuff no one takes the time to learn about, and sometimes it's the more interesting stuff, to be honest."

Joanne smiles. "I agree."

"I'd love to come back and pick your brain some more. I mean, you know, about what I told you about my great-grand-father. I just feel like I'm supposed to know more about Mr. Creighton. I'm sure there's other, more personal stuff that isn't on the official tour." Kat gives her best smile, hoping to get an invitation back to find out a little more.

Joanne sighs, not an annoyed sigh, one that lets Kat know she's thinking over what she said seriously. Kat waits. No pressure.

"How about this? We officially close at six every night. I usually go home and eat dinner then. If you come back with some spaghetti and meatballs from one of the Italian places nearby, we can sit and eat, and I'll see if I can give you the unofficial tour. People aren't usually this interested in the house, and I don't get much company for dinner. Might be nice to eat with someone else for a change," Joanne says and pats Kat on the arm.

"That sounds perfect," Kat says. "Is there any restaurant you like more than another? And what can I bring you to drink?"

"*Dominic's* is the best. When you're there ordering, just ask the bartender what wine goes best with the spaghetti and meatballs and ask for a bottle of that. I have glasses." Joanne winks at Kat, who laughs and smiles back.

"Okay, see you tonight." She exits out the front door and smiles to herself. Mission accomplished.

Kat uses the rest of the day to give herself a tour of Elk Hills. She gets a ride back into the center of town and walks around. Her first stop is the train station. Although she can't tell exactly where the fire was that killed her great-grandfather, she wants to be able to tell Gramps she saw the site. Following that, she finds a diner—*Louise's*—and has a small lunch. Kat doesn't usually eat that much in the middle of the day, and she knows she's having a dinner with Joanne later on, so she keeps it light. Then she walks around the rest of the downtown area and finds herself sitting at the library until it's time to pick up the food and the bottle of wine.

This time, when she arrives back at the Creighton house, the gate is open, and her driver takes her all the way to the door.

With a bag of food in one hand and a bottle of wine in the other, Kat knocks softly on the door of the house. The sun is low in the sky, but it's not dark yet. The shadows fall the opposite direction they did this morning. Long shadows lead away from the house and make it seem larger than it looked earlier. The house is ominous, sitting there, as if growing throughout the day. Kat studies it, scanning it once more as she waits for Joanne to open the door.

There is no sound of movement from the other side of the door, but Kat waits, not wanting to seem impatient. After a few more minutes, she knocks again, louder this time. She hears Joanne approach right away after this second knock. The door clicks, and Kat is greeted by Joanne's smiling face.

"There you are, dear. I honestly didn't know if you would

show up. It's a bit of an unusual circumstance." Joanne lifts her arm and motions Kat inside. "I hope you weren't waiting out here long. I finished up some work and had to clean up before you got here."

"No, no, I just got here," Kat says. She holds up the bags of food and wine. "Lead the way!"

Kat follows Joanne down the hall and then surprisingly into the kitchen.

"In here?" Kat says when they enter the kitchen. The table is supposedly the same table that was in the house a hundred years ago. Kat isn't comfortable eating and drinking at the thing, much less sitting on the chairs.

"Yes, yes of course. Where else would you eat other than the kitchen?" Joanne takes the bag from Kat and places it on the table along with the bottle of wine. There are already paper plates and plastic utensils on the counter, as well as a bottle opener and napkins.

"But, but what about the table?" Kat looks at it, mortified.

"I guess this is the first part of the unofficial tour. In the late 1940's, after the war, they began the process of turning the house into a preserved home. Much of the furniture was salvaged, but this table was not. The table that was here when preservation began is identical to this one. Yes, this is still an antique table, but it's a recreation made specifically for the Creighton House. There are a few other pieces of furniture here that are exact matches of the original furniture, but not many."

Kat nods, standing at the table while Joanne twists a corkscrew into the wine bottle.

"This isn't in the official tour either, but when Mr. Creighton disappeared, Mrs. Creighton was left here in the house, largely by herself. Before he left, Mr. Creighton fired all the workers that were usually in the house, and became very secretive. Most attribute that to the fact that he knew his life was in danger and he tried to close himself off. Didn't work. But anyway, he let all the workers go and then when he was gone, there was no one really to watch the wife. She had mental problems, which was why she never came down from the upstairs very much, that was the claim anyway. Most people believe she had a drug problem. Opium or cocaine probably; no one really knows for sure, but also drank heavily. The furniture that was replaced was all damaged by her after Mr. Creighton was gone. The kitchen table was soaked in rum, same for a few of the mattresses upstairs. We still have all of the pieces in storage, but in order to give tours of the house, we had to get them out of here. I've heard the whole place smelled of rum when they came to take Mrs. Creighton out of here. Shall we eat?"

Kat nods, and Joanne moves the plates and plastic silverware over to the table. Then she gets two plastic cups and fills them about halfway with the wine. Joanne smells it before she has a sip.

"Ah, this is good stuff."

"Only the best," Kat says. "Plus, I wanted to thank you for letting me back. I just feel like there is so much to learn about the house, Mr. Creighton, and maybe even my Great-grandfather, that isn't possible to learn in a forty-five-minute tour."

Kat helps Joanne get the food out. Two orders of spaghetti and meatballs. Kat also added cheesy garlic bread to the order. They begin eating, and Kat makes sure to fill any silences with questions.

"So, you know a little about my family, what about your family?" Kat asks, wanting to seem interested and hoping the conversation and the wine will help Joanne open up a little more.

"Oh, not much to tell really. I have two brothers. One of them lives close by, the other moved out to Massachusetts twenty years ago and only comes back now with his kids a couple times a year. No kids of my own, so my nieces and nephews are like my kids now."

Kat nods, knowing the feeling.

"But you didn't come here to learn about my family, Kat. There's a lot of history here in this house, that's what you want to know about, and I want to know more too. One thing I've never heard about that I'd like to know more about is your great-grandfather. What else can you tell me about him?"

"I only know what my Gramps told me, which is not that much. The basic story he told me was that my great-grandfather, Michael Jacobs, died in a train fire on the way here to do a story about Mr. Creighton. That was what the police told his wife anyway. She never believed it though. She told Gramps that Michael was writing a story that Creighton was doing all kinds of shady things up here. He was going to expose them. Next thing she knew, Michael was dead. Not long after that, Creighton disappeared. That was it. My Gramps' mom told him that and he never really looked into it. Stories, you know." Kat goes on between bites, hoping that laying it all out there is the way to go. Joanne listens and nods when the time is right, but says nothing. Kat can't tell if she's just listening to the story or if she knows something about any of what Kat is saying. "My Gramps—he's kinda nearer the end now, um, and doesn't have much time left. He felt like he needed to look into it before it was too late. So, he sent me."

"That's an amazing story. I can't say that I've heard

anything about most of the details, but it's very likely your great-grandfather, Michael, was it? It's likely he was on to something here. Mr. Creighton did a lot of good in the community. But it was the 1920's, and the super-rich, like Mr. Creighton, didn't get super rich by following the rules all of the time. I'm sure he cut corners here and there."

Kat nods and listens to some of the business corruption that occurred during the 1920's. It's nothing most people don't learn in high school and, though she feigns interest, Kat's mind wanders. It's only then that she hears a squeak coming from somewhere outside the kitchen. She stops chewing and listens harder, trying her best to tune out Joanne. It was too loud, too definite, for it to just be the old house settling.

"But I don't know exactly what Michael might have been looking into." Joanne finishes whatever she was saying and takes a final bite of her dinner. Kat is done and leans back in her chair.

"Are you here much at night? Must be a different place when the sun isn't out." Kat listens for the sound again but hears nothing.

"I'm usually not here after dark. I try to be gone by the time the sun is down. It's a little harder in the winter because it gets dark so early, but we close earlier in the winter, and it's usually pretty empty around here. We stay open, though. There is enough money in the foundation to keep me and Rebecca paid year 'round. Neither of us really want to leave. It's a good job and not terribly stressful."

"Rebecca?" Kat asks, her eyebrows raised. She tries to pretend that she's just curious but wonders if it comes across that way.

"She helps me out. Works three days during the week, plus the weekend days. It can't always be me." Joanne laughs.

"That's true, I guess you'd never leave if that was the case." Kat smiles, but now she wants to talk to Rebecca. "So, what else isn't on the tour?"

"Oh, not that much actually, come this way." Joanne stands up and refills her wine, then does the same for Kat's cup, draining the bottle.

Joanne leads her out of the kitchen and into the office.

"Over here." Joanne brings Kat into the far corner of the room to a book set against a wall sitting on the desk. "This book was here. We've never really been sure what the names in the book are for, but most of the other ultra-rich that disappeared around the same time as Mr. Creighton have their names in this book. The police at the time figured when Mr. Creighton and the others disappeared, and the fact that they acted like it might happen, meant that someone had a list of people who could be potential targets of the Chicago mobsters. Mr. Creighton, maybe, was able to get his hands on the list. It obviously didn't help him, or anyone else, because they all ended up gone."

"Correct me if I'm wrong, but it seems like the police didn't put too much effort into the investigation of these disappearances. They didn't even take the book," Kat says.

"You're right, follow me." Joanne brings Kat back through the office, out to the hallway, and into the library. "It was widely known back then that there were two kinds of police officers in the area, especially here in Elk Hills. There were police who took money from Creighton and did whatever he asked. He paid more than they got paid to be cops, so they did what he told them first. Then there were police who hated the guys who took money from Creighton. There was a long-time police chief here. He supposedly took money from Creighton. It helped him get the job, and he just never let it go. Even after Mr. Creighton disappeared."

"That's probably true any time there are dirty cops some-where. Just like anything else, good guys and bad guys." Kat follows Joanne into the library as they talk.

"Right. The problem was the chief and the town's most well-respected cops were all in Mr. Creighton's pocket. From what I know, they never really did anything illegal, but they did shirk their responsibilities as police officers to help Mr. Creighton whenever they could."

"Like how?"

"Oh, you know." Joanne tilts her head to the side, reading the spines of some of the books on the shelves like she's looking or something specific. "Instead of patrolling a certain area, they would come up here and make sure everything was safe. If Mr. Creighton had a delivery of alcohol, they would accompany him and make sure it went smoothly. Again, it's not like they killed anyone for Mr. Creighton, but they helped him out when they could."

"I get it." Kat nods. She opens her mouth to ask why they are in the library again, but a low scraping sound and a long squeak comes from the far end of the room. Both women stop their conversation and look in that direction.

Kat shifts her gaze from the door to Joanne, at first thinking maybe this is Rebecca, but the look on Joanne's face tells a different story. Not only is this not Rebecca, she's never heard this sound before in her life. Whatever is happening behind that door, it's not normal. The natural response, the one that Joanne makes almost immediately, is to get up and take a couple steps toward the exit.

"What was that?"

"I don't know," Joanne says.

Kat's response—the way she's been her whole life—is not to take a step back. She doesn't back away from anything that catches her curiosity. Once the noise comes from the closet, she needs to know what it is. The fact that Joanne can't tell her what made the sound only intensifies her need to know.

As Joanne backs up to the door, ready to run if something comes charging out, Kat stands up and takes a few cautious steps toward the closet. There are more sounds behind it, shuffling and scraping, and then, as if in slow motion, the door opens.

"Wha—" Joanne utters half a word, but as the door swings open, the word is stolen by her shock. Even Kat, who feels there is nothing on earth that could scare her, takes a step back. Nothing she has ever seen in her life could prepare her for what she sees as the door swings open the rest of the way.

Two figures step out. Rail-thin bodies appear in the doorway. The two human-like figures stand, mouths agape, and stare at her. And Kat, frozen in place by shock of the whole thing, just stares back at them.

"Kat, Kat I—I think we should, I think..." Joanne stammers but doesn't move or leave or finish her sentence. "What are they?"

Kat doesn't know what they are. They are skeletons with skin, but just barely. One of them, the one in the back, looks like an old person who hasn't eaten. Skinny, clothes hanging off of its bones. Long white hair cascading down past its shoulders. On both heads is a device of some sort. Blinking lights indicate it's operational, but she has no idea what it might be.

The thing in front takes a slow step forward, and then

another. As it does, Kat takes a step back, keeping the distance between her and the things the same. She waits, expecting the thing to crumple to the ground from the impact of its movement. Different devices are attached to both their arms and legs, and they let off a quiet hissing sound when they move. The slow thing with the dark eyes and peeling lips moves to the side, and the second thing steps forward. When they take a step toward the women, it looks as if their legs and arms might fall off of them. It's hard to tell from this distance what is actually holding them together. It's as if death itself draws closer to them.

Torn between an urge to leave and her curiosity, Kat backs up another step. When the second thing steps forward, it holds its hands palm out, not like it wants to attack them, but like it wants to talk with them. Kat stops. Joanne has positioned herself half outside the library, holding the door open for Kat if they need to run. Kat holds her position. These things look old and weak. If they do have to run, she is sure they can outrun the walking skeletons. It doesn't hurt to give them a chance to speak.

"What the fuck are you?" Kat says.

CHAPTER 25

Michael's eyes almost pop out of his head when he sees the two women standing in the library as he and Clyde step out of the closet. In all the time they've been doing this, first on their own, and now more frequently with the knowledge of the rest of the group, they've never come across another person.

When the younger one speaks, he realizes how he and Clyde must look to them. Though Michael has been eating as much as possible, it is still not much, and it doesn't make up for decades of starvation beneath the house. Their hair is long and white and they have devices attached to the top of their heads. They are far from looking human in any sense.

The older woman backs up out of the door to the library. The younger one takes tentative steps back, but she isn't as quick to flee. She is terrified, and rightly so, but she also wants to know more. Michael relates to this. The younger one could be the person he's looking for. A representative in the outside world. Before he can convince either of these women to be on their side, he's got to convince them not to run out of the room and call the police.

"Wait, wait," Michael says. His voice is scratchy, and, for the first time in a long time, he realizes how weak he is—how weak they all are.

The younger one looks at him. She looks familiar, but only in a passing sense. He hasn't seen anyone but the skeletons for such a long time. It's probably just seeing a normal looking human. At the same time, there is something about her eyes. He has trouble pulling himself from them. The older one, now completely out in the hall ready to make a break for it, stares back at him, eyes wide. Then she surprises him by being the one to break the silence.

"D-do you need help? I'll call the police, and then we can all wait together. You shouldn't be here." She spins and turns, not toward the front door like Michael expected her to, but the complete opposite direction, probably back to the office.

"No, please don't," Michael says. He tries to move toward her, but he doesn't want to physically stop her because it would be counterproductive. Could he even stop her if he wanted to? He's surprised again when the younger one calls out.

"Joanne, wait."

Joanne. Michael knows that name. It's her office. She's been unknowingly feeding him for a while now, helped him to gain a little bit of his weight back, even though she has no idea.

"What?" Joanne's voice calls from the hall.

"Just—let's just give them a second here, maybe there is some sort of explanation," the younger woman says. Curiosity again. Michael likes it. He can work with curiosity. He and Clyde have enough secrets to satisfy almost anyone's curiosity.

Joanne comes back to the doorway, she's not in the library,

but also not running down the hall to call the police—it's a step in the right direction.

"I gather you're Joanne," Michael says, trying to keep his voice clear and even, but aware of how it must sound. He gestures to himself and then to Clyde, who has not moved much since they first entered the room. "My name is Michael, this is Clyde."

"I'm Kat," the younger woman says with a faint smile on her face.

"Why were you in the closet?"

"And how long have you been there?" Kat follows up.

The two women stand by the door, curious but cautious. Still, something about the younger one is familiar to Michael; he can't figure out why. He knows he's never seen a photograph of her before, but can't figure it out. Even her voice reminds him of someone he's known.

"It's..." Michael starts, then clears his throat before starting again. "It's actually a very long story. Can—do you think it's possible for us to sit and talk? I promise we won't hurt you. If you still want to call the police after you hear our story, then you can go ahead. But our story is rather unique, and we're not looking to hurt anyone. If anything, we want to help you, and need your help." His words are genuine for the first time in a long time, and it feels good to be truthful with someone other than Clyde. They must have been able to see his honesty because even Joanne's face softens.

Kat looks to Joanne, who nods.

"Okay," Joanne says.

"Can we use the kitchen?" Kat says. Joanne nods again. Joanne is in charge of the house, that much is clear, but Kat is more comfortable with the whole situation.

"Is there, maybe, a glass of water we could have?" Michael asks. The women say nothing but turn and exit for the kitchen. Michael gives a look back at Clyde, then follows the woman out of the room, Clyde shuffling along behind. Michael enters the kitchen; two bottles of water sit on the table. The women, it seems, are not going to sit. They stand and lean against the counter. That's fine with Michael. He sits at the table and looks to the door, waiting for Clyde to enter.

"Where is the other one?" Kat asks.

"He's on his way," Michael says. He can almost place the voice, and then he realizes it reminds him of Mary. It's been so long since he's heard an actual woman's voice that isn't scratchy with age and decay, that any female voice would remind him of Mary. He can barely remember what her voice sounded like, but there's a hint of familiarity he can't push away.

Michael gets up and opens the door to let Clyde come in. Slowly, he sits at the table opposite Michael, and they talk to the women.

There's been a lot of thought put into what he would say in this situation, but, now that it's here, Michael doesn't know exactly how to start. Should he give them all of the information up front, or should he slowly give them information until they know the full story? They sit in silence, the women content to let the silence continue. He's the one who asked for a chance to explain himself. He's the one that needs to talk. Once again, it's the younger woman, Kat, who breaks the silence between the four of them.

"Okay, this is your chance. Joanne here is freaked out. She wants to call the police, and I don't really blame her. I'm curious, and I want to know your story. If you don't start talking soon, we can just call the cops, and *they* can figure everything out and hear your story."

Direct, to the point.

"It's... it's kind of hard to explain, but I'll do my best," Michael says.

"It's hard to explain old guys who look like skeletons coming out of a tiny closet in a library closet. Yeah, you're right, it is. Try anyways," Kat says. Joanne nods, her arms crossed across her chest.

"Right." Michael looks over at Clyde, who gives a slow nod. Michael pushes his hair back away from his face, a habit he's picked up over the years, and starts at the beginning. "My name is Michael Jacobs. I was here to write a story on Mr. Creighton, I'm sure you've heard of him."

Joanne's head snaps, her eyes widen. Kat's knees buckle, she catches herself by putting an arm on the counter. She exhales loud enough for Michael to hear.

"I'm sorry," Kat says. There is a quiver in her voice. Her eyes narrow, her face tightens, and she looks down. "Just got dizzy for a second. Please go on."

"We're actually members of a group called the Elk Hills Research Society." Here goes nothing. He's going to leave the part out about how he was forced into his immortal state by the Doctor and Mr. Creighton. That part can come later. Other than that, he's going to stick as close to the truth as he can. "I was born in 1896, and, along with the rest of the research society, I've been living underneath this house for the last ninety-two years. Back in 1926, Mr. Creighton and our Doctor, devised a way to allow people to continue living for a lot longer than nature intended them to. *A lot* longer. Since we've been down there, none of us have died, and we don't expect to die any time soon. The device on our heads," Michael taps his head. "It keeps the electric current running on our brains so that they cannot turn off. I don't know all of the medical aspects of it, but the Doctor could explain it to you.

"These devices on our chests keep our lungs and hearts operational as well. My heart will never stop beating as long as the device is running. Same thing for my lungs, they will continue to work for as long as the device works. The contraptions on my arms and legs produce and store electricity to operate the other devices. With all of these devices working together, we have remained alive, although with very little food, for nearly a hundred years beneath this house."

"You're, you—" Kat stammers.

"Why? Why would you do that?" Joanne asks. Her face is white, her hand over her mouth. She stares at him and Clyde, studying the devices attached to them. Kat does the same, but there is something else there, he doesn't know what it is, but something has thrown her.

"Profit." Michael is uncertain how much to tell them, so he doesn't bring up the way Creighton has basically kept them captive all these years. For now, he will keep things positive. "Mr. Creighton believed, back when we first did this, that if we waited long enough, since we had the ability to, we would see a larger profit than if we just tried to sell the technology back then. We've been keeping tabs as best we can from under there and we think he's right. We actually think this is the best time two show our faces again and ultimately try to sell our equipment."

Michael stops. He studies the women and is confused. Kat was the curious one, but now she's gone silent.

"This was probably a bad idea, maybe we can—" he starts.

"You're Michael Jacobs?" Kat blurts.

"Yes, do you know me? Have you heard of—"

"I'm Katherine Jacobs, my... my grandfather is Joseph Jacobs, and you're... you're—"

"Joseph? He— did he get—"

The room fills with silence, except for the hiss and hum of the devices keeping Michael and Clyde alive.

No one speaks.

Tears draw lines on Michael's cheeks. He can't remember the last time he cried. Kat is crying, too. Katherine, his great-granddaughter, that's why she looks and sounds familiar. She *is* familiar. She is family.

Michael looks up at her, and blinks away the tears in his eyes so he can see her more clearly. He looks at her now as a person he helped create and not as someone he just met.

Kat wipes tears from her eyes. He can see she's not sure what to do.

"I understand," Michael says. "How can you believe me? But— but I looked Joseph up a few weeks ago, maybe more than that now, I sent him a note. I didn't think it would work, but I told him to investigate this place."

Kat digs in her pocket, pulls out a piece of paper, and unfolds it.

"Yes, that one. He got it, I— I can't believe he got it and that he's still alive and that— that you're here."

"This can't be real. It's just some sort of trick. You— you're supposed to have died in—"

"In a train fire, I know. My friend, well, not really my friend, Ronald Weaver, set it up to make it look like I was killed. He burned up bodies to make them unrecognizable."

"Ronald Weaver? He was the Chief of Police here in Elk Hills for a long time," Joanne chimes in.

"Not back then. He was a detective then. In Creighton's pocket, apparently, along with half the force here in town. I was —" Michael stops short, realizing he's going to end up telling the whole story. Clyde gives a slow nod next to him, and a smile grows on his face.

"Look, I wasn't totally truthful before. Now that, now that we're family, there is more I can tell you." He couldn't have planned this any better if he tried. One note led his great-granddaughter here to be the person he shares the story with. If he needed someone to trust, he found her. He can tell her everything and hopefully, get the Doctor and Creighton and the rest of them arrested, and maybe sell the technology himself. "But I also want to know about my— my son."

Kat nods at him. "Please tell me what you need to tell me first, and then, then we can figure out the rest. I don't know if I can really believe all of this. There's no way this all can be true."

"It is true, Kat. I mean look at us. Look at this. It's all true. I came to Elk Hills to investigate and write a story on grave robberies that occurred here and in other surrounding towns around the same time." Michael recounts the tale, the truth this time, including how he was taken captive by the Society. "But even when they took me, I still had two questions: What had they been working on up here? Why did they need the bodies?"

"Why *did* they need the bodies?" Kat asked. She reminded Michael of himself, digging for another small piece of information.

"They were reanimating them," Michael says. The words hang in the air and no one says anything,

"Like, back to life?" Kat says.

Michael nods. "But it wasn't the ultimate goal of the group. They wanted immortality and money. They kidnapped me, made me their test subject. Clyde here was the first live subject. He had some obvious side effects. I was the second, no side effects."

"Holy shit," Kat says. "So, why are you up here now then?"

Michael smiles. It's a different time—he's not used to hearing a woman swear so openly like that.

"We're supposed to be here learning about the world today. I was chosen to find someone who will help us get a business deal with a major technology company, or even a medical company. We want to— Creighton and the Doctor—want to sell the idea to the highest bidder and make lots of money off of it. Clyde and I had a different idea. We want to turn Creighton and the Doctor, and the rest of the group, in to the authorities. They took me and experimented on me against my will. The reanimated people down there are all suffering, but were never given a choice. We want them to serve time for what they've done. All of them, but Creighton and the Doctor are more evil than the rest. They've kept us all down there all these years. They are the only ones that knew how to maintain these things and keep us alive. We had no choice. Second to all of that, maybe as a bonus, Clyde and I, along with the rest of the reanimated people, can make any money that is left if we can sell these things." Michael points to the device on his head.

"Jesus." Kat rubs the side of her head and takes a long breath in. "This is a lot to take in."

"Kat, do you believe him?" Joanne says. Kat is more intimately involved, but Joanne is the one he needs to convince not to call the police. When it comes to the museum, she's in charge. She will do whatever she wants, even if Kat disagrees.

"I mean, look at them," Kat gestures. "They look like they've been alive for a long time, don't they? What else am I supposed to believe?"

Kat steps away from the counter and moves toward them. She studies Michael for a second and then backs up.

"Yeah, I actually do believe him. He looks a lot like Gramps," she says to Joanne, then looks at Michael and continues. "Gramps says his mother always thought Michael's death—*your* death—was suspicious. He said she thought something strange was going on up here with Creighton, but at the time your friend, um, Weaver, assured her that it was just an accident. She trusted him at the time and believed him, but there was always something in the back of her mind that made her question it. I guess she was right. Gramps is in the hospital now, but before he went there, he got your note. He never told anyone about his mother's thoughts on the train fire and your death. He did some research but everything pointed to the train accident being the truth. The disappearances of the members of your Society were chalked up to mob hits at the time. He never would have told me about any of this if it wasn't for the note. I flew in from DC yesterday when I heard he was sick. So, he told me all this last night. He asked me to come here and figure stuff out, see if there was anything here *to* figure out, and find out who sent the message."

"What do we do?" Joanne asks. She looks at all of them, but her gaze settles on Kat.

* * *

A silence fills the room. Clyde moves from his seated position to standing, the hiss of the contraptions on his arms and legs echo with each movement. He steps forward, gives Michael a look. He can't even begin to calculate the chances of this happening. It's almost too perfect. But it happened. They need to get someone to be on their side. Who better than Michael's own great-granddaughter? But there is still cautiousness on both sides. He fears Michael may be too trusting, too quick to give over control of everything to Kat because she is family. They don't know anything about her other than the fact that she must look something like his wife, given the way he keeps studying her face. Michael will listen to Clyde. He knows he will, so he has to put in his opinion now, before it's too late.

"Private." Clyde makes eye contact with Michael before continuing past him into the hall.

"Ah, excuse us. Just one moment, please. He...he just needs extra time sometimes." Michael gives a smile, steps around Clyde, and leaves the room. Clyde plods along and eventually follows him out.

"What is it, Clyde?"

"Be...safe...help...do...what...we...need...and...bring...family...together...but ...don't...know...her...yet...plan," Clyde says.

"We don't know enough about her yet. Just because she's family doesn't mean she will see things from our side. We need to keep to our plan, even with all of this," Michael translates. It's not exactly certain what Clyde was trying to say, but it's close enough. He gets the point, and Clyde thinks he'll go along with it.

"I agree, Clyde, but this is my family. I know if it was your family, you'd feel the same way. She looks just like Mary. Sounds like her too. I just..." Michael trails off. "You're right, you know.

I need to stick with the plan to get her to help us, not just assume that she will."

Clyde nods. They return to the kitchen. The women were having a private conversation of their own but stop when the two men return. Kat makes eye contact with Michael.

"Joanne still wants to call the police. I understand. Is there a reason we can't do what you want and still call the police? It seems the police would have to get involved at some point anyway," Kat says.

Clyde sees her point but knows the sooner the police get involved, the more likely it is that they will never see a dime from the experiments they underwent and the technology they helped create. He and Michael came up with the plan together many years ago, but he's worried that the purpose of the plan has switched in Michael's head. If the point is to find justice, then they could let them call the police right now, but the second it becomes a legal matter, they lose some of their rights to the technology. Creighton, the Doctor, and the rest of them will be in custody, and once that happens, the police, the government and the legal system will have more control over the devices and the technology than anyone else. They could replicate the Doctor's devices and claim them as their own. Creighton would be in prison, but Michael and Clyde, and the rest of the reanimates, would be out of luck. Michael needs to keep his eye on both things equally, with family involved it complicates things. Clyde needs to make sure Michael stays focused on what they are up here to do. Family or no family.

"I understand that," Michael says, looking only at Joanne. "But we can't be too quick with that. There will be a time. Believe me, I want to see Creighton and the rest of them in jail for what they did, but we need to wait. We need to get ourselves a deal on the technology first. Once we do that, we can get the police involved. If Creighton and the Doctor, and all the rest of them down there get involved before we get a deal, it will blow everything. It will make the years, the decades we've waited down there, all for nothing."

"Just because we're family doesn't mean I have to trust you. I *want* to trust you. But I don't know that I can just yet," Kat says. "Creighton, you said he wanted you to find someone from up here to help you. To bring you all back into society, right?"

Michael nods. He looks to Clyde, who can tell his longtime friend has no idea where she is headed.

"Listen, I guess I followed you in the family job. I'm a reporter, and I have to tell you, a story like this, from a reporter like me, will get lots of attention."

"You're a reporter?" Michael grimaces. Clyde is the only one in the room who knows it's a smile, and it's the biggest smile he's ever seen on Michael's face.

"I write for a website in Washington DC. It's a political website. I broke a few big stories over the years, and I guess I'm a big name in the DC press, even nationally. Oh jeez, I'm sorry, you don't know what a website is, do you?"

"We do. Like I said, we've been preparing for this for a while, including using your computer, Joanne. Sorry about that."

Joanne smiles. "I guess I know where my Snickers went now."

It seems as though she's only going along with this because Kat seems to trust them for now. They need to keep Joanne happy too. He makes a mental note to tell Michael this later.

"What does this have to do with our little predicament then?" Michael asks.

CHAPTER 26

"It has everything to do with it, because if you tell Creighton that you found someone to help you, I can get down there and see what is really underneath this house. Once I do that, I can write a story about you and the devices you're trying to sell. It will be seen by millions of people, and you'll get all the interest you want. After that, I write more stories explaining how you were the victims. Before you know it, you'll be suing Creighton and the Doctor and everyone else that you want to sue for everything they have. I'm the right person to have as your great-granddaughter right now," Kat says. She knows she's asking a lot. Probably more than either Clyde or Michael envisioned when they hatched their plan, but she has two sides. One side would do anything for family, the other would do anything for a story.

While Michael told his story, Kat saw the headline on the site. The story wrote itself in her head. But when she starts to see the story take shape, it's hard for her to stop. The fact that she *knows* Gramps would want her to follow this through only makes it that much more appealing.

The long silence in the kitchen is broken when Kat looks to Joanne. "Are you okay with that? You don't have to come down with me if you don't want to. I'm used to going into places that are unsafe and uncomfortable to be in. It's all part of getting a good story. For me, it's worth it."

Joanne nods. "I don't want to go down there, but I have to see what's under the house. I'm as much a part of this house as Mr. Creighton ever was. I think I owe it to myself to go down there."

"What do you say, Great-Gramps? Do we have a deal?" Kat gives a half smile and looks from Michael to Clyde, and back again.

"Just like that, huh? I guess you *are* my great-granddaughter. You might even be better than I was at this. Clyde, what do you think?"

There is a long pause, and Clyde nods. "Up...to...you."

Kat knows she has it now. She doesn't know the dynamic between Michael and Clyde, but it seems as though they don't make any decision on their own. If she has Clyde's approval she's halfway there.

"We need to preserve what Clyde and I have planned for."

"Of course," Kat says. She's got him. "We will stick with the first story. You recruited us to help you sell your technology. You and I are *not* related. I am here helping my aunt Joanne rearrange some things in the office to better display Mr. Creighton's things. That's it."

"Alright, let's do it." Michael smiles. Kat is getting used to the death-like faces of the two men. Their eyes both look almost gray, as though the life has drained out of them. Even if she is able to find someone to purchase these devices from them, one look at the two men, or any of the others down in the basement, and no one would want to buy anything. Maybe if they lived a better lifestyle. With proper food and rest they might look somewhat human, but that is a long way off for these two men. Still, their appearance is less shocking than it was when they first saw them.

Joanne leads the group back into the library and to the closet door, Kat follows closely behind her. Michael shuffles past them but stops.

"It takes some getting used to waiting for Clyde. His brain works at full speed inside his head, but the messages from his brain to his muscles take extra time. The Doctor corrected it with me, but Clyde was supposed to be the first success. He ended up being just another test subject." Michael stops talking as Clyde enters the room. "Okay, Clyde and I will go down first. Creighton and the Doctor are usually there at the bottom of the stairs withing for us. You can just follow us down. Trust me."

Michael pulls open the closet door, and then Kat watches him lean his body against the right-hand wall and step back. A hidden, inner door swings out toward him. The smell hits Kat immediately, but it dissipates quickly. It's not as bad as she feared, making her wonder if there is some sort of ventilation system down there.

"Oh, my gosh, I can't believe it. I've only looked in this closet a few times, but I would never think to push on that wall."

"I believe that was the point," Michael says. Then, looking at Kat, "Let me do all the talking to start. And no lights. Not yet."

Kat nods as Michael descends the stairs into the awaiting darkness. Clyde follows at his slow pace, then Kat with Joanne behind her.

"You're back early," a voice says, and Kat realizes it's probably Creighton or the Doctor, startled by Michael's early return.

"Actually, Edmund, there's been a major development," Michael says as Kat follows Clyde one step at a time. It's darker than she thought it would be, but light from the library illuminates the space enough for her to see the outline of two shapes at the bottom of the stairs. She can't make out any features, but she can tell both figures are just as skeletal as Michael and Clyde. Everyone looks the same. Part of her head warns her that this is a huge mistake, and a risk she shouldn't be taking. Joanne exhales loudly behind her. Kat reaches back, finds Joanne's hand and squeezes it, knowing they feel the same nervousness.

"It's going to be okay," Kat whispers.

"—telling you this girl is perfect," Michael says to the person Kat still assumes is Edmund Creighton. It's obvious they are talking about her. It's almost her time.

"Well, let's meet her— or them—and see where we're at," the second voice says.

Clyde reaches the bottom step and then moves to the side.

"Michael," Kat says, unable to see more than an inch in front of her face.

"I'm here," Michael says. There is movement next to her, a hand on her shoulder. "We can see a little bit better than you can down here, I guess."

"I can't see anything," Kat says.

"Me neither," Joanne echoes from behind her.

"Do you have something we can use for a light?" a new voice asks.

Kat doesn't reply but finds her phone in her pocket and flicks the flashlight on. "There," Kat says.

The light illuminates the area around them. There are four of them standing there. Michael, Clyde and two new rail-thin forms. Both of the men stare back at her. Like Michael and Clyde, their hair is long and ash-grey, their faces sunken. The effect is so extreme that Kat is certain the skin will fall off their faces if they open their mouths too wide. But they don't open their mouths at all. They both stand there and stare at Kat and Joanne. Their mouths hang open in a way that makes Kat think they can't control it.

"Apologies," the taller of the two men says, finally breaking the silence. "It's been a while since we've seen someone from out there."

"I've heard. Michael filled me in on what you all have been doing for the past...well, for a long time."

"Good, good, I trust you understand our dilemma," the man says, but continues without waiting for a response from her. "I am Edmund Creighton."

He holds out his hand to Kat. She grips his hand gently. The papery skin slides against her flesh, individual bones in his hand moving when his fingers enclose around hers. The handshake lasts less than a second, but far too long for Kat. She's relieved when it ends, and Creighton looks past her to Joanne.

"Mr. Creighton," Joanne says. "I have been the caretaker of your home for the last thirty-five years. It is an honor to actually meet you. When I heard the story from Michael, I couldn't believe it. I didn't really *want* to believe it. But when he said we could come down here and actually meet you, I couldn't turn my back on that opportunity."

"Thank you, I appreciate everything you've done," Creighton says, looking right into Joanne's eyes. She is star-struck. The woman has dedicated her life to keeping up this person's home and learning everything there is to learn about his life. When you begin research on someone who has been dead for almost a hundred years, you know deep down that you're never going to meet that person, but you still think about what questions you would ask them given the chance. Joanne must have thought about what she would say to Edmund Creighton if they ever invented time travel. They didn't do that, but this is close. Now the older woman doesn't know what to say.

"We've kept the house just like you left it. Everything that could be restored has been restored. I think you will find it's not that much different up there than it was when you left," Joanne says.

Creighton looks to Michael and Clyde, who both nod at their own separate speeds.

"I truly appreciate everything you've done for my house and my land. When we were down here, I hoped the best for all of the property, but you can never be sure. I'm glad to hear it has been in such good hands the past thirty-five years. And Michael says this is your niece."

"Uh, yes, this is Kat, my niece. She was here helping me get some work done tonight when your two friends surprised us."

Creighton turns back to Kat. He seems to know that she is the one who has offered to help them.

"Michael says you can be a huge help to our cause. He wouldn't say that unless it were true. So, tell me, Kat, how can you help us?" Creighton smiles as he talks, but the lips that stretch across his teeth hardly move. Instead, the thin cheeks on his face just pull up and back slightly, exposing more of his teeth.

"Yes, yes. I think I can. I am a reporter for a web— a newspaper that gets a national run. If I can write a story about you all down here, we can get the exposure you need to sell your equipment to anyone you want, probably for any price you want. I think it would be a win for both of us."

"I agree, she could help us," says the only person that has remained quiet the entire time. Kat knows this is the man Michael only called the Doctor. His eyes are wide, and there is something behind them that makes Kat uneasy. Michael and Clyde, and even Creighton, are all emaciated and look close to death. This man looks this way too, but his eyes are different, wild.

"Kat, Joanne, this is the Doctor," Michael says. He moves closer to her, almost as if he is worried about what the Doctor might do and needs to protect her. Of course, she realizes all of that is probably just in her head. "He's the reason we're here, all of us. Creighton and the rest funded it, but he's the person that made it possible. He changed it from just an idea into a reality."

Kat nods and looks to the Doctor, but his eyes flick up behind her and Joanne.

"No!" Michael shouts in his gravelly voice, but it's too late. Before she realizes what has happened, bodies move in behind them, skeletons draped in skin and the tattered remnants of clothes. Hands wrap around her, and though she struggles, there are too many of them—weak as they are—for her to stop them. The same happens to Joanne, and Kat can hear her screams for help over the scuffling of her feet against the stone floor.

"No! Let me go!" Kat shouts.

The skeletons don't listen.

Kat tries to push herself back against the mob at her back, forcing her body into them, but they hold her tight. Her feet slip against the floor as they pull her backward. She twists her body from side to side and tries to push an elbow, a shoulder, a knee, anything into the skeletal monsters, but their bony hands are too many, their grip too tight.

In her attempts to break free, her phone, her only source of light, clatters to the floor. They plunge into absolute darkness.

There are grunts and groans next to her, then silence. Even as she tries to break free from the dozens of hands that hold her, she can hear the shift. At first, Michael protested, but now there is silence.

"Listen to me, Michael, it's the only way." It is Creighton's voice. "We had a vote while you were up there. The Doctor convinced me, convinced all of us. *This* is the only way to get them on our side. Sorry I couldn't tell you."

A long silence fills the darkness. Kat twists and thrusts her body in any direction to try to break free, but nothing works. She blinks, forces her eyes open, but still sees nothing. The total darkness makes her blood pump faster, her stomach drops. She is at their mercy.

"You will become a part of us, and then you will be as invested in this as we are. You can take your place alongside us, and you can live forever. Then, and only then, will you really be able to help us," the Doctor's voice echoes from the darkness.

"Okay, okay, let go," Michael says.

With that, Kat feels the fight drain from her body, and she lets the many hands drag her backward. The emaciated mob pulls her into a separate room. There is light in there, though it isn't entirely clear where it is coming from. Kat watches Joanne get strapped down to a bed, her body thrashing and fighting back as much as possible. One of them gets hit in the face with a knee and drops to the floor. Seeing one of their attackers fall gives her newfound strength. Kat kicks and thrashes along with Joanne. Even as they get one of her legs strapped to a bed, she still lashes out, knocking two of the human-like things down. Kat stops thrashing about long enough to look over at Joanne, who is still fighting them off, but has both her legs strapped down.

"Michael, what the fuck are you doing? Help us!" Kat shouts, hoping the sound of her voice, the voice that sounds too much like his wife's voice for him to ignore, will snap him out of it. Undo whatever trance Creighton has put him under.

"But, do you realize," Creighton's voice shouts over the noise that fills the room. "By not helping you, he is making you immortal? We are making the best decision for you. You will live forever!"

"No, no, I don't want that!" Joanne shouts, but when Kat looks back at her, she is fully strapped onto the bed. Kat fights harder, but the entire length of her arm is restrained by the things around her. They have faces, but they look so much alike that they might as well be aliens. She can't move her arm, and the more she tries, the tighter they hold. The cold leather envelops one wrist, then the other. She's losing. It is happening.

Now that they are both strapped down, Kat and Joanne fight against the leather that binds them, but neither is successful. The cuff tears at the skin of Kat's arm. Each time she tries to tug against it, pain shoots through her body. She tries to rock back and forth, but the mob returns and steadies the table so it doesn't tip. Her screams and swears echo through the lab, but the words go unheard by those around her. Before long, she becomes too exhausted to fight back. Joanne goes through a similar shift. Breathing heavy, sweating on the beds, they lay there until the Doctor finally speaks from behind them. He's no doubt chosen this position so that Kat can't see anything he is doing, and she bets Joanne can't either.

"Everyone out, except Edmund, Michael and Clyde," the Doctor says. A grumble rolls though the others in the room, but they eventually exit. The door slams shut; Kat forces her head up to take in as much as she can now that her bedside is not surrounded by half dead human bodies. She glances back in the direction she thinks Michael is, and she catches his eye, but only for a moment. Something in the look tells her it might, *might* be okay. She can only trust that he will help her when the time comes.

"As you've already heard, I've done this many times before, but we entered into our seclusion shortly after the procedures were performed." The Doctor stands between the two beds and looks back and forth between his two captives. Joanne's whimpers echo throughout the room. "You will never look like we look, ladies, if that's what you're worried about. We suffer from severe malnourishment. The devices are all that keep us alive. You, *you* will eat regular meals and live regular lives. You will never look like us. You will age, but you will never die. And you will be the perfect face for our sale." He runs a bony finger along Kat's cheek.

"The sale of these devices by two healthy looking *immortal* women will bring in a lot more money than anything we could hope to do. The people will need proof that the devices work, and we are not proof. *You* will be the proof they need."

"But what if we don't want this?" Kat shouts, making the volume of her voice match the fight she has inside her.

"You just don't know you want it," Creighton's voice carries over from the far side of the room. "Once completed, you will understand what it means to be immortal. Ask your new friend, Michael. He didn't want it at first either, and now he is part of the inner circle of the Elk Hills Research Society. It may take time. Think of the money."

There is a long pause, no one talks. The only sounds in the room are the continued quiet wails of Joanne as she tries to process what is about to happen to her.

"I think these are set, Doctor," Creighton says, from the table on the other side of Joanne. The Doctor leaves the spot he's held between the two beds and moves to examine whatever Creighton has on the other table. As soon as his back turns, Kat catches movement out of the corner of her eye. Michael is moving toward her fast but silent. He reaches her and leans over. The Doctor and Creighton both still have their backs turned and haven't noticed him yet. Michael brings his mouth close to her ear, whispering as he starts unbuckling her right hand.

"You're stronger and faster than them," he whispers. "If they don't gang up, you can take them out. Tell Joseph I love him."

"No," Kat replies, but the sounds of the leather strap being undone turns Creighton's attention toward them.

"No, Michael!" the rich man shouts.

Kat glances in Creighton's direction as Michael works on her other strap.

"There," Michael says. Her hands are free, but Creighton and the Doctor are headed toward her. Michael moves in front of the two mad-men and slams his shoulder into both of them. It slows them down, but Michael is as weak as they are, so it doesn't do much.

Kat sits up and gets one of her legs unstrapped. As she moves to the other one, the Doctor reaches her and grabs for her arm. The advice Michael gives her echoes in her head. She is stronger than them. She shoves the Doctor back, slamming her palm against his chest, narrowly missing the device attached to his heart. The skeletal body goes sprawling to the floor, and Kat gets back to work unstrapping her second leg.

The second strap slips free, and Kat is off the bed faster than she thought possible. She's on her feet with Creighton barreling toward her. She looks at Joanne and then back at Creighton. She runs toward him and lowers her shoulder into his abdomen. She doesn't really feel the impact of the light, old man against her. He's taller and his shoulders are wider, but she still probably outweighs him. The hit knocks Creighton to the floor with an audible thump. Kat doesn't stop to admire her handiwork and instead begins removing Joanne's right arm from its strap.

The Doctor works his way back to his feet, and Kat slams a foot down against his shoulder, putting him back down on the floor.

"Get the other arm, and I can get my feet! Let's get the hell out of here!" Joanne shouts. Kat turns her attention to Joanne's other hand, focusing only on that task. She doesn't know what is happening around her.

"Kat! Behind you!"

She starts to turn, but is too late. Two bony arms wrap around Kat's chest and searing hot pain explodes from her shoulder, almost on the side of her neck. She turns her head and sees only the long, bright, white hair on the top of Creighton's head. And his teeth clamped down on her skin.

"They can't get away!" the Doctor shouts from the floor.

CHAPTER 27

The girl's blood fills his mouth, the warm, coppery fluid coats his tongue, her salty flesh a delight against his taste buds. She is stronger than him, and he needs to even the playing field. Taking a chunk out of the girl is the fastest thing he can think of, and his hunger gets the best of him. Creighton holds her tightly against him, but his muscles are non-existent. Her body twists, and he feels his grip on her loosening. She is too strong; when her elbow connects with his ribs, his arm lets go of her, his teeth, however, remain clamped down on her neck. He isn't going to let her go. Even if she breaks every bone in his body, it will only make him clamp his mouth closed around her flesh with more force.

She elbows him again in the ribs, harder this time. The crack of his ribs breaking is followed by dazzling, dizzying pain. Creighton groans, air is expelled from his lungs, but the devices attached to them continue to pump his breaths when any normal person would need a few seconds to gasp.

The older woman, Joanne, is free now and kneeling on her

table. She pulls at Creighton's hair, but it only succeeds in him pulling at Kat's flesh, tearing at it. She screams louder than before.

"Get off me, you son of a bitch!" she shouts, and slams her elbow into the same spot a third time. Creighton groans, his mouth opens; only slightly, but it's enough for her to twist away from him.

"No!" Creighton takes a step toward the two women, who are already on their way to the door. The others—Creighton hopes the others might be able to stop them like they did before. But they are not prepared, the door was closed, chances are they probably have no idea. The women will be faster and stronger than them and they will get away. Then what? Then what?

The sweet, coppery blood drips from his mouth. Creighton licks his lips, smiles then takes a step forward, to chase them even if only to warn the others, but the women are already out the door of the lab. Two arms wrap around him and hold him back.

"No, Edmund, it's done!" Michael says.

Clyde can't do much but watch the scene unfold in front of him. He already knows what he will say and do, no matter what happens. The girls run out; he is happy to see them leave. He doesn't know if they will contact the police or what will happen to them when they leave the room, but he hopes they make it to the surface.

Michael's hands wrap around Creighton. When Creighton

turns, Clyde sees rage like he's never seen before. Creighton stops his pursuit and rips Michael's hand from him. Both men stand facing each other, but Creighton is still the taller of the two. The Doctor gets back to his feet, looking like the eldest of all of the Immortals. His long hair is matted to his forehead and hangs down his back as his chest heaves.

"What is wrong with you, Michael?" Creighton glares down at the former reporter, blood dripping from his mouth and leaving a pink coating on his otherwise yellow teeth.

"They didn't deserve that, and you know it. They would have helped us. *Would* have helped."

"You're right. They *would* have, had you not let them go!" Creighton rises up and steps closer to Michael. It doesn't have the impact that it had in the days when he was physically larger, but even after all these years, he still has a way of commanding attention. Clyde approaches across the room.

"I had to," Michael says. He raises himself up too, like few people have ever done to Mr. Creighton.

"There was a vote, Michael. A vote! We have always listened to the group. Always!" The Doctor takes a place behind Michael. They've successfully boxed him in. Creighton on one side, the Doctor on the other, and the beds cutting off any chance of escape.

"But we've never voted on something like this before. They have a right to choose this."

"We *have* voted on something like this before. Haven't we, Doctor? Clyde?" Creighton asks. The Doctor nods and then Clyde does as well, still making the slow walk to the others.

"When?"

"You, Michael. We took a vote, and it was decided you

would join us, whether you wanted to or not. The vote was unanimous, just like this one." Creighton smiles, and the blood on his mouth and his pale skin turn him into a grotesque clown.

"That was a long time ago. Things have changed," Michael says. The Doctor moves in closer. Clyde watches. Seeing the worry on the old reporter's face, he turns his body to try and give himself more room.

"Some things haven't changed. At first, I thought it was a mistake keeping you alive. We were going to kill you that night, you know? I grew to like you. It wasn't a fake thing, Mike; you were my friend. But it seems my first thought was correct; I should never have kept you around."

There is a moment of silence. No one says anything. No one moves. They all just look at each other. Clyde is nearly there, but he still doesn't know what he will do when he gets there. Creighton makes the decision easy for him. As fast as Clyde has seen any of the Immortals move in the time they've been down here, Creighton's arm springs out. Creighton extends his hand and, through the fabric draped over Michael's delicate chest, his large—if frail—hands grip a device. Clyde can't see which one it is. Then he realizes, it is the one in the middle. The heart. He wants to shout, wants to rush over and help Michael, wants to stop this. But his body won't respond in time. He wants to shout 'No!' but he doesn't because, by the time the words get out, his friend will be dead.

"No, Edmund—" Michael shouts, but it's clear Creighton's mind is already made up.

The once rich man presses his bloodied lips together and glares at Michael. Then he squeezes the device and tears it downward hard. The device and Michael's shirt end up in Creighton's hand, and he holds them up above his head. Michael Jacobs, who never got a chance to finish his last story, crumples to the floor.

CHAPTER 28

K at and Joanne sprint down the long hall toward the stairs up to the house, their footfalls echoing in both directions. Blood drips down Kat's arm and shoulder. Her hand presses hard against her wound. If she doesn't, she fears a chunk of her will end up on the cold brick floor.

"We've got to get back up there," Joanne gasps. Her words echo as loud as their footsteps. The last thing they need is for the mob of skeletons to chase after them again. One or two at a time they can deal with, but together, the large group is too much to overcome.

"Come on, let's go," Kat says, in what she hopes is a whisper. They get to the stairs, however, and one of those things is waiting for them.

"I can't just let you go," a scratchy voice says from the darkness of the stairway. The thing's face is illuminated, and Kat realizes the thing is holding her phone. Kat and Joanne barely slow down. Joanne shoves a shoulder into the creature, and the thing falls back onto the stairs. It drops her phone, and Kat snatches it up before they step over it. It gives a weak grab at

Kat's leg. She shakes the hand off and pushes herself up the stairs. As they reach the top, yelling erupts from below.

"They're getting away. We have to stop them! Help me! We've got to get them back!" It is the thing that grabbed her, getting the rest of the group, but there is no way they can catch up to them now. Kat reaches the top and Joanne is already there with her hands on the heavy stone door that leads down below the house. When Kat steps out of the way, Joanne starts to pull it closed.

"Come on, help me!" Joanne looks back at Kat.

"I... I can't. Michael..." she says.

"Kat, he might be family, but he's supposed to be dead. He might already be dead for all we know. This is our chance, before they get here."

"I know, but..." Kat trails off. She knows Joanne is right, but she can't figure how she would tell Gramps she left Michael to die. The sounds of feet coming from below get louder, and Joanne strains against the door.

"Kat!" Joanne pleads, the door sliding closed, but not fast enough.

"Fine," Kat says, and she grabs the door with Joanne. A look down the stairs tells her the things are closer than she thought they would be. She has to close it, but it doesn't have to stay closed.

Kat pushes on the door with Joanne, and it slides closed faster. The sound of rock scraping against rock is almost drowned out by the shouts and yells from below. A thin hand juts out from the narrow space between the door and the wall. No. Are they too late? Kat groans and leans harder against the door, forcing it back with all her weight. She grabs the hand and pushes it back into the basement and then pushes harder against the door. It shuts, but she can feel the force of the human skeletons pressing on the other side.

"We've got to wedge it closed somehow!" Kat shouts to Joanne, who is sitting on the floor, her back against the door, holding it closed.

"How? With what?" Joanne says.

Sweat drips down Kat's face, her blood makes her shirt stick to her as she does her best to keep the door closed. She scans the library for anything they could use to keep the door closed. There isn't much; chairs and small tables won't do it, it needs to be bigger, heavier.

"I don't know. What's in there? It's got to be big and heavy." Kat strains.

There is a silence as both women hold their own and the pushes against the other side of the door weaken.

"They're running out of steam. One of us can hold it now. They aren't strong enough," Kat says.

"I got it," Joanne says. "The bench by the entrance. The one you sat on. It's big and heavy, and it will fit right in here. I bet it will hold the door closed, at least until we can find a better option."

"Can you move it?" Kat leans harder against the door, pushes her hair out of her face.

"I— I think so. I've moved it a few times to clean, but never this far."

"Let's try it. What have we got to lose?"

"Have you got this door? We can't let them out. I— I know it's family, but you know what they'll try to do to us if they get the chance. We have to keep them down there."

"I know. It's okay. I'm with you. They should never come out of there," Kat says. She's sad but knows she's right.

Joanne nods and stands up, watching the door for movement. They both do. It remains stationary. Kat isn't even sure she needs to lean on it anymore, but she doesn't dare back away. She hears the creaks and scrapes as Joanne moves the heavy bench through the library's open doors from the entry way.

"You've got this," Kat shouts, encouraging Joanne. Eventually, Joanne gets the bench in the door of the closet and lines it up.

"I think it will just fit. They won't be able to open the door once it's in place," Joanne says. Kat nods. Joanne was right, the bench touches both the hidden door to the basement on one side and the wall on the other. The door isn't able to be opened.

With the bench holding the door closed and the skeletal monstrosities stuck in the basement, Kat slips out of the closet and maneuvers past the high back of the bench.

"We did it!" Kat says.

Joanne nods. "Sorry about Michael. I know it would have meant a lot for your grandfather to meet him."

Kat doesn't say anything, nods, and collapses on the bench. Joanne does the same next to her. They suck air in and out quickly, but eventually their breathing slows and resembles something normal.

"I think I've learned all I want to learn about this house, Joanne," Kat says with a smile.

"So have I." Joanne smiles.

"Should we call the police?" Kat asks, knowing Joanne has wanted to do that from the beginning.

"You know, I thought that was the right thing to do, but now I'm not sure those things should ever be allowed out of there again. My brother's a mason. I can have him here in the morning. He'll have the whole closet bricked up by lunch time."

"You mean brick over the door?"

"No, I mean brick up the whole closet. He won't ask questions, and if he does, I'll tell him it's something Creighton said he wanted in an old paper we found. We wanted to go ahead and fulfill his wishes."

"You think he'll buy it?" Kat asks.

"Even if he doesn't, he'd do it for me."

That is good enough for Kat. She realizes now that the story will never be written. It is the story of a lifetime—of many lifetimes—but one that will remain untold.

Kat waits at the Creighton house with Joanne while she calls her brother. At first, he's worried because she called so late at night. She gives him a story about doing research late at the house and finding a paper about Creighton's wishes to have the closet bricked up. After some hemming and hawing about wanting to do other jobs first, she convinces him to come first thing in the morning. Kat agrees to stay in the house with Joanne for the night, but Joanne assures her she will be fine by herself. After some hesitation, Kat leaves.

On the ride to her parent's house, Kat finally checks her phone. Messages from her parents and her brothers, none of them urgent. She still doesn't know what she is going to say to Gramps when he asks her what she found at the Creighton house. She also isn't quite sure how to explain the bite marks on her neck.

Back at her parents' house, which doesn't feel like the house she grew up in anymore, she is comforted by the distance from the Creighton house. The house is deserted when she gets there, and she's relieved. After a shower, she finds a baggy sweatshirt she'd packed and throws it on, hoping it will cover the teeth marks. She's exhausted and surprised no one has come here looking for her. Her brothers, she assumes, both stopped by the hospital today and are back home with their families. Her parents must both also be at the hospital, which is where Kat should be, but it's closer to morning than it is midnight—a short nap can't hurt. She sits on the couch and flips open her phone with the intention of moving to her old bedroom, when she feels a little more tired, and she falls asleep before she can get up.

The ringing of her phone wakes her up as sun pours in the front window.

"Oh shit!" Kat says. She blinks a few times and answers the call. It's her Dad.

"Dad? Hey, sorry, I guess I overslept."

"Hey, Kat. Gramps told us you were checking on something for him, so we figured we'd let you be for the day. I'm sure whatever it was, it was important, or he wouldn't have asked you to go," he says. But Dad sounds serious, more serious than usual. As soon as he starts talking, Kat gets up and starts to gather the things needed to go to the hospital.

"Yeah, I did some digging, but I couldn't find anything." She hates lying, but she hasn't had time to figure out what to tell Gramps. For now, it has to be a lie. "How's everything there?"

"It's not good, Kat." He sighs. "He's still with it, but the pain is getting worse, and the meds aren't keeping up as much as they were before. He doesn't want to be in that much pain, so he...he wants to unplug everything. The doctor agrees. Says it's a matter of hours once they turn it off. Are you close? Can you get here soon?"

"Yes, yes, I'm at your house. I got in late, just needed to crash for a few hours. I'm up and ready to go now. Please tell him I'm on my way, it's important."

"I will. Jeremy and Simon are on their way too, but they won't be here before you. Wish we could all get together for some other reason."

"I know, Dad, me too." Kat ends the call and scrolls through her phone looking for the ride-share app. Her six unread text messages catch her eye, and she realizes she hasn't checked on work in almost twenty-four hours. Kat hesitates, then moves on. There will be time for work later.

When she is walking down the hall toward Gramps' room less than an hour later, Kat hears what sounds like crying— probably because she expects it—but it's laughing. She smiles, sticks her head in, and is greeted by Dad and Gramps with grins across their faces.

"Ah, there she is," Gramps says.

"I heard hospitals can be depressing, but I guess I heard wrong," Kat says.

"Oh, I was just telling your father about the time I tried to catch him smoking out behind the shed in our backyard with his friend, Johnny Milton, from next door. I slipped and fell down the hill back there, but not until after I stepped on a bee's nest in the ground and got stung twice," Gramps says, trying to catch his breath, a smile plastered on his face.

"I had no idea until just now. We moved around the other side of the shed just as he got to us. We knew the nest was there and were trying to get away from it," Dad says, in between small laughs.

She knows the story is funnier because of the situation and laughs along with them. However, she makes eye contact with Gramps, and he gives her a small nod.

"Listen, David, I need a few minutes to talk to Kat. Just a few. Then hopefully the boys will be here. I'm feeling a little lightheaded. We really should get the boys in here."

Kat's sure he'll be gone soon. She can feel it inside her somehow, like a connection has grown between them. She still doesn't know what she should say.

"Yeah, sure, Dad. I'll step out and give them a call. Christine should be back up from the cafe pretty soon too," Dad says. Gramps just nods at him.

Dad leaves, and Kat turns to look at Gramps.

"So," he says. He smiles, his eyes twinkle, like always. She remembers sitting on his lap in the living room of his house growing up. The same twinkle was there. She wants to sit on his lap now, to feel his arms around her and know that she will be safe forever. She wants him to tell her what to do, but she's got to figure this out on her own. Gramps always knew what to say to her. Now she has to know what to say to him, and she has no idea. She takes his hand.

"I went," Kat says, still unsure if he really wants to hear all this. But once she starts, she can't stop. The whole story comes out. Gramps sits silent through the whole thing, tears and happiness in his eyes. When she tells him about meeting Michael, there are even more tears. And more still when she shows him her neck.

"Kat, I'm so sorry," he says.

"No. No, don't be. It's part of the job. I'll be fine and move on. I had to learn the truth, so there's nothing else I could have done."

"Well, then thank you," Gramps says. "What was he like?"

"He was," she stops for a second and feels tears welling in her own eyes. She tries not to blink so Gramps won't see the tracks as they run down her cheeks, but they run down in spite of her efforts. "Just like you, Gramps. All he wanted to do was meet you. I'm sorry that didn't happen."

"It's okay. I'm—I'm glad you got to meet him." His tears flow, his breathing labors—more than just the heavy breathing of an emotional person. The machines start to beep, and Gramps looks at her, twinkle still in his eye. His face changes, contorts almost, and he barks out a groan of pain. Gramps coughs and seems to calm himself. "Please keep this between us. Meds are wearing off. You better get them now, kid."

She nods and sticks her head out the door and shouts for her father. He comes rushing in with Mom and her brother, Simon—Jeremy is on his way but doesn't know if he will make it in time.

They stand around the bed as the machines beep and flash, and a nurse comes in and tells them it's time. Gramps nods, and so does her Dad. They disconnect everything from him—turn everything off. The devices keeping him alive no longer connected. The noise stops. Beeping stops. Hissing stops. The room is silent except for the heavy breathing of the man who brought them all here. Kat doesn't know if it will take hours or minutes for him to die, but she knows it's coming. The medicine can't keep him alive; it just kept the pain away. He seems stronger. Maybe it's the lack of medicine or the pain that keeps him more coherent, but he is stronger than he's been since Kat got there. They sit and talk and even laugh a little, but his breathing labors more with each passing second. Kat can't watch his face contort and wince when the pain gets too much, and she looks away.

Jeremy arrives and Gramps holds it together long enough to make a joke and give him a hug, but Kat just watches and knows the hours Gramps once had have turned to minutes, maybe seconds.

"Getting real tired," Gramps says, his voice low and strained against his chest.

The nurse gives Dad a look. This is it.

They each take their turns. They hug him and say their goodbyes.

Kat goes last and leans in close to him.

"I love you, Gramps," she whispers in his ear.

"I love you, Kat. And thank you." She can barely hear him, even with his lips touching her ear. She stands back and watches him. His chest rises less and less with each strained breath. Out of the corner of her eye, Kat can see her Mom shaking, her hand over her mouth, crying silently, watching the man die. He looks at each of them, his eyes blank, dry, not really his. His chest stops moving, and his mouth hangs open. There is one more exhalation of air. Joseph Jacobs, son of Michael, closes his eyes one final time.

CHAPTER 29

They try. All of them try. The reanimates too. All pushing against the door or against each other at the same time. But they can't get the door to move. It won't open. Not anymore. Clyde sits in the large, cavernous room and looks around. They attempt civility. There has always been, all this time, something keeping them focused on a goal. They could leave any time they wanted. They were here by choice.

This is no longer a choice.

They are here now because they are imprisoned here. Clyde watches, silently, as they all begin to lose their minds.

The Doctor was first. Creighton right behind him. Michael is dead, along with at least three others, ones who had a chance to stop the women and failed. Pull the devices off these bodies, and the person dies almost instantly. Others are starting to fight. It won't be long now before almost everyone is dead. In the end, there will only be one person left down here, and if no one is around to kill that person, he or she will live forever. Clyde wants that person to be anyone but him. He doesn't think he can kill himself, but he doesn't want to live forever.

* * *

Creighton takes the device he pulled from James Wallbeck's chest and throws it in a pile with the others. Wallbeck makes four, but there will be more. He and the Doctor have a plan. Anyone who doesn't agree to go along with the plan will die. They've tried this once and it didn't work, but they are immortal. If the first Immortal Night didn't work, then the only thing that makes sense is to have another one. It won't be now. They have to figure out how to get out of the room. But it's never too early to start getting ready.

"Once we harvest the devices from the people we don't trust, we can start planning a way out of here, Doctor."

The Doctor looks back at him, eyes wide as he pulls the rest of the devices off of Wallbeck's corpse.

"We will still be able to sell this, Edmund. We will be alive forever."

CHAPTER 30

2025

"You know what's best about moving into a new place together?" Kat says from behind an overflowing laundry basket filled with clothes.

"No, what is it?" Laura puts down her own overflowing laundry basket.

"Instead of me having a pile of shit I don't really need but don't want to get rid of, and you having a pile of shit *you* don't want to get rid of, we have one big pile of shit that neither of us want to get rid of."

Laura laughs. "I guess you're right. I'm glad we are finally doing this."

They've been living together at Kat's old place for two years, but it always felt like *Kat's place* and Laura was just staying there. Neither of them wanted that anymore. They needed a place that was theirs together; this new condo was it.

Still in the Washington area, but a little bit further outside of town. It was good for Laura because she worked outside of town. Kat could get into the city when she needed to, but she didn't have to commute to work every day because so much of what she did for work was remote. Being close to work wasn't a necessity.

"What's the plan for dinner? I'm starving," Laura says. The laundry baskets are the last of the things they need to bring up, and, though all the boxes are in the condo, it still feels empty. There is no food, but at least they have a place to sit.

"I don't know, pizza?" Kat says. She already has her laptop in her hand and is sitting on the couch and plugging it in to do her evening news check. Laura is okay with her nonstop work schedule and understands that when she's reading articles on her phone or on the computer, it's all about work for her. They both know Kat will never change, and they are both okay with it.

"Why don't you do your read through," Laura says, nodding at the laptop, which is sitting at the home screen and waiting for Kat's password. "I'll run out and get some pizza. Then we can stuff our faces when I get back."

"Sounds perfect," Kat says.

Laura orders the food and leaves Kat to her news websites and text messages.

Kat checks all the regular sites and then moves to ones that she's been checking more frequently lately, even though they have very little to do with work. The local news websites around Elk Hills have been hard for her to stop checking. She's kept her promise to Gramps and never told anyone what happened the night before he died. She will take that secret to her grave, though it's probably the only one. Too many good stories out there. She's kept in touch with Joanne, who has also kept the information to herself.

As she scrolls though the Elk Hills local news, a headline catches her eye and almost makes her drop the laptop off her legs.

'MYSTERIOUS GRAVE ROBBERIES REMAIN UNSOLVED,' the headline reads. Her eyes widen. She wants to know everything in the article, but she can't stop her eyes from scanning it, looking for references to Creighton or the Creighton House. Of course, there aren't any. Chances are it's not connected, but Kat can't help but wonder what might be going on in Elk Hills. Joanne would be able to ease her mind. She makes a mental note to contact her as soon as she gets a chance. Kat sighs and the front door opens, Laura enters, pizza box in hand.

Kat snaps the laptop closed and stands up.

"Just finished. No big news today," Kat says. "Let's eat, I'm starving."

Printed in Great Britain
by Amazon